'How are you feeling?' the voice growled.

'Nick?' she whispered, reaching out a hand as tentative as her voice to touch his shoulder and confirm his substance.

'Who else?' he barked harshly, and her fingers dropped back on to the bed.

She felt the palm of his hand, cool and slightly roughened, against her forehead. He *had* to be a hallucination.

'Maybe I am dead!' Callie muttered to herself. 'And he's dead, too! Now wouldn't that be a joke? Both of us in hell together, because that's certainly where he always said I'd end up!'

Having pursued many careers—from school-teaching to pig farming—with varying degrees of success and plenty of enjoyment, **Meredith Webber** seized on the arrival of a computer in her house as an excuse to turn to what had always been a secret urge—writing. As she had more doctors and nurses in the family than any other professional people, the medical romance seemed the way to go! Meredith lives on the Gold Coast of Queensland, with her husband and teenage son.

Recent titles by the same author:

FLIGHT INTO LOVE
A SUBTLE MAGIC
UNRULY HEART
A DIFFERENT DESTINY
WHISPER IN THE HEART
A TESTING TIME
HEALING LOVE

PRACTICE IN THE CLOUDS

BY

MEREDITH WEBBER

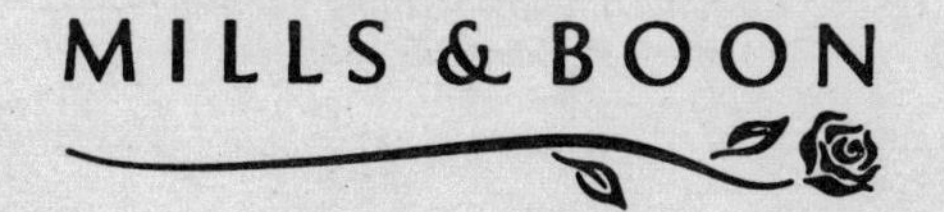

All the characters in this book have no existence outside the imagination of the author, and have no relation whatsoever to anyone bearing the same name or names. They are not even distantly inspired by any individual known or unknown to the author, and all the incidents are pure invention.

*Harlequin Mills & Boon Limited,
Eton House, 18-24 Paradise Road, Richmond, Surrey TW9 1SR
This edition published by arrangement with Harlequin Enterprises B.V.*

ISBN 0 263 79460 1

*Set in Times 10 on 11½ pt. by
Rowland Phototypesetting Limited
Bury St Edmunds, Suffolk*

03-9601-53537

*Made and printed in Great Britain
Cover illustration by Peter Oakes*

CHAPTER ONE

HOURS earlier the sun had glinted off the shiny corrugated-iron roof of the new health-post building, and Callie had fixed its position in her mind, trudging up towards it with a mindless, almost fanatical, determination. All around her now, the last rays of the sun were striping the mountains—gold, mauve, rose and crimson—turning the towering Himalayan peaks to a giant backdrop of incomprehensible beauty.

Three days ago it had left her breathless, and she had insisted they stop and watch nature's magic show. Three days ago, as the sky above the impossible peaks had deepened to purple and the sunset had lit the snow to fiery beauty, tears had coursed down her cheeks. That so much beauty could exist in the world! That she, Callie Ward, was alive and actually here to see it! The wonder and sheer joy of it had filled her heart and mind and soul until she had ached with the might of it.

But three days ago the blisters had only been a slight burning sensation, unnoticed as she drank in all the splendours of the mountain kingdom of Nepal, and marvelled at the towering peaks, luring her up and onward. Tonight those blisters were going to kill her! She knew that as surely as she knew her own name.

Driving her on was the thought that the health post might have a bed. Last night, as she'd tossed and turned feverishly on the hard ground outside a 'tourist camp', she had decided that her last wish was to die in a bed. Somewhere up there, she reminded herself, shuffling one foot forward and dragging the other up to meet it, somewhere up there, under a new, shiny roof, is a bed.

'This is a health-aid post, not a trekkers' rest camp! Of course she can't have a bed,' a voice was saying, and in her trance-like, pain-numbed state it sounded like Nick's voice.

Callie sank to the ground outside the stone building, and rested her head on her knees. Was it because the man sounded cross and for the last few years of their friendship, Nick had always sounded cross? Well, nearly always!

When he had first gone away to university ten years ago she had missed him dreadfully, but he had still been 'the boy next door'—her first, best and most special friend—and during his weekend visits home and holidays they had picked up their friendship as if they had never been parted. Until. . .

Tears welled up again as she thought of Nick. If only she hadn't lost touch with him! If only she'd been able to talk to him before setting out on this impossible journey. He'd have been exasperated with her, of course, but he might have talked her out of it. He was good at telling her how stupid she was! Frowning at her with his dark eyes blazing yellow fire. . .

She dragged her mind back to the present. Her guide, Sonam, was speaking now, softly and urgently, as if trying to explain something, but the man who sounded like Nick only snorted derisively.

'You can set up camp out the back,' he offered coldly. 'The area's well-grassed, and sheltered from the wind, but don't think I'm going to let this place become an unofficial resting place. There are tea houses and a so-called hotel in the village, just around the corner, barely ten minutes' walk away!'

'But Kelly coming here!' Sonam explained. 'Before all dying talk, she was coming here!'

She should stand up and explain to the man, Callie realised, but her body refused to unfold from its hunched position on the ground, and her feet throbbed so badly that she didn't think she could put weight on them. Besides, it wasn't much use telling the man that she was here to assist him when she was going to die anyway.

'That's how she knew there would be a bed,' Sonam added helpfully, and, even though she was dying, Callie's sense of humour was still sufficiently active to wish she could see the man's face. 'She has sore feet now, but she'll be better soon. We leave her here and go now. Friends in village waiting.'

'What's happened? Has she run out of money for food, or have you discovered she can't pay you?' the man demanded, suspicion biting the words to an acid sharpness. 'If you're a registered guide you should have sorted all that out before you left Kathmandu or Lukla or wherever you met up with her. You know you can't desert your party, and you definitely can't dump her here and walk away.'

So that's why he's so angry! He thinks I'm an impecunious trekker about to be abandoned by my guide and porter. Understanding broke through the muffled fog of pain, and Callie moved, trying to force her body into an upright position so she could tell him who she was.

The movement brought one foot into the gentlest of contact with its partner, but the pain pounded up along her nerves and exploded in her brain. Someone cried out—a long, wailing lament that echoed from the mountains—and she wondered if she had made the noise.

She came to on a bed, but couldn't appreciate the luxury of being off the hard ground because someone was tearing the skin from her feet, and obviously relishing the job if she understood his muttered imprecations correctly.

'Please don't!' she whimpered. 'I'd much rather die with them as they are!'

The torturer ignored her plea and continued, moving his body into a sitting position so he could hold her legs still with one heavy forearm. In the dim light he was simply a back, a hunched, darker shadow in the shadowy room.

'I'd let you die, but that would be too easy an escape for you!' The words sliced through her pain. Even his intonation—those deep, dark tones of baffled anger—was like Nick's! 'No, this time, my girl, you're going to suffer. This time, Callie, you might finally learn something from your madcap behaviour and irresponsible escapades.'

It was quite a relief to hear him call her Callie, because it made her realise she was hallucinating. Her guide and the porter had both called her Kelly, and would have given this man that name. She sighed. Now she knew that Nick was no more than a dream, she could stop trying to wake herself up to get a look at the stranger. She could get on with dying in peace!

She smiled as she slipped back into the half-world between sleep and unconsciousness, because Nick was in it with her, nagging at her as he had time and time again in their shared childhood.

She woke to darkness so absolute that it frightened

her. Movement brought pain, suggesting that she wasn't dead after all. Then she remembered similar awakenings at the beginning of her trek, when she'd felt so totally alive that her body had filled to capacity with excitement and happiness. This darkness was the time immediately before dawn, when the stars and moon were gone and the mountains waited for a new awakening. She lay tensely for a moment, telling herself she was in a bed at a health post—that she was safe.

As her panic eased she peered around, searching for the faintest shading of grey that might indicate a door or window, but could see nothing. The room she was in must be better built than the rough stone houses and bamboo-sided 'camps' they had used on the trek if the windows and doors fitted so neatly!

Then a finely drawn yellow rectangle appeared, and a sharp wedge of light spilt into the darkness as the door was pushed quietly open. The light widened, then pooled, shining down into her eyes as the lantern the man carried was lifted on to a hook in the centre of the room.

As he bent towards her she frowned and blinked, trying to banish the dream and re-establish some reality in her life. If she was not going to die, and she certainly didn't feel as if she was at the moment, then she had better get on with living!

'How are you feeling?' the voice growled.

'Nick?' she whispered, reaching out a hand as tentative as her voice to touch his shoulder and confirm his substance.

'Who else?' he barked harshly, and her fingers dropped back on to the bed.

She felt the palm of his hand, cool and slightly

roughened, against her forehead. She tried to shake it off, unable to believe such an impossible, bizarre, implausible coincidence. No! It couldn't be possible! He *had* to be a hallucination!

'Maybe I am dead!' she muttered to herself. 'And he's dead, too! Now wouldn't that be a joke? Both of us in hell together, because that's certainly where he always said I'd end up!'

She turned away from the intruder, but the movement restarted the fires in her feet, and she curled into a ball to hold the pain inside her.

'Not only not dead, but also probably well enough to get up by tomorrow,' the implacable voice continued. 'And certainly well enough to answer a few questions, my girl!'

She felt his hand settle on her shoulder.

'And before you go back to sleep, I'll get you a cup of tea and some porridge. I want to start you on a course of oral antibiotics and they'll be absorbed better it you've eaten something.' The fingers tightened for a moment, then he added, 'I'll leave the lantern. There's a bathroom of sorts through there. I'll carry you in when I've got breakfast organised.'

Like hell you will, Callie told the retreating back. She unzipped the enveloping sleeping-bag, and eased her legs up and out of it, ignoring the flare of pain from her protesting feet. When they emerged she blinked at them, two large white blobs, professionally swathed in bandages.

Twisting around, she slipped them off the edge of the bed and down on to the floor. The pain was no worse! Gritting her teeth, she pressed one more firmly against the hard, bare ground, and felt the fiery response lick up her leg. She glanced at the open door, then looked across the small room to a darker shadow. She would crawl to the bathroom!

The 'bathroom' was a space the size of a large cupboard, but it had a tap above a plastic dish, and a small chemical toilet that made Callie shake her head in wonder. It had not taken her long to realise that everything but the food grown locally was carried into these mountain villages on yaks or in the woven bamboo baskets the men and women carried on their backs, much of the weight taken by a thong around their foreheads. The thought of the toilet's journey made her smile!

She was back on the bed, shaking with the aftermath of the exertion when he returned.

'Put something warm on!' he snapped, then he cursed softly and looked around the room before depositing the tray he carried on an upturned box, and reaching up to remove her jacket from a hook above the bed.

As he bent to wrap it around her shoulders she peered at his face: dark olive skin that tanned easily, thick black eyebrows, complete with small white scar across one where she'd thrown a rock and struck him accidentally. Tears blurred the straight line of his nose and the lovely symmetry of his lips. She blinked them away and sniffed.

'You look so like my Nick,' she whispered thickly as memories of the days when Nick had been her hero, her guide and protector—always there when she had needed him—came tumbling out of her misery and overwhelmed her.

'Stop your nonsense and eat!' he ordered. 'And make sure you drink all the tea. Your whole system's been poisoned by those blisters, and you're dehydrated as well. Fine doctor you're going to make, if you can't even take care of yourself! Or have you given up on that idea and set out to drift aimlessly around the world?'

She blinked again and peered at the phantom. As well as looking so like Nick, he spoke to her in exactly the same way—with a mixture of exasperation and anger that was still slightly softened by the fondness of their childhood.

'You are William Wilcox, aren't you?' she whispered, nodding at the same time as if to confirm her own question.

He frowned down at her so ferociously that she shrank back, and when his hand reached out towards her she flinched away.

'I'm not going to hit you, you stupid girl,' he uttered, 'though, heaven knows, you deserve a beating.'

His hand settled again on her forehead, and he shook his head, the frown deepening.

'Tell me who I am, Callie!' The commanding tones told her he would brook no argument, so she answered, as she would have answered the real Nick if he'd been there.

'You look like Nick Grant, an old friend of mine,' she whispered, 'but he's in Colorado, in America, so I know that's wrong. My letter came from a Dr William Wilcox, and if that's not you then I'm sicker than I feel or I'm lost.'

She felt the tears, as fat and hot as blobs of melted butter, sliding down her cheeks, but she was too tired and too confused to even try to stop them.

'What letter?' the tyrant demanded.

'It's in my wallet with my passport,' she sobbed, reaching automatically for the zip of the pouch in the silk belt she wore around her waist. Her fingers touched bare skin, then scrabbled around under her bulky tracksuit top.

'It's gone!' she accused. She felt her eyes widening as the horror of this final loss hit her, but a healthy anger flared, burning away her misery as surely as the sun burnt the mists from the valleys each morning.

'You've stolen my money and passport!' she snapped. 'You or some thieving servant of yours.'

Rage pushed her upright before she remembered her feet. As the agony shot through her she slumped back down again, clutching at her legs as the referred pain twisted in her calf muscles and reduced her knees to jelly.

'This what you've lost?' he growled, reaching over the bed again and lifting the silk belt from the hook that had held her jacket. 'And I'd keep off your feet if I were you!'

She glared at him, then bent to find the letter. 'There!' She thrust the folded missive towards him, and turned away, too disturbed by her ambivalent feelings towards this stranger in the body of Nick to watch him any longer. Instead, she felt her own forehead, although she knew if she had a high temperature she wouldn't be able to tell because her hands would also be hotter than normal.

Then she tried to think of all she had learnt about acute mountain sickness, or AMS as it was known. Delirium could occur if the person was suffering from HACE, high altitude cerebral oedema, but, at fourteen and a half thousand feet, she wasn't sure she was high enough for that. Besides, she had spent a day and two nights at Namche Bazar for acclimatisation and walked up slowly—very slowly as her feet had got worse—so she should have become accustomed to the altitude even if she was one of the people who could be affected more easily.

'No one mentioned an assistant,' the man who should have been William Wilcox muttered. 'And what made you decide to take on a volunteer job like this?'

'I love mountains,' she told him simply. 'And these are the best you can get, aren't they?' She tried a tentative smile, although she wasn't certain of the protocol of smiling at ghosts. Nick had been responsible for her fascination with high places, she remembered. Nick. . .

'And you didn't know I was here?'

He sounded so suspicious that she tried looking hard at him again, to see if he'd changed into someone she didn't know.

'Only if you're William Wilcox,' she offered hesitantly, and was rewarded with a scowl that would have melted ice. Then he bent down and took her shoulders, shaking her as if to wake her up, while his so-familiar face hovered only inches in front of her eyes.

'Do I look like William Wilcox?' he growled. 'Do I, Callie? Do I?'

'You look like Nick!' she murmured, unable to control her trembling lower lip and the tears that prickled again in her eyes. 'Like a. . .a boy who used to live next door to me back home in Toowoomba, but I know he's in America and so I must be seeing things, and I wondered if perhaps I might have AMS or something. . .'

The man turned away from her pitiful explanation, muttering under his breath about impossibilities and calling down curses on fate and the absent William Wilcox. Then he swung back to face her, suspicion glimmering like candlelight in his eyes.

'I'll check this out, Callie!' he warned. 'As soon as I get back to civilisation I'll contact Mum and Bill Wilcox and discover the truth! If I find this is another of your wild schemes——'

'You are Nick?' she gasped, interrupting the threat. 'A real Nick, not a ghost? I'm not delirious?'

She shook her head, not knowing whether to laugh or cry as the unreality of the situation overwhelmed her. She reached out to touch him, but he moved abruptly away, as if afraid of the contact.

'But you're in America!' she objected. 'I saw your mother six months ago when Mum was shifting to Perth. She said you were there for two years studying haematology.' And that Jane hadn't gone with you! That Jane was no longer part of your life! The silent postscript echoed in her head.

'I was there, and will be going back after my two months here,' he told her. 'But I'd been trying to fit another trip to Nepal into my schedule, and, six weeks ago, I heard on the mountaineering grapevine that Bill Wilcox had become ill and was forced to drop out of this project. I arranged two months' leave to come over and finish the job. The work he was doing here fits in neatly with my own studies, so the hospital in Colorado was happy to let me go.'

She frowned up at him, still unable to believe in an incredible coincidence that could put two childhood neighbours together in a health outpost high up in the remote Himalayas. Then the reality dawned on her.

'Oh, Nick!' she breathed, and smiled mistily as a sense of security and well-being flooded through her. An answering smile, rueful but welcoming, flickered on his lips, before they tightened again.

'It still doesn't explain how your mother let you take on such a ridiculous assignment, or how you allowed your feet to get into such a state, especially when, according to this letter, you claim to be continuing your medical studies. Or why you're wandering the mountains dressed like a demented hippie, or why you cut off all your hair!'

The expostulation had begun in a typical 'exasperated Nick' tone, but by the time he'd listed all her current short-comings it had deteriorated into a gruff roar. Callie's smile widened. It was so familiar, Nick scolding her like this! So familiar, and so *dear*!

'My rucksack got stolen or lost or something. It never arrived in Kathmandu and I had to buy whatever I could find to wear at the markets.' She plucked at the tracksuit top that nearly obliterated her slight figure. 'A man's tracksuit and some Nepalese saris for skirts, and some tops, and this jacket—but it's yak hair and it's heavy and scratchy, so it wasn't an exceptional bargain.'

The words came rushing out, apologetic and placating, but she knew Nick would see the lost rucksack as simply one more disaster she had brought on herself. One more example of her ineptitude!

'And I had shoes made,' she rushed on before he could fire his first salvo, 'because Sonam, my guide, said that would be best, but somehow they didn't quite fit, so I bought another pair along the way that will fit me when the swelling from the blisters goes down.'

She grinned at him, hoping to divert the storm of censure she was certain would be building behind the grim mask of his face.

'And Mum's gone to Perth to live, so by the time she had my letter I was practically on my way,' she added. 'Besides which——' she drew herself up as tall as her five feet six would allow while still sitting on a bed'—I am now twenty-three years of age and no longer need to ask my mother's permission for everything I do.'

Another pert smile flickered towards him, and she thought she caught an answering twitch at one corner of his shapely lips.

'Don't you, brat?' he asked mildly, then he reached out and flicked her inch-long hair with one slender finger. 'And?' he prompted as she moved cautiously away from him.

'Well, I could hardly come traipsing around the mountains with long blonde curls floating in the breeze. I do have some common sense, you know!' She ignored the derisive snort and continued her defence, although what her hair had to do with him these days she could not fathom. 'I know there's a water problem up here, so regular washing was out of the question, and I also know——' she flung a haughty glare in his direction '——that it can be dry and dusty at this time of the year, so, all in all, cutting off the lot seemed wisest!'

He made a noise that she was fairly certain would have been written 'Hmph!' then turned and walked out of the room.

Relief flowed through her like a warm, healing tide, transporting her back to the carefree childhood when Nick had been her best friend, comfort and support. She stuck her tongue out at his retreating back, then quickly covered her cheeky gesture with a bland smile when he swung back to face her.

'Well, kindly remember that you're here to work. You can have today off to recover, but after that there are file cards to prepare, and case-notes to type. Plenty of things you can do that won't involve hobbling about on those disgusting feet.'

'Yes, sir!'

She snapped a two-fingered boy scout salute at him, and chuckled when she saw his frown.

'If I find out this is one of your devious plans, Callie. . .'

The threat was implicit in the words, but before she could argue he was gone.

You shouldn't have used that boy scout salute! she chided herself. Things are bad enough without reminding him of that little effort!

But the smile that had settled on her lips couldn't be wiped away. If anything, it deepened as she thought of the time she'd smuggled herself aboard the bus that was bearing Nick off to scout camp. He'd been so mortified—the big-time patrol leader!—when the scout master had summoned him to the headquarter's tent and presented him with a small grubby girl in an overlarge khaki shirt and a pair of his cast-off shorts.

She reached out and picked up the teacup. The unidentifiable liquid inside it was now cold, but she drank it anyway, welcoming the sweet, milky taste. Definitely better than the hot liquid the locals called tea, with its skim of rancid yak butter, that she had been drinking on the trek at tea-houses.

The tea finished, she reached for the bowl of porridge. It looked more like rice, and a tentative taste confirmed her suspicions, but it was sweet and filling and she ate ravenously, unable to remember when she had last had solid food. In spite of what Nick might think, she had forced herself to drink copious amounts of liquids all through that long final day on the trail, but eating had been beyond her as pain from her infected blisters had twisted her stomach into knots.

'If you've come under the auspices of Bill's research scheme you would have received a list of basic medical supplies to carry on the trek up here.'

The suspicion still lingered, Callie realised, when the words preceded his tall, gangly form into the room. He had ducked his head to get through the door, and now bent lower to hand her two bright red capsules and a cup of water.

'And a warning not to pack medicines in your baggage but keep them in your hand luggage at all times.'

Hearing the accusation in his voice, she fluttered her eyelids closed and sighed. Maybe finding Nick wasn't the blessed miracle to end all miracles! Not now she remembered his tendency to nag at her, to go on and on about every little misdemeanour and mistake she ever made.

'It wasn't in my baggage, Dr Know-all!' she snapped. 'It was in my hand luggage because even a moron like me can read instructions and follow them as long as they are numbered one, two, three! It just so happened that the customs people became overly interested in me once I'd yelled a bit about my baggage being lost. . .'

The instant the words left her lips she regretted them, and, as she felt her cheeks colour to a bright vermilion, the air between them cooled perceptibly, and Nick's lovely brown eyes hardened into rock-hard pebbles.

'They didn't strip-search you, did they?' The words whipped past her ears like knife-edged swords, but the dreadful, shameful memory of the ordeal came flooding back and wiped away any confusion she might have felt about his strange reaction.

Again the tears that pain, exhaustion and fever made

hard to hold back welled up, then brimmed over and slid across her scarlet cheeks, wetting the fingers that lifted to wipe them away.

'It's OK, Callie!' he said roughly, and now, at last, he sat down beside her on the bed, and pulled her hard against his chest. 'It's OK now, brat. You're here, and safe, and I'll look after you!'

The familiar childhood promise made the tears flow faster, and he rocked her gently, letting her cry away the pain and despair, until the flow had eased, and a few pitiful sniffs sent him searching through his shorts' pockets for a handkerchief.

'And I suppose the drugs disappeared from your hand luggage at the same time,' was all he said, but the voice in which he added, 'I'll put in an official complaint about it!' boded ill for the person who would be on the receiving end of his carefully controlled displeasure.

She sat very still in the circle of his arms, feeling his warmth seeping through into her bones. For too long a time she had missed this closeness; had thought she would never again have him hold and comfort her. She snuggled into his side, pressing against the hard bones that made up his lean frame.

Old skin and bones! she used to taunt him, especially when he had mocked her childish chubbiness. . .

Then the substance of the warmth changed, charging through her blood, firing to life the yearning hunger she had tried to kill. Surely she couldn't still love him——

'Now, brush the tears out of those bright blue eyes and take those capsules.' He spoke suddenly, breaking into her thoughts and levering his body away from hers with a stiff formality. 'You can drink all the water—

it's been purified. It's kept in a drum in the little laboratory-cum-office, so don't drink from anything else.'

He stood up and studied her for a moment, then rubbed the tip of one long forefinger across her cheek, collecting the moisture. It was a gentle gesture, although his face revealed nothing.

'I'll come back and dress your feet later, but right now I've a radio schedule to keep, and, by the time that's finished, I usually work in the lab until my first patients arrive.'

'Patients? Are you actually treating people?' She would have liked the finger to linger but his words diverted her. She hadn't thought much about how William Wilcox would fill in his day.

'Of course I am!' he replied, shaking his head again. 'A doctor wanting to research something in a remote area like this can hardly come barging in and demand the local people make blood samples available to him. Although I'm not working under the auspices of the Himalayan Rescue Association, I am offering a service similar to that which their aid posts offer in the trekking season. I'm treating locals and also trekkers who are going through to Gokyo.'

'Oh!' Callie muttered as the magnitude of a research project in such an isolated area suddenly struck her. 'Do many people trek up this valley? Namche Bazar was overflowing with tourists but I thought they were all headed towards Base Camp Everest or the monastery at Tengboche or the Everest View Hotel. No one seemed to take this trail.'

She peered upwards, sorry he had moved away from her side, but glad that she could study him dispassionately now she knew he was real.

'It's early in the season, and there's still a chance of

more rain, but next month you'll find quite a steady stream of visitors passing through Machherma. It's on the way to Gokyo, which offers spectacular views of Everest. With about ten thousand trekkers a year taking the Everest Base Camp trail, and even more trekking in the Annapurna region, many people are looking for quieter and less commercialised trekking routes, and Gokyo is becoming a new favourite.'

As he spoke she saw a glimmer of the old excitement lighting his thin, aesthetic face. He had hungered for adventure as others hungered for money, and the same drive that made some people rich was, in Nick, diverted into finding new challenges—both physical and mental.

'Have you been on up the trail to Gokyo?' she asked, and watched him shake his head.

'No, but I'll go!' he promised. 'There are a couple of nice little peaks up that way just waiting for me to climb them.'

He must have seen her smile, for his own lips widened and a self-deprecating grin lit up his face. He shrugged.

'Well,' he muttered, 'there had to be some compensation for coming all this way.' There was a pause before he added, 'And for putting up with trouble like you for an assistant!'

CHAPTER TWO

CALLIE woke again to bright sunshine streaming through a glass window and the low murmur of voices from somewhere beyond her room. Her body felt refreshed, and an experimental wriggle of her toes inside their enveloping wrappings produced less pain than she had grown to expect.

She sat up, pushed away her sleeping-bag and examined the bandages. Nick had said he would dress her feet again later. Surely she could do that for herself? She was unravelling the first bandage when his head appeared around the door.

'Feeling better?' He grinned, and Callie's heart flipped over. Would she ever get over whatever it was that made her insides react like that?

'Well enough to do whatever has to be done to these revolting feet of mine,' she told him. 'If you could give me the cream or ointment you're using and some clean dressings, I'll fix them.' She smiled apologetically at him. 'After all, I am supposed to be assisting you, not adding another patient to your load!'

He nodded and disappeared, but not before she saw his dark brows knit. What was worrying him now? Was he still suspicious of her arrival in the village? Did he still believe she'd found out he was here and followed him? Surely not! Not even in her most infatuated days would she have done something like that! Would she?

He was back before she had time to think about answers to his annoyance.

'I'll use sterile, treated gauze on the open wounds and cover that with clean lint, but keep the bandages on top of your bedding there and I'll re-use them to hold the gauze in place.'

She nodded, understanding the need to maximise the use of all dressings, and began unwrapping one foot while he worked on the other.

'What on earth had you put on them?' he asked as he examined the torn and still-inflamed skin. 'They were a bright, glutinous green when you arrived!'

Callie looked at his face, bent over her foot and examining it carefully. He looked stern but so very dear! she thought, then shifted her mind back into gear. Getting sentimental about Nick would do her no good whatsoever!

'I flew into Lukla and they were sore by the time I'd walked up to Namche Bazar. I spent two nights there, and climbed both days because I knew if I went up to higher altitudes then came back down to sleep it would help me acclimatise faster.'

His nod of approval produced a disproportionate pleasure.

'But the shoes weren't softening and the blisters were getting worse so I went to one of the local health posts and was given some leaves to use as a kind of poultice.'

His head shot up, and his eyes narrowed.

'You got whatever did this to your feet from a local health post? I find that hard to believe, Callie. The local practitioners' knowledge is usually excellent.'

He sounded so incredulous that she hurried to explain, although she knew what she was about to say would prompt yet another of Nick's 'you haven't the sense you were born with' lectures!

'Not exactly!' she mumbled. She finished her

unwrapping but the sight of the dressings made her feel ill, so she lay back on the bed and propped herself up on her elbows. 'The leaves they gave me were fantastic, and soothed the pain enough for me to sleep. It made me feel that I could continue on up the trail, but the next day the blisters burst and. . .'

Maybe seeing Nick again wasn't as wonderful as she'd thought!

'And?' he asked silkily.

'Well, the leaves they'd given me looked like dandelion leaves——'

'Dock,' he interrupted. 'Traditional Ayurvedic medicine makes good use of it! Go on.'

'Well, I hadn't thought to get some more to bring with me, but I saw something I'm certain was the same thing in one of the meadows near where we camped. . .'

'So you picked some unidentified leaves, wrapped them around your feet and waited for them to become so infected you're lucky you're not going to be walking around on stumps for the rest of your life!'

Now she knew she wasn't pleased to see him! This was Nick at his most scathing. She clenched her teeth together and counted to ten before replying carefully, 'I'm not entirely stupid. I knew they were likely to be dirty and dusty. I washed them carefully before I put them on my feet.'

'Washed them where?' he demanded, glaring down at her wilting form.

Callie opened her mouth to speak, then thought about what she was going to say. 'In the river!' she whispered. 'I washed them in the river! I knew about the infections spread through water in the mountains but I didn't think about——'

'Didn't think! You wouldn't drink the water out of the river, yet you think it suitable for sterilising leaves you used as dressings on open wounds!'

The scornful tone brought back her fighting spirit. That was the thing with Nick, you had to stand up to him.

'That's ridiculous!' she argued. 'I washed our eating utensils and the porter washed the pots and pans in the river, and I washed my clothes and myself. Any germs from the water could have got into my feet when I was bathing them each night.'

'And most water-borne infections only affect the intestines anyway,' he agreed, surprising Callie more than another burst of anger would have. 'So maybe it was the leaves. Did the plant you used have distinct yellow dandelion flowers on it?'

Callie shook her head, and waited. He didn't reply immediately but bent over, removed the soiled lint and gauze, and examined her other foot.

'Well, whatever it was didn't do you a whole lot of good, but I think they're getting better.' He turned towards her as he spoke and Callie smiled her relief. For a moment she thought he was going to smile back at her, then his lips tightened, and the softness disappeared from his eyes, replaced by something she couldn't identify—a kind of hunger almost. . .

The air grew still, invaded by tension that zapped along the skin.

'I'll get you some antiseptic solution. I want you to soak them in it for ten minutes, then dry them carefully before putting on fresh gauze and wrapping them up again.' His brisk words broke the strain and interrupted her tangled thoughts. She watched as he placed the kidney dish he'd brought into the room on to the upturned box within easy reach of her, then he stood up and walked away.

Is he going to go cold and hard like that every time I smile at him? she wondered sadly. If so, it was going to be an agonising month. She was overwhelmingly glad to see him again! Couldn't he have been just a little bit glad to see her?

Or was she overwhelmingly glad? Wouldn't a month working closely with him tear away her layers of scar tissue, reopening painful old wounds?

She sighed and shook her head. Puberty had slashed a deep rift in the friendship between herself and Nick. To try to cross it would be as precarious a task as crossing some of the swaying suspension bridges she'd experienced on her trek. And probably twice as dangerous! she warned herself, remembering her body's reaction to his touch.

'Here! The water's been sterilised and I've added some tea-tree oil, so soak them then pat them dry. Can you manage?' He bent and placed a bowl on the ground by the bed, then dropped a clean towel onto her knees.

'Of course I can,' she replied gruffly, her mind still snared in the new problems that had arisen. 'If you could lift my pack over to the end of the bed, I've some big, thick socks in it. I'll pull them on over the bandages when I finish, and I'll be as good as new.' She caught the speculation in his eyes, and added, 'Well, almost!' with a grin that won a slight response from his stern face.

He crossed the small room and reached under the second bed, to drag her pack from beneath it.

Second bed! Callie blinked and shook her head. She'd been so absorbed by the pain and the sudden reappearance of Nick that she hadn't noticed her surroundings! The bed was neatly made, if you called spreading a heavy down sleeping-bag tidily along its length bed-making. Obviously there was someone else sharing the room—or was this a 'hospital' ward of sorts in the new health post?

Nick dropped her pack by her bed, and disappeared before she could ask questions. Well, that was OK. She'd fix her feet then go exploring—even if she had to crawl as she had earlier.

She dropped them into the warm water and wriggled her toes gingerly. They were probably the worst affected parts of her feet, as the regular downhill stretches as the trail crossed ridge after ridge on its upward path had forced them into the hard, unyielding leather of the hiking boots. The constant friction had rubbed the blistered skin away until the small digits were like raw, bloody stumps.

While they were soaking, she pulled on the new rubber gloves he had left in the small dish and checked out what he was using. Would she have used treated gauze or medi-powder, she wondered, if she hadn't lost all her medical supplies?

Close examination as she dried each foot tenderly revealed a great deal of improvement in their condition. She would lose her toe-nails, but the angry red inflammation had gone and with it the worst of the pain. Tearing open a new packet of medicated gauze, she found the scissors Nick had provided, and cut strips to wind around the raw wounds. With one foot covered, she picked up fresh lint and padded it into place on top of the gauze, then re-wrapped the bandages to keep everything in place.

'You finished?'

Nick's head appeared in the doorway again, and she caught back the involuntary smile that fluttered on her lips. 'Five minutes!' she told him, bending to concentrate on the second foot.

'Good. There's a lull between patients, so I'll carry you out to what I euphemistically call "the surgery" when you're done.'

Like hell you will, she thought, but she contented herself with an absent-minded nod and pretended she was totally absorbed in dressing her toes.

With the padding and her thick socks, she found she could stand, providing she took some of her weight on the end of the bed. A stout stick like the one she had used while trekking and she would be mobile again! She peered under the second bed where her pack had been, but there was no sign of the stick. Still, she could hobble along holding the wall for support!

First to the bathroom. Once there, she was sorry she had made the effort, for, in daylight, she could see herself in the small mirror that hung on a hook on the wall. Her face looked as if it had lost all its flesh, so thin and drawn that the bones threw shadows on her cheeks. And the skin, clinging tautly to those bones, was drained of its soft, golden-brown tan and had become white and dry-looking. Dark smudges beneath her eyes contributed a bruised look, and the eyes themselves, half-hidden behind dark fringing lashes, gave no hint of the lively glint that could transform them from ordinary blue to sparkling sapphire.

She grimaced at the ghostly image, then ran her fingers through her inch-short hair. There must be a comb in her rucksack. She made her way back to the bed. A quick rummage through her rucksack produced clean underwear, a long, floating skirt and a T-shirt with a Nepali inscription on it that made the local people laugh. One day she would find out what it said, but, for the moment, it was clean, and it would cover her. She dressed hurriedly, anxious now to explore her surroundings.

The next room was combination ward and examination-room, by the look of it. Two sets of double bunks were set against the far wall, and a low wooden bench ran along the outside wall. To her left was a flimsy-looking structure that must have been an examination and possibly operating table. Made from tubular aluminium, it was evidently designed to come to pieces and pack into a small bundle to enable it to be carried into isolated places or flown into emergency situations. On top of it, a thin slab of dense foam beneath heavy plastic sheeting would provide minimum comfort for the patient.

Beyond the table, a door led into another room which would be similar in size to the minuscule bathroom off her bedroom, and complete the rectangular shape of the building. Using the table as support, she inched her way towards it. The sight made her blink in surprise, for it was set up as a miniature laboratory, rough, to be sure, but easily recognisable, with a wide stainless-steel bench, a microscope and slide boxes, and two locked metal cabinets, stacked one on top of the other.

So, where was the surgery? And the doctor?

Voices led her towards the outer door. There, on the low wall surrounding a sunny courtyard of hard-packed earth, sat a motley group of Nepalese, three Japanese trekkers, identifiable by the state-of-the-art camera equipment they carried, and a white man who had obviously ignored warnings to wear a hat and sunscreen and was a mottled red and white colour on all visible parts of his skin.

Beyond them, the unbelievable, massed array of snow-dappled peaks pushed their grey crags into a brilliant blue sky. Callie caught her breath, then sucked in the clear, crisp air. Once again the majesty and might of the scenery struck her like a physical blow, and she could only shake her head and marvel at it.

The Nepali conversation intensified, and Callie realised they were probably discussing her sudden appearance, and her sock-clad, oversized feet. Hearing the chatter, Nick looked up from his examination of a small child, and nodded to her.

'If you're well enough to be useful, find out what the Japanese party want.'

She smothered an urge to pout! Of course, he was too busy to greet her properly, or congratulate her on making it out this far!

She found a stick propped against the wall near the door of the hut and hobbled across to the Japanese group.

'Do you speak English?' she asked, and was relieved when all three nodded. 'Then how may we help you?'

'We go on to Gokyo,' one of them explained. 'Back in Namche Bazar we are told you will give us talk about acute mountain sickness before we go further.'

His two friends nodded, and one of them added, 'We have read that no one dies of this problem after listening to talks at health posts.'

Not so far, but the research that provided that information is connected to talks given at the Himalayan Rescue Association health posts, Callie wanted to tell them. An explanation of the difference would probably prove too much for the language barrier to handle.

She looked at Nick, then decided it would reveal her ignorance if she yelled her question across the courtyard. Excusing herself, she crossed to his side and whispered, 'Do you do AMS lectures?'

He looked up and smiled and the world stood still.

'No,' he told her, 'but my assistant does! Make it for three o'clock. It's after twelve now. They can climb around here if they want to fill in a few hours, and come back then. If they're going on to Gokyo it won't hurt them to stay at this altitude for the day.'

I can't still feel like that about him! she chided herself, his pronouncement about her new job lost in the whirling chaos of her reaction to a simple smile.

She crossed back to the tourists and explained the situation to them, pleased to find they would be quite happy to come back at three. She said goodbye and turned her attention to the sunburnt man. She couldn't let these erratic physical responses to an old friend distract her, and she certainly couldn't let that old friend see any hint of such reactions!

'The lame helping the blind!' the man joked as she approached him, and it was only then she realised that his eyelids were so puffed up that his eyes were closed to narrow slits.

'What happened?' she asked, wondering if her initial assessment of sunburn was wrong and he had been injured in an accident.

'Stupidity!' he responded through blistered, blackened lips. 'Reached Luza yesterday and decided to stop, although it was only lunchtime. I set up camp by the stream. Had a swim and lay down in the sun—woke up three hours later!'

'Have you put anything at all on it?' Callie asked as her training asserted itself.

'Only a cold cloth,' he told her, and waved a thick wadded handkerchief. 'I keep wetting it from my water bottle and dabbing the most painful bits.'

'Best thing you could have done,' Callie assured him, bending closer to look at the man's lips. 'I'd say it's only superficial. Apart from your lips, there's no blistering. Your body has probably reacted more strongly because of an altered supply of oxygen to the skin due to the altitude. Sit tight for a moment while I speak to N—Dr Grant.'

Again she crossed the courtyard, bending to explain the situation while Nick debrided dead tissue from a nasty leg ulcer.

'Should I lie him down on one of the beds and cover the burnt areas with wet towels? And what about an antihistamine, and pain-killers? Do we provide those or should I see if he has some in his own personal first-aid kit?'

Nick glanced up, his face intent. 'Yes to the bed and cold compresses. Wet them every hour or two. Use the treated drinking water from the drum in the office. You'll find glasses, bottles and sachets of salts on a shelf above it. Put a litre of solution by his bed and check his intake, give him a mild analgesic if he thinks he needs something but use paracetamol from our supply in the top metal cabinet. Most trekkers leave their medical stuff at health posts on their way out. If his trek is finishing at Lukla, he can pay us back on his way down if he has anything left over. I'll check him later to see if he needs antihistamines to reduce the swelling.'

Callie scurried away, glad to have her diagnosis confirmed. She led the solitary trekker into the 'ward' and watched as he stowed his rucksack under the bunk.

'Is it very painful? Have you taken pain-killers?' she asked.

'It's sore, but I've got such a terrible headache I've been more worried about that than the sunburn.'

'The headache could be a reaction to the sun or the effect of the altitude. Acute mountain sickness in its most benign form usually starts with a headache. I'll tell Dr Grant, and in the meantime I'll see what I can do to make you comfortable.'

Still hobbling about with the help of her stick, Callie found keys to unlock the cabinets, and took out three small hand-towels. It was good to be working! Apart from anything else, it took her mind off her sore feet. She followed Nick's instructions to the letter, then, while the man who had introduced himself as Jack Ryan relaxed beneath the wet clothes, she walked back out into the sunshine.

'You up to another job?' Nick asked. He had been walking towards the hut and paused as she appeared in the doorway.

'Of course!' she said crisply, determined to show him how good an assistant she could be.

'Then I'll get you to dress that leg ulcer. I've cleaned the wound and bathed it in a sterilising solution. Use the same gauze we used on your feet. You'll find it in the bottom cabinet. Then lint, then a waterproof dressing, taped tightly around the edges. If we use a bandage the whole thing will get wet the next time he wades through a stream and the wound will never heal.'

'But he should keep off it!' Callie protested, remembering the angry redness of the wound she'd noticed earlier.

Nick slanted her a peculiar look, but his voice, when

he explained, was kind, not sardonic, or derisive of her naïveté.

'He's a porter, Callie. He's with the Japanese party, so at least he'll have today to rest. But you can't ask these men to stop, or, if you did, they would smile politely, thank you, and ignore you. His livelihood depends on the work he does during the trekking season—six months at the most.'

She nodded and hurried back inside to fetch the dressings. She would make sure the cover was so darned watertight, his leg would have to get better!

'You very good doctor,' the man told her when she had finished, and she smiled at his careful English. Many of the porters practised other languages whenever they could, aspiring to be elevated to guides in the future.

'Not quite a doctor,' Callie told him as he departed with loquacious thanks.

'I've checked your sunburn patient and given him antihistamines. He's going to walk back down and find a lodging in the village. All he can do is keep up cold compresses and drink plenty of fluid.' Nick appeared like a genie beside her as she watched the porter walk down the trail towards the village. 'Do you know why we've got to be careful with any pain-alleviating drugs up here?'

She shook her head, too busy absorbing the beauty of the place to be fazed by his closeness—this once!

'Drugs could mask the onset of AMS or one of its more serious manifestations.'

'HAPE and HACE,' she offered, remembering the special lectures on altitude sickness she'd attended before leaving home.

Nick nodded. 'Do you understand enough about

them to speak to the trekkers this afternoon?'

Callie was inordinately pleased by the casualness of the question. He was assuming she had studied the subject before coming to Nepal. Which, of course, she had, but she hadn't expected Nick to credit her with so much common sense!

'I know the rule of thumb—like never ascending more than one thousand feet a day once you're over ten thousand feet, or taking an extra acclimatisation day before a two-thousand-foot ascent. I know about climbing high, maybe on a rest day, then returning to sleep low that night to help adapt to the altitude.'

'And the symptoms of AMS and the early-warning signs of HAPE and HACE?'

It was like being back at university, Callie decided, but she responded promptly, knowing he had to check her knowledge before he could allow her to lecture to the trekkers.

'AMS usually shows as loss of appetite, nausea, headache, sometimes vomiting, difficulty in sleeping and sometimes people complain of a fullness in the chest. It may not be serious in itself, but should always be taken as a warning signal, and if it isn't improved by rest the patient should descend—but never alone.'

'That's right,' Nick told her with a smile that made her forget all her resolution not to react to him. 'And what about the more serious manifestations?

'High altitude pulmonary oedema is a build-up of fluid in the lungs. People feel breathless, even when resting. There is a cough, beginning with white sputum, and usually some cyanosis of the lips.'

He nodded, as stern and serious now as any senior lecturer. She bit back the 'sir' she would have liked to snap at him and continued.

'High altitude cerebral oedema is the most potentially dangerous. And unsteady gait, impaired ability to make decisions and abnormal behaviour may give warning signs, but generally the onset of unconsiousness is rapid. If the person experiences drowsiness or any unsteadiness on his or her feet the party should descend rapidly. If the person loses consciousness, then he or she must be carried.'

'Good girl!' he said and the mild praise brought a disproportionate pleasure surging through her. 'Emphasise that they must all watch each other, and they must also be responsible for their staff. Many trekkers assume that because their guides or porters are natives of the mountains they have some inborn immunity to altitude sickness. People living permanently at high altitudes may develop some compensatory techniques, but sudden ascent affects them as much as anyone.'

'That's what you're working on here, isn't it?' she asked, pleased that they seemed to be able to conduct a medical conversation so amiably. As long as she could keep her physical reactions to him under control, this might be an enjoyable adventure, after all!

His shrewd brown eyes studied her face for a moment, and she fancied she could hear the painful rearrangement of previous judgements going on in his mind. Would 'Callie the Irresponsible' be given another chance? She waited, hoping, yet not hoping. The way her body was responding to Nick's presence in its orbit, it might be better if they remained at loggerheads.

'You saw the kharkas on your way up?' he asked.

'The summer settlements? Sonam explained that the sherpas bring their yaks up to the high pastures and live in the small houses. The tiny villages seemed to appear wherever there was a flat bit of ground.'

She watched him as she spoke, remembering her amazement, years ago, when the strong bony profile of a man had developed from the boy's thin, sensitive face.

'The houses all belong to people from Khumjung, a village across the ridge from Namche Bazar. Some family members move up for the summer and Bill wanted to compare their health, and particularly changes in their blood, with that of their relatives at lower altitudes, and also with that of the people at Luza, which has a permanent high-altitude population.'

'But summer's nearly over; what's your job?' she asked, caught up again in the limitless possibilities in her chosen vocation.

'Our job!' he corrected with a smile that reminded her of old times. 'We're the follow-up team, and there's a heap of paperwork, and files and figures to correlate when you're ready. Bill spent the beginning of the monsoon season with these people in the Khumjung region, then came up here with them when they brought their animals up. He's been looking in particular at the increased coagulation of blood, so the samples I take over the final months will be to see if the viscosity increases or decreases after a prolonged period at the higher altitude or remains constant throughout their stay in the kharkas.'

A tiny trickle of excitement warmed Callie's body, but this time it was the thrill of the chase, of being part of a team that might, by some miracle, discover something new. And the fact that Nick was part of the team?

He turned away at that moment, to greet a new

arrival, and she studied his back with a peculiar intensity.

Her hero-worship of Nick had pushed her to work hard through high school and made the study of medicine her ultimate goal. In adolescent dreams she had pictured the two of them working together—just like this! But four years of study had awakened a genuine love for the work she had chosen for the wrong reasons, and made success at it a goal in itself. As she'd grown up and matured—albeit slowly and painfully—she had put aside her foolish dreams of 'happy ever after' with the boy next door, and concentrated on her studies.

There's still no happy ever after, she reminded herself firmly. Nick will always see you as the flibbertigibbet of a girl he was always rescuing from scrapes, the nincompoop who always leapt before she looked! He has made it abundantly clear—more often than you care to remember—that he is not interested in you as a woman!

But the joy of working with him—even for a short time—was not so easily dimmed. It was part of the dream, and if it was the only part that she could have then she would make the most of it.'

CHAPTER THREE

'THIS is Solti. He cooks for us and looks after the hut.' Nick's voice made her blink away her thoughts.

'Cooks? Cooks where and what?'

His smile slid into place and she responded carefully, giving him an 'old friends' smile that he could not mistake for anything else.

'Come and see,' he suggested. He took her arm and supported her as she shuffled on her bulky feet through the courtyard and around towards the back of the hut. A smaller stone building butted against the hut, sharing a common wall with what would be the bedroom and the so-called ward.

'When the place was built, Bill wanted to be sure it could be used in many ways. This kitchen hut is similar to local houses, except that the fire is against one wall instead of in a fire well in the middle of the room.'

'So the fire heats the stones and transmits the heat to the other building,' Callie marvelled, stooping to enter the small, smoky room.

'And we get to keep the smoke and food odours out of our clinic. Quite a bonus when you consider the earlier health posts were set up in old houses and horribly unhygienic conditions!'

He waved her towards a rough-hewn table and pulled out a long wooden stool.

'Dahlbhat for lunch?' she asked with a grin, knowing that the watery lentil and rice mixture was the staple diet in the mountains. Over by the wall, Solti was pushing his pots and pans around above the fire with all the mastery and verve of an orchestral conductor.

'Dahlbhat with a difference,' Nick assured her. 'Solti is one in a million—and we have a table and a chair of sorts!'

'Real luxury!' Callie agreed, remembering the meals she'd consumed squatting on the ground, or slumped against the hard stone walls of a smoky, over-crowded house. She dropped down to the stool and slid along as Nick folded his long legs and settled beside her.

For a moment her heart raced, but she quelled the excitement sternly, and tried to pretend that the intimacy of sharing a meal with him like this meant nothing to her. After all, they had eaten together, at one or other of their homes, from the time she could toddle! Right up until he'd gone away to university.

'How are your studies going?' he asked, fitting neatly into her thoughts, as Solti placed a tin plate filled with an aromatic mix of vegetables, rice and lentils in front of her, and gestured towards an empty can that held an assortment of old spoons and forks.

'Terrific!' she told him, and enjoyed the look of surprise that crossed his face. On the regular occasions she'd seen him during her high-school years, she had complained constantly about the amount of work she was expected to do. 'And so's this meal!'

She ate hungrily, scooping up the spicy stew with obvious enjoyment. He was so close that she was aware of every movement he made, and out of the corner of her eye she could see his arm lifting and dropping as he ate.

The silence between them was broken by Solti clattering his pots and the soft hiss of the fire, but Callie could feel tension building up inside her old friend again and wondered if his original suspicions about her sudden reappearance in his life were still simmering beneath his calm exterior. What else could be making him so edgy?

'I'm doing paediatrics first semester next year,' she said brightly, knowing they were on safe ground only when they discussed their common interest. 'Then obstetrics—yuk!'

That got him! His head spun towards her.

'And what's wrong with obstetrics?' he enquired in the voice he used when he lectured her on something 'for her own good'. The topic could range from eating pumpkin, through the benefits of learning the four times table, to 'boys don't like promiscuous girls', but the tone was always the same.

'It's one field of medicine that should receive more focus in general practice. Not so long ago GPs delivered all their patients' babies, referring on only when there was an anticipated problem.'

'Which doesn't alter the fact that it's my least favourite subject,' she goaded, her lips twitching with delight at how easily he'd taken the bait. 'So messy! And only women patients!'

She saw his quick frown, and watched his lips half form words, then suspicion flared in the dark gaze that slanted towards her, and his own lips twitched, then widened into a familiar grin.

'Did I fall for something there?' he asked ruefully.

'Not entirely!' she conceded. 'I do agree with you about its being important in general practice, but it is the subject I like least of the entire curriculum.'

'And this is the girl who was going to grow up so she could get married and have a dozen children!' he teased.

'Only when I thought you bought them at the hospital,' she reminded him. 'And you told me that little fable, so don't try looking superior. I probably found out the real story before you anyway, girls maturing so much younger and being more prone to talk about such things than boys!'

Solti reappeared before Nick could respond. He placed a pot of tea on the table and spoke rapidly, gesturing towards his neck, and rolling his eyes heavenwards at intervals.

'I'd better go!' Nick told her. 'You drink your tea—it's the closest you'll get to the real thing anywhere in Nepal. Solti cooked for an English family in Kathmandu for many years, and brought a teapot back home with him.'

'But what's happened? Can't I help?' Callie asked as he hurried to finish the last few mouthfuls of his meal.

'Not this time, brat,' he said easily. 'You have some tea, then rest for an hour before the Japanese arrive. And make sure you sit down to talk to them. You've been on those feet too long today as it is!'

And that's that! she thought as he nodded to an excited Solti and left the room. But she was warmed by his use of the old nickname, and reassured by the more relaxed conversational level they had managed to find.

She drank her tea, realising that the idea of a rest was more appealing every moment, but, as she made her tortuously slow way back to the other building, she knew it might not be possible. An excited group had gathered in the courtyard, three women, with miscellaneous children hovering around their skirts, and the centre of attention a small baby, cradled in the sari of one of the women.

Knowing that her lack of anything more than basic politeness in the language was going to be an insurmountable problem, she called to Solti, and, when he appeared, waved her hand towards the women.

'Could you find out what they want?' she asked him. 'It might be something urgent that we can't leave until the doctor gets back.'

He went ahead of her into the sunny space, and was soon asking questions, listening, shaking his head, and peering doubtfully at the baby.

'Baby very hot, very. . .' He flopped his arms up and down by his side and Callie hazarded a guess at 'limp'.

'That right. Not eat or drink either for two days.'

He held up two fingers to emphasise this, and Callie nodded. 'Will the mother let me look at the baby?' she asked, and listened to the incomprehensible rattle of conversation.

'You can look!' he told her, and she walked towards the group, then realised she couldn't hold the baby and prop herself on her stick at the same time.

'Ask her to bring the baby inside,' she suggested, and turned to make her slow way into the hut. Once there, she gestured to the examination table, and waited for the mother to put the baby carefully in the centre of it, then step back, every angle of her body indicating her apprehension.

Propping herself against the table, Callie dropped her stick, and unwrapped the shawls from around the tiny infant. Its little body was hot, but there was no sign of a rash. The pulse was racing but it was strong and regular. Mucous filled the tiny nose, but she had realised soon after her arrival in Nepal that respiratory-tract infections and the resultant nasal discharge were endemic in the country.

Gesturing for the mother to hold the baby, although she doubted it had the strength to roll towards the edge of the table, she crossed to the cabinet and found a small rectal thermometer.

The reading was one hundred and five, and she felt her own pulse accelerate. She had seen liquid paracetamol in the cabinet earlier, but hesitated over giving it to such a small infant. Yet she must do what she could to reduce the temperature.

'How old is the baby, Solti?' She waited for a reply.

'She four,' he told her confidently.

Callie looked at the tiny infant—more the size of a premi baby than a child of four, and decided they must be counting months. She would start with medically reducing the fever, and getting some liquid into the little one's system.

Retrieving her stick, she left the mother rewrapping the child, and hobbled back into the side-room. A large plastic syringe, still in its protective Cellophane packet, caught her eye and she grinned to herself.

First she mixed the paracetamol elixir with a little sterile water, then made up another mix of electrolytic salts and water. Using a book as a tray, she carried both solutions back to the table and motioned for the mother to pick up the child. She leant against the bed, and, using the syringe, dropped liquid into the baby's mouth, holding it closed after each drop and stroking under the tiny chin to encourage her to swallow.

The other women watched this process for a short time, then nodded and smiled. Once the medication was finished, Callie started on the salts solution, and one of the women gestured that she wanted to take a turn.

Callie passed her the syringe, and watched as she mimicked the process that would replenish the moisture in the tiny body. Satisfied that they would manage, she went back into the cubby-hole and mixed up more medication and another, larger amount of liquid. A search of the lower cabinet uncovered an assortment of glass bottles, obviously gathered from a range of sources, and sterilised ready for re-use.

She tipped the medicine into a small one, and the liquid into a larger one, then found a third that would hold the syringe. Into this she tipped some sterilising liquid, diluted it with water, and left the lid off it. Now all she had to do was explain!

She called to Solti, who was still supervising the baby's feed. 'If I write the times and amount on a label on the jars, will they understand?' she asked. She lifted the medicine. 'The baby should have three millilitres of this every four hours,' she explained, 'and a little of this every hour until she is well enough to suckle again.' She touched the larger container and wondered how much English Solti understood.

'We put mark on tool!' he said, and she frowned at him. 'On tool' he repeated, and made a pressing motion with his thumb as if he were working the syringe.

'Of course we can!' Callie said delightedly. She searched through a box on the make shift desk and found a black felt-tipped pen.

Solti had disappeared, but he soon returned, bringing with him the mother and baby, and the other woman who had taken over the feeding. Speaking rapidly, he pointed to the medicine, then took the syringe and handed it to Callie. She marked it with the pen on the three-millilitre mark, then, holding it, she turned to Solti.

'Could you please tell them that when they finish each feed they should wash the syringe—' she washed it under the tap that protruded from the wall, catching the waste water in the plastic bowl beneath it—then put it into this bottle to keep it clean? No germs!'

It was two o'clock now, so she used the black pen to write '6pm, 10pm, 6am, 10am' on the jar of medicine. If they missed the late-evening dose, it wouldn't matter much; her main concern was rehydrating the baby.

'And tell them the liquid is most important!' She lifted the large jar. 'Keep trying to get as much as they can into her, and also trying her on the breast whenever she cries.'

She listened to Solti's translation of her words, and heard the stern admonitory tone he used. As she watched the women nod almost humbly she realised that they would probably take orders from the man they knew more easily than from a strange woman! Maybe learning a smattering of Nepali was not as urgent a consideration as she had thought.

By the time she had packed off her patients, the Japanese party had arrived, built up to seven with the addition of four Swedish trekkers. She found some paper and took the pen with her to illustrate the levels of altitude on their ascent to the village of Gokyo and the peak of the same name beyond it.

The courtyard was perceptibly cooler as the sun moved to the other side of the valley, and she considered going back into the bedroom and getting her jacket. She hesitated for a moment, but the dull throbbing pain from her feet decided her. She *had* been on them for most of the day, and the extra journey seemed too much to contemplate.

'Sit over here!' she suggested, leading her class to a sheltered but still sunny corner. Dropping on to a bench, she leant back against the sun-warmed rocks, not minding the hard roughness while her body could absorb their heat. The trekkers settled themselves on the ground in front of her, and she smiled to herself. The irresponsible Callie Ward as teacher? What had Nick been thinking when he gave her this job? Banishing the fleeting pleasure even thinking of him provided, she launched into her description of acute mountain sickness, cautioning her listeners to consider even the slightest of symptoms as a warning.

An hour later she thought she had finished, and was looking forward to getting out of the cold wind when her students began to ask questions.

'If judgement is impaired and the person who is sick doesn't know he is sick, how do we tell?'The question, in faultless but attractively accented English, came from one of the Swedes.

'With HAPE, you won't have a problem. You will hear the person coughing, notice his laboured breathing, see white or pinkish sputum. If you suspect HACE, the balance is impaired, so a simple test is to draw a line on the ground and ask the person to walk along it.'

One of the group stood up and drew a line with the side of his shoe, then staggered drunkenly along it.

'Maybe I'd better stay in hospital,' he suggested, winking suggestively at Callie.

'If I fill up hospital beds with malingerers like you I'll be in trouble with my boss,' she told him, joining in the general laughter. The conversation turned to social chatter, trekking experience being the main topic. Then the sun began its nightly show, painting the mountains gold before it disappeared behind them and the softer hues of the sunset took over.

They sat transfixed, their silence a communication in itself. Then, as the darkness began its brisk descent, the visitors stood up and moved towards the track to the village. Callie stood with them, then staggered as the pain shot up from her feet. One of the trekkers reached out to steady her, and held her arm while she stepped tentatively forward.

'Why don't you come down to the village and eat with us?' one asked. 'We're staying at the hotel.'

It would be fun to join them, she realised, but she was already tired, and so cold that her body was shivering involuntarily.

'Yes, do come!' the young man who had helped her up added. He must have felt her shivering, for he drew her close against his body and rubbed his hand up and down her arm to warm her. 'We can play cards, or sing songs, or tell each other lies about what great mountaineers we are!'

She laughed as she remembered evenings like that in Namche Bazar, when people of every nationality shared meals and sleeping space, drawn together by the one thing they had in common—a love of the mountains they had travelled so far to see.

'It sounds great, but no,' she told them. 'These feet might get me back to the bedroom, but I doubt they'd take me any further tonight.'

A slight lessening in the general jollity made her turn towards the trail. She watched as the group parted and Nick strode into the courtyard. Even in the dimming light she saw his quick glance take in the scene, and read the condemnation in his eyes as they lingered on the stranger's arm still slung around her shoulders.

'I hope you fellows know all about altitude sickness now,' he remarked without breaking step in his forward progression towards the hut. 'Solti will probably have dinner ready,' he added crisply to Callie, then nodded to the departing trekkers and vanished into the dark interior.

A light flickered behind her as she waved goodbye and she knew he had lit the lamp. She reached out for her stick, and made her painful way inside.

'Looking after your health is essential in isolated areas,' he grumbled as she entered the bedroom. 'And sitting outside without a jacket after the sun goes down is plain stupid. I don't want to be spending half my time here looking after you.'

He slung her jacket towards her, and disappeared into the little bathroom, his bare back stiffly proclaiming a new aggravation. The annoyance did little to deter the thoughts his pale skin and knobbly spine provoked, and she had to drag herself back to reality with deliberate force.

His down waistcoat, checked shirt and silk vest were neatly folded on the end of the second bunk, and, for the first time since early morning, she considered the significance of that other bed. Of course medical staff would be expected to share a room! But to share it with Nick? To have him sleeping so close to her?

She shivered in the enveloping folds of the jacket and shuffled towards her bed, slumping down on it to relieve her aching feet of the burden of her weight. She heard the scrape of a match and looked up to see a soft light gleam from the bathroom, then Nick appeared in the doorway, a tall, rangy shadow, backlit by the lamp now hung from a long chain that dangled from the rafters.

'Solti boils up a big kettle of water when he finishes cooking dinner. I'll carry it across for you after we've eaten, but your pre-dinner wash will have to be cold.'

You must always wash your hands before eating—she remembered him saying that to her a thousand times in the past, going into lengthy scientific detail about bacteria that had gone right over her head when she was three but annoyed her intensely by its repetitiveness. She had always washed her hands because Nick had told her to, not because of any mysterious, invisible back-whatevers that might have been lurking on her skin.

'Right now I'd settle for a couple of small bouts of cholera and typhoid if it meant not having to stand up and walk into that bathroom,' she told him as the pain in her feet became more and more insistent.

'You've overdone it,' he scolded, bending to feel her forehead, then frowning down at her feet. He squatted beside her on the floor, pushing up the concealing skirt to feel her ankles and the lower part of her legs. 'You should have been in here resting, not hanging round the courtyard cuddling total strangers!'

She opened her mouth to deny his furious assertion, then closed it again. Arguing with him when he was in this kind of mood was a waste of time. Besides, she quite liked the proprietorial tone he had used, although she knew he hadn't meant it the way her mind received it.

'I won't re-dress your feet until you're ready for bed, but in the meantime you'd better stay put. I'll bring you a bowl of water to wash in, and Solti won't mind serving your dinner in here.'

'Proving that I'm more bother than I'm worth,' Callie said bitterly. 'Don't worry about looking after me. I can make it to the bathroom to wash, and I'll crawl to the kitchen if necessary.'

'Don't be stupid!' he snapped, and walked away, back to the bathroom. 'You'll have a wash where you are, then, if you insist on going to the kitchen to eat, I'll carry you.' She heard water splash into the basin, but, above the noise, heard the muttered addition of, 'It won't be the first time!'

She bit back the retort that hovered on her tongue, and, when he returned, obediently soaped her hands then rinsed them in the basin of water he held, with too patent a patience, above her knees.

'Did you notice a drum in the corner of the bathroom?' he asked as he moved away.

'Half full of water? It looked like a slop bucket, so I emptied the basin into it this morning,' she replied.

'Bright, aren't you?' he said as he re-emerged. 'I treat it then re-use the water for washing clothes. The waste water from the lab is also treated—with a large concentration of iodine—and Solti sprays it on the grass out the back. By the time it's seeped through shale and rock and found a water course, it should be purer than most of the river water.'

For the first time Callie realised how modernisation could produce its own new range of difficulties in these mountain regions. People who had no running water, but carried it in buckets to their homes from the river or a village tap, would have little problem disposing of the small amount they used.

'How come we've got taps, anyway?' she asked.

'Where does our water come from?'

'It's come down through a black PVC irrigation pipe from a snow melt higher up the mountain. The taps were installed as modern conveniences for the visiting doctor.'

'Well, I'm glad Dr Wilcox didn't overdo the modern conveniences,' Callie told him, 'if the installation of two taps produces a problem of waste disposal.'

'And the local people feel set apart if foreigners living in their midst bring their own lifestyle with them. I've visited a research station that had all the comforts of home, including a kerosene refrigerator well stocked with imported bottled beer!'

He bent down as he spoke and lifted her into his arms. She wanted to protest, but her breath had trapped itself in her lungs, and her lips had stopped working. She looked into his face, so close that she could see where his beard stubble emerged from his skin. Her fingers reached out involuntarily and traced the tiny scar that marred the straightness of one eye-brow. She felt his reaction as the hands holding her tightened, and his breath hissed out from between his teeth.

For one incredulous moment she thought the eyes that caught and held hers had softened, but she knew she'd imagined it when he said, 'That will be enough of that!' in a voice that would vie with the mountain peaks for hardness.

'Stop being so twitchy!' she retorted, unreasonably annoyed by his over-reaction. 'I'm touching your scar, not taking liberties with your body. And I didn't ask you to carry me—you insisted!'

'You didn't ask me to carry you the day you broke your leg doing ballet on the water pipe across the creek,' he muttered, stooping over her as he ducked through the door. Outside the air was cold and crisp, and overhead the sky was a deep purple. Soon it would darken to a velvety blackness, with bright jewels of stars flung across its rich mantle. 'Or the time you sprained your ankle jumping off the bus before it stopped.'

He hadn't even noticed the beauty of the early evening, she realised. He was far too busy listing her past imperfections. She opened her mouth to argue, to point out—for the fortieth time—that she'd only jumped off the bus because she'd seen him lying on the footpath and thought he was hurt, but then shut it again. The Nick who went on and on about her little misadventures was infinitely preferable to the cold stranger he'd been in the last few years—less puzzling than the new stranger she'd glimpsed, for a fleeting second, inside the hut when she'd touched his scar.

He carried her into the kitchen and put her carefully down on the bench.

'Thanks,' she muttered as the warm places where his body had been touching hers felt the coldness of his physical withdrawal. But it was a coldness of the soul, she realised. A sense of loss for what had been between them, and all the things she knew could never be.

'I looked at a sick baby while you were out.' She blurted out the words, knowing that work would divert her mind from pointless regrets. She explained the symptoms and what she had given the infant. 'No prescribed drugs, so I didn't break any rules in using them,' she assured him, but the words didn't seem to penetrate.

'Did you have a polio booster before you left home?' he demanded, and she nodded.

'I had everything on the list,' she told him, 'although why polio was on it is beyond me. I thought doctors began introducing first Salk and then Sabin vaccine in Nepal soon after Hillary climbed Everest—and that's over forty years ago.'

'And have you noticed many medical teams walking the hills with refrigerated packs of live vaccine treating every new baby within three months of its birth?'

'Then it still exists in these parts? But that's dreadful! Couldn't you have brought frozen vials with you and given it to people on your way up here?' A sardonic grin and raised eyebrows greeted her question. 'Not a very scientific approach, eh?' she muttered, shrugging away her embarrassment. 'Is there a programme in place? Is something being done?'

He stretched his back then leaned forward, resting his elbow on the table and his head on his hand, so he was turned towards her as he replied.

'There is a programme, and it's been an effective means of control, but the immunisation teams move through most of the country on foot, so it is often a year between visits. Newborn babies are at risk of all the normal childhood complaints, plus things like diphtheria and polio, until such time as a team revisits their village.'

'But if all the adults were immunised against polio at some stage in the past,' she argued, thinking back to the immunology studies she had done earlier in the year, 'they can't be carriers.'

'Not if they've received vaccine at some time in their lives,' he agreed, 'but think of the lifestyles of these people. What if the team came to the Khumjung region during summer, when many of the local people are up here in the high pastures. Or if sherpas from a village were away supporting a mountaineering group when the team passed through. These people are nomads, remember. They drift through these mountains as easily as fog drifts down a valley.'

'So there are still carriers in the community?'

'And babies who catch it. The only consolation is that it's usually mild enough to be treated as another infant illness.'

'But what about paralysis later? The polio virus is attracted to nerve cells. If the motor-neurons are destroyed——'

'Infection in infancy and adulthood rarely results in paralysis,' he assured her. 'There's an age-linked risk of paralysis in children after infancy and before puberty. Babies who contract it will develop their own immunity, and a vaccination team would come regularly enough to ensure that most young children are covered by the time they are two.'

'So my baby shouldn't be affected?'

'My baby, is it now? Such concern for a child you will never see again after these four weeks,' he teased, but there was a gentleness in the words that pierced the armour she was trying to erect around her heart.

'She was my first Nepalese patient,' Callie explained, then sat back as Solti reached between them to put a plate of steaming stew on the table in front of her.

'And that's very special!' he agreed. 'Well, don't worry too much about her. Most young babies carry some of their mother's antibodies, so the disease will not affect them much more than a common cold, although with a high temperature there are always other associated risks.'

They discussed febrile convulsions while they ate, and Callie felt an irrational happiness. This is how I'd always imagined it, she thought, then she chuckled at her own stupidity. The vision of herself and Nick, both suitably bespectacled, soberly marching through the future like a pair of modern Curies, was a little extreme for even her vivid imagination to handle.

'Good joke?' he asked, but she shook her head and turned away from the eyes that gleamed down at her. There could be no pretence about a fairy-tale future, no matter how often she glimpsed a softening in his attitude towards her, or how much she longed for all the misunderstandings of the past to be erased!

One false move on her part, one look or touch that would betray that she was still attracted to him, and he would shy away. And, no doubt, it would also re-ignite his doubts about her reappearance in his life, and make him withdraw back into his cold, supercilious shell. If they were going to live and work in harmony together, she must devise a way to keep her emotions in check, and, more importantly, to allay the suspicions that hovered like a cloud of insects in the forefront of his mind.

CHAPTER FOUR

'. . .so I stitched it up as best I could. I hope the darned thing lives. I'd hate to be blamed for not saving the man's best breeding bull.'

Nick's voice penetrated her thoughts, and she blinked, trying to guess at the rest of the conversation. It must be to do with Solti's urgent conversation and Nick's subsequent disappearance from the lunch table.

'What about infection?' asked Callie. It seemed a fairly safe question, and should convince him she had been listening avidly.

'It will have to take its chances with that,' he told her. 'Our medical supplies are limited as it is, and to waste enough antibiotic to cure ten humans on one ungrateful yak would be taking public relations too far.'

His easy grin told her he had relaxed in her presence—at last—and she crossed her fingers superstitiously under the table, willing the mellow mood to remain.

'What are the plans for tomorrow?' She lifted one hand to hide a yawn as she asked the question.

'Lab and office work in the morning. I've found the local people rarely arrive for consultation before midday. They must get their chores out of the way first, then drift up here the moment I start thinking about lunch.' He smiled again, but she refused to acknowledge it.

'And speaking of lunch, what about meals? What

time do you get up and eat? Should I offer to help?'

'And offend the best cook in the mountains? No way! Solti makes tea and brings that in with porridge at about six, then he cooks a hearty brunch—omelettes and rice—at about ten. He also makes his own flat bread—the best chapattis north of India—and you can fill up on those. You slept through that meal today.'

'And if I've any sense I'll sleep through tea and porridge at six!' she wailed. 'You can't be serious! I'm on holiday!'

'A working holiday,' he reminded her, laughing at her protests, 'and you'll be in bed and sound asleep before ten. Believe me, that bed might be a comfortable alternative to some you've slept on recently, but after eight hours your body will be pleased to leave it. Bare boards covered with an inch-thick layer of foam soon lose any illusion of softness.'

It *was* like old times, laughing and joking with Nick, but, tired as she was, she knew she couldn't take it for granted, or relax her self-imposed vigilance until she'd struck on some way to convince him that he meant nothing more than an old friend to her.

'Now, I'd better get you back to the hut, and take a look at those feet.'

He stood up, and as he moved his arm brushed against hers, igniting all the fires she was trying to deny. And she was tired! Too tired to fight it?

'I'll hobble back on my stick,' she told him when he reached out to take her in his arms. 'My legs are cramped. The walk will loosen them up.'

She saw his reaction as his arms grew taut and his hands clenched into fists before dropping back to his sides.

'Your stick's not here. I'll take your arm,' he said

coolly, stepping back while she pushed herself painfully to her feet and regained some balance.

He helped her carefully back towards the hut—too close for her peace of mind—yet not close enough to give any relief to her aching, wanton body. She kept her eyes steadfastly on the ground, refusing to acknowledge the magic of the night, or risk a quick look at the beauty of the stars that burnt so brightly above them. Stars and velvet nights were for lovers.

Lovers! The word leapt and jangled in her mind, and she hobbled on, trying to capture the glimmering of an idea it had started.

He led her into the bedroom, and, as she dropped on to the safety of her own bed, she looked at the second rough structure, so close to hers, and her insides trembled.

Lovers!

'I don't know how Howard would feel about this!' The words had popped out before she realised the idea had fully formed.

'Howard?' He sounded surprised, but he couldn't be more surprised than she was. The flash of inspiration had come like a lightning bolt from the heavens, but, as the seed of thought grew and blossomed in her fertile brain, she recognised it as a stroke of genius. The old subconscious mind at work!

'My fiancé,' she said, sounding sickeningly coy. She was wearing at least ten rings on her fingers—all pretty but cheap adornments she had bought in Kathmandu. Nick would never know that one wasn't an engagement ring. 'He's an architect in Brisbane. I met him through——' her imagination faltered for a moment '—the Freedom for Hunger appeal—forty-hour famine thing—he was one of the starving volunteers whose health I was monitoring.' She felt quite smug with her own brilliance, but Nick's voice diverted her self-congratulation.

'And what "this" might Howard be concerned about?' The words were delivered through tightly compressed lips, the voice colder than the water from the snow-melt.

Callie's heart quavered but she stood—or sat—her ground. It was for the best, she reminded herself. 'This sharing my room with a man!' she answered lightly, waving a casual hand towards the second bed. 'But when I tell him it was only my old friend Nick, he'll understand.'

The 'old friend' turned away from her, his stiff back disappearing through the ward towards the equipment-room. She thought she heard him mutter 'Old friend' under his breath, but she couldn't be sure. Besides, now the danger was averted, why should she care what he muttered under his breath?

She found her stick and hobbled to the bathroom. The promised pitcher of hot water was sitting on the floor. Stripping off, she washed her body all over, using soap sparingly as she knew it was hard to remove with the soft water. She tipped the soapy water into the drum, then used fresh warm water to rinse herself off. It was an awkward process, as she had to keep water off her feet, but she managed.

It was bliss to be clean, but the cold air was biting into her skin and she towelled herself quickly dry then pulled on a clean thermal singlet and the warm tracksuit she used as pyjamas. Clutching her discarded clothes, she shuffled back towards the bed, where Nick waited with another basin of water.

'I'll do my feet,' she offered. 'You use the bathroom while the water's still hot.'

'You managed to bath without using all the hot water?'

The sarcasm didn't bother her. 'No trouble at all!' she assured him. 'Howard would like to work in under-developed countries, so I've been practising my bird-baths!'

She heard him grit his teeth together and warned herself not to overdo things! He'd get suspicious if she overplayed the enthusiasm.

'Off you go. I'll do my feet,' she repeated when he continued to hover over her. The silent vibrations from his body surrounded her senses and tormented her nerve-endings, and for a moment she wondered if he was as impervious to the invisible currents as he liked to pretend. Could such a vital attraction be all one-sided?

'I'd like to have a look at them. Unwrap them, and bathe them, but don't dress them until I get back.'

It was an order—peremptorily delivered—but she didn't lift her hand in a cheeky salute this time. Instead, she watched him step stiffly away from her, and told herself it was better this way.

Her feet looked healthier, and Nick must have agreed, for he dispensed with the treated gauze, and contented himself with using antibiotic powder and clean lint beneath the bandages. She suffered the long fingers probing at her toes, and tried to ignore his physical closeness, holding her body tense as if her very stillness might stop the flow of warmth his touch generated.

'Have you got clean socks?'

The question startled her out of her reverie. 'Two

pairs,' she told him, pointing to her rucksack. She watched him reach out and lift it, then realised he was going to search through it. 'Pass it here—I'll get them,' she said, so abruptly that he spun around to face her.

'Afraid I'll find Howard's love-letters?' he asked nastily, and she felt a tide of colour wash into her cheeks.

'Something like that,' she mumbled, grabbing the rucksack from his hand. He blinked his surprise, then frowned ferociously down at her, and walked across to his bed.

Callie ignored him, rummaging through the contents until her fingers found a firm leather rectangle. She held it tightly for a moment, thanking the fates yet again that it had been in her hand luggage on the flight to Kathmandu, then she slid it out and pushed it under the thin mattress before searching through the jumbled clothing for clean socks.

I'll never sleep, she told herself as she settled into her sleeping-bag and curled on her side so her back was turned to the room and its other occupant. Then she woke to movement in the blackness, and Nick's voice saying, 'Tea's made,' with a hateful enthusiasm.

Her body ached, her bones felt bruised from the slatted bed, and her eyes were matted closed. 'This is ridiculous!' she complained. 'It's still pitch-dark and those lanterns don't give enough light to see by, let alone write reports or study slides. Why get up now?'

'So we can see the sunrise,' he told her heartlessly. 'Sit up and have your tea, then hobble out to the courtyard. When you get a spare moment, you can write and tell Howard all about it. I'm certain an architect would be more interested in the magic of the mountains than tales of cell culture and blood coagulation.'

'And post it in the little letter-box down the road?' she muttered scathingly, but the lure of the sunrise was strong and she struggled into a sitting position and picked up her cup of tea. Once warmed by the hot, sweet liquid, she found she was hungry, so attacked the porridge with gusto. Maybe six o'clock wasn't such a bad time to wake up!

Outside, the light was getting stronger, but the mountains looked bleak and forbidding until the sun rose high enough to touch them with its rays, turning them a rosy, unbelievable pink. Callie felt the sigh slide from her lips, and knew Nick must have heard it, for he turned towards her and nodded.

'Worth it, brat?' he said, reaching out to ruffle his hand in her cropped curls.

'Just!' she told him, but she softened the admonition in her voice with a smile, and caught the memories reflected in his eyes.

Ten years ago he'd dragged her to the top of Mount Cordeaux, not far from their home town of Toowoomba, insisting they must be there to see the sunrise over the fertile coastal plain. She had complained bitterly throughout the cold, dark, misty climb, and only grudgingly conceded him right when the splendour of the winter sunrise had stolen into her heart, and brought tears to her eyes.

She walked back inside the hut, anxious to escape the weakening effects of familiarity. At the door she paused, and turned towards him. 'I'll have a quick wash and change, then be ready to start.' She hoped her brisk, businesslike voice would impress him.

More than her wardrobe would, she realised as she rifled through her rucksack again for a clean T-shirt to wear with the flowing 'hippie' skirt she'd worn the day before.

He was working in the small laboratory when she returned, sitting on a rough stool, his long back bent forward as he peered into the eyepiece of a microscope. 'I've pulled out the file cards,' he told her, without looking up. 'They should be in the same order as the slides.' He waved to a pile of envelopes beside him on the bench, and she opened one and peered in to see the blood-smeared slide. 'It will save me a lot of time if I can call out the findings and have you jot them on the cards. This fellow is Mingma Three.'

Callie picked up the first file and saw 'Mingma Three' written at the top. 'That's a name?' she queried.

'What do you know about this region?' he asked, still concentrating on the slide as his long fingers manipulated the tiny screws that would move it around beneath the strong lenses.

'It's Eastern Nepal, Sherpa population, semi-nomadic people.'

'Who share about twenty surnames, so we have Tserings and Tenzings all over the place, but not necessarily related. Also, many of the people call their sons after the day of the week on which they are born. Dawas, Pembas and Mingmas abound!'

'So how can you correlate the results and look at family connections?' Callie demanded.

'Look at the next file.'

She lifted the second card and smiled. 'Pemba, Son of Mingma Three'!

'We have six families involved in the studies. Two of the senior men have worked as porters on expeditions and spend a lot of time at extremely high altitudes—one was on the Russian ascent of Cho Oyu a few years back. The next two are men who bring their families up to Machherma each year to run their yak herds on the summer pasture, and the final pair are merchants from Namche Bazar, who make fortnightly trips up to Gokyo during the trekking season to bring stock for the shops and tea-houses they open to catch the passing trade.'

'Entrepreneurs?' Callie asked, and saw him smile his assent.

'All have sons who work with them, so we have widened the age group, but our work with women is confined to the Sherpanis who are here for the summer. Now, go back to Mingma Three and write this.'

Callie bent obediently over her work, realising as she wrote that the last entry was in Nick's handwriting and dated a month earlier. She hadn't thought to ask when he'd arrived—the shock of seeing him in this unlikely spot had swept such mundane considerations from her mind.

They worked peacefully together, but she was glad she had invented Howard, for she felt his presence like an invisible curtain between them. It might not be strong enough to stop Nick's nearness affecting her skin, or an accidental touch zapping her nerves to riot-point, but it had certainly made normal conversation between them possible.

'Dr Nick, you needed on trail below village. Girl very sick.'

Solti was shifting from one foot to the other, and a man in the ragged dress of a porter shuffled nervously beside him. Callie felt a wave of panic sweep across her. It must be something bad to cause such obvious anxiety.

'Could you pack these back into that metal case?'

Nick asked, waving towards the solid aluminium trunk. 'Heaven knows when we'll have time to work on them again.'

He went to a cabinet and took out a small doctor's bag, incongruous in the primitive surroundings of the mountains.

'Hold the fort!' He smiled at her as he spoke, and for Callie it was like the sunrise all over again.

This is ridiculous, she scolded herself, and busied her hands packing away the slides, files and microscope. Through the window she could see Nick's tall figure bent low to speak to the porter, and as they disappeared she realised he must have been speaking Nepali. Had he learnt it when he trekked here during his university holidays? Had he always intended coming back?

'Breakfast ready ten minutes,' Solti told her, and her stomach growled obligingly. A second breakfast at ten o'clock now seemed an excellent idea.

Without Nick, the rest of the morning dragged. She washed and dressed her feet, reducing the bandages to more manageable proportions.

Now what?

She went back to the lab, opened the case that held the file cards, and looked through the other papers in it. Unfolding one, she saw a large graph. Remembering the notations on the cards, and recognising the names on the graph, she worked out what the absent Dr Wilcox had been trying to do.

None of the notations was in Nick's writing. She spread the sheet of paper on the desk. Perhaps she could start transferring information from the cards to the chart. Within minutes she was absorbed in the task, so Solti's lunch call surprised her. No patients? No

interruptions? She looked at the chart and pride surged through her. Well, at least she'd accomplished something this morning!

She had finished lunch and was spreading some washing to dry on a low stone wall beyond the huts when a commotion brought her back to the courtyard. Nick was there, surrounded by a chattering, giggling gaggle of young European women—most of them far too nubile and attractive for their own good, Callie decided.

'Ah, such bliss!' one of them said, her accent proclaiming her Australian nationality. As Callie watched in amazement the girl dropped her light day-pack on to the ground beside the building, then sank down beside it, using it as a pillow while she raised her face to the sun. Others settled themselves on the benches or stone walls, slipping out of their jeans and unbuttoning their shirts to reveal minuscule bikinis. Within minutes, the space where they had treated patients the day before resembled an Australian beach in high summer, with near-naked sunworshippers spread all over every available surface.

Nick looked across at Callie and grinned, but her answering smile was forced. If she had ever behaved as these girls were doing he would have been furious, and lectured her on respecting other people's customs, skin cancer and probably morality as well!

'Sick, are they?' she sniped as he came towards her.

'The sick one's still coming,' he explained, but she saw his glance dart across the group and felt fury mounting inside her. 'It's a school party, and one of them has developed chickenpox.'

'Nearly everyone gets chickenpox at some stage of their life!' Callie bit out the words. 'It's not something

that requires hospitalisation! Or an emergency dash down the mountain by the only doctor for hundreds of miles!'

She saw his eyes darken and the quick frown that drew his brows together. 'Will you ever learn to think before you open your mouth?' he snapped, and she stared at him in surprise. 'The porters knew she was sick and when they saw the blisters most of them panicked and fled. The guide stayed, and he had the sense to send one of the remaining porters up here to get me, but the others could be back in Namche Bazar by now!'

'They thought it was smallpox,' she said slowly. 'Vaccination only started after the country was opened up to foreigners. I suppose most of the older men had seen smallpox outbreaks when they were young.'

'Exactly!' Nick agreed, ushering her into the hut as the chattering voices of the teenagers became distracting. 'So when a porter tells me there's a case of smallpox, of course I go rushing down the mountain!'

'But it isn't smallpox,' Callie objected. 'So why are all those young women sunning themselves in our courtyard?'

If he noticed the proclamation of ownership in her 'our' he said nothing, but his frown deepened. 'Think!' he ordered. 'In another two years you will be let loose on an unsuspecting public, so you must learn to use whatever brains you've got inside that fluff-filled head of yours.'

Fluff-filled head, indeed, she thought, but when she tried to work out what he wanted to know she realised the description was curiously apt. Her head did feel fluff-filled—not at all like the clear, unclouded space

her brain usually occupied. And it was all his fault!

'Contagion?' she tried meekly, but when he nodded she remembered something else and had to argue. 'But the incubation period is two to three weeks. You can't keep them all here for that long—they'll have planes to catch, return schedules to meet. And they won't all catch it. Some will have had it when they were younger and still carry immunity.'

'And the villagers?' he probed, and Callie slumped down on to one of the beds.

'Oh, hell!' she muttered. 'I didn't even think of them. What if my sick baby caught it? Unless it's common in the mountains it could sweep through these isolated villages like the plague.'

'So, what do we do?' He was looking down at her, his face stern, as he forced her to consider all aspects of what had seemed a simple case.

'Isolate all suspected carriers,' she told him, feeling stupid that she hadn't immediately thought of this. 'That's why you've brought the group here. But how long can they stay here?' And some of them could still be carriers whenever they leave, because they won't all start incubating it at the same time.'

'So our job will be to make certain we put in place procedures they can follow to prevent it spreading.'

'Masks,' Callie suggested, pleased that her brain was beginning to function normally. 'It's spread by droplets from the respiratory tract, isn't it?'

'And contact with the lesions, or clothes or bedding that have been in contact with the lesions,' Nick added. 'I've brought them all up here, rather than allow them to stay in the village. Fortunately they overnighted at Luza and camped by the river well away from the village. They were on the trail early this morning, hoping to get beyond Machherma today because they are already behind schedule.'

As he was speaking Callie sensed movement outside and the chattering of the girls became shrill cries of welcome. Nick walked to the door, then hurried outside, leaving Callie to follow more slowly. Two sherpas carried a makeshift stretcher, and two young women walked beside it. One held an umbrella over the girl who lay on the stretcher, while the other held her hand and seemed to be talking quietly to her.

'Bring her through into the hut,' Nick said, waving the excited girls away from the small party. The porters lowered the stretcher, and the girl rose shakily to her feet.

'I feel so stupid!' she said, and Callie's heart responded instantly. It was the kind of silly thing that had always seemed to happen to her.

'It's not your fault,' she said swiftly, stepping forward to lead the girl to a bed. 'Now, would you like a wash? Do you want to change into clean clothes before you hop into bed? Would you like a cup of real tea?'

She could feel Nick hovering behind her, then heard the amusement in his voice as he said, 'The Florence Nightingale is my assistant Callie Ward. She's finished four years of medical studies so qualifies as a beginner nurse. I suggest we leave the patient in her capable hands and sort out your camping arrangements.'

Callie spun around, remembering words he'd used when she had arrived, half-dead, on his doorstep. He'd been adamant that the health post did not become some kind of unofficial trekking camp.

Then she saw the raven hair and sparkling smile of one of the women, and glimpsed the youthful, suntanned flesh spread about the courtyard. Would a less attractive group of trekkers have received such prompt, preferential treatment?

'This is Ellen Rice, and this is Amanda Quirk,' Nick said. 'Teachers in charge of the girls.'

Then he was gone, and all Callie could do was ignore the jealous pounding of her blood and turn back to her new patient.

'I'm Callie,' she introduced herself. 'Who are you and what are you all doing up here in the mountains?'

The sick girl introduced herself as Linda, and explained that they were pupils at an all-girl school in Brisbane, the capital city where Callie was studying. Exclaiming over this new coincidence, she led the girl through to the bathroom, leaving her to strip off her dusty clothes while she sought out hot water and ordered tea from Solti.

'And are all fifteen of us going to use the one little toilet?' she muttered at Nick when she passed him in the courtyard. 'That will be fun!'

Without waiting for his reply, she limped into the kitchen hut, annoyed with herself for allowing her irritability to show. And why was she so irritable? It would be fun to have company for a few days.

As she emerged with a metal pitcher of water, one of the girls came towards her.

'I'll carry that for you,' she offered, making Callie feel even more guilty about her inhospitable thoughts. 'I'm Helen. Linda's my best friend and we've been sharing a tent, so if I'm going to get it I'm probably incubating it already.'

Callie smiled at her. 'I'll carry the water—it's boiling hot and I'd hate to have another patient if you slopped it on yourself. You could go back into the kitchen,' she nodded her head back towards the smaller hut, 'and wait for Solti to make the tea then carry it across. You'll know how Linda likes it.'

The chaos in the courtyard continued, and Callie felt her temperature surge at the sight of Nick surrounded by the young women, the majority of whom were gazing adoringly up into his face while he explained the basics of pit toilets. Well, at least he's doing something about that little matter! she thought grudgingly, but the lovely oval face of the dark-haired Amanda made her feel sick with apprehension. How could he not fall in love with someone so beautiful?

She walked away from the sight, feeling pain in her feet for the first time today. Looking for sympathy, that's all that is, she told herself firmly, and shuffled into the bathroom, where Linda waited.

By the time she had tucked the girl into her sleeping-bag on one of the hospital beds, given her two analgesics for her headache, and washed out the discarded clothes in disinfectant and water, the courtyard was empty, waiting for the village patients to come straggling in. Walking around the end of the hut to spread the washing on her stone 'washing-line', she blinked in amazement.

A small village had been set up on the grassy area in the lee of the two buildings. Two-man sleeping tents were erected in a neat line against the stone wall, and a larger cooking tent stood in the angle of the hut walls. A kerosene stove was already lit and a large pot of water was heating on it. Fifty yards away, beyond the compound, the two porters who had carried the stretcher were digging a hole in the iron-hard ground: the pit toilet Nick had promised.

Surveying the activity and its results, Callie realised that the deserting porters must have rejoined the party, or new men been employed, for the girls had carried little more than snacks and warm clothing in their day-packs, and all this equipment had arrived here somehow.

'We seem to have taken over your hospital,' a voice said, and she turned to see the teacher called Ellen standing beside her.

'It's best to keep you all away from the villagers,' Callie told her. 'That way we might keep the infection under control.'

'We're lucky you're here,' Ellen said. 'Our guide tells us the health post has only opened this year.'

Callie nodded, then turned towards the courtyard as voices heralded the arrival of more visitors or patients. 'Back to work—I'll see you later,' she said, and Ellen smiled.

'I'll make sure the girls keep out of your way,' she promised, as Callie looked around for Nick, and, not seeing him—or the lovely Amanda—she called to Solti to come and translate for her.

It was another messenger. Once again Callie recognised an anxious, excited, and rather breathless porter.

'He is from group who walked through to Gokyo three days earlier. One man get lost on black mountain there, and spend night in open. They carry him down, but need doctor to look at him sooner so this man run on ahead.'

'Hypothermia!' Callie muttered, her mind racing through the symptoms and treatment of the condition. Apart from gradual warming, if necessary by the introduction of warm fluids into the blood, the only on-the-spot first aid a doctor could give would be oxygen. Would the party have any hot pads or an insulating silver blanket? she wondered.

'Find Dr Nick,' she told Solti, then hurried into the lab. Grabbing a small backpack, she opened the cabinets and squatted down to search through the contents. First she took out the six small heat pads. One flex and they would produce instant heat. Packed around the extremities, they might do some good. Next she added a slim silver packet—the blanket designed for NASA and space research. Folded around the patient, it would keep in whatever heat was being generated. Then she added the small oxygen cylinder and a sealed mask and tube-attachment pack.

'Good girl!' She looked up to see Nick checking the contents of the bag. 'If you put your hand right through to the back of the cupboard you'll feel a plastic packet of what looks like balloons.'

Reaching in, she found the packet and pulled it out.

'And I'll take a kero stove, billycan and some extra water, and a bag of IV fluid, to heat and drip into his veins.'

'You'll never carry it all!' she protested, still looking dubiously at the balloons.

'I'll give the bulk of it to the porter who came with the message, and carry the light pack on ahead myself. Amanda's coming as well; she can take the fluid and venous catheters in her day-pack.'

Callie felt her lungs constrict, and clamped her lips tightly shut lest some unladylike comment escaped.

'It could be dark before we meet up with the party. We'll take a tent and sleeping-bags, and will stay the night. A person suffering from hypothermia shouldn't be moved until he's been stabilised. He will be losing more heat while he's being carried, and even the most careful movement puts an added strain on his body and distracts it from its job of trying to keep the central core warm enough for all the organs to function properly.'

'So you'll set up camp and warm him where he is?' Callie asked, trying to ignore the dismay escalating within her body.

'As best we can. Hopefully, we'll find somewhere near water. Those balloons are long rubber hot-water bags. They can be filled with warm water and packed around the body to help raise the skin temperature and ease the pressure on the body core. If necessary, we'll sleep with him and use our body heat to warm him. All the guides know that trick, but the group's leader refused to let them try it.'

'And if anything urgent arises here?' She hoped she didn't sound as bitter as she felt.

'You'll handle it!' he told her, sounding so confident that she gaped at him, unable to believe it was the same man who, only hours earlier, had called her fluffy-headed. 'At least you'll have company while I'm away!' he added.

And so will you! she thought angrily.

'I'll be back as soon as I can be—tomorrow evening at the latest. Once I've seen the patient through the night, and shown whoever's with him the routine, I should be able to leave.'

He reached out as if to pat her on the head, but she ducked away, fiddling with the simple lock on the cabinet as intently as she would a complicated locking device on a bank vault. Patting her on the head as if she were a child, while he headed off up into the mountains with the nearest thing to a beauty queen Machherma could offer. . .!

But the simile was not a good one. It reminded

her of her own fleeting moment of glory—queen of Toowoomba's Carnival of Flowers, no less! The honour every little girl dreamed of from the first time she saw one of the spectacular floral parades. She'd been so excited! So lit up by the thrill of it all!

Until she'd danced with Nick.

She pressed her head against the cold metal of the cabinet, and forced the memories away.

CHAPTER FIVE

'LINDA's sores are itchy!'

Helen's voice brought Callie back to the present.

'I'll get some soothing lotion to spread on them, but it won't completely alleviate the problem. The best thing to do is try to divert her mind from the misery. Talk about things that interest her—clothes, boys, whatever!'

Helen grinned, and Callie pushed herself to her feet, rocked back on her heels to take her weight off her painful toes, then searched through the top cabinet where all the medications were kept.

'Someone foresaw the most surprising eventualities,' she muttered, coming across a bottle of tablets labelled 'Ergotrate Maleate'. As far as she could remember from pharmacology lectures, they were used to help contract the uterus and prevent haemorrhage after childbirth or abortion. She pushed them aside, and finally located a bottle of tried and true calamine lotion. She reached back into the lower cabinet and brought out a pack of cotton balls.

'Here,' she said to Helen. 'Dab this over them. If she's still uncomfortable tonight, I'll give her an antihistamine. That should ease the itchiness and the mild sedative effect will help her sleep.'

Should she hand out prescription drugs without Nick's consent? She was puzzling over the medical proprieties when Ellen appeared.

'I think you've got a patient in the front yard. And a good-looking one at that.'

'Maybe word's spread about the bevy of bathing beauties we have up here,' Callie remarked, and saw the other woman's wry smile.

'We've tried to keep them covered in public!' she exclaimed. 'You'd think with all the emphasis on skin cancer these days they'd have more sense, but no. The moment we reach an even partially secluded spot they all strip off and plant themselves like carpets out to air in the sun!'

Callie chuckled, then followed Ellen out to the courtyard, denuded now of the sunbathers. The Swedish trekker who had asked her to dinner in the village was sitting on the wooden bench, one leg pushed out in front of him and the other tucked away under the bench. Twenty feet beyond him, the girls had clustered to peer at the new arrival.

'I'll take the girls for a walk up the hill,' Ellen said. 'It will keep them out of your way and hopefully tire them enough to make a good night's sleep possible.'

'And what's your problem?' Callie asked the newcomer as Ellen shepherded the girls away.

He levered his second foot forward and pointed towards it. The foot was bound less professionally than Callie's pair, but the sock that encased the bandages was a far brighter specimen. He forced a smile, and said in his beautiful accented English, 'I think the frost has bitten my toe.'

'What did you do? Sleep with it stuck out of the sleeping-bag and tent?' She bent down and was about to pull off the sock when his hands caught her shoulders.

'I'll do it!' he told her, and she saw the paleness of

his lips and guessed at the pain he was suffering.

What on earth was she going to do with a frostbitten toe? She looked up at the clear blue sky and felt the warmth of the sun on her shoulders. Surely he was wrong!

'Shall I help?' she asked as he peeled the bandages away from his foot.

'Very, very sore!' he told her.

I bet it is, she thought, remembering the clinical progress of frostbite when ice crystals formed in the tissue. Water was then drawn out of surrounding cells, causing an increase in intracellular electrolytes, and subsequent destruction of cells and damage to blood vessels.

'When did it happen?' she asked as he dropped the discarded bandages in a pile.

'Last night. We were in camp, asleep, and it became too painful to bear. I look at it this morning, and walk back to see you.'

He would have passed Nick on the trail, Callie thought, but she had no time to pursue the notion as the foot was now revealed. His big toe was swollen and an angry red. Even before she touched it, Callie could feel the heat emanating from it.

'It's not frostbite,' she told him. 'Wrong colour!' She tried a smile, but her friend of the previous day was eyeing her warily. He's either wondering if I know what I'm talking about, or it's so painful that he's terrified I'll touch it and hurt him more, she thought. 'Frostbite begins with a firm white plaque, and the digit is cold to touch. That's not cold, is it?'

Her patient shook his head. 'But it might be worse frostbite,' he offered.

'No,' Callie said, bending closer to see if she could

see any evidence of an insect bite. 'Second-degree frostbite has white blisters, while third degree has purple blisters. And the skin is always cold. Could something have bitten you?'

'I don't think so,' the man said, and lifted his foot to peer underneath the toe.

'Well, hobble inside and get up on the table. I can have a closer look at it without having to handle it and cause you more pain.'

She led him into the ward and introduced Linda and Helen.

'I am Carl,' he told them politely, but Callie recognised the extent of his pain when he failed to flirt with—or even smile at—the two girls.

Once he was lying comfortably, she looked at the toe from all angles, using magnifying glasses to see if she could find a sign of a bite or an infection site.

'The only thing I can think of is gout,' she told him bluntly, 'but that's unlikely in someone of your age.'

'Gout?' he queried. 'What is gout?'

'It's a form of arthritis,' she explained. 'It's caused by a build-up of uric acid, which forms crystals in the joints. The pain and inflammation is caused by your body's defence system attacking the crystals. I can give you some pain relief, but you'll have to wait until Dr Grant returns for any other treatment.'

Carl frowned, and Callie felt perversely annoyed with the man. He was lucky there was a health post here at all, she felt like telling him.

'It usually gets better in a week without treatment,' she told him heartlessly, then crossed to the cabinet to find more pain-killers. A dispenser of aspirin, that's what I am, she decided as she poured water into a glass. As she watched the water flow slowly, a possible explanation occurred to her. She hurried out and gave him the tablets.

'Do you drink plenty of water as you trek?' she asked him.

'More chang!' he said, referring to the local beer.

'Well, beer is a diuretic. It makes you urinate more frequently and helps to dehydrate you instead of supplying your body with liquids. The build-up of uric acid could have been caused by not drinking enough water for your kidneys to function properly.'

Her patient nodded, but she didn't know how much he was taking in. His English was excellent, but would he understand scientific theorising?

'You'd better stay here tonight, so I can make sure you get at least three litres of fluid into you,' she suggested. 'I'll put Linda, who's infectious, in my room and you can have this bed.' She waved her hand towards the bunk furthest from Linda's. 'If you lie down, I'll make a cradle to hold your foot up, then between us we'll work out some way to keep you covered without having bedclothes resting on your toe. With regular pain-killers, you should make it through the night, and Nick will be back tomorrow and will have some suggestions about anti-inflammatory drugs.'

She closed her eyes for a moment and prayed she was doing the right thing. Then she shrugged philosophically. Even if it wasn't gout, it was painful, so pain relief couldn't do any harm.

It took her an hour to get Linda settled and a makeshift sling knotted from the upper bunk to elevate the foot. Carl nodded his appreciation and drifted off to sleep as the pain-killers worked and the effects of an anxious and sleepless night caught up with him.

Back in the laboratory, Callie found some blank

patient cards, and, using completed ones as a guide, began filling in one for Linda and one for Carl. She would have to get some more details—like surnames!—she realised and smiled at the casualness of the consultations compared to the hospital sessions she had witnessed during her studies and practical work.

Her next patient was a man with a tooth so rotten that it made Callie feel sick to look at it.

'You must have someone in the village who pulls teeth,' she told him through Solti.

'Only in Khumjung, where they live,' Solti explained after a rapid conversation. 'Dr Nick do it here last week, that's why this man came to see him.'

Well, he can just go away again, Callie thought, but she kept her dismay hidden. 'I can give him something for the pain,' she said, smiling inwardly that once again she was dispensing pain relief, 'but he'll have to come back tomorrow if he wants it pulled out. Dr Nick will enjoy doing it,' she added wickedly. 'And Miss Quirk might assist him!'

The man was leaving the courtyard when another porter appeared, and Callie closed her eyes for a moment and pleaded with the heavens that it wasn't another emergency somewhere on the trail. He approached her diffidently, asking for Nick in passable English.

'He's not here,' she explained. 'Maybe I can help you.'

The man smiled shyly, then rummaged in his clothes and produced an empty bottle with a prescription written on it in Nick's handwriting.

'Was this for you?' Callie asked, studying the date and working out that it was ten days earlier.

'I get it going up to Gokyo, but cough still bad.'

The man demonstrated, spraying sputum all over the courtyard.

'Wait here,' Callie told him, and fled inside, anxious to escape further contamination.

She studied the name scrawled on the bottle's label, then rifled through the cards until she found one that matched. Sure enough, the man's visit was recorded on the given date, his temperature, blood-pressure and pulse-rate were noted down, the prescribed tablets were described, and, right at the bottom, was a final note: 'Query TB, suggest Khunde for tests.'

Callie read it aloud, horror flooding through her. Not only polio but tuberculosis as well! She knew TB was still common in many tropical countries, but had not connected it with Nepal. She shook her head, grabbed a thermometer and the sphygmomanometer and hurried back outside. It was the isolation of these people that made them so vulnerable, she realised, strapping the cuff of the blood-pressure machine around the man's arm and inflating it.

'I must do this and take your temperature to put it on the card,' she explained. 'That way, Dr Grant will know how you are getting on, and what I have given you.'

Walking back into the lab, she realised that his blood-pressure was stable but his pulse-rate seemed alarmingly low to her. Consulting his card, she realised it must be normal for him as it was the same as the last notation. But his temperature was much higher—three degrees above normal. She tried to remember what she had learnt about TB and wondered if she was imagining it or if she had read that the patient's temperature would soar towards evening.

She noted it on the card, and re-filled the bottle

with the same antibiotics Nick had prescribed. It was a broad-spectrum tetracycline, not one of the three drugs of choice for tuberculosis but extremely effective for chronic infections of the respiratory tract.

'Will you be in Machherma tomorrow?' she asked as she handed over the bottle.

'No, I go to Dole in the morning, taking trekkers back to Lukla,' he explained.

'Well, when you get to Namche Bazar, go across to the hospital at Khunde. They can do tests for you.'

It was all she could do, but her heart quailed at the thought that it was so little. Was he walking round with the killer disease inside his body—forcing himself to keep working, because that was the only life he knew?

She looked out over the mountains. It was a hard life, carrying heavy loads up and down the winding trails, but it had its compensations, surely. The peaceful beauty of the scene caught at Callie's heart again. She remembered the sunrise she had shared with Nick only this morning, then she remembered Amanda, who would be sharing tomorrow's sunrise with him. . .

Turning away from the view, she hurried back inside the hut. Linda had drifted off to sleep and Helen was lying on Callie's bed, reading one of the paperbacks she'd bought in Kathmandu.

'Would you like to walk a little way up the hill and meet the others? They should be coming down soon.'

'No chance!' Helen told her, sitting up and swinging her feet guiltily off the bed. 'I'm enjoying this lazy break. I'll head out to the camp shortly and get the first hot water for a wash, then get ready for dinner. Do you want the bed?'

Callie shook her head. 'If I lie down I might never

get up. I've got to find the lanterns and make sure they're filled, and that I can light them, or we'll have a dark hospital tonight. I'm new here myself,' she explained.

Solti produced four filled lanterns for her, and demonstrated the lighting technique. They were similar to the old kerosene lanterns her mother had kept at home for power failure.

Returning to the ward, she lit the first and hung it from the ceiling hook. She saw Carl stir, and bent towards him.

'Would you like something to eat?' she asked.

'Very much!' he assured her. 'Are you also cook as well as doctor?'

She smiled at the question. 'No way!' she assured him. 'But Nick tells me we have the best cook in the Himalayas and, after only a few meals, I'm inclined to believe him.'

'Will you eat with me?' he asked with a winsome smile that showed even white teeth and pressed a dimple into his suntanned cheek.

'Not tonight,' she told him. 'I've got work to do.'

She left him to go through to the laboratory, where she lit another lamp and hung it high. She checked that the cabinets were locked, then slipped the keys into her pocket. Opening the big metal trunk, she took out all the patient file cards.

She didn't want to eat in the laboratory for hygienic reasons, but with the fire and more lantern the light in the kitchen hut was stronger than the light in her bedroom. While she ate she would go through the cards and familiarise herself with the patients Nick had already treated—and with the treatments he had used. If she was going to be left to make her own decisions—and hand out prescription drugs—at least she would have his decisions to guide her.

It was midday before he returned. Callie heard voices and looked up from her squatting position from which she was smearing ringworm ointment on a child's foot to see him laughing at something his lovely companion had said.

Fury pounded in her blood, and she held her breath to stop herself blurting out her irrational anger. She bent lower over the affected area and pretended she hadn't seen them. This is stupid, she told herself, appalled at the emotional disarray churning within her.

'Cover it with a bandage if you want it to do any good!'

His voice brought her head spinning up, and the teasing smile on his lips made her want to cry. It must be the altitude affecting me, she told herself as she returned his smile with a false one of her own, and muttered a cool, 'Welcome back.' Then she smiled again, a real smile this time, as she picked up the bandage from the kidney dish and waggled it about so he would see she had already decided to use a bandage.

'I'm looking forward to using a real bathroom!' Amanda's cooing voice destroyed Callie's moment of triumph. She supposed the woman was entitled to a proper wash after the extra miles she'd covered, but. . .

A quick glance upward showed her an unwelcome scene as Nick reached out an arm to usher the teacher through the door.

'I'll finish with this patient then come and fill you

in on what's been happening,' she told him. 'There's a patient in the hospital, so I shifted Linda with the chickenpox into your bed.'

The surprise on his face brought a moment of minor triumph, but then she wondered gloomily if he'd offered Amanda his bed as well as his bathroom, and a hideous dismay rushed through her again.

He was examining Carl's foot when she walked back into the ward, and, seeing his face clearly, she realised how tired and strained he looked. She stood beside him, longing to reach out and touch his shoulder, to offer him comfort, although she couldn't say how she knew he needed it. But the imaginary Howard and the very real Amanda and far too many memories stood in the way, so she waited silently, hoping her closeness might help.

'I might be able to find something that will hasten your recovery,' he said at last, and motioned with his head towards the laboratory door.

'I didn't want to give him anti-inflammatory drugs without your approval,' she explained quietly when they reached the seclusion of the little room. 'I've been giving him pain-killers four-hourly.'

He slumped down on to one of the stools and gave her a tired smile.

'And fixed up a sling! You've done well, Callie.'

The words were kind, but lifeless. She moved closer to him, and reached out to touch his arm.

'What happened, Nick?' she asked, looking into his pale, tense face.

'He died, Callie!'

The words were filled with such despair that she reacted automatically, stepping into the space between his knees and reaching out her arms to draw him close so his head rested on her shoulder and her fingers could massage his scalp.

'Before you got there?' she asked, knowing he would need to talk it through.

'No, but he was in a deep coma when we arrived, and I imagine there was already a crippling degree of irreversible damage,' he explained. 'I started gradual warming with all the means at my disposal—body heat while water was warmed, warm fluid injected into his veins, even mouth to mouth to get warm air into his lungs, but it was all useless! He died soon after midnight.'

She felt him shudder convulsively, and dropped her fingers to massage the tense muscles in his neck and shoulders. Knowing Nick, she could understand the depths of his despair, for he was intolerant of failure in himself although willing to concede imperfections in other mortals.

'You must have seen it happen before,' she whispered. 'The first thing you learn in practical work is that you can't save every life.'

He lifted his head to look into her face, and the pain in his eyes shafted through her like a knife wound. 'But he was young and fit and healthy. He was adventurous or he wouldn't have been here. He loved mountains and peace and solitude or he wouldn't have climbed alone. He could have been me, Callie, with all his hopes and dreams still floating like bright balloons ahead of him, beckoning him on into a limitless future. Then, one day later, it's all gone! How can I look at him as just another body? Just another failure?'

His eyes closed, as if, that way, he would not see the grim phantoms that danced in his mind. His shoulders slumped and his head dropped back against her. Her arms tightened, and she held him to her breast, and rocked him as a mother rocked a child in silent empathy.

'You're exhausted,' she told him later, still shocked by this Nick who was showing his vulnerability. 'Why don't you grab one of the ward beds and sleep for a few hours?'

'We slept for a while last night before starting back,' he said, lifting his head and nuzzling his face against her cropped hair. 'But I was worried about you here on your own, and. . .'

Her hands moved across his back as his grief filled the little room. 'You did all you could, Nick,' she whispered. 'No one on this earth can do more than that.'

Now he sat back, and she saw the tired smile that lit up his face. 'Using my own words, brat?' he teased, and her heart leapt when she realised she had got through to him.

'Oh, someone said it to me once!' she replied, hiding her jubilant reaction under an elaborately casual shrug. 'Now, if you're tired, you'd better have a sleep, because a man's coming back to have a tooth pulled, and I've some other things I want to discuss with you.'

She studied him closely and saw some colour come back into his cheeks as he was visibly shrugging off the depression that losing his patient had caused.

'I won't try to sleep, but I'll get Solti to make me some coffee and one of his special omelettes instead. With that inside me, and perhaps some chapattis and honey, I'll be a new man.'

He eased upright, and she dropped her arms and stepped backwards as the invisible barriers Nick had erected between them five years ago slid silently back into place again. She watched him reach out for the patient cards she had left on the bench so he could check what she had done in his absence.

'Bathroom's free!'

Amanda's voice told Callie she had moved just in time. She looked up to see the dark beauty smiling in the doorway. Her hair swung like a silken curtain on her shoulders, and her dark eyes seemed to gleam secret messages at Nick.

'Thanks, Amanda.' His voice was preoccupied, which provided Callie's jealous heart with some consolation, but then he added, 'I'm going over to the kitchen in about ten minutes to get Solti to cook up a late breakfast. Will you join me?' Of course she needs a meal, Callie told herself, but common sense held little sway against the green-eyed monster jealousy.

'So Anuag came back.'

Callie blinked, and the card Nick was waving at her came into focus. 'I gave him the same tablets you'd given him——'

'And added a big question mark? Doubting my prognosis or my treatment?' His brown gaze caught and held hers, but the communion they had shared a few moments ago had vanished.

'The question mark was to remind me to ask you about the antibiotics. I looked them up in your pharmacology book and they don't mention TB.'

Was it approval that glinted momentarily in his eyes?

'TB is treated most successfully by a combination of three drugs. I have streptomycin here, but not isoniazid or myambutol, and, if you use one without the others, the bacteria can become resistant to it.'

'And the regimen becomes ineffective?' she asked, following what he was saying carefully.

'That's right, and, if we add the fact that the treatment should continue for six months, it's not the kind of case we can, or should, tackle here.' He rubbed his fingers tiredly across his forehead, as if this was one more failure he had to add to his present burden.

'I told him to go to the hospital at Khunde. Surely, if he's feeling sick enough, he'll do that?'

That won a smile. 'I wouldn't count on it,' he told her, sliding off the stool and stretching to his full height. 'The people in these parts can be very stubborn when it comes to seeking treatment for their ailments. Maybe stubbornness is a trait common in people of short stature.' He grinned at his weak joke, then patted her on the head, and left the room.

'Five feet six is not short,' she yelled after him, rising to his bait with her usual ferocity. 'And six feet two is overdoing things in the height department!' she added, but she smiled to herself as she returned the patient file cards to their box.

Working with Nick might be disastrous for her emotional equilibrium, but she was gaining invaluable medical experience, in a place of incomparable beauty. And it was fun when they both relaxed and forgot the tensions that had plagued their friendship during her late teens and killed the closeness that had once existed between them.

Friends are as important as lovers, she told herself, but it was hard to believe it when she walked outside and saw Amanda hurry across to Nick's side as he made his way towards the kitchen.

Then philosophy was forgotten as another excited group of villagers made their way up the trail. As usual, Callie heard them before she saw them. When they did appear she was surprised to see that they were children—or perhaps teenagers, although their slight build made it hard to tell.

Two of the boys carried a young girl sitting upright on their crossed arms. Blood seeped through a grubby bandage on her leg. Motioning them towards the bench, she followed, crouching to unwrap the wound while her stomach churned at what might lie beneath.

The wound was a clean gash, about four inches long, bleeding profusely but with no sign of an arterial spurt.

The girl's friends made appropriate gagging noises then withdrew to sit along the low, stone wall, the boys producing cigarettes and lighting up ostentatiously as they searched the camp beyond the hut for a sign of the young trekkers. Would they all have accompanied the girl if there had been no secondary attraction at the health post? Callie wondered.

'I'll have to clean it, then stitch it up,' she told her young patient. She had done simple suturing like this during her hospital practicum last year, but should she call Nick?

She found antiseptic, a five per-cent xylocaine solution vial and needle for a local anaesthetic, sutures and a sealed pack of saline solution. Carrying them back outside, she began work, cleaning the area around the wound with the antiseptic but being careful not to intrude on the exposed tissues to avoid further damage to them.

She was flushing the wound with the saline solution when she heard Nick's voice greeting the young people behind her.

'Happy to do it yourself?' he asked quietly, and she bit her lip and thought for a moment, then nodded.

'I've sutured longer wounds than this, and it's only a primary closure, no blood vessels affected or deep layers to be closed.'

He bent over, so close that she could feel the warmth emanating from his body. He examined the wound, checked on the contents of her stainless-steel dish, then straightened up.

'I'll take over if you'd like to do the tooth,' he teased, then walked away before she could think of an answer.

'I hope it's not the effect of Amanda that's turning him back into a human being,' she muttered, then blushed when her patient uttered a shy,

'Pardon?'

She was halfway through the stitching when she realised that she would have been far more comfortable standing up to do the job, and that she should have asked the girl to lie on the examination table. Why hadn't she? Because Nick treats all the local people in the courtyard, she reminded herself. That's why he calls it 'the surgery'. Did they feel more at ease in the open air, with their mountains ranged like guardians behind them?

She finished the sutures and wrapped the wound securely. 'Leave it like that for two nights,' she told the girl, who seemed to understand what she was saying. 'Then come back and I will put a clean bandage on it.' Again her patient nodded. 'If it becomes tender or the skin goes red around the bandage, come back straight away.'

The girl limped over to join her friends, who were carrying on a loud and laughing conversation with the trekkers across a no-man's land about twenty feet wide.

Callie gathered up her gear, and stood up, noticing Ellen standing by the line of girls, keeping a close eye on the proceedings. Beyond the doorway, Nick was bent over the man with the bad tooth, and Amanda was nowhere in sight. Probably asleep on my bed,

Callie thought uncharitably, and the uneasy notion made the smile she gave Carl far brighter than was strictly necessary.

'I'll bring my lunch over with yours,' she promised him, 'and keep you company. Solti will have it ready shortly.'

She walked on into the laboratory and dropped the used disposable equipment into the metal drum they would carry out with them when they eventually left the mountains. Used syringes were hardly the things to leave lying around in remote areas. She washed and dried the bowl, then locked the antiseptic away, juggling the keys in one hand for a moment while she wondered what she should do with them.

While Nick was away she had kept them in her pocket, terrified lest something go missing while she was responsible. She wrote up a patient file card for the young girl, Aya, still clutching the keys in her left fist, then Nick walked in and she threw them thankfully towards him.

'They're all yours,' she said, and saw his surprise reflected on his face. 'With all these strangers around, I didn't like leaving them on the bench where they usually are,' she explained, uncomfortably aware of an intentness in his scrutiny.

'And I called you fluffy-headed?' he teased, shaking his head in mock reproof at his lack of judgement. 'Is it Howard's influence that's developed this new sense of responsibility in you, Callie? If so, the man has my most fervent admiration.'

The words were lightly spoken, but beneath the joke Callie sensed a brittleness, and she shifted uneasily in the small room. 'I don't know what you're talking about,' she said stiffly. 'I've always been responsible for myself when I've had to be. Just because you ordered my life about for years and years and never gave me the chance to think for myself doesn't mean I'm not capable of it!'

'Responsible?' he echoed. His grin widened and once again his hand reached out towards her, but she ducked before he could touch her head again. 'It was a joke, brat!' he said softly, then left the room, leaving Callie staring after him.

He was certainly a different man from the angry, suspicious Nick who had greeted her arrival at the health post, and far more relaxed than he'd been yesterday when any light-hearted banter had brought a cool response or quick rebuke, but there was something else about him. Something behind the façade that she sensed but could not define.

She puzzled over it for a moment, then thrust the uncanny concept away. Today he was back to the teasing, casual friend he'd been years ago, accepting her comfort when he needed it, and ruffling her hair in affection, that was all.

But she didn't want that Nick any more, and the Nick she did want, didn't want her! And what had caused the change in his attitude?

One answer loomed larger than any other. There was only one variable in the equation—and that was Amanda!

'Where's that lunch you promised?' Carl's voice broke through her reverie.

'Coming right up,' she assured him as she hurried through the ward. Psychoanalysis was a sixth-year subject, so further pondering of her problem would have to wait.

CHAPTER SIX

'MY FRIENDS will be coming into Machherma from Gokyo tonight,' Carl told her as they ate Solti's delicious lunch together. 'Do you think I will be able to join them on the trip back down the mountains?'

'You're the one who knows how your toe feels,' Callie told him. 'You have to make the decision.'

'It's much better since I have been resting it, and, of course, the pain-killers and the new tablets the doctor gave me have helped. I think I could walk slowly on my own if necessary and catch up with them at night.'

Callie nodded. Carl would be better off staying with his party in case he needed support later on in the journey. A solitary hiker was always more at risk and there was a multitude of problems that could arise.

A burst of laughter from Linda and Helen interrupted her thoughts.

'You be quiet, girls, or the yeti will get you!' Carl threatened, and Callie smiled. The conversation and arguments between the two rooms went on all day, passing the time more easily for both her patients. She had also noticed that Linda's stream of visitors would dawdle through the ward towards the bedroom, exchanging smiles and joking remarks with Carl.

'He lives here in Machherma, you know!' Carl added, bringing Helen to the door between the rooms, her lunch plate clutched in her hands.

'Yetis don't exist,' she said, but her tone was doubtful.

'Oh, yes, they do!' Carl told her. 'Haven't you seen the sign on the Machherma Hotel? "Scene of famous yeti sighting", it reads.'

Carl grinned and Helen turned to Callie for a denial.

'Well, I haven't got down to Machherma yet,' she told the girl. 'But I did read all I could find about the area before I came over here to work. It seems that the most authentic yeti story came from a young woman who was watching her father's yak herd. She says a yeti came from nowhere, killed one of the yaks, and threw her and a calf into the river.'

'But it's not true, is it?' Helen asked, and Callie shrugged.

'No one else saw it, so we don't know!'

'They say that yetis only appear for young virgins,' Carl said nonchalantly. 'You girls should all be OK!'

Helen shrieked her outrage at this comment and disappeared back into the bedroom to share the joke with Linda and tell her this latest bit of information. Callie heard them laughing together and smiled.

'And would Howard approve of all this togetherness?' Nick ducked through the door and strode past her, dropping the words like a brick on her head, before disappearing into the laboratory. Carl mustn't have heard, for he continued to discuss the yeti sighting, oblivious to Callie's sudden silence. The changes in Nick's temper were becoming too volatile for her to follow!

The afternoon was quiet, so Callie took advantage of the lull to pull on the sloppy, flat-heeled shoes she had worn over on the plane and make her way down to the village. Each of the rough dwellings was surrounded by low stone walls, pens for the herds that were brought up to the summer pasture. In what might euphemistically be called the main street, a tumble-down building bore the inscription Carl had quoted, and Callie smiled at the self-importance of it.

The smile faded when she met Amanda coming out of the 'shop'.

'Walking back?' the other woman asked, and Callie resisted a childish urge to say no. Telling herself she was being unreasonable, she fell in beside the teacher, who immediately began probing Callie's presence at the health post.

'Nick tells me it's pure coincidence,' she said in a voice that told Callie how unlikely *that* story was! 'I did wonder if he believed it, considering how you threw yourself at him all through your teenage years.'

Callie pressed her lips together as pain squeezed her insides into a tense ball. How could he have discussed her with this stranger?

'You covered a lot of conversational territory on your walk,' she said, hoping an off-hand remark would hide the hurt.

Amanda smile smugly. 'It was a long walk, and an even longer night,' she said, then sighed so theatrically that Callie wanted to push her off the edge of the path. 'Plenty of time to talk and to. . .'

'Teacher's Body Found At Bottom Of Ravine. . .' Callie could see the headlines. They hadn't set off together, so why should anyone assume——?

The murderous thoughts shocked her back to reality.

Four excited girls were waiting for them where the trail widened before entering the health post courtyard. 'Is there really a sign? Couldn't those of us who've had chickenpox when we were kids go down and have a look?'

'Couldn't we go, Miss Quirk? Couldn't we?'

News of the yeti had spread, Callie realised, smiling at the girls' enthusiasm.

'What do you think, Callie?' Amanda asked. 'Could they go down?'

Put on the spot, Callie hesitated. If they had had chickenpox as children they shouldn't be carriers, but Nick had put a blanket isolation order on the trekking party—with one obvious exception!

'You'll have to ask Dr Grant,' she replied, glad to dodge the responsibility. Then, when she saw Amanda's eyes brighten and her steps quicken as she hastened to find Nick, Callie regretted her words.

That evening they were invited to eat with the campers. Carl's friends had arrived and helped him on his way back down to the village, and Linda had decided she was well enough to join her friends for dinner, so they all sat around a fire built up on stones in the centre of the camp, eating, talking and laughing.

'I think Miss Quirk likes your Dr Grant,' Helen whispered to Callie.

'He's not my Dr Grant,' Callie told her. 'She's welcome to him!' If only the pain in her chest didn't belie that!

'But he's very dishy!' Linda whispered into her other ear.

'A bit thin, don't you think?' Callie asked, looking across the fire to where Nick sat between Ellen and Amanda. His craggy face was thrown into harsh relief by the firelight, and she couldn't see the wide brown eyes that usually softened its angularity. He wasn't conventionally handsome, yet somehow she still judged all men's looks against his clean, strong profile.

'Oh, no,' Helen argued. 'He's kind of hard and lean, but strong. I saw him helping Miss Quirk up the hill behind the camp. He practically lifted her over the tough bits. I like men with those hard flat muscles, more than men with bulgy ones!'

Again Callie had to bite back a retort, while her mind searched for a less painful subject. Linda and Helen had adopted her as a special friend, and insisted on sitting either side of her. At first she'd been flattered and pleased to have their diverting company, but if this was to be a sample of the evening's conversation, the sooner she excused herself and went to bed, the better.

Across the circle, the flames threw shadows across Nick's face, blurring any expression that might reveal his thoughts. But Amanda's body language, her slight movements and seemingly casual touches, proclaimed an ownership that made Callie squirm with irritation.

'Do you think boys like girls to make the first move?' Linda's question jolted her.

'The boys I knew didn't!' Callie told her firmly, frowning across at the 'boy' who'd made that fact abundantly clear to her years ago. At sixteen, she'd decided she was finally grown up. She had dressed herself in her most provocative outfit and ambushed Nick when he'd returned home from university for the long summer holidays. It had been early evening, dark enough to hide her in the shadows of his garden, but not dark enough to hide her tears when he'd pushed her roughly away from him and told her to behave herself and grow up!

'I think boys still like to do the chasing,' Helen stated. 'It makes them feel more of a man, although a girl can show she likes a fellow in a lot of subtle ways.'

Like leaning all over him to speak to someone else! Callie thought bitterly, her eyes still on the scene being played out opposite her. Well, if Amanda lacked subtlety, so had she! Subtle as a sledge-hammer, she'd been, she remembered. Especially once Nick had spurned her advances.

The fire glimmered with memories, and she half smiled, remembering the anger of the boys she had teased, tempting them to drive her home after parties and insisting they park outside Nick's house rather than her own—'in case her mother looked out'! Then she'd sat and talked to them, often for hours, carefully repelling wandering hands and passionate kisses, until she had deemed it long enough for Nick to have noticed the car and become annoyed with her. She had always made sure she emerged from the car tugging at her clothes and patting her hair into place, so he couldn't help but assume she'd been indulging in some heavy petting. And she had allowed the boys to walk her to her door, bribing them with the promise of a single, tight-lipped kiss!

'I think if you've been going out with your boyfriend for a few months, you could have sex with him.'

Callie blinked. The conversation had certainly covered some ground while she was lost in the past with the girl she had been.

'What do you think, Callie?' Linda asked.

Callie shrugged uncomfortably. 'I think it's an individual thing, and depends on how the two people feel about each other, where they want their relationship to go, how deep their commitment is—a whole host of things!'

'But is it OK to have sex with your boyfriend?' Helen persisted, and Callie groaned inwardly. I'm probably the only woman in this valley over twenty who might still see a yeti, she thought, and they're asking me!

Forcing her own feelings aside, she concentrated on the question, trying to give it proper scientific weight and consideration.

'Well,' she said slowly, 'given that the relationship is long-term, that you've got to know each other as people, beyond the sex-objects stage, and you've talked it over and *both* agree it's what you want——'

'Not just what the boy wants from you,' Linda interjected.

'Exactly,' Callie told her. 'Then I think you should talk to your parents or some older friend about it, and get them to help you with contraception. Or go to your local doctor or family-planning clinic—but go together so your boyfriend finds out as much about it as you do.' She heard the girls gasp and took a deep breath. Theory always sounded good, but in practice it was ever so much harder! 'If he loves and respects you, he should be willing to do this. It's his responsibility as much as yours. Why should you be the only one to go through all the embarrassment of asking to be put on the Pill, and you be the only one to listen to the warnings about prolonged use, and when it's safe and not safe?'

'I think that's a jolly good idea,' Helen exclaimed, but Linda was shaking her head.

'I can't imagine my boyfriend, Tony, fronting up at the family-planning clinic with me!' she said, then added gloomily, 'Always supposing he's still around when I get back!'

'Well, if he's that fickle, you don't want him,' Callie told her. 'And if you're so uncertain about his feelings for you, then sleeping with him would be a mistake!'

'He's a ratfink!' Helen declared succinctly. 'You'd

be better off if he did find someone else over the holidays.'

They began to argue, and Callie could hear undertones of herself in their argument. It had been when Nick, asked by her mother, had come up to escort her to the Carnival of Flowers ball—when she'd been high on her success as the golden-crowned queen—that she'd offered her body to him, hoping to entice him into loving her as much as she loved him.

Stupid, that was what she'd been. Stupid, stupid, stupid!

It was after that he'd brought Jocelyn home, then Caroline, then Jane. And Jane had stuck, becoming a familiar sight around his house on weekends and holidays. They had all thought he'd marry Jane. . .

And suddenly Callie had remembered too much! She excused herself, struggled to her feet, and walked away, out of the circle of light, and back towards the dark bulk of the hut. As she rounded the corner, light spilled out to welcome her, but the soft glow of the lanterns could not banish the loneliness that battered against her heart.

With a quiet determination she prepared for bed, slipping thankfully into her sleeping-bag as if it might provide an escape from her turbulent emotions.

She woke to high wailing screams and a dreadful sobbing, and pushed herself out of bed. A lantern still burned in the ward, throwing light through the open door. Linda lay asleep in the spare bed. Nick had intended sleeping in the ward. Did the light mean he was still working?

The noise outside was escalating, and she hurried through the ward, registering his absence but assuming he had also rushed to investigate the disturbance. Her main aim was to calm whoever was out there before the whole camp was aroused. Whole camp aroused? As she turned the corner from the courtyard, she realised she was too late to avoid that little problem. The girls, clad in a weird assortment of sleeping attire, were clustered by the dying fire while Ellen tried unsuccessfully to calm them.

'Quieten down. I don't want Linda woken by all this commotion,' Callie said loudly, and was pleased when the noise level dropped. 'Now, what's going on?'

'It's Carol. And we saw a yeti!' The girl who was crying on Ellen's shoulder sobbed out the words. 'He's got her! He's taken her away!' she whimpered.

'Yetis don't exist!' Callie said firmly. 'Now, this Carol—where did you last see her?' Her stern voice had some effect, for the girl stopped sobbing and raised a tear-stained face from her support.

'We were going to the toilet. We had a torch and went together like we always do, then Carol yelled, "Yeti! Run!" and I turned and ran back but she didn't come!'

'And has someone gone to look for her?' Callie asked as the absence of both Nick and Amanda sank into her consciousness.

'Not yet,' Ellen replied, her face grim in the orange-red light. 'Those are the first coherent words Sally's spoken.'

'And where are your guide and your porters?' Callie asked, looking around and seeing only the girls. 'A couple of them should go across immediately and see if the girl is over there somewhere.'

'They've gone down to the village,' Ellen whispered. 'They go every night to have a drink and play cards.'

'Well, you take Sally into the kitchen and wake

Solti—if he's not already awake. Get him to make warm cocoa for all the girls. I'll take a torch and walk across to the toilet.'

'You can't go over there on your own!' Ellen objected, but she passed Callie the torch she had held in her hand.

'I'll be within yelling distance,' Callie assured her, wanting company on this venture but not willing to put any other girl at risk, or delay while Solti was woken. 'Anyway, any self-respecting yeti would have run away when all the noise began! Leave your most sensible girl out here, and I'll blink the torch three times when I find Carol, and five times when I need help to bring her back.' She hoped the common-sense words made her sound braver and more in control than she felt.

She climbed over the stone wall, heading towards the slope of the hill and the dark oblong that was the plastic shelter around the toilet.

'Carol! Carol!'

She kept calling, although every instinct told her to be quiet, to creep across the dark, deserted landscape and not draw attention to herself. She swept the torch over the ground in front of her, then in wider arcs to cover either side of the faint path worn by the girls.

'Carol!' she called again, and heard the word picked up and flung against the mountains by the wind that tore down their precipitous slopes.

Then the light picked up a patch of white, and Callie felt her breathing falter, then stop as she moved the torch and saw it reveal the fallen figure of the girl. She turned and blinked the torch three times.

As swiftly as her still painful, sock-clad feet would allow, she crossed the rough ground, then knelt beside the still form, her hand going first to the limp wrist. A definite pulse brought Callie's breathing back under control, but her heart still thudded erratically as she played the torchlight across the girl's body, seeking any sign of external injury. Propping the torch on a rock, she ran her fingers over Carol's skull, then down her arms, and legs. There was no wetness of blood, nor any depressed fracture of the skull or obvious fracture of her limbs, but the girl was definitely unconscious.

Should she turn her over so she could use the torch and examine her eyes' reaction to light stimuli? Was a neck or back injury likely? One that would be exacerbated by moving her?

She picked up the torch and shone it around. The girl had obviously fallen forward, either tripping over a rock as she hurried away, or possibly fainting when whatever it was had frightened her. Either way, the most likely scenario was that she had struck her head on a rock when she had fallen.

Pleased with her deductions, she cleared the ground beside the girl of all large rocks, and was about to roll her over, when a low moan told her the patient was recovering.

'It was a yeti!'

Callie felt the fear in the words even before a shudder shook the slim body. 'It's OK! You're OK! There's no one and nothing here with you but me!'

The girl pushed herself up, one hand going to the side of her head. 'There was a yeti!' she moaned. 'There was! I saw it!'

Another virgin, Callie thought, relieved by Carol's movement.

'It was over there in front of the toilet!'

Callie stood up and turned back towards the camp. She blinked the torch five times, and heard a shout that told her help would soon be on the way.

'Have you got a torch?' she asked Carol.

'I did have one,' the girl replied, and Callie swung her beam of light around, and found the torch beside a rock. Had the bulb been broken in the fall or would it still work? She bent down and retrieved it, turned it on, and smiled when she saw the brave light.

'Your friends are coming to help you back to the camp,' she told Carol. 'You can hear them and see the light from their torches.'

The girl nodded.

'Now, I want you to sit here and shine your torch towards them so they can see where you are. I'll go on up to the toilet and make sure nothing is lurking up there!'

'Don't leave me on my own!' Carol whimpered, clutching Callie's arm in a vice-like grip. 'I did see a yeti! I really did!'

Callie looked up at the bright, starlit sky and around at the dark, brooding mountains. I don't believe in yetis, she told herself, but her pulse had quickened and the dark beyond their torch lights seemed to be alive with lurking dangers and whispering spirits.

Ellen was one of the pair of rescuers, and Callie explained what she was going to do.

'Wait for the porters to come back!' Ellen protested.

'And if they don't come back till morning, and one of the girls gets up later in the night and. . .' She didn't know how to finish the sentence; she only knew she had to walk the final fifteen yards to the sheltered structure and check it out.

'I'll come with you,' Ellen said, but Callie shook her head.

'You take Carol back to the hut, and put her to bed in the ward. I'll be back in a few minutes and I'll examine her then. She has probably got a mild concussion but we can't do anything for that except bed-rest. If she's fully conscious and able to talk sensibly, you can give her a hot drink.'

She helped Ellen and the girl lift Carol to her feet, and watched as they stood either side of her, to take some of her weight on their shoulders. Then, as they headed back towards the flare of the now brighter fire, she turned her back on the beckoning light and walked hesitantly towards the toilet.

Her torch picked out the shape within seconds, and she sank down to the ground with a helpless little whimper.

'Yetis don't exist!' she whispered to herself, hunching her body into a tight ball while she tried to will it to stop shaking. With trembling fingers she raised the torch again, and this time the stillness of the figure made her reaction less overwhelming. True, her hand trembled uncontrollably, and her mouth was dry, but she willed her eyes to remain open.

It was drawn there, she realised, crying with relief. She pushed herself to her feet, and, still cautious although she knew it was a hoax, she made her way towards the sheltering plastic.

The rough sketch grew less and less real, until close up, it was only a series of rough chalk marks on the black plastic, but it was a cruel trick and could have had far more serious consequences.

Using the sleeve of her tracksuit, Callie rubbed out the offending marks, then flashed her torch around inside the structure to make certain there was no other trap set for unwary night-walkers. It was only as she made her careful way back towards the camp that she began to wonder about the absence of Nick and Amanda.

Forget it, she told herself. It's none of your business if they are interested in each other. But her heart didn't listen, and the velvety night, made for lovers, became a bleak and lonely place.

Training kept her going while she examined Carol, tucked the long balloons filled with warm water around her body and covered her with an extra sleeping-bag. Then, as the camp settled back down and the injured girl drifted off into a natural sleep, reaction set in, and Callie began to shiver uncontrollably.

She crept towards her bed, but her teeth were chattering so loudly that she was afraid the noise would wake Linda. Reaching up above her bed for her jacket, she pulled it around her shoulders, and headed back outside. A fire burned in the kitchen all night. She would go and sit by it until she was warm.

Solti was asleep behind a screen beyond the table. She stole quietly in and thought about making a hot drink, but her hands were trembling too much to be lifting boiling water.

Crouching by the glowing embers, she wrapped her arms around her shaking shoulders and peered into the tiny spurts of flame, letting them mesmerise her with their constant, dancing beauty. She sat there silently, not thinking, until voices outside distracted her for a moment.

Ellen, sounding displeased, she registered dimly. Had she found the artist who'd used her talents to destroy the peace of the night? Callie thought about investigating, but her own fears were still too close for her to think much about what was happening elsewhere. She turned back to the hypnotic solace of the fire.

'You OK?'

Nick must have come soft-footed into the kitchen, for he spoke before she realised he was there. He dropped down to kneel on the ground beside her, his eyes so full of concern that she felt the heaviness of tears behind her eyelids. She turned back to the fire, and nodded, but the shivering had started again and she could not control it.

'Oh, Callie!' he whispered, and gathered her into his arms, sitting down on the ground and drawing her on to his knees. 'It's OK now, darling, you're OK!'

He rocked her back and forth, one hand pressing her head to his chest, and the other stroking her back, her arms, her neck.

'I'm all right,' she said gruffly as the dreadful shuddering began to ease, and the word 'darling' beat like a drum in her brain. 'It was only a drawing on the plastic. I wasn't scared, just got a bit cold, that's all.'

'Little liar,' he murmured tenderly into her hair, his hands moving constantly over her body, warm and reassuring. 'Do you think I don't know how much courage it took for you to walk out there into the darkness on your own? Do you think I've forgotten how that vivid imagination of yours peoples even the mildest of nights with bogey men?'

He held her tight, then added in a tone of self-recrimination, 'I should have been here! Should never have left you alone to face those kind of demons! Amanda forgot the film she had bought down at the shop, and wanted to walk down to get it. I thought I should go with her because the trail is rough and difficult in the dark!'

Did she ask, or did you offer? Callie wondered, but the feel of Nick's body hard against hers was too good to risk losing it with a bitchy question.

'We met your Swedish friends down there and stayed talking to them. There was a bit of a dance going at the hotel, and time slipped away.'

Dancing or lingering in the darkness on the walk back up? the jealous imp wanted to ask.

'You didn't know it was to be a demon kind of night,' she said, and wondered why she needed to offer excuses.

'No, I suppose not, but I'm sorry, Callie.' The whispered words, tender in the firelight, floated past her ears.

It's OK now, she wanted to say as her body warmed itself against his and the feel of his arms around her was so exactly what she wanted that she stayed motionless lest she break the spell.

'I wasn't very brave about it,' she admitted at last, and felt the arms hold her even more tightly. 'I just kept telling myself that yetis didn't exist, the same way I used to tell myself that there were no lions and tigers in Toowoomba back in the days when you used to make me walk between our houses after dark as a kind of test.'

'I always walked behind you, though!' he murmured, brushing his lips across her hair.

'Did you?' she asked, surprised and inordinately comforted by this new scrap of information.

'Just in case one had escaped from a circus!' he said, and she felt his chest move as he chuckled.

She snuggled into his lap, a warm sleepiness relaxing

her limbs and feeding her sense of well-being. She wanted to ask about Amanda, but she and Nick had not been this close for too long for her to spoil it with unwanted questions. She would take whatever he would offer her—she'd realised that sad fact long ago—and, if all he could give was comfort, at least she was in his arms, and while she was there no one else was!

'Ready for bed?' he asked, and she wished the simple question had a more romantic meaning. She shifted uneasily now. The fear had dissipated and his nearness teased at her senses and filled her with an aching hunger.

'I suppose so,' she mumbled against his chest, not realising that her movement had pushed his shirt open and her lips were moving on his warm skin.

She felt him stiffen in reaction, and waited, breath held, for the explosion that was sure to follow. But all she heard was the crackling hiss of the fire and a closer hiss of indrawn breath, then his head bent over her and she felt his lips touch her hair, her neck, her ear. Warm caressing kisses, firing her senses as they licked and nibbled and pressed against her skin.

Dared she turn her head up to look at him or would seeing her face remind him it was his old friend Callie he was kissing? She trembled within the circle of his arms, her blood pounding through her veins as all her erotic fantasies threatened to come true at once.

Then the kisses stopped—right at the base of her neck, on track towards the breast where his hand curled protectively. His head lifted, and his hand dropped to her waist, then moved away as if the contact stung.

'Damn Howard!' he muttered, then he hoisted her

into his arms and carried her out of the kitchen and back to the hut, where he dropped her, with every sign of relief, back on to her bed. 'Get into your sleeping-bag, and make sure you're warm,' he growled. 'I'll check on Carol then come back and see that you're OK.'

Then he was gone.

Callie ran her hands over the skin he had kissed, trying to recapture the magic of those moments. Once before, he'd nearly kissed her properly—had brushed his lips across hers and started fires she could not hide—but that time she had believed the disgust that followed their embrace had been directed at her. This time, he seemed more angry with himself!

CHAPTER SEVEN

A LIGHT gleamed in the darkness, not bright enough to be coming from the ward, so it must be in the laboratory. Callie worked this out as she eased her body out of the sleeping-bag and stretched sleepily. Had Nick left it on in case she woke to darkness in the night? Or was he up to see the sunrise, and letting her sleep in after the dramas of the previous evening?

She found her torch, and shone it on her watch. Definitely morning. Any minute now the sun would be bringing its warmth to the high mountains, and, if she didn't get moving, she would miss the spectacle.

She scrambled out of bed and headed on her bulky feet to the bathroom. Yesterday's walk in lighter bandages and her sloppy shoes had not done any harm. Maybe today she could try her new boots. And Ellen would find out who was responsible for last night's prank. And Nick. . .? Well, who knew how Nick would behave?

In the light from the laboratory, she saw his empty bed. The small office was also empty and suspicion flared, fuelled by an anger she had no right to feel. She stormed out of the door, colliding, as she emerged into the cold morning air, with a tall, rock-hard body.

'What are you doing out of bed? You should be sleeping in after all that fuss last night.'

'And I'm pleased to see you, too!' she snapped as her body's reaction to the physical contact pushed her temper beyond control. 'As far as I know there's nothing in my job description that tells me when not to get out of bed. You've woken me at this ungodly hour on other mornings, so why wouldn't I be up?'

She pushed away from him, heading for the kitchen and the cup of tea and porridge Solti would have prepared, but then she remembered Nick's absence the previous evening when she had needed him, and the rage turned to fury. She spun around.

'Were you thinking of sharing the sunrise with someone else? Are you worried I'll get in the way?'

Without waiting for a reply, she strode around the corner of the building, moved soft-footed past the sleeping camp, and entered the friendly warmth of the kitchen. As Solti poured her tea, and spooned his special porridge into a bowl, she thought about sitting at the table to eat it. There would be other sunrises while she was here.

She hesitated, then picked up her tea and porridge and left the kitchen. Why should she miss it? She marched back to the front of the building as the light gathered strength, and sank down on to the bench a good three feet from where Nick sat. There were a few clouds in the sky, already tinged with palest salmon, and, as she watched, the colour deepened, and the sun's rays dropped lower, brushing each mountain with colour.

The magic filled her, blotting out all conscious thought, and calming her jangling nerves.

'Show's over, so, seeing you're up and about, let's get to work!'

Callie blinked in the feeble sunshine, but Nick was on his feet, bending to collect her cup and bowl. She watched him walk away, and shook her head. For 'back to work' read 'back to normal', she realised. The closeness of last night might never have been. She sighed, then stood up and headed for the laboratory, glancing at the sleeping Carol as she passed.

'You've done a good job on that chart,' he told her as he came into the room and took up his position in front of the microscope. 'Now, let's see if we can get the rest of these slides done. The merchants come up today, so I take fresh samples from them, and do the two families in the village at the same time.'

So it's all brisk business, Callie thought, bending to write his findings on a card. Well, I can handle that.

'If you're taking fortnightly samples from four of the six groups, does it matter that the porters' blood is taken at less regular intervals?'

'I think not. The changes seem to be correlated with time spent at altitude. We know that the body's first reaction to the decrease in atmospheric pressure and subsequent decrease in oxygen in the body is to produce more erythrocytes, the red blood cells.'

'That shows clearly on the chart,' Callie agreed. 'The red-cell count in the samples taken at Namche are much lower than the first samples taken here.'

'That's right. Did you notice any other marked differences?'

Callie thought for a moment, visualising the chart. 'An increase in deviant shapes?' she guessed. 'The words fazed me—poikilocytosis is not something you say three times a day——'

'But you remembered it!' Nick interrupted, sounding so pleased with her that she felt a blush mounting to her cheeks.

'Only because I had to look it up in the pathophysiology book,' she admitted. 'The text mentioned a number of atypical red blood cell shapes, but the most common deviance in the files seems to be spherocytosis, where the cells take on a round shape instead of their normal biconcave shape.'

Nick nodded. 'Bill thinks that might be genetic, not altitude-induced. There's a slight increase in acanthosis—the thorny-looking formation that tells us the cell is about to collapse—but whether that's because there are more cells being produced so more are dying, or because they are made to work harder in the thinner atmosphere, I don't know.'

He bent over another slide, then dictated his findings, before straightening up. 'The increase in the number of red blood cells means that more oxygen can be carried to the lungs and brain—which are both crying out for it, but what else could it mean?'

'Clotting!' she said promptly, and smiled at his surprise. It was hard to stay annoyed with Nick when they were working together like this. She had always enjoyed the challenges he had set for her—well, most of them!—and this new intellectual puzzle was a game she hoped she could win.

'I read up everything I could find on mountain sickness before I came,' she explained. 'Chronic mountain sickness occurs in some people who live permanently at high altitude. They have an over-abundance of red blood cells and develop clots in their veins and lungs. Descending to lower altitudes will correct what is often a fatal illness.'

'And I think your mate Mingma Three might have symptoms of it. He's one of the herd owners, so we'll do his blood today and check it immediately. He might have to go down and leave his son and the rest of the family to mind the beasts.'

They worked on until they heard movement in the ward.

'I came to check on Carol and Linda.' Amanda's lovely head appeared around the door jamb.

You would, when you knew Nick was here, Callie thought uncharitably.

'If Carol's awake I'll have a look at her,' he said, following the teacher out into the ward. 'Linda can get up if she feels like it. No one else feverish or coming out in spots?'

'I don't think so!' Callie heard Amanda's voice and wondered how such a mundane conversation could be made to sound so provocative. 'Ellen's checking on all the girls now. She's reading the riot act and demanding to know who drew the figure on the plastic. Such a fuss over a harmless prank!'

'It was hardly harmless when one girl was injured, another terrified out of her wits and my assistant put in danger having to investigate it!'

Nick's voice dripped icicles, and Callie grinned to herself, then felt ashamed of her delight. She moved across to the microscope and looked at the blood he had already studied, noticing the differences in the cell shapes that he had mentioned earlier. With a concentrated effort, she searched the slide, finding the things he had told her to write down. The slides he was viewing at the moment were all films made from a fresh drop of blood, and stained. They told him the size and shape of the cells, while poor staining of them could show iron deficiency.

Carefully, she made her own notes, counting the deeply stained cells and those with bluish colouration.

I can do this, she realised as she studied the round and thorny cells. The work she had done in physiology and biology in her first year at university came flooding back into her mind, and she picked up another of the slides and studied it, remembering the categories on the file cards.

'Nick can check the first few,' she told the microscope as she scribbled her results on a scrap of paper. 'And if I'm right then it's another job I can do when he is called away.'

'More chickenpox!' It was Ellen's voice this time, and Callie left the fascination of the slides and walked out into the ward.

'How much longer can you stay here?' Nick asked, and Callie noticed that he spoke to Ellen, not Amanda, although she was hovering close to his side.

'Two more nights at the most,' Ellen replied. 'Our guide tells us we can get down Phortse in a day quite easily, and maybe make it on to Namche Bazaar. Another long day would take us down to Lukla, and still give us a day to spare before the flight out.'

Callie thought of the horror stories she had heard about delayed flights out of Lukla, but she said nothing. Ellen had enough problems.

'It will all depend on how much walking the sick girls can do,' Ellen added worriedly. 'Linda hasn't been at death's door with her bout, but she's been lying in bed, being waited on, not traipsing down a mountain.'

'It won't do them any good to be walking when they're feverish,' Nick agreed, and only Callie knew how worried he was underneath the casual words.

'Let's get the sick ones into bed first,' she suggested as Carol and Linda appeared to join in the conversation.

'Good idea,' Nick agreed. 'You go and get them, Amanda, and settle them in. Ellen, I want you to get your guide and bring him to the kitchen. Callie and I usually eat at this time of the morning. We'll hold a conference over coffee and breakfast.'

Amanda looked affronted, but she walked away, and Callie felt obscurely sorry for her.

'I can stay here and take temperatures, check the girls in,' she suggested, but Nick took her firmly by the arm and led her away.

'You can do that later,' he said. 'Right now we need all the brains we can muster to sort out this little problem.'

Ellen and the guide followed them into the kitchen. She introduced him as Tashi, and they sat down at the table, Solti offering breakfast to the two visitors.

'The sick girls shouldn't over-exert themselves, and who knows when the well ones who are still vulnerable will start running a temperature?' Nick said. 'So what do you suggest?' He turned to the guide, knowing that he was the one who would have to find part of the solution.

'We are already short of porters, after the stupid smallpox scare,' he explained, 'or we could have arranged litters and carried the sick ones. I think we should try to get yaks.'

'Yaks?' Callie asked. 'I've seen some loads carried on yaks, but people?'

'At this time of the year there will be more yaks than porters available. Most of the good men in Namche are booked through the trekking season. Even in winter when the snow comes, the visitors still trek. I might get some porters from Phortse or Jorsale, but it is a day down there to ask and another day back. Local men or yaks would be better.'

'If we leave tomorrow and walk more slowly, would

that help?' Ellen suggested, as if the idea of the girls being carried by the hairy long-haired creatures of the high mountains was appallingly awful.

'If the sick girls can keep up!' Nick agreed, but he sounded so dubious that they all shook their heads.

'What about the merchants coming up today?' Callie asked. 'Do they use yaks to bring their supplies up to the shops? Perhaps we could hire them.' Nick smiled his approval of the suggestion—warming Callie's heart to a fever of its own—then turned to the guide. 'They might have yaks or mules, but usually porters,' Tashi said. 'I will go and ask. Would we go after one night or two?'

'I'd prefer to leave tomorrow and take it more slowly,' Ellen told him, her face tight with worry.

'I could walk down with them.' The words were out of her mouth before Callie realised she'd said it, but Ellen's concern had prompted them and she did not regret her offer.

'With those feet?' Nick asked, peering under the table at her socks.

'They're just about better, and I've got good shoes,' she told him. 'Even if I only stay with them until Phortse. By then they'll be close enough to get someone from Khunde hospital to help if there's an emergency. And if some men from the village go down as porters, I can come back up with them.'

'It would be wonderful to have medical help.' Ellen offered the words very tentatively.

'It's only two days, three at the most, Nick,' Callie pleaded. 'One down and maybe two back up if I take it slowly.'

'You can't go!' he exploded. 'It's ridiculous to even think about it. Ellen, I think you're right deciding to leave tomorrow. I'll go down to the village with Tashi and see if we can find some men with animals willing to help, and, once we know numbers, we can make our decisions from there.' He pushed away his half-eaten breakfast and left the room.

'We're being such a nuisance for you!' Ellen muttered, but Callie shook her head.

'That's what these aid posts are set up for,' she told her. 'No one can plan to avoid illness and accident. Dr Wilcox had this place built for his own purposes, but he offered his services to the Himalayan Rescue Association at the same time. They have permanent buildings at Pheriche on the Everest trail and at Munang in the Annapurna area, and staff them with up to four volunteer doctors right through the trekking season. As other trails, like Gokyo and Annapurna Sanctuary become more popular, temporary aid posts are set up at the height of the two main trekking seasons.'

'I'd read about the Himalayan Rescue Association,' Ellen admitted, 'but I'd imagined it was formed to rescue mountaineers injured during their climbs. It isn't until you come to these places that you realise how important it is to have medical people in place in the mountains to keep an eye on the health of all the trekkers.'

Callie finished her breakfast, then walked back to the ward with Ellen. The two sick girls were in bed, but Carol was gone, and Linda had evidently shifted back to camp.

Callie took temperatures, then went through her usual routine of dispensing analgesics to reduce the fever, and putting jars of water beside the girls' beds. Nick returned as she was dropping the thermometer into the sterilising liquid they used.

'It's all set; we'll leave in the morning,' he announced, hovering over her in a most distracting manner.

'We'll leave?' she echoed frostily.

He put a friendly arm around her shoulders and drew her close for a moment—behaving like old-pal Nick when she wanted to kick him!

'I've got a couple coming up from the village to sleep in the hospital ward. The woman has done some nursing in Khunde, and will give you a hand during the day, and they will both give you peace of mind at night.'

Callie stared blindly at the jar of sterilising liquid, but her mind saw a vivid picture of Nick and Amanda, tripping hand in hand down the mountain. It doesn't matter, she told herself. He was only ever a friend to you, never more, no matter how much you might have wanted it!

He must have sensed her hesitation, for he rubbed his hand up and down her arm as if to comfort her.

'You were right in the kitchen, Callie. Someone has to go down with them, if only to call a halt if the girls show signs of stress,' he explained huskily. 'And nearly better isn't good enough with those blisters of yours!'

He turned her in his arms, and looked down into her face. His eyes were soft, but unreadable.

'I'll get back as soon as I can,' he promised. He leant forward, dropped a kiss on her forehead, then walked out of the room.

'And what do I do about prescription drugs?' she yelled after him, blinking away invasive pictures of the beautiful Amanda by the nightly campfire.

He spun around and frowned, as if he had heard

aggression in her voice and was puzzled by it. 'I'm not going yet, Callie! We've all day to go through procedures here. If you could get some needles and syringes ready to take the blood samples, and some slides and all the staining paraphernalia, I'll let Ellen know what I've organised and then we'll go down to the village as planned.'

'I'll need the keys,' she muttered, then couldn't stop herself adding, 'And does "we" mean you and I, or you and Amanda?'

For a moment his frown deepened, and he stepped towards her, one hand lifted as if he was reaching out for her. 'Callie——' he began, then Ellen called to him, and whatever he had been about to say was lost. As he turned to answer the call he fished in his pocket, found the keys, and tossed them on to the bench.

Callie picked them up and fingered them, feeling the lingering warmth of his body on them. Last night he had held her in his arms, jolting all her over-active hormones back into action. Not that they are usually over-active, she reminded herself. Rather the reverse, in fact, if all the fellows she'd been out with over the years were to be believed!

You are being stupid, she told herself. Stupid, and unreasonable, and irrational and neurotic. If you can't treat Nick like an old friend, which is all he is willing to be, then treat him as a colleague!

She unlocked the cabinets, found syringes, phials to store the blood, and slides stored in ethanol to use for fresh smears. Forceps to handle the slides were dropped into the pack, then some clean cloth for wiping them. Searching through the boxes on the bench, she found envelopes and adhesive tags for labelling, and added them to the pack. What else?

The slides would have to be stained, he said. She went back to the cabinet. There was a bottle of Leishman's stain in the cupboard, and a container that must be used to hold the stained slides while they were being treated. Reading the directions on the bottle, she added a jar of distilled water, and decided it would be far easier if the men came to Nick to give their blood, instead of him going to them and having to stain the films down there while the blood was still fresh.

Antiseptic solution and cotton balls for cleaning the skin. Tape to close the wounds. She worked quickly, pleased to have her mind fully occupied by work.

When Nick returned, he checked what she had packed, then led her towards the trail.

'The two merchants go on to Gokyo today, so they don't have much time,' he told her as they walked down to the village.

Old friend Nick, Callie reminded herself, nothing more.

'I was wondering why we took all the gear to them,' she told him. 'Couldn't the village men come up to us?'

'I suppose so,' he said, turning to help her down a steep pinch, 'but Bill didn't like to set them apart. It might have made them feel less important, he thought, so he did all of them at once. The villagers know which days the merchants come, so they wait at home for their needles.'

'And the porters?' she asked, repeating 'old friend' over and over in her head to keep her body in check as he helped her over the rocky outcrops that littered the path. 'Do we have to worry about their sensibilities?'

'Most of them call at the aid post anyway. They bring their trekkers for a talk on AMS.'

'So if some come while you are away, do I take samples?'

He smiled again and shook his head, stopping his descent to turn and look at her. 'Determined to prove me wrong, aren't you, brat?' he said softly. 'Yes, you could. In fact, I'd be grateful if you did. And I apologise again for the "fluff-filled head" remark.' He shook his head, and for a moment she thought he was going to touch her—hold her. 'It's not easy for me to accept that you're not my little Callie any more. I keep being surprised by what you know and what you can do, although I know I shouldn't be.'

A gruffness in his voice disconcerted her, and she grinned uneasily, before replying, 'I only know as much as any fourth-year student would, but it might help if you could remember I'm a grown woman, not a child!'

She saw something flutter in his eyes, then his dark lashes descended, hiding whatever it was, and he turned back towards the village. 'Oh, I don't have any trouble remembering that and it's not a help at all. Rather the opposite, if anything,' he informed her harshly and strode away, leaving her almost running to keep up with him.

The merchants were both worldly, loquacious men who greeted Nick as an old friend. While he took blood from pin-pricks for film on the slides, he chattered away in a mixture of English and Nepali.

'He is trying to show how good he is at our language,' one of them told Callie. 'We speak better English, but still he insist on speaking bits and bits of our language.'

'Have you ever prepared counting chambers to do a red blood cell count?' Nick asked her quietly as he drew up a small quantity of venous blood, then carefully labelled the vial.

'Back in second year,' Callie told him, 'but I remember the procedure.' She saw the flash of brown as his eyes grazed her face, and knew she had surprised him again.

'If I don't get time to do the slides this afternoon, would you have a go?' he asked. 'There's a box of pipettes in the top cabinet and the counting chambers are near them. If you need some revision, all the instructions are on the box. I had to read them step by step the first ten times I did it.'

'Poor old man,' she teased. 'Memory fading already?'

The merchant laughed, and Nick smiled, but shook his head. 'Too much technology available nowadays. I send blood to the lab and it comes back as pages and pages of computer print-out! It was a long time since I'd dabbled with the real red stuff, or made slides and film of it.'

'I'd be delighted to do it,' Callie assured him. 'I suppose we have to do the count as soon as possible after taking the blood, but the examination of the stained film can wait.'

If his hands hadn't been busy taking blood from the second merchant he would have patted me on the head again, Callie realised, but she was pleased that he had accepted her competence. More than pleased, she admitted silently as her blood skidded through her veins and delight stretched her lips into a wide smile!

'That's right. I use the special battery-operated theatre light to work at night at these times. With an assistant who can check my calculations, I'll get through the work in half the time.'

Callie remembered the formula for changing the number of cells in a specially marked square of the slide into an approximation of total cells. 'He's talking about counting things to the nearest half-million,' she explained to the bemused audience. 'He'd need a woman to check that for him, wouldn't he?'

The men laughed again, then called to their sons to come forward and donate their blood to science. Callie worked and talked easily, content that Nick was near. Even if it wasn't quite the dream she had wanted to come true, it was close, and she had to be satisfied with that.

Leaving the merchants to make their way on up the trail to Gokyo, they walked through the village to a house on the outskirts.

'I take blood from three people here,' Nick told her. 'And it's the changes in the blood viscosity of these people that's proving more interesting.'

Before she could ask why, and in what way, he called a greeting to the family and ducked to enter the low-set cottage. Callie followed him, automatically adjusting her breathing to shallow gasps so the first lungful of smoky air didn't start a paroxysm of coughing. Even during the day, when the fire died out to preserve the precious supply of fuel, the smoke hovered in the houses like an unexorcised ghost.

Nick introduced her to the woman of the house, and then the children who clustered, bright-eyed and curious, about her long tunic skirt. Callie pressed her palms together and bowed her head in greeting. She looked around the small hut, seeing the shining stainless-steel and copper pots on a shelf along one wall. Another shelf held a motley assortment of packaged food that made her wonder about the changes the increasing number of trekkers had brought to the region. At the end of the shelf were four large Thermos flasks, used for keeping tea or water hot during the day, Callie assumed.

The woman spoke rapidly to Nick and sent one of the children dashing out of the door.

'Her husband will be here shortly,' Nick explained. 'He's one of the men who will lend an animal to go down with the school party tomorrow, and he's bringing his dzopchuk into the house yard.'

'How nice!' Callie said politely, and Nick grinned at her.

'To us, all yaks are yaks, but a dzopchuk is a male animal that's a crossbreed between a cow and a yak. They are docile and easily trained, which makes them much better for use as plough animals or for carrying loads.'

The woman was nodding her head while Nick explained, and Callie wondered how much English she understood.

'Ready?' Nick asked. 'We'll take a drop of blood from her finger and make a film first, then I'll draw some up for the RBC count.'

Callie produced the necessary paraphernalia, and spread it on a clean cloth on a small square table. Nick bent over and drew a slide from the ethanol solution. Using a second cloth, he dried it carefully then selected a needle. The woman came forward, holding out her finger to Callie, who swabbed it clean, then held it steady while Nick pricked it and squeezed a drop of blood on to the slide. Using a second slide held at an angle, he smeared the blood across it, then handed it to Callie to stain, while he swabbed the woman's arm and carefully drew up a small phial of venous blood.

They had been through the motions five times already, with the store-keepers and their sons, so they worked silently, their actions orchestrated into an uncanny precision.

'All done!' he said at last, and Callie, glancing at her watch, saw that it was past their usual lunch-time.

'Let's hope there isn't a queue of patients up there in the courtyard,' she said as they made their way back up to their temporary home.

'There shouldn't be,' Nick assured her. 'The locals always know which day we're busy, and trekkers going into Gokyo rarely arrive until mid-afternoon, while those going back down rarely stop!'

'You love it, don't you?' Callie asked as the deep warmth in his voice spoke more clearly than the words.

He paused and turned back to look at her. 'Wouldn't anyone?' he asked, waving a hand towards the mountains that rose around them. 'And it's not only the peace and majesty of the mountains that's so special, it's the beauty of the people, their kindliness, and their simplicity. They laugh when they are happy and cry when they are sad, they work to produce enough food to keep their families fed. In the Western world, we hide our tears and our laughter too often, lest others think us weak, or stupid, and most of us work to make more money to buy not necessities, but bigger and better luxuries.'

'Could you live somewhere like this?' Callie asked, wanting to prolong this rare moment of sharing.

'No way!' he told her with a conspiratorial smile. 'My needs are different. Not so much materially, although my bones are used to more softness in a bed, but intellectually. But I will always come back—to here or to some other place—to remind myself how little I need to be happy.'

And this time, when his hand lifted, she did not

duck away, but felt his fingers slide into her curls, and grip, then tug! She felt herself drawn closer and was about to move towards him when the fingers relaxed, ruffled across her head, and dropped away.

He turned back towards the trail, and climbed swiftly away from her, and she followed his strong, well-muscled legs on and up.

She'd followed Nick from the time she could toddle, bonding to him as a motherless duckling would bond to a human surrogate. Before she was three she would escape her fenced yard and follow him up the road to school, unable to understand that he could go while she had to remain at home.

Time after time, he'd taken her back home, scolding her all the way. But his arms had always been gentle, and she had always known that, beneath his surface anger, he had loved her as much as she had loved him.

CHAPTER EIGHT

'HAVE you heard one word I've said?' Nick demanded, spinning around to face her as they reached the courtyard.

Callie shook herself back to the present. 'Not since you stopped the philosophy lecture!' she admitted, and her memories spilled over into the happy, cheeky grin that accompanied the words.

For a moment he said nothing, and she thought she saw a faint shadow cross his face and hover in the intentness of his gaze. Then his eyebrows twitched together, and his eyelids dropped to hide his eyes.

'There's a pharmacology book there. You can give out antibiotics for bacterial infections, or prescription drugs like Lomotil for diarrhoea, but make sure you read all the warnings, adverse reactions and interactions before you give even the mildest of drugs.'

'Is this legal?' she asked, surprised by the amount of latitude he seemed to be giving her.

'When you consider that most trekkers carry a medicine chest that's as comprehensive as ours, and that most drugs we issue prescriptions for at home are available over the counter in Kathmandu, I don't think there's much illegal about it in these circumstances.'

'What about penicillin and people with allergic reactions to it?'

He sighed, and the furrows in his brow grew deeper. 'People have allergic reactions to so many drugs. Often there are indications, like allergies to a number of other things. I know that many people who are allergic to peanuts are also allergic to penicillin.'

'But how could anyone possibly connect the two?' Callie argued. 'Who would think of correlating tests between peanuts of all things, and penicillin?'

'Maybe not peanuts themselves, but what about peanut butter?' The question was accompanied by a teasing grin, and she knew how badly she would miss him when he left in the morning. 'I noticed it first when I was in a children's ward during my training, and something in my subconscious mind has always followed it through. Kids with peanut butter on their allergy list—and you've got to remember a lot of young children haven't tried oysters of shellfish, so their lists weren't all that long—well, they usually had penicillin listed as well.'

'So I do what I can to find out about allergies, and treat all allergy sufferers with grave suspicion?'

'Exactly,' he agreed. 'And warn people to return immediately if they feel at all sick after taking medication. Most of the villagers who attend the clinic bring friends and relations with them. If they don't speak English, get Solti to explain that they must watch their sick friend in case the medicine reacts badly for them.'

He looked so serious that she reached out and touched his arm. 'I'll be fine,' she said.

He looked down at her hand for a moment, small and pale against his suntanned skin, then he dropped his arm as if her touch had grown too hot to bear, and turned towards the hut.

'I wouldn't go, but if I don't I could be risking the health of those sick girls,' he said, the words drifting back over his shoulder, faint and insubstantial, as if he was talking to himself as much as to her.

In the small ward, Amanda was playing nurse, or, Callie thought uncharitably, pretending to care for the sick girls while waiting for Nick to return. She was standing close to him now, whispering into his ear, and Callie's stomach somersaulted. All the pleasant feelings towards Nick that her mental journey into the past had engendered disappeared, swept away by the jealous anger she found impossible to control.

'Just drop the gear in the office then have a wash and go over to the kitchen; I'll be there as soon as I've checked the girls.'

It was an order to be followed meekly, Callie decided. There'd be time enough to argue with him about his peremptory attitude when they didn't have an avid audience. But, when Amanda followed him into the kitchen, and dropped on to the bench beside him, the meekness disappeared.

'Do we start making up the counting-chamber slides immediately after lunch?' Callie asked, in case he needed a reminder about why he was in Machherma.

'Making them up and labelling them. I can't tell you how good it will be to have assistance with that little job. Bill had trained a local man from Namche to help, but he went with Bill to make sure he got safely back to Kathmandu, and was never seen again.'

'For a man from Namche Bazar, Kathmandu must seem like Paris,' Amanda said. 'I can quite understand his refusing to leave.'

Squashed on the bench beside him, Callie couldn't help but feel Nick stiffen in response to the artless comment, but she refrained from uttering the argument that had sprung to her lips.

'Don't trust me to make the slides?' she asked instead, bringing the conversation back to work.

'You could do it,' he told her, 'but it takes practice and a steady hand, and I've had more recent practice. We've eleven slides to prepare, then all the counting to do. Whichever way we divide the work it will be a long night.'

'But you said we were leaving early in the morning, Nick.' Amanda broke into the conversation. 'The girls are planning a special sing-song around the campfire tonight.'

Once again Callie felt him stifle his surge of impatience.

'The girls can have their sing-song, Amanda,' he said carefully, 'and Callie and I will still hear it. But we're not on holiday like most of the foreigners you meet in the mountains, we're here to work.'

And that's put you in your place, madam, Callie thought, then felt ashamed of her feeling of triumph—until Amanda whispered, loud enough for her to hear, 'Well, at least you won't be working quite so hard on the trek back down. We'll have plenty of time to spend together.'

'I'll go and unpack the stained slides!' Callie announced, sickened more by her own furious reaction to the words than by the words themselves. She pushed away her half-eaten lunch and left the room, but not quickly enough to miss Amanda's parting shot.

'I thought she'd never go, darling!' the husky voice said, and Callie fled before Nick's response could twist the skeins of jealousy within her any tighter.

Back in the lab, she worked with a will, storing all the completed slides in the metal case ready for examination later. She stacked away the unused equipment and disposed of the needles and syringes they had used. By the time Nick returned, she had twenty chamber slides and their special ground-glass covers out ready for him to use. If it was as tricky as he said, there would be mistakes. She printed the eleven names on adhesive tags, so they needed only to be peeled off and placed on the correct slide.

'Blood, diluting fluid, slides, names—all ready to go! What a clever little assistant you are!' Nick grinned his pleasure and Callie felt the air come to life around her, and saw the sun beyond the window take on an extra sparkle.

He loves his work so much that he'd enjoy working with anyone who was competent, she reminded herself, but the warning could not dampen her disproportionate feeling of pleasure.

They worked together until the light was gone, she shaking the glass tube of blood then holding it steady while he drew up the blood and plunged the pipette into the diluting fluid, drawing up enough to dilute the blood two hundred times. Once he had dropped the diluted blood into the counting chamber of the slide and was satisfied there were no air bubbles, the slide was labelled and set aside.

'We'll break for dinner, then come back and use the battery light to do the counts,' Nick told her when the last slide was labelled and stacked. 'I wonder what lucky break gave us a patient-free afternoon.'

He stood up from the stool as he spoke, and stretched his arms as high as the low roof would allow. Callie felt the tug of his physical attraction sweep across her and blinked her surprise. They had worked together for four hours, touching and brushing against each other, but her involvement in the work had kept her safe from her nagging awareness of Nick the man.

'Tired?' he asked, and the gentleness in his voice

made her heart twist within her.

'Not at all,' she said heartily. 'I was thinking.'

'Of Howard?' he snapped, and the change in his voice was so marked that she had to shake her head before she remembered who Howard was.

'Well six weeks is a long time to be away!' she muttered. 'Of course I think of him.'

She stalked out of the door and headed for the bathroom, more confused than ever now that Nick was treating her like an equal—and, occasionally, like a woman. That was even more disconcerting.

The girls were getting ready for their evening meal as Callie crossed the edge of their camp to get to the kitchen. Nick was there, head and shoulders looming out over the usual group of adoring girls that clustered and chattered around him every time he appeared. Until Amanda came on the scene, Callie thought spitefully. When she appeared the teenagers melted like shadows into the dark.

She asked Solti to serve her dinner, then ate quickly and hurried back to her bedroom while he was still in the camp. She would write to her mother and to a few friends and get Ellen to post the letters when she returned to Australia.

She was still bent over her writing pad, head low to make the most of the lamplight, when Nick returned.

'I'm ready when you are,' he announced, and she knew the harmony of the afternoon was gone.

'I'm certain the herders' blood is changing quite perceptibly,' he said a little later, breaking the tense silence that had developed between them. 'If so, it will bear out other studies that have been carried out that claim major changes only occur after a person has been at altitude for six weeks or more.'

'But all the subjects have higher RBC counts at Machherma than they did at Namche Bazar,' Callie argued, remembering the figures she had transcribed on to the chart.

'Yes, but that figure fluctuates fairly consistently,' Nick pointed out. 'It could be possible to make a table showing the increase in RBC development as people climb. The real differences are in those who live part of the year here, and how long it takes for their blood to go back to normal when they return to lower altitude.'

'You'll need someone in Namche doing follow-up work,' Callie suggested, pleased to concentrate on work and distract her mind from other unprofitable speculation.

'We already have a doctor at Khunde hospital taking samples of the merchants before and after each trip. He'll do the follow-up on the herders if Bill is still not well enough to return.'

'Hi, you two, may I interrupt for a moment?'

Ellen spoke from the doorway and they both spun around to face her.

'No more problems,' she assured them quickly. 'You should have seen both your faces!' She chuckled quietly, and Callie felt her racing pulse subside. She had expected trouble! 'I wondered what time you want us to get away, Nick, and also if either of you would like mail posted.'

'I've got letters,' Callie said, and hurried out of the room as Nick explained that he would arrange for Solti to give them all early-morning tea so the porters could pack up the kitchen tent and head off ahead of the main party.

'That way, you can have a late breakfast on the

trail,' he was explaining when Callie returned.

She saw his quick frown as she handed over six letters to Ellen, who put them into the pocket of her jacket and promised not to forget them.

'Better not,' Nick said silkily, 'or the boyfriend will think she's deserted him.'

'He would not!' Callie argued, defending her mythical fiancé. 'He knows there's no reliable mail service from these parts, and what's more——' she drew herself up to her full height and added haughtily '—he trusts me!'

'I've a letter I'll give you.' Nick's words were deep and harsh, as if they hurt to say, but Callie was too disturbed by the reminders that he was leaving in the morning to try to work out why he was upset. As he pushed past her, she returned to work, multiplying out the count to get an approximate figure.

'I'll finish in here—you go to bed,' Nick told her when he returned a little later.

'You're the one who should be in bed,' she objected. 'You've got two days' trekking in front of you.'

He was standing close to her stool, and she wanted to put her arms around his waist and nuzzle her face into his flannelette shirt, to ask him not to go—or to at least say goodbye properly.

'I can walk down that trail half-asleep, but you'll be making medical decisions. Don't expect more days with no patients. Today was the first time that's happened in the month I've been here.'

'Maybe they won't come if they know you've gone,' she argued.

'And maybe they will,' he countered, and she felt him move a fraction closer and wondered if he also felt the need for physical contact before he left. She held her breath, then heard him sigh. 'Go to bed, brat,' he murmured, and, when she remained stuck to the stool, he finally reached out and touched her shoulder, his fingers biting into the flesh before giving her a little shake. 'Now!' he ordered.

She went, knowing that he was right and she needed sleep, but wanting so badly to stay with him that her legs trembled as they carried her away.

She woke to a clatter of boots against the rough stones on the trail and knew only an emergency would bring someone up to the aid post in the early hours of the morning. As she felt for her torch she was aware of the sound of Nick's breathing and knew he must be deeply asleep to have missed the noise of a new arrival. Using the torch to light her way, she crept out past the sleeping girls.

The man was one of the herders she had met when they had taken the blood, but she was unable to follow the mixture of Nepali and English that poured from his lips.

'Wait!' she said, holding up her hand. 'I'll get Solti.'

Solti appeared at that moment, and soon explained the man's agitation: his wife was having a baby.

Remembering the woman with the tribe of children playing around her skirts, Callie shook her head. 'That woman wasn't pregnant,' she said to Solti. 'At least not noticeably so.'

As Solti questioned the man, she thought about the long straight tunic the woman had worn, and the coloured apron over it, and wondered, certain it couldn't have concealed a pregnancy nearing full term.

'He says another wife, not the one you saw. It is her first baby, and already she is unhappy all day and some of last night.'

'Unhappy? After more than twelve hours in labour? Now there's an understatement,' Callie muttered to herself as she headed for the laboratory and began grabbing equipment they would need.

The aid post was hardly equipped for emergency childbirth, she realised, in spite of the ergotrate maleate. She added the pills to the doctor's bag. No special electronic equipment to monitor foetal heartbeats, but a stethoscope would do. She checked that one was already in the bag. She added plasma and an IV catheter, then searched through the medical cupboard to see if there was anything else that they might use. Drugs were available to promote uterine contractions and actively manage the third stage of labour, but oxytocin was the only one that she remembered and there was nothing in the cupboard that included it, or mentioned the management of labour on its label.

Solti hovered in the doorway.

'I'll have to wake Nick,' she told him. 'If the woman's in trouble, I might not know what to do. Do you know which house she's in?'

'Yes, I take you there,' Solti assured her.

'Then send the man home to be with his wife. Tell him Nick and I will follow.'

She crept back into the bedroom and shook Nick awake, muttering his name in a frantic undertone.

'It's OK, darling!' he mumbled sleepily. He reached out with one lean hand and tried to draw her down against his chest. 'It's OK, I'm here.'

'Wake up!' she muttered, tugging at his shoulders as if her puny strength might be able to lift him forcibly out of bed. And who was he calling darling? her distracted mind wondered. 'There's an emergency,' she hissed, while her body fought an urge to let the hand pull her down. He felt so warm and snuggly, and smelt so male and virile and—— 'Wake up now!' she ordered, and flashed her torch in his eyes.

He blinked in his sleep, his eyelids reacting to the brightness, then he forced his eyes open and sat up.

'There's a woman in the village been in labour since last night. Solti's waiting to take us down there.'

'I'll go,' he said, struggling up through the layers of sleep and shaking his head as if to clear it. 'You go back to bed.'

'I'm coming, Nick!' she told him. 'I've packed everything I could think of into the bag, and have put clean towels and a sheet into a backpack. I'll put on my boots while you get ready.' She eyed his bare chest, now fully exposed above violently coloured boxer shorts. The sight of so much skin made her regret not lying down against him—even if it had only been for a brief moment.

'All set?' he asked moments later, and took her arm to help her down the track.

They reached the house, and the husband led them inside. For a moment Callie could see nothing in the smoky dimness, then, as her eyes grew accustomed to the gloom, she saw the woman she had met before bent low over a moaning bundle in the corner.

Nick crossed the room swiftly, and knelt to examine the patient, a slight young woman, barely more than a girl. Callie leant above him, shining her torch down to provide more light. The young woman was certainly pregnant, but her barely distended abdomen would only put the foetus at five or six months—not developed enough to survive without a heap of unattainable medical equipment!

She watched as Nick slipped on gloves, and leant

forward to palpate the abdomen. The girl was curled towards them, her knees drawn up to her chest. As Nick bent over her she stiffened, and rolled away. As he followed her with his hands to feel the abdomen, Callie saw Nick's shock registered on his face.

'It's rigid and hot to touch. Take her blood-pressure, Callie, and pulse-rate, while I see what I can find. Is the pain there all the time?' he asked the girl, then must have realised his mistake, and translated the words. The herder repeated Nick's question, then turned back and replied.

Callie lifted the girl's wrist and felt the rapid heart-beat, then strapped the blood-pressure cuff around the thin arm and began to pump.

'I think it's appendicitis, not labour,' Nick said quietly. 'There's no indication of labour, and her belly's as taut as a drum. She practically leapt through the roof when I touched her abdomen. I'll inject a sedative that should begin to work shortly and act as a pre-med. We can't do anything here. We'll have to get her up to the aid post.'

Callie turned to Solti and asked him to arrange to have the patient carried up the hill.

'Can you still remember how to do an appendec-tomy?' she hissed at Nick, knowing he had been in research for at least a year.

'I've heard stories of yachtsmen operating on their mates with rusty penknives,' he replied. 'I'm certain I can do better than that!'

They watched as the girl was lifted on to a makeshift stretcher, then hurried out, anxious to get back to the little hospital and prepare for the operation.

'I'm more concerned about what we'll find,' he added. 'Chances are it's burst and there's peritonitis.

That will stretch Bill's medical chest to its limits.'

'We've plasma, IV fluid, saline and antibiotics,' Callie reminded him.

'And general anaesthetising agents, I assume. I did go through it all when I first arrived, but since then I've only opened it to get out something I needed immediately.'

'I know there's Diprivan,' Callie told him. 'I suppose because most emergency procedures are covered by a short anaesthetic period.'

'It's a good product,' Nick assured her. 'We'll set up a drip and put in a Y-piece in case we need a repeat bolus injection. Diprivan can be infused with five percent dextrose, and I'll check the analgesics and sort out what we can add to the cocktail.'

'She's lucky you were still here,' Callie told him. 'If it had happened tomorrow night I think I would have loaded her on a yak and sent her down towards the hospital at Khunde, and, if it has burst, she would never have made it.'

Nick chuckled, then said, 'Ah, but she would have met up with me and the school party, and I could have made a hero of myself with my rusty penknife!'

The joke lightened Callie's anxiety, and calmed her fluttering nerves. She led the way through the ward and re-lit the bright lamp in the office; then she went back to the ward and woke the two sick girls.

'You'll have to go through and sleep in our bedroom,' she told them. 'We need to use this room for an emergency.'

As they stood up she picked up the thin foam mattresses off the bunks they had been using, and followed them in to remake the beds. Dragging her own and Nick's bedding on to the floor, she spread the mattresses, then helped the girls, still cocooned in their sleeping-bags, back into their new beds.

They were both drowsy, and, as she shut the door on them, she was certain they would drift back to sleep. Nick was still busy in the lab, so she pulled a mattress down off one of the top bunks and made up a clean bed for the new patient.

Nick came into the ward and looked around, nodded once, then disappeared again. Callie followed him into the small office, and he handed her a sterile plastic sheet in a sealed packet.

'Put this over the foam on the table,' he said, 'and try to keep it up the top. She's only small, so I'll use the end of the table as a tray for the instruments. I can regulate the oxygen flow to a minimum, so you'll be able to be a second pair of hands when I need them for retracting the skin, mopping up or irrigating the wound, but your prime concern is to check her pulse, blood-pressure and breathing.'

'Is she definitely pregnant?' Callie asked as the enormity of what they were about to do hit her with the force of an avalanche.

Nick nodded. 'That's why we can't afford to dally,' he told her. 'I'll get in and out as quickly as I can, but I'll have to tie off all the small bleeders, as there's no cautery machine. I'll also have to use antibiotics both during and after the operation.'

'But the baby—' Callie objected, cutting short the words when she realised how ridiculous her protest was.

'I'm using a tetracycline, Reverin,' Nick explained. 'Tests have shown that all tetracyclines cross the placenta and are stored in bone. They may lead to a discolouration of teeth in unborn infants or babies, and can produce a slowing of bone growth. But the bone growth reverts to normal as soon as the drugs are discontinued,' he hastened to assure her. 'Let's hope the foetus is developed enough to be unaffected.'

Solti interrupted them, leading his little party into the room. Nick crossed to the girl who was already asleep. Callie watched as he lifted her tenderly off the litter and stretched her out on the unmade bunk.

'We'll have to take her clothes off and sponge her down, Callie,' he said. 'I daren't risk additional contamination from her clothes or organisms on her skin.'

'I'll do it,' Callie told him. 'Then I'll wrap her in one of the clean sheets from the cabinet, and tie her hair up in a small towel.'

She hurried off to get water and antibacterial lotion to wash the slight body. Action stopped her worrying about what was to come!

'I'm ready,' he announced at last, carrying the bright battery light into the ward and hanging it on the hook above the operating table. 'You have a good scrub in the lab and get gloves on.'

He crossed to the bunk and lifted the girl again, taking the weight as easily as if she were a child. Watching his gentleness, Callie wondered why he had left practical medicine and contact with people, to go into something as removed from human contact as haematology research. Could she ask? She hurried away to clean her hands and arms and prepare for this bizarre surgery.

'IV catheter, Callie!'

She pushed intrusive, personal thoughts aside and snapped back into work-mode. She found the needle at one side of the laid-out instruments and passed it to him. He used the blood-pressure cuff as a ligature around the thin arm, and finally raised a vein to take the drip. Callie picked up the bag of fluid he had chosen, and attached the tubing to it. For the first time she noticed hooks set in the wall above the table, and realised that they were there for a purpose. She walked around the end of the table and hung the bag on the lowest of them.

Nick flushed the tube then fitted it into the canula, watching to make certain the fluid was going into the vein, not the surrounding tissues. He checked the fluid flow, fiddled with the oxygen tank held by a clamp to the end of the table, and settled the mask over the unconscious girl's face.

'I'll inject the Diprivan and I've drawn up a second dose in case it's needed,' he said quietly. 'You use the stethoscope to monitor her breathing and heart-rate, and check her blood-pressure now, then every ten minutes. There's a card by her head—record every finding.'

To Callie, the night took on a dream-like quality. Nick cut neatly through the skin, and she pulled it apart with retractors while he split the flat external muscle, then found his way through the internal muscle to the smooth membranous lining of the abdominal cavity. The next cut was crucial, Callie realised, holding her breath as the scalpel sliced through, revealing the soft pink curves of the caecum.

'It's still intact!' he murmured, and Callie watched tensely as he manoeuvred the caecum and the swollen, inflamed appendix out through the incision. This was the critical moment when one false move could cause it to rupture and release infective material into the abdominal cavity.

'It's OK now,' Nick said, as if he felt her tension. 'See the membranous tissue here.'

Callie became interested in spite of herself and leaned forward to look more closely. She had watched hundreds of operations from a gallery above the theatre at the teaching hospital where the students did their practical work, but hadn't got this close to one before. Nick worked with the intentness he brought to all tasks, and she admired the swift certainty of his fingers.

'I have to cut it and tie off the blood vessels. Pass me a catgut suture from the left of the instruments, then check her pulse, blood-pressure and respiration. Once I've tied these off, I'll snip off the offending appendix and put a ligature around the stump, then, to make certain that any possible leak goes into the gut rather than into the cavity, I'll do a purse-string ligature around that part of the caecum, and push the stump back into it and tie it in there.'

Satisfied that the young woman was stable, Callie turned back to watch Nick do his fancy work, then check his instruments and the bloody swabs before flushing the wound with a saline solution and closing it securely.

'Would you normally leave a drain in an appendix wound?' she asked as he taped a dressing over the wound.

'Probably,' he admitted, 'particularly when the appendix was so swollen and her temperature indicated that some infection may already have been present.'

'But?' Callie prompted, hearing the lingering doubt in his voice.

'But a drain and the open wound it necessitates are like highways for outside infections to enter the body.

If she was in hospital, in reasonably sterile conditions, I wouldn't hesitate, but here?'

He gestured to the dirt floor and the pile of soil-encrusted clothes they had removed from the young woman.

'I am not condemning their lifestyle,' he said quickly, 'but they have different standards of hygiene, and, as their medicine is less invasive than our surgical methods, there is little chance of the cure being worse than the disease. It's only when we try to make Western medicine work in cases like this that the difference in lifestyle becomes a threat to healing.'

He sounded so earnest and committed and caring that Callie felt a wave of love sweep up from her toes, invading every cell of her being with its wondrous warmth.

'Would you have such a thing as a nightdress?' he asked, and Callie jerked her tired mind back into gear.

'I'm afraid not,' she muttered, disconcerted by the heat she knew must be flaming in her cheeks.

'Then go in and find a clean flannelette shirt in my bag. We'll dress her in that and open up a sleeping-bag to tuck around her and keep her warm.'

Callie found the torch and crept into the bedroom. Muffled snores and snorts told her both girls were sleeping, but she moved carefully, dragging the bag inch by inch from under the bed, then shining the torch into its depths to find a large, clean shirt.

'I'll dress her, and, once you've lifted her across to the bed, you should get some sleep yourself,' Callie told him. 'I'll clean up, then sit with her and do regular observations.'

'Giving orders, are you?' he said softly, but the brown eyes that looked down into her blue ones seemed to be saying something else.

'Nick?' She stepped hesitantly towards him, and saw the strange light strengthen to a burning intensity, then fade and die.

'She's waking, Callie!' he whispered. 'Get her dressed, and I'll settle her into bed. After that I think I might take your advice and get some sleep myself.'

He moved with her towards the table, and started gathering up the instruments, while Callie lifted the young woman's shoulders and slipped the shirt up her arms. She rolled up the sleeves as far as the wrists, then fastened the buttons. Nick lifted the child-like figure across to the bed, checked her pulse, then stepped back.

'Is our bedding on the floor next door?' he asked, and, when Callie nodded, he added, 'I'll sleep in there, then. Unless you need me earlier, wake me at five. It will still be dark enough for your body to think it's night-time, and you can sleep through until about ten. I won't need to leave before then.'

And that's that, Callie thought as the door closed behind him.

CHAPTER NINE

'Do you think all those people waited deliberately until Nick was gone to get sick?' she asked Solti as she attacked with a ferocious hunger the lunch he had served her. She had slept through the confusion of the girls' departure, waking at ten in time for Nick to introduce her helpers, Ang and Kanti, and to witness the arrival of the first patient, a man with severe colic.

Nick had stayed to examine the man, palpating his stomach and diagnosing severe constipation. He had sent him home with a packet of suppositories and strict instructions not to eat them, and left Callie with the comforting words, 'Let's hope that's all it is, not a total gut obstruction of some kind.'

'Would you operate if it was?' she had asked, and watched his face darken.

'It would mean a resection of the bowel, which is a complicated business in the most up-to-date and totally sterile theatre, but I suppose I'd have to think about it. Now, about our other patient. . .'

He had led her across to where the young woman slept, and shown her the notations on the chart.

'The foetal heartbeat is strong and regular, so we can only hope the operation did not harm the unborn child. Her fever has subsided, but I want you to give her another injection of Reverin at six this evening, and again at six in the morning. I've left the vials at the front of the cabinet.'

He had finally left about three hours behind the

girls, knowing he would catch them up soon after their breakfast stop. As she had watched him stride away from her, his pack carried easily on his strong shoulders, she'd felt a sadness that was hard to define.

'They think you a good doctor.' Solti's voice broke into her thoughts. 'They would not come to you if they did not think that.'

'I suppose that's a compliment,' she said doubtfully. So far, all the patients had been suffering minor complaints that a few tablets or some cream could ease. 'I've a group of climbers coming at three,' she added. 'They are going up to Gokyo, and will set up a weather station there for an English research project.'

'Maybe you should get their blood if they will be there for a long time.'

Callie started in surprise, then felt a wave of shame sweep over her. Why shouldn't Solti know about the project? He had been here since Dr Wilcox had begun it, he was an educated man who spoke a smattering of four languages that she knew of—three more than she could speak!—yet she had never given much thought to his intelligence.

'Maybe different race reacts differently,' he offered quietly, and she nodded.

'Maybe they would!' she agreed. 'I know they will be up at Gokyo for two months, and Nick has another few weeks here. If he has time he wants to do some climbing in the Gokyo area. He could do follow-up studies.' She smiled at Solti. 'I'll ask them,' she said. 'Thank you for the idea. I'd never have thought of it myself.'

His small face wrinkled into a hundred creases as

he smiled his delight. Smiling back at him, Callie realised that he had become more than just an excellent cook—he had become a friend.

The English climbers arrived while she was finishing lunch, and when she started her lecture Callie realised that they knew as much about mountain sickness as she did.

'What are you fellows doing here?' she demanded, breaking off from her increasingly confused explanation of HACE.

'We heard there was this beautiful white female doctor up in the mountains, but that the only way to get to see her was to break a leg or come to her AMS lecture, so here we are.' The man who spoke had twinkly blue eyes peering out above a bush of reddish beard.

'So you're here to waste my time!' she said, and, although she tried to look stern and reproving, her smile broke through.

'We walked in from Jiri, although all our scientific gear was flown to Lukla—so it's a long time since we've had a chance to sit down and talk to a real, live woman,' a dark-haired, dark-bearded young man explained.

'Well, make the most of it,' Callie told them, 'because I fully intend to use you all as well!' There was a shocked silence, followed by a little uncomfortable shuffling, then Callie smiled, and explained. 'For scientific purposes only,' she said quickly. 'I'm going to take a little blood from each of you today, then, any time any of you come down for more supplies——'

'But Gokyo's a town,' red beard interrupted.

'Of six houses,' Callie explained. 'The merchants do take stock up there every fortnight, but you'll find Machherma a bustling metropolis compared to Gokyo.'

'I'll come down for supplies,' one of the group volunteered, sparking an argument that went on for ten minutes.

'As I was saying,' Callie broke in when the noise abated, 'if you come down we'll take another sample, and we will try to make at least one trip up there.'

She went on to explain what they were doing and why.

'If you give me some slides and phials, I'll do it for you!' A slight, dark-looking man who had been sitting quietly at the back of the group stood up as he spoke. 'I'm Liam Strong. I trained as a doctor first then switched to aeronautics.'

'That switch is about as logical as your presence in the mountains with this group of balloon-flying reprobates,' Callie said with a puzzled frown, but she smiled when they all laughed. 'No wonder you knew more about mountain sickness than I did—you've got your own doctor!'

'And one of our porters could bring the samples down,' Liam said. 'You want them fortnightly?'

'Fortnightly would be great!' Callie told him. 'Why don't you come through to the lab and I'll show you our set-up, and get some cards to fill in for those nice volunteers!'

After taking his friends' blood, Liam stayed when the others drifted back to their camp. He made up the counting-chamber slides from the five samples while Callie stained the films.

'You'll have to excuse me,' she said as the shadows warned her that night was approaching. 'I'd better check on my resident patient.'

Kanti was sitting with the young woman, who was alert and chattering brightly. Callie could only marvel at the resilience of these mountain people.

'She wants to know if the baby is all right,' Kanti asked, using a combination of fractured English and mime.

'We think so,' Callie told her, nodding to underline her words. She knelt beside the bed and asked the girl to roll over so she could inject the antibiotic into the upper quadrant of the gluteus maximus. Her patient might be slight, but the muscle was well-defined, and Callie remembered seeing other sherpanis walking up the steep trails with a baby on top of the sixty-pound loads they habitually carried.

Once satisfied that all was well with the woman, Callie spoke to Kanti about her dinner, suggesting potatoes or rice and some not too spicy vegetables for this, her first proper meal after the operation.

'I know, I fetch,' Kanti told her, and hurried away.

'And could you please tell Solti that Dr Liam will be staying to dinner?' Callie called after her.

'And what can I expect from that invitation?' Liam asked when she re-entered the laboratory.

'The best meal you've had since you left Kathmandu!' Callie promised him. 'We'll finish counting then go across to the kitchen.'

'Where's your offsider?' Liam asked as they settled themselves at the kitchen bench.

'I'm the offsider,' Callie explained. 'I'm still a student, while he's the real thing.'

She told them about the school party and about their concern that the girls' high temperatures could lead to organ damage if they over-exerted themselves in the thin mountain air.

'We passed that group,' Liam told her, 'but they were packing up after a meal, so we didn't stop to talk. The porters were so far ahead of them that we guessed they were trying to make Phortse in one day. Will you be all right up here on your own?'

Callie smiled, and thanked him, then explained the arrangements Nick had made to ensure her safety and peace of mind.

'He sounds like a good man,' Liam remarked, and she felt a thrill of pride, as if his praise was intended for her. 'I'll look forward to meeting him later in our stay.'

He is a good man, she repeated silently, her heart still hungering for him.

They returned to the office and completed the file cards before Liam left. Callie tucked them away into the box with a feeling of satisfaction, then walked out into the courtyard to see Liam on his way.

'I'll be in the village tonight, and could stay another night if necessary,' Liam told her. 'Save me all the trouble of helping to set up camp at Gokyo if I found an excuse to stay.'

He smiled, and for a moment she wondered if he was flirting with her, but a wave of tiredness swept over her before she could think about it, and she promised to contact him if she needed him, then waved him on his way.

With Kanti determined to sleep beside her friend from the village, and Ang installed on an upper bunk in the ward, she finally made her way to bed, crawling into the welcome folds of the sleeping-bag with the last skerrick of energy she could muster.

Had she slept for a minute or an hour when the wailing woke her? It certainly only felt like a minute, but as she shrugged on her jacket and thrust her feet into her flat shoes she didn't bother to check. Someone needed her now, whatever the time.

Ang lit the lamp as she entered the ward, and by its soft light she could see Kanti bent over their patient. The wailing had ceased, but, as Callie hurried across and bent over the girl, she cried out again.

'Baby come!' Kanti whispered to her.

'Get Solti!' Callie said to Ang as she hurried into the laboratory to get the brighter lamp and a stethoscope.

Even a fourth-year medical student who disliked obstetrics knew that Kanti's diagnosis was correct, Callie admitted as she waited for the next contraction to finish before bending to listen to the foetal heartbeats.

Solti was hovering behind her by the time she straightened.

'Could you go down to the camp in the village and find Dr Liam?' she asked him, then she remembered the yak herder and wondered if he would want to be present or if childbirth was still women's work in these parts. 'You decide what to do about telling the father,' she added to Solti, who nodded and padded softly away.

'I think this baby is coming far too soon,' she told Kanti, wondering how much English the other woman spoke. 'You watch her and I will see if I can set up a crib of some kind so it can breathe extra oxygen without risking a damagingly high concentration.'

Callie's stomach fluttered as she spoke. The contractions were lasting sixty seconds and were four minutes apart, which indicated, even before she checked the dilation of the cervix, that the woman was in the second stage of labour. Had intermittent earlier contractions been put down to wound pain, or had she simply borne it stoically, not wanting to make a fuss?

Back in the laboratory, she looked around, and decided that the metal trunk in which they kept the files would make the best crib. Opening the cupboard, she found clean towels with which to pad the chest, and some sterile gauze in which she could wrap the baby. She could fashion a tent above the crib with a sheet, she decided, then saw a roll of plastic wrap. Two layers of that would be even better! Now all she needed was a frame to hold it up, and some tape to prevent the vents she would need from tearing the makeshift tent apart.

'Problems?'

Liam's voice was the most welcome sound she had ever heard.

'Do you want her shifted to the operating table?' she asked when she had given Liam an outline of the situation.

'It would certainly make both the examination and the delivery easier,' Liam said, 'but I wonder if it will upset her. Do you know what position these people usually adopt to deliver their babies?'

Callie looked at him, surprised by the question, but even more surprised that this stranger could be so perceptive about another person's feelings. She crossed to Kanti, and asked her.

'Use table,' Kanti told her. 'More important that way!'

Callie blinked, then smiled—here was more perception at work!

Between them, she and Kanti lifted the young woman to the table. The appendix scar was still securely covered by the taped dressing.

As Liam crossed to examine the patient, Callie

followed him. 'You know it's only twenty-four hours since Nick took out her appendix,' she reminded him. 'What will the contractions be doing to the repairs he made to the peritoneum and muscle layers?'

'Not much good, but we can't be worried about that. All we can do is help her through the birth, do whatever we can for the baby, then wait and see what happens.'

Callie went. Back in the lab, she looked around again, then realised that she could prop the lid of the trunk in an upright position, and use it as a frame to hold the plastic high above the crib.

The next danger was fire. Last night, during the operation, Nick had pointed out the inherent dangers in using oxygen near the naked flames of the lamps. Oxygen contained by a face mask was one thing, but oxygen leaking out of a makeshift humidicrib had all the potential for disaster.

He had shown her where the battery lights and fluorescent torches were stored for use in emergencies, and she thought of him, longing for his calm competence, as she brought them out of the back of the cabinet and ranged them on the bench. A solar panel on the roof of the building kept the batteries charged for the bright light they used in the lab at night, and smaller solar cells recharged smaller batteries for use in the other emergency lights.

She carried the bright light through to hang above the operating table, and hung a smaller battery-operated light in its place in the lab. She then removed all the lanterns from the hut, taking them around to the kitchen to make certain no one inadvertently struck a match to light one. She stood another light beside the patient's bed, and explained her precautions to

Solti, asking him to impress on Ang and Kanti the need for extra care.

Liam checked the equipment he had chosen from the cabinets, and watched the woman's progress with anxious eyes. When Callie had finished her preparations, he drew her to one side.

'Everything seems OK,' he whispered. 'The contractions are down to two minutes and she's fully dilated. Do you know what to do if I faint?'

'Don't you dare!' Callie threatened. 'I've watched fifteen deliveries, and assisted at three, and it's not my favourite subject!'

A call from Kanti brought them back to the table in time to see the small dark head appear. Liam moved in, hands ready to assist the turn that would release the shoulders, but the tiny bundle slid out easily. Callie's heart was beating so fast that she could not move. She held her breath and watched as Liam used a small tube to suck mucous out of the infant's mouth.

A frail cry alerted her to her own duties, and she rushed back into the lab to find towels to wrap the little scrap of humanity now resting on its mother's breast.

The young mother was reluctant to part with her prize, but, when Callie shivered realistically, she nodded and raised herself enough to take one small towel and swaddle the baby in it. As she lifted the tiny infant to her breast she smiled, and Callie felt tears trickling down her cheeks.

'I look after her now!' Kanti announced, and she waved Liam away from the table.

He beckoned to Callie and walked into the laboratory. 'It's obviously women's work from here on in,' he told her. He looked at her little crib and smiled. 'I don't think we need it after all!' he told her. 'I know the baby is much smaller than we would consider normal in a neonate, but these are small people. From the look of it, I think it's close to full term.'

'Just as well,' Callie told him, dismantling her plastic cover but leaving the soft towels in the trunk, 'because I don't think that young woman is going to be parted from that infant for any reason! I'll leave this by her bed later, but I doubt if she'll use it. A baby's place is definitely next to the mother in this culture.'

Voices outside told them that the family had arrived and were being introduced to the new son of the house.

'Should we let them stay?' Callie asked. 'She's still weak from the operation yesterday, and who knows what internal complications giving birth might have caused?'

'Give them half an hour with her then send them off,' Liam suggested, stretching and yawning as he spoke.

Callie glanced at her watch. It was three o'clock!

'I'll sit up with her,' she said, 'but I'd be grateful if you would stay in case I need you. There are beds through there.' She gestured towards the bedroom door. 'I think Ang may be sleeping in one—he disappeared early in the drama—but take the other. The bathroom's on the right.'

'You did say bathroom?' Liam joked, and Callie nodded.

'I did indeed! Here, take this torch and make the most of it!'

Kanti and one of the other women had lifted the woman and child back to the bed. Callie looked at the pale, drawn face and decided the visitors should leave.

'She must rest,' she told them, miming sleep with her hands under her head, but she needed Kanti's firm help to herd them out of the door. With the visitors gone, she checked the woman's blood-pressure, knowing that would give her the first clue if the contractions had caused any internal haemorrhaging. She would check it and her pulse half-hourly, she decided, and hoped the patient would sleep through the disturbances.

By the time dawn broke she was feeling quietly confident that both mother and child were progressing normally. She stood in the doorway and watched the sun rise, then made her way quietly around to the kitchen. Solti had been up with them for most of the night, but, even if he was still sleeping, she had to have a cup of tea.

The bright fire told her he was up and the smell of his special porridge made her mouth water.

'Patient well?' he asked.

'I think so,' Callie told him as a great wave of tiredness washed over her.

'You will be glad when Dr Nick comes back,' Solti said soothingly, and Callie nodded. More than glad!

By the time she returned to the ward, Kanti was up tending mother and child. 'I will get her food and tea with butter. . .good for *ojas*,' Kanti announced.

'*Ojas*?' Callie asked.

'Goes in milk to baby,' Kanti explained. 'Keeps baby well and makes him happy.'

Is it like immunity? Callie wondered, but she did not pursue the subject, knowing she needed to read a lot more about Ayurveda before she could hope to understand even the simplest of its concepts. It had become evident during the night that Kanti had a great deal of experience in traditional medicine, and could probably have acted as midwife if Liam had not been present. She could leave the nursing care of the patients in her hands.

Callie checked the woman one more time, wrote up the chart, then cautiously pushed open the bedroom door. Ang was gone, but Liam was sleeping peacefully in her bed. She closed the door again and walked outside. The courtyard was just catching the first high rays of the sun, so she sank down on the bench and leant back against the stones, tilting her face up to its warmth. Sleep stole silently upon her.

'Long night!' The voice jarred through her dreams of babies, and she jerked herself awake to find Nick glowering down at her.

'Oh, Nick!' she whispered, and smiled a fuzzy welcome, unaware that the soft glow in her eyes and the radiance of her smile were imparting a special beauty to her tired face. She reached out a hand to pull him down beside her, but he turned away before she could touch him and strode around the corner of the hut, rage emanating from his body in almost visible waves.

He's not carrying his rucksack, her tired mind thought, and she knew this should worry her, but she couldn't think why. Anyway, now that he was back, she could relax. Even an angry Nick would look after things for her.

She closed her eyes and drifted back into oblivion.

She woke in a bed, and stretched luxuriously before prising open her sleep-sticky eyes and peering around at her surroundings. It was her bed in the hut. Then Liam must be gone! She smiled at the silliness of her reasoning.

Stiffness told her she'd slept too long sitting up outside the hut, but she clambered up and shuffled through to the bathroom, where a brisk cold-water wash brought her totally awake.

Nick had come back! Her heart hummed a joyous refrain, although her brain knew his presence should mean nothing to her. And he'd been angry! The joy faded as she recalled the stiff-legged stride and ramrod-straight back. What had she done to annoy him this time? Why do you bother? she asked her traitorous heart. Can't you accept that you irritate the man immensely, and your youthfull dreams were just that—dreams?

Wrapped in her towel, she pottered back into the bedroom to find clean clothes. The subject of her silent cogitations was sitting on the second bed. It was his own bed, she admitted to herself as she halted mid-step and looked at him, but she'd be much happier if he wasn't there at all. She wasn't quite ready to argue about whatever was bothering him at the moment.

And neither was she dressed for confrontation. She needed every bit of protection she could muster when Nick was around—and that began with several layers of clothes!

He looked at her and frowned, then stood up and turned to leave the room. Every movement was slow and strained, as if his limbs were locked with pain. Concern flooded through her, and with it came an anger of her own. She stepped forward, reaching out a hand to stop him.

'Sit down and rest!' she ordered. 'How did you get back so soon? Have you walked all night? Are you mad?'

'I think I must be,' he said slowly, looking down at the bare skin of her shoulder as if mesmerised by its pale sheen. 'I think I must be stark, staring mad!'

His hand lifted and he brushed it across the whiteness. Callie felt her flesh tingle at the touch, and she stepped hastily away.

'Well, go to bed!' she snapped. 'It might be a passing phase that sleep will cure!'

She crossed to her bed and bent to collect the clean clothes she had laid out on it. Behind her, she sensed him moving, but it had only been to close the door, before he walked back to stand in the middle of the room.

'I wanted to kill that chap.' The words were delivered in such a conversational tone that she thought she must have misheard them, but, when she spun around to face him, she saw his fists clenching and unclenching and knew she hadn't.

'What chap?' she whispered, frightened by this tense, pale stranger who had once been her friend.

'The one in your bed!' he rasped, and sank back down on to his bed, clutching his head in his hands and rocking backwards and forwards as if trying to obliterate the memory with motion.

'Liam?' she gasped. 'You wanted to kill Liam? The poor man had been up all night doing your job while you trooped off down the trail with the lovely Amanda, and you wanted to kill him? Is it too much to ask why?' Callie's voice was high, and she hoped she didn't sound as hysterical as she felt.

'I went down the trail because I had to,' he roared, lifting himself back to his feet and looming over her, 'and then turned around the moment we met up with someone halfway competent who could keep an eye on the girls, and headed back up here because I was worried about you!'

'And since when have you worried about me?' Callie demanded. 'Where were you when I had to fight the yeti? Out with your precious Amanda, that's where!' She tilted her chin to meet his eyes, and her own flashed the fire of her fury.

'It wasn't a yeti, and she's not my Amanda, and I've already apologised for that,' he fumed. 'We're not talking about my behaviour now, my girl, we're talking about yours. And I've always worried about you, right from the day you moved in next door. You had no more sense than a kitten—and that hasn't changed much!'

'I was ten months old!' she yelled back at him, infuriated by an argument she could not understand. 'And I've got more sense than you!'

'Well, that's not saying anything,' he announced, turning away from her to pace the small room. 'No one with any sense at all would have risked his stupid neck walking up that blasted trail in the darkness. And what do I find on my arrival? Only a new protector tucked up in your bed!'

The full implication of his suspicions hit Callie like an avalanche, forcing the air from her lungs, but she couldn't let him get away with this. 'It's none of your business who's in my bed!' she shrieked in outrage. 'None—do you understand?'

She saw him move towards her, his eyes glittering with a strange light, and she shrank back towards the bed, her clean clothes clutched in one hand in front of her, while the other hand held the towel firmly in place.

'Oh, no?' he whispered, and his hands reached out and gripped her shoulders, drawing her inexorably towards him. 'Isn't it?' he groaned, and his head came down so slowly that she was mesmerised into immobility. When his lips brushed across hers and the fiery heat licked through her blood she could only tremble, clutching at the flimsy protection of the towel and willing her body not to respond.

Responding to Nick would cause more trouble than she could handle. That was one lesson of the past she remembered vividly and it held her stiff and unrelenting in his grasp!

But the kiss went on so long that she thought she might have to weaken, to open her lips to his questing tongue, to taste him and let him taste her, to put her arms around him and draw him close, and let her knees give way to their weakness, and her body fold itself into his.

Then, at last, his hands released their cruel grip, and she felt the coldness of her response cool the heated skin that brushed against hers. He raised his head and looked down into her eyes with such anger and disbelief that she wanted to smile. Then he turned away.

'If you've been walking all night, you should have a sleep,' she suggested, her voice shaking from the tension of their silent confrontation, and the aftermath of the iron control she had been forced to exert. 'You won't be much use to any patients as you are.'

She watched as he crossed to the bed and dropped down on to it, and something in the slump of his shoulders made her want to go to him, and comfort him.

But that would be tantamount to admitting defeat. And she'd just won, hadn't she?

CHAPTER TEN

NICK reappeared for lunch, and, as she slid along the bench to make room for him at the table, Callie eyed him warily.

'It was a good idea of yours to take blood from the English group going up to Gokyo. With that doctor's help we can collect more samples while we're still here and I can get the chap in Khunde to do a final blood test on them when they leave.'

'It was Solti's idea,' Callie told him stiffly. The switch back into formal working mode should have been welcome, but it worried her, particularly as her skin was reacting uneasily to his presence, and her body was still regretting that she had not responded to his kiss.

'The baby's small but he seems fine,' he continued in a bland, professional voice.

'If you're making polite conversation for my sake, Nick, then don't bother. I'd just as soon eat in silence.' The words were blurted out as tension twisted into knots beneath Callie's skin. 'In fact, I'd prefer it!' She bent her head over her plate, but the appetising meal no longer appealed to her, and all she wanted to do was get away from him.

'I'm sorry if I upset you earlier.'

The gruff words brought her head up with a jerk, but he was studying his lunch as if it might hold all the answers to the mystery of the universe.

'Well, if that's a genuine apology, at least you could look at me!' The words were bitter, forced out by the turmoil within her, but when he did lift his head and look at her, she was sorry she'd spoken.

He was a stranger! A tired, defeated stranger!

Her Nick was never defeated. Maybe set back occasionally, but finally invincible. Her Nick was a man of action, a man who made things happen. He was a man who yearned for new experiences, who wanted to see and do all that this wonderful world had to offer. Her Nick carried his enthusiasm for life ahead of him like a bright golden banner. And he might get tired—but he'd never be defeated.

She pushed her plate away and left the table.

Back in the ward the new mother, who had finally been introduced as Shusi, was holding the infant to her breast. The image of the girl-woman with the baby in her arms burnt into Callie's mind and she longed for all the things her unrequited—unwanted—love for Nick had denied her. Surely she could put all that behind her now? When she returned home she would start building new relationships, go out with her fellow students—get a life, as the teenagers would say.

Then Nick walked into the ward and her heartbeats began their silly syncopation, and she wondered if she would ever 'get a life'.

'Every hour that passes lessens the chance of internal bleeding,' he said briskly. 'You can extend Shusi's obs to two-hourly.'

He continued on into the laboratory, leaving Callie staring at his back. Dutifully she took Shusi's blood-pressure, temperature and pulse and recorded all the figures on the chart they kept on the top bunk. Then Shusi lifted the baby and offered him towards Callie. She reached out and took the tiny bundle, drawing him close into her cradling arms and looking down into the tiny perfection of his face.

'He's so beautiful!' she murmured, and both Kanti and his mother smiled at the silly tears that glittered on her eyelashes.

'If you're finished there, you might add those new blood donors to Bill's chart.'

Her head jerked sideways when she heard Nick's voice, and her eyes met his. The defeat was gone, and something different blazed in the brown depths. At first she thought it was more anger, but the voice that added, 'When you're ready, Callie. There's no hurry,' was soft, and deep, and full of an unfamiliar undertone that an idiot might have taken to be love!

Callie handed the baby back to his mother, and was moving reluctantly towards the lab when the sound of voices made her turn towards the outer door.

'Patients arriving for afternoon surgery,' she called to Nick, then she walked out into the courtyard to greet the new arrivals.

'Three bad, bad stomachs for you,' the sherpa guide informed her, pointing towards a middle-aged man and two younger women. All were European, and, when they greeted her with unbridled enthusiasm, she realised they were American.

'"Bad, bad" is putting it mildly,' one of the women said. 'We've tried everything our tour guide carries in his medical kit, but nothing is working.'

Callie settled the three patients down on the bench, and looked towards the door. But, as Nick emerged, a group of villagers arrived, and Callie knew he was better equipped to deal with them.

'What have you been eating and drinking?' she asked them, knowing water was the main culprit.

'Only purified water,' the man assured her. 'We've all got nifty little water purifiers and carry them with us all the time.'

'That's not quite right, Herbert,' one of the women argued. 'Some of the group still use ordinary water bottles and those iodine tablets.'

Callie raised her eyes to heaven and muttered a silent thank-you for the clue. 'You've probably picked up a water-borne bacterium,' she told them. 'There are any number of the little blighters, and, while water purifiers filter the larger bacteria from the water, they can miss both parasites and smaller bacteria, especially if the filter material is getting old, or is cracked or damaged in any way.'

'Well, I never did!' the second woman exclaimed, then Callie saw her face pale and knew she was suffering a severe cramp.

'I'll get some cards, take your pulse and blood-pressure, then we'll go through what you've taken already,' Callie suggested. 'That should help eliminate some of the nasties.'

She hurried away, leaving the three arguing over which pills they'd already tried. By the time she returned, Herbert had obviously been elected spokesman.

'When we first got sick,' he told her, 'the guide suggested we go straight on to antibiotics. He had some in his medicine chest, but Dolly and I had some Bactrim that our doctor at home had given us, so we took that.'

'Strike one for the bacteria,' Callie murmured under her breath.

'Then he thought it might be amoebic dysentery!' he said in a tone of great importance.

Strike two, Callie thought. No one ever gets simple diarrhoea any more, it's always amoebic dysentery!

'So we took. . .'

'Fasigyn,' offered the woman who wasn't Dolly.

'Well, that should have got rid of Giardia or amoebic dysentery,' Callie assured them. 'And you're all still suffering.' Three unhappy nods greeted this remark, and Callie had to smile at them. 'It's miserable, isn't it?' she sympathised. 'And I think maybe the cure has been worse than the disease. Most cases of bacterial diarrhoeas run their course in a week or so, but if your intestines are already upset, and are then hit by an assortment of drugs, they don't quite know how to react.'

'Are you saying we have to keep suffering?' Dolly demanded, and Callie shook her head.

'No, but you've probably suffered longer than you need have. Unfortunately, Bactrim, which is used so frequently as a broad-spectrum antibiotic in Western civilisations, is no longer so effective in Nepal. Tests have shown that up to fifty per cent of the bacteria here are now resistant to it. The drug of choice is now Norfloxacin. I'll give you it as Noroxin, large white tablets which you take twelve-hourly.'

As she walked through the ward, Nick joined her, and she explained the symptoms, previous treatment and her tentative diagnosis and solution.

'Sounds spot-on,' he told her, pausing to let her walk into the lab in front of him. 'You did do your homework well before you came!'

The note of pride in his voice brought a flush to her cheeks, and she buried her head in the drug cabinet to hide her confusion.

'There should be some Cantil in there as well,' he

said, standing so close behind her that the breath of his words lifted her hair. 'It's an anti-spasmodic and will help ease the pain of their cramps.'

If she turned around now she would be as close as she had been earlier. If she turned around now and lifted her head, would he kiss her again? The thought hammered in her head while her fingers fumbled for the drugs she wanted. Why hadn't she responded earlier? Why had she thrown away the last chance she would probably ever have to show Nick how she still felt about him?

'I'll find them, Callie,' he said softly, and his hands settled on her shoulders and moved her gently out of the way.

The new, considerate Nick remained, more removed from her than he had ever been—even when they were fighting all the time. His unfailing courtesy and consideration were a source of wonder for a few days, but it could not last, she told herself.

Or could it? Within a week, this passive, quiet, imperturbable stranger was starting to drive her mad, and she longed to provoke him, to test his equanimity and bring back the complex, emotional man who lurked beneath this false veneer.

She found herself growing testy over minor inconveniences, responding sharply to his suggestions, and arguing with his decisions. And all the time the longing within her body grew stronger and stronger, until she stormed around the too-small hut with a feverish ache burning through her.

At night, she lay sleepless in the hard bed and listened to him breathe, wondering what they would be doing if she had responded to that kiss. She imagined herself in the narrow bed beside him, her head rising and falling on his chest, her body, heavy with love, held to his by the film of sweat sheened across their skin by their lovemaking. In the darkness, her cheeks would flush, and she would wrap her arms around her shoulders and shudder away the images that tormented her.

'Hello, the house!'

They were working in the laboratory after dinner, making up new slides from their fortnightly blood collection, when Liam's voice broke the silence.

'Come through!' Nick called, his attention focused on the pipette he held in his right hand.

'Good timing, I see!' Liam said. 'I've five more samples for you.'

'I hope you're going to help,' Callie said, an added warmth tingeing her welcoming smile. It would be a relief to have another person breaking the constraints Nick's attitude had drawn around them—and good to have a normal conversation!

'I'm intending to do more than that,' he announced. 'I'm intending to stay here and give you two a break for a few days. Those chaps up there can manage without me, and the thought of a bed and a bathroom was too tempting to resist.' He paused, and watched Nick examine the slide for bubbles, then fix it in place on the microscope. 'You did say you wanted to go up to Gokyo before you left, and, if the action I witnessed in twenty-four hours here was any indication, you could both do with a break.'

'Nick can go; he works far harder than I do, and he's been here a month longer——' Callie began, but Nick was talking over her and the words were lost.

'Callie needs a break,' he was saying. 'Why don't

you take her back up there to stay with the fellows for a few days?'

'Are you kidding?' Liam exclaimed. 'Those fellows have been on the trail for weeks. I'd have to throw them in the lake twice a day to keep her safe! You'll have to go as her protector.' He paused, and then he added quietly, 'You've come this far; you owe it to yourselves to go. It's quite spectacularly beautiful, and the view of Everest is something you could never imagine.'

Callie heard the wonder in his words and felt it stir her oneness with the mountains. Had she been so wrapped in her own confusion that she had begun to take her surroundings for granted? She looked from Liam to Nick, and knew that the dawning excitement within her was probably reflected on her face.

'You want to go, brat?' Nick asked softly, and the old nickname warmed some cold and lonely places in her heart.

Too full of hope for words, she nodded, and then heard Liam chuckle.

'I'll help Nick with these slides; you go and tell your cook to pack some food. I can stay three nights, which gives you two nights away. Get moving!' he added, shooing her with his hands when she hesitated.

She nodded, but doubt kept her feet glued to the floor. Walking up to Gokyo with her old friend Nick would have been a marvellous, exciting, dream-fulfilling experience, but, she realised sadly, sharing it with this stranger might be more than she could bear.

'It will be all right, Callie,' he said quietly, as if he had read her doubts and knew she needed reassurance. 'Tell Solti, then pack whatever you'll need. We'll divide the food between us, and I'll carry a tent.'

'Go on, get moving!' Liam repeated, and Callie smiled at him, then hurried out of the room. He would be disappointed if he thought his kind offer was not being enthusiastically received.

They left immediately after sunrise, intending to be well on the way before the day became too hot for comfortable walking. The morning air was cold and crisp, filling Callie with such a sense of well-being that she wanted to sing and dance along the trail.

'Take care!' Nick warned when an unwary movement sent small stones skittering down into the valley below them, but nothing could dim the joyous excitement that frolicked in her soul. All around her the mountains loomed, the rising sun silvering their slopes and turning their crevasses and gullies to a rich purple. Beyond the worn trail, brightly coloured moss and clumps of stones made miniature gardens that surpassed the beauty of anything a landscape gardener could achieve, while above them the sky turned a surreal blue, and the sun grew warmer on her shoulders.

'Need a rest?' Nick asked over his shoulder, his feet barely breaking stride in front of her.

'Today?' Callie replied. 'Not on your life! I could go on and on forever!'

'You always feel that way,' he reminded her. 'Then you overtire yourself and are exhausted next day!'

She smiled at the admonition in his voice. Was the real Nick finally emerging from the false shell he'd worn for the past ten days?

'It's a long time since we walked together,' she argued, speaking loudly to make sure he heard her. 'I might have changed.'

'And the mountains might move!' he teased, and

her heart skipped a beat because she knew for certain the cool, considerate stranger was gone, and the real Nick Grant was back.

They hiked on in silence, pausing now and then to look back along the trail, or look up towards the encroaching peaks.

'Second breakfast!' he announced when the path levelled out and a patch of bright green grass would provide a place for them to rest. 'Knowing Solti, it will be cold omelettes rolled up and chapattis.'

'With honey, of course!' Callie added, remembering how he always liked to finish a meal with something sweet.

'Honey gives you energy,' he informed her pedantically, then he grinned, and, for Callie, the world stopped turning.

He opened his pack and pulled out a Thermos and cups, then a battered billycan. Inside this, Solti had packed their first meal, already cooked so they did not need to light the small stove.

'You pour the tea, woman,' he ordered, 'while I set the table.' Two tin plates appeared, then a tea-towel, which he spread with great precision on the grass.

They ate in a companionable silence, while the sun warmed the air, and the mountains filled their eyes with beauty too spectacular to be absorbed by a single sense.

When Callie had finished she leant back on her elbows, and lifted her face to the sun, closing her eyes and enjoying the peace and contentment that even temporary freedom from all responsibility offered.

'I think perhaps I've always loved you,' Nick said, in such a conversational tone that she did not take in the words at first. But when they had been absorbed, she knew they weren't what she wanted, but they would have to do.

'I love you too, Nick!' she said drowsily, repeating a litany of their childhood.

'Not like that,' he said—again in the same clear, quiet, contemplative tone.

The air burst from Callie's lungs, and for a moment she wondered if she would ever be able to breathe again; then all the repressed emotions of the last ten days began to seethe and simmer in her mind, turning the confusion to a bubbling mass of anger.

'Not like what?' she demanded, sitting up straight and frowning down at him as he lay on his back on the grass. 'Not like what "that"?'

He looked up into her furious face but didn't smile. He studied her in silence for a moment, then he lifted his hand and traced the outline of her mouth with one long finger.

'Not like I loved you as a child,' he said, his face as blank as she had ever seen it. It was as if the words were coming from a pre-recorded tape whirring somewhere inside his chest, the voice deep and faraway. 'Oh, I still love the child, Callie, but I love the woman she became in a very different way. I suppose, subconsciously, I've known for a while, but haven't been game to admit it, even to myself.'

'Oh, and when did this miracle occur?' Callie asked sarcastically, her eyes snapping her disbelief. 'I seem to remember being told to grow up, when I mentioned we might fall in love with each other. And another time, when you told me you weren't the slightest bit interested in my new woman's body. Surely a man in love would feel some lust towards the loved one?'

His eyelids fluttered down as if to close out her

words, but she was only warming up.

'And what about Jocelyn and Caroline and Jane? And even Amanda? Does a man in love flaunt all his conquests in front of the supposed loved one? Is this how relationships work? You've let the altitude get to you, Nick Grant. . .' Her breath seized in her throat and the words became tangled in a soft but solid lump that had suddenly made swallowing difficult. 'And now you've spoilt my lovely day!'

She tried to blink away the tears which accompanied that final, despairing wail, but they wouldn't be contained, so she let them slip while she rummaged in her knapsack for a handkerchief.

Even through the tears she saw him grow tense, as if he was holding himself on a tight rein.

'You were barely sixteen, Callie, when you decided you were in love with me. You'd never been out with a boy. I knew what you were feeling was an adolescent crush. And I suspected that what I felt was probably lust!' The words grated harshly out of his throat, as if the memory hurt. 'What sort of a man would I have been to take advantage of your innocence—and of the trust you had in me?'

He'd always had these warped chivalrous ideals, she thought, blowing her nose angrily on the crumpled handkerchief.

'I'd been out with plenty of boys by the time we went to the carnival ball together!' she reminded him bitterly.

His angry laughter startled her so much that she wiped away the tears and peered at him. He didn't look particularly cheerful. 'And sat in the car and talked to them,' he growled, stunning her to a momentary silence.

'How did you know that?' she demanded, anger simmering again.

'I waited for the first of them to come back from walking you to the door,' he told her, his voice still rough with memories. 'I grabbed hold of him and gave him a lecture on how to treat young women, and was ready to strangle him before he finally gasped out the truth.'

'You don't know that I only talked to all of them!' she retorted, although deep inside her something was irrationally pleased with his confession. 'I hardly saw you after that—and you never came home alone!'

'I was pretty sure there was no one special in your life when your mother asked me to take you to the ball.'

And now the words were out they reared up between them as solid and immovable as the mountains that surrounded them. Silence so absolute that it couldn't be comprehended pressed against Callie's ears, and she felt the mountains waiting, as she waited.

'You were so beautiful!' he said at last, his voice barely a whisper stirring the air. 'So beautiful that it frightened me! You weren't my little Callie any more. Weren't even the tomboy who'd grown into an enticing siren flashing your golden cloud of hair, your slim tanned legs, and lithe body around the back yard to torment me.'

She heard him suck air into his lungs, but she couldn't speak, as half a shadow of hope began to shimmer in her heart.

'You were a woman, so alive and full of pride and joy and laughter that you took my breath away. You were suddenly way beyond my reach, and I, who'd always been the leader—the one who gave the orders and took control—lost every bit of confidence I'd ever had. I fell apart, Callie, torn to pieces by this beautiful butterfly who'd emerged from the chrysalis of the girl next door.'

'You still said no!' she reminded him in a hard voice, not willing to listen to the hope now beating a refrain against her ribs. She'd been hurt before; she couldn't let it happen again. That got to him, she realised as he sat up straight and finally looked at her, his eyes flashing with the golden fire she knew so well.

'What was I supposed to do? Whizz you off to bed in some motel room? I could barely touch you for wanting you so much, barely bear to feel you touch me in case I lost control and frightened you with all the passion I'd held bottled up too long. Damn it, Callie, you were still too young, too trusting, too inexperienced! You were about to finish high school. . . you'd never been away from home. . .the whole world was due to open up for you in the next year when you went to university.'

He dropped his head on to his knees and groaned, then continued, the words muffled against his legs. 'How could I take what you so innocently offered? How could I start an affair with you? I was twenty-three—a man! I had two months to go in my course and was booked to leave for Nepal to climb for three months after that. I knew when I returned I had an appointment in a hospital two thousand miles away from Brisbane. Would you have given up your chance to study and come with me? It didn't matter, because I knew I couldn't ask. I knew the timing was all wrong again, and probably always would be.'

Callie felt the words penetrate her skin, bringing her more uncertainty than the joy she would have expected.

'Well, you certainly hid your feelings well,' she said stiffly, remembering the agonies of jealousy she'd suffered when his tall, long-legged beauties had followed him around the house, starting conversations she couldn't follow and talking of things so far beyond her experience that she had wondered if she would ever understand. 'Especially once Jane appeared on the scene.'

He straightened up at that, and looked around, as if taking in their spectacular surroundings for the first time. Glancing at his face, she saw the deep frown on his brow, and the tight set of his lips.

'I am not proud of what happened with Jane,' he told her, each word weighed and measured before being offered to the air. 'Especially when I persuaded us both that I loved her.'

Callie felt a tide of sadness sweep over her, sadness for herself, for Jane—for Nick.

'Once we were physically involved, I tried to make it work,' he said, 'but whenever things were going smoothly and we began to talk of marriage, an image of you in that damned ballgown would come slamming into my mind, and I'd hear your silvery laughter, and that little gurgle in your voice when you were teasing me. Jane deserved far better, but it took a long time for me to accept that, and even longer for me to persuade her it was true.'

Now the words were whirling through Callie's mind, dancing with the hope that had filtered up from her heart. But inconsistencies kept jangling the keys of the music.

'I was grown up before you went off to America,' she pointed out with a gruff belligerence, 'without even saying goodbye! And if you'd broken off with Jane, what excuse do you have for not coming to see me then and telling me how you felt?'

She saw the words hit home in the darkening of his eyes, but when he half-smiled at her, a shamefaced, lop-sided kind of grin, she felt the tension slide out of her body and knew it would all be all right.

'I was afraid, Callie!' he admitted. 'Afraid of making a fool of myself! Afraid you might have grown up too much, might have grown up and fallen in love with someone your own age.' The grin became a grimace, and his voice dropped several octaves. 'Believe me, brat, if it was murder loving you, not knowing how you felt, I was certain loving you but knowing you loved someone else would be a million times worse.'

He turned away from her then, and stretched back out on the grass, covering his face with one arm.

'I was wrong, of course,' he said, in a strained, tight voice. 'It's a zillion times worse!'

Callie's head spun. Could he possibly be saying what she thought he was saying? Hope made her want to reach out and touch him, but her sense of self-preservation, well developed where Nick was concerned, held her back. 'You weren't very pleased to see someone you were supposed to love when I arrived at the aid post. You yelled at me!'

A deep groan answered this accusation, but she stayed silent, knowing he would have to answer her eventually.

'You were half-dead with the most badly infected feet I'd ever seen, and I was terrified I might not be able to save your toes.'

Another groan, and a longer silence.

'And, sick as you were, I still found you so desirable that it was all I could do to keep my hands to myself.

I wanted you, Callie, as I've never wanted anyone, but was it love or lust? Was it some hangover from our youth? I knew you deserved better than that. I thought about wooing you, began to hope. . . Then you told me about Howard.'

Callie ran the words through her head, testing them for truth against an instinct she had not known existed.

'But if that's how you felt about me, why did you keep going off with Amanda?' she demanded, and heard the sigh that preceded his reply.

'Self-protection!' he muttered. 'How do you think I felt sharing a room, working so closely with you, knowing, all the time, that you loved another man? Every time you mentioned your precious Howard it was like a knife stabbing into my heart. Amanda was an excuse to escape for a short time, to pretend I didn't care.'

'You told her I'd been chasing you for years, and that I'd followed you over here.' The pain of his betrayal made the words gruff, but they must have struck home, for he shot back up into a sitting position and looked across at her.

'I said nothing of the kind,' he fumed. 'I told her we were old friends, next-door neighbours, and probably told her about you following me to school when you were young——' He smiled at the memory, and his face softened, and it was all Callie could do to stop her hand reaching out to touch him.

He leaned a little closer, and she saw the smile hadn't reached his eyes, which were sad, and strangely vulnerable.

'Well, brat,' he said softly. 'Now I've made a complete fool of myself, and poured out all that sob stuff, I suppose we'd better get on our way!'

She stared at him in horror, unable to comprehend

that he considered the matter closed.

He must have seen her reaction, for the rueful half-smile left his face, and he frowned across the valley at the mountains.

'You needn't worry that there'll be a repeat of that kiss, Callie.' The words were deep and held a haunted echo of pain. 'You didn't need words to tell me that my feelings weren't reciprocated.'

Now she did reach out, and her fingers brushed across his arm, as soft as the wind that lifted his hair and ruffled through her curls.

'Kiss me again, Nick,' she whispered, but he shifted angrily, and brushed away her touch.

'I don't want your pity, Callie!' he declared. 'Heaven knows, I upset you often enough in the past when you were young and fancied yourself in love with me. You should be pleased to see me suffering, not feel sorry for me.'

'I don't feel sorry for you, you stupid man!' she yelled. 'I love you! I've always loved you!' She paused and gulped in the crisp mountain air, knowing the importance of what she was about to say—the importance of getting it right. She began slowly.

'The only thing that changed was the quality of my love, Nick. It didn't seem to matter how often you told me you didn't love me that way, my feelings stayed the same, tucked away like wine in a cellar, maturing with each lonely, passing year.'

Now his eyes mirrored his disbelief. 'What about Howard, then?' he growled. 'How do you explain him?'

It was Callie's turn to feel embarrassed, and she felt the colour sweep into her cheeks. 'I made him up!' she told him, her eyes sparkling with defiance. 'There you were, rabbiting on about my following you, flinching every time I touched you. I knew we couldn't work like that for four weeks, so I invented Howard.'

Suspicion flickered in his face. 'You've got his photo, letters. . .I saw you take the folder out of your rucksack and push it under the mattress where I couldn't see it.'

Callie sighed, letting out air that seemed to have been trapped way down in her toes. She reached for her rucksack and pushed her hand deep down into it, feeling for the hard leather folder she carried wherever she went. 'This folder?' she asked, drawing it out but not daring to smile. Not yet!

He turned away as if the sight of it pained him, but she thrust it in front of him. 'Take it, Nick. Open it!' she said softly, and thrust it into his resisting hand. She held her breath while he ran his fingers over the surface, and wondered if he remembered giving it to her years ago. Then he opened it, and looked down at the two photos inside—looked down for so long that she thought she might cry with the tension.

'I've never seen that photo,' he muttered, pointing to the one of himself. His voice sounded as if it might break at any moment.

'It was taken the night of the carnival ball,' she murmured. 'If I couldn't have you, at least I had a photo to remind me of what I'd lost.'

And now he turned towards her, shaking his head as if still unable to believe the truth. 'You never lost me, Callie,' he said, and reached out to pull her into his arms. 'But when I kissed you in the hut I thought. . .'

His lips were achingly close, but still they didn't touch hers and she realised how badly her lack of response had hurt him.

'I had to make you think that,' she told him. 'I was sure you didn't love me, and I couldn't bear for you to know how I still felt about you.'

She shifted closer, snuggling up against him, and lifting her smiling face to his.

'Try me now!' she challenged and heard an answering groan, then felt the only lips she'd ever wanted settle on hers like a benediction.

'I think we'd better move on or the next group walking up or down this trail will find me making love to you in broad daylight.'

He muttered the words huskily into her ear about an hour later, and Callie chuckled.

'Is making love OK with you?' he added, in a tone so full of doubt that she held him tight and nodded against his chest. 'Before we're married?' he persisted, and she pushed herself away from him.

'Married?'

'Of course we'll get married. We've wasted enough time as it is. The only problem is I have to go back to the States. Would you mind finishing your course over there, or deferring it until we get back at the end of next year? You could study something else maybe, or work in the lab with me. . .' He sounded worried and uncertain again, and she lifted her head and kissed him softly on the lips, excited by this new role of comforter.

'We don't have to decide all the details right now,' she murmured, tangling her fingers in his hair to draw his head down to hers. 'We don't have to decide anything! Isn't this enough for the moment?'

She pressed another kiss against his lips, and this time her tongue teased at their outline, and she felt the thudding acceleration of his heartbeats.

'Enough!' he agreed, responding with a passion that left her shaking with desire.

TAKE A DEEP BREATH

BY

MARGARET O'NEILL

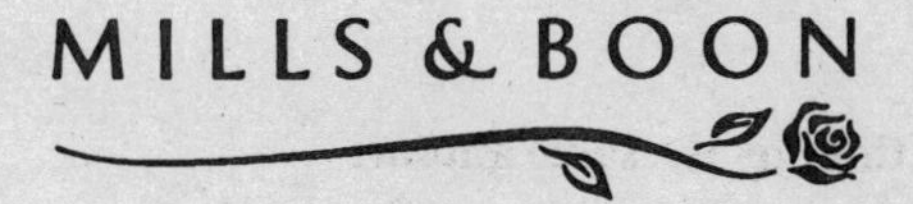

MILLS & BOON LIMITED
ETON HOUSE, 18–24 PARADISE ROAD
RICHMOND, SURREY, TW9 1SR

First published in Great Britain 1994
by Mills & Boon Limited

This edition 1994

ISBN 0 263 78478 9

Set in 10 on 12 pt Linotron Times
03-9403-52388

Typeset in Great Britain by Centracet, Cambridge
Made and printed in Great Britain

CHAPTER ONE

JULIA knew the moment she went on duty that it was going to be 'one of those days' in Accident and Emergency.

An ambulance, lights blazing, sirens wailing, passed her as she walked up the long drive from the sisters' residence, an enlarged, converted lodge at the foot of the drive. A motor accident victim, probably, losing a lot of blood, or someone injured in a fire, or a cardiac arrest, an emergency situation. Whatever it was, it would be dealt with efficiently by the night staff still on duty, Julia reminded herself, slowing down her automatically quickened pace. She had no need to rush; everything would be taken care of by the time that she got there. It was only half-past seven, and she wasn't on duty officially until eight o'clock. Not that one clock-watched in her job.

It was hard to learn the first lesson of administration, the art of delegation. After three months as managing sister in charge of A and E at Princes Park Hospital, Julia still had trouble coming to terms with the fact that she was there largely to direct and advise, and not to give hands-on nursing care to every patient who was admitted to the department. Somebody had to tell everyone else what to do and where to go, and that someone was her. There were, of course, enough occasions for her to get stuck in and apply her very practical hands to the nursing side of the job; she just had to keep reminding herself that that wasn't her only duty.

She loved the responsibility of running the busy accident and emergency department; even the juggling of staff to cover sickness and holidays was a challenge to which she readily responded. Keeping stock of equipment and the replenishing of every item used there was down to her, from syringes to bandages and waste bags, and disposable sheets to blood and plasma supplies; all came under her control.

So did training new nursing staff, students who were sent to do their stint in Casualty as part of their general training. Sometimes it worked out well and a student would take to the particuarly specialised work of the department like the proverbial duck to water, but sometimes it didn't work at all. Some nurses just weren't right for the cut and thrust of Casualty, which could see-saw in a short space of time from the high drama of resuscitating a dying patient to bandaging a sprained ankle.

Today two new students were due to start work in A and E. One was a third-year student, with a reputation for being quick and bright, but the owner of a rather caustic tongue, and at times too clever by half. The other was a first-year, with very little nursing experience at all, as she had so far worked only on geriatrics and women's medical wards. Reports from these wards suggested that she was a good little worker, tender-hearted, but rather slow.

Julia groaned as she entered the building by the rear entrance. An over-quick one and a slow one, and neither would be much use for several days, perhaps even weeks. The first thing she must do when she got in, was sort out whom each of the girls would work with. That was one of the headaches of the job, pairing off the right people. Work went so much more smoothly if one got the mix right.

By the time she reached her office she had made her decision. The third-year would work with Dan Beatty, the charge nurse, in his early forties, and virtually unflappable. He would not be affected by Nurse Black's sharp tongue, and he would keep her busy and out of mischief if she tried to be too clever. As for the first-year student, Celia Ponting, she would put her in the care of Niri Patel, the Indian staff nurse, who was quiet and understanding. She wouldn't try to rush the girl and make her lose confidence, something that could so easily happen in those first few bewildering hours in Casualty.

Julia was happy with her decision, and concentrated on taking the report from the night sister, her friend Sonia Jansen.

'You'll be delighted to hear,' said Sonia with a wry smile, 'that there was a message from Staff Nurse Stevenson's mother to say that she's sick. My guess is too many late nights and boyfriend trouble, but who am I to cast aspersions?'

'A hard-working nurse, like what our Stevenson should be,' replied Julia facetiously, pulling a face. 'It's no good; I shall have to see the powers-that-be about Stevenson. This going off sick has happened once too often. It's a pity she lives at home; she couldn't pull this stunt if she lived in.'

'Yep, that's for sure,' agreed Sonia. 'Now to get on to the nitty-gritty. At ten o'clock we admitted. . .' She read through the list of patients who had arrived during the night, not many by A and E standards, but making enough work to keep everyone on duty steadily at it for most of the night. Some had been admitted to wards following primary treatment in the unit; one had turned out to be ruptured appendix and had been whisked off to Theatre for an emergency op.

'And the emergency that's just come in?' asked Julia.

'I've got to write that up, but you may have to finish the report, unless things have been sorted before I go. Two men, head-on collision, just off the motorway. One a windscreen job, I'm afraid, old car, no laminated glass.'

'Oh, no,' groaned Julia. Everyone hated 'windscreen jobs' when victims were thrown at, or sometimes through, the front of a vehicle and sustained horrific facial and head injuries. 'He's still here, of course.'

'Yes, but due to go up to Theatre any moment. We've begun cleaning him up, and set up a drip, but Luke said not to do any more. There's a cardiac problem; it may have been the cause of the accident. He'll have to go under a general if he's up to it, for removal of debris and so on. That'll be up to them upstairs.'

At that moment there was a sharp knock at the door, and Luke Steel, the unit consultant, entered.

He looked tired in a hawkish, rather distinguished way, thought Julia, but that wasn't surprising: he'd been on duty till late the night before, and had been called out at five a.m. to look at the burst appendix that Sonia had reported. The emergency had caused the houseman on duty, Imelda Robbins, some anxiety, and she had sought advice from the much more experienced and well qualified consultant. This was the right procedure, as an abdominal emergency of this nature was a tricky one. The fact that Imelda had probably been glad to ask for Luke's help for non-professional reasons was neither here nor there. She had acted properly.

'Would one of you kindly and beautiful Florence Nightingales please supply a cup of tea or coffee to your poor old exhausted consultant?' pleaded Luke, his deep-set grey-green eyes gleaming, the skin crinkling at the corners. His grey-speckled black hair, thick and wiry, looked slightly ruffled, but then, since he had just come from dealing with the accident victims, this was not surprising. The protective plastic apron that he was wearing was smeared with blood, which made him look somewhat piratical, thought Julia with a secret smile; and, what with his rather forbidding pose and strongly marked eyebrows, he looked every inch a commanding, story-book pirate captain. A strong, authoritative man, capable of anything that life demanded. He lowered his large frame on to a chair, and gave a sigh of relief.

'I'll make it,' offered Sonia, disappearing through the door to the little kitchenette that opened off the office. 'I wouldn't mind a cup myself, before going to my supper.'

'What an upside-down life we do lead when we are on night duty,' said Luke. 'Supper at eight o'clock in the morning—what a nonsense it makes of normal living.' He gave Julia a smile and lifted one eyebrow expressively.

She realised quite suddenly how very handsome and sexy he was in a rugged and at the same time sophisticated way. How extraordinary that she hadn't noticed it before, in the months that they had worked together.

It was almost as if she were seeing him for the first time.

Before she could reply, Sonia reappeared with a tray bearing three mugs and a plateful of biscuits. 'Tea,' she said cheerfully. 'I thought it would be a change from the everlasting coffee.'

'Splendid,' said Luke, reaching out a hand for a biscuit. 'Exactly what the doctor ordered,' he added, biting into one with strong white teeth. 'That's better; a boost to my sugar levels.' He grinned at them. 'Now don't let me disturb you doing the report.'

'I was just going to fill in the last bit about our two accident cases,' said Sonia. 'And then I'm away.'

'The windscreen chappie has just gone up to Number One Theatre. I don't think he's going to make it; he's deteriorating fast. There's a policeman with him, by the way, and with the other man, for what it's worth.'

'What about him, the other one, Sidney Carter? Will he do?' asked Sonia, busily writing on the report card.

'Not very happy about him either,' said Luke looking sad. 'Definitely fractured humerus and radius and ulna, right arm, and a wrist fracture, left arm, plus left leg fractured femur, and maybe lower leg bones there too. Can't be sure of damage—they're such a bloody mess that it's difficult to tell. He's in shock, of course; intravenous fluids are being given, and there are superficial wounds caused by glass and metal. That's all I can tell you, I'm afraid. He's going up to Intensive Care; they'll have to sort him out.'

Sonia finished writing up the report card and clipped it into the folder.

'Right, I'm off. Will I see you tonight when I come on, Julia?'

'Yes, I'm doing a split. All being well, I'll be off for a couple of hours this afternoon.'

Sonia hooted derisively. 'You should be so lucky,' she said.

'Well, one can always hope.'

'Sweet dreams,' said Luke, smothering a yawn.

'You look like the one who needs a bed,' said Julia in a gentle voice. 'Can't you take a bit of time off? Imelda's on duty and I'm here with a strong team. We can give you a shout if necessary.'

Luke returned her smile. 'You temptress, you,' he said. 'There's nothing I'd like more, but there's always paperwork or phone calls to make when things quieten down a bit, and I've a lecture to give some of the nursing students later this morning. But I tell you what I would appreciate.'

'Name it.'

'Time to nip off and have a shower and shave.'

'Your wish is granted, and throw in a breakfast while you're about it.'

'What a brilliant idea.' He stood up, unfolding his long body from the chair, and leaned across the table and looked straight into her smoky blue eyes. 'You're an angel, Sister Julia Manning, such an asset to the department.'

Julia felt herself blushing, something she didn't do very readily. He'd never complimented her like this before, even in a half-teasing fashion. She put up a hand and tucked a tendril of chestnut hair into her smooth chignon, and straightened her cap. It was an unconscious gesture that she frequently made when thrown off balance.

'Oh, get away with you,' she said brightly. 'You're maudlin for want of sleep and food.'

'Glory be, and I thought that I was being romantic,' Luke said with a laugh. He was about to open the door when somebody tapped it from the other side, and, before Julia could open her mouth to invite whoever it was to enter, it was pushed open and Dr Robbins came in.

She looked angry, and stalked straight into the office without seeing Luke, who was partly hidden by the half-open door. She began speaking before she reached the desk.

'Sister Manning,' she said in a high, cross voice, 'if you could bear to drag yourself away from your tea and biscuits, you could perhaps organise your staff so that one could get some sense out of them.'

Julia caught Luke's eye. He raised an eyebrow as he stared at the back view of the pretty young doctor. He didn't seem surprised at her outburst, thought Julia, though Imelda was usually sweetly reasonable when he was around.

Imelda realised that someone was behind her, and turned swiftly. When she saw her boss standing there, she flushed with embarrassment, or perhaps it was annoyance at giving herself away.

'L-Luke, I'm sorry, I didn't see you there. I didn't realise that Julia was talking to you.' She turned, flustered, back to Julia, obviously furious that Luke had heard her being so belligerent and rude. 'Julia, I do apologise, I didn't really mean anything. That was a silly remark about you having tea. Heavens, you work hard enough; you're quite entitled to. . .' Her voice drifted off under Julia's quizzical stare. 'Sorry,' she mumbled, and began to back towards the door.

Julia felt quite sorry for her. 'It's all right,' she said. 'You're busy, and it is time that I surfaced, anyway. Now do tell me what's wrong.'

Luke said silkily, with a half-grin, though his eyes when he looked at Imelda were more coldly grey than green, 'I'll leave you two ladies to it, to sort out your differences amicably, I trust.' He nodded, and gave Imelda another hard look, which made her flinch, as he stalked out of the office.

It was clear that he was angry with his houseman for losing her temper with Julia, who ran the unit like clockwork and always had everything under control.

As Luke drove down to his cottage on the edge of the little market town of Princes Hollow, spreading southwards from the foot of the drive to Princes Park, and which was still frequently called 'the village', he wondered about the episode that he had just witnessed. He was aware that Imelda, though she appeared to be behaving out of character to him, was readily understood by Julia Manning. In other words, he mused thoughtfully, Julia's used to dealing with Imelda's tantrums. I wonder why the tantrums?

He had a good idea. He knew that his craggy good looks made him attractive to women, and that he was considered one of Princes' eligible bachelors. Up to now, at thirty-nine, he had been working so hard for his consultancy that he'd indulged in only the most fleeting of relationships, nothing heavy, nothing demanding on either side. But now. . .he wasn't sure how he felt. It really was time he settled down, thought in terms of a wife, home and family, but this meant falling in love, or being drawn with great certainty towards a woman.

He thought, as he let himself into the house, of the facetious remarks about being romantic that he'd made to the delicious Julia Manning earlier, when he'd paid her a compliment.

A picture of Julia's oval face sprang to mind: the finely arched brows over those most unusual smoky blue eyes, the small, but definitely aquiline nose, like that of a distinguished Roman matriarchal figure, and the wide, generous, full-lipped mouth, curved into a delightful smile. Not a beauty exactly—her features were too strong for that—but handsome, in a peculiarly feminine fashion. And, of course, concealed under that dark blue sister's uniform dress was a stunning figure, and long, shapely legs.

He pulled himself up with a jerk. What was he doing, fantasising over a woman with whom he had worked for three months and hardly noticed, except to appreciate her efficiency and sense of humour? Thinking back, he realised how often this had surfaced when things had got really trying and everyone was under pressure in A and E. It was Julia who, by word and deed, had pulled everyone together. When a splendid woman she was, and what a super nurse. She could handle anything.

Her went to shower and shave in thoughtful mood.

Dr Robbins' complaint about staff inefficiency had arisen because, as Julia suspected, she had picked on Celia Ponting, the first-year student, to fetch something for her. The young girl, having arrived only minutes before to report on duty, had been shattered by a request from a doctor to produce an instrument of which she knew nothing from a place that she didn't know existed.

She tried to explain, but had been ignored by the impatient houseman, who had blown her top in the middle of Casualty, to the mixed interest and embarrassment of those waiting for treatment. Celia had burst into tears, and rushed off to the duty room, and Imelda had hurried to report her to Julia.

This was the situation that greeted Julia when she left her office after Luke's departure. She soon sorted everything out, and sent an experienced nurse to assist a subdued Dr Robbins. Then she arranged for the rather arrogant third-year, Pat Black, to work with Dan Beatty, comforted the first year-student, and introduced her to the gentle Staff Nurse Patel. She then looked in on the various patients in cubicles to check on them and their treatment, before going along to Reception to find out how many patients were waiting to be seen.

It was relatively quiet. Only six people were waiting, and two of them she recognised as local tramps, who appeared every few weeks, wanting treatment for bronchitic infections or unhealing cuts and sores. It usually meant that they were looking for bed and board for a few nights, and, when possible, they were accommodated. Luke, Julia was sure, would take pity on the men and find beds for them, as would his registrar, John Peak, but John was off at the moment on compassionate leave, and Luke not yet returned. Imelda, thought Julia, would not be as kindly as her two male colleagues, and would probably send the tramps away after treating their obvious ailments. She was inclined to give short shrift to those patients she considered malingerers, unless her seniors were around, when she would turn on the charm.

A difficult lady to deal with, Dr Imelda Robbins.

Julia spoke to the receptionist, a constantly harassed-looking lady in her late thirties, Rita Winter.

'Rita, keep back our old friends the tramps for a bit, please. I'd like Dr Steel to see them when he returns. And here. . .' She slapped some coins down on the counter. 'Get one of the porters to get them tea or coffee while they're waiting.'

'Will do, Sister,' said Rita with a smile. 'You are an old softie, aren't you?'

Julia grinned with embarrassment, and returned to her office to tackle the equipment request slip.

She was halfway through the list when Dan Beatty knocked at the partly open door and entered.

'Sister, I think you had better come,' he said in his calm voice. 'We've a wee bit of a problem here.'

The 'wee bit of a problem' turned out to be a father protesting against his daughter being given blood, on religious grounds. The child was ten years old, and had been involved in a road accident. The mother of the child had not yet arrived. One or the other of the parents' signatures needed to be on the form before the blood could be given. In the face of the father's objection, this was going to be difficult to obtain.

Luke had returned and was with the child.

'Do something,' he said between gritted teeth, 'to make this man understand that his child might die if she's not given blood. I've got my hands full and can't waste time arguing with him.'

'What's the child's name?'

'Amanda Forrester.'

Gently Julia drew the distraught but unyielding man from the child's side, compassionately aware of his awful dilemma, having experienced a similar situation before.

'Mr Forrester,' she said, 'neither you nor your church want to see your child die, do you?'

'Of course not,' the man almost shouted. 'God won't let her die; he'll save her without all this man-made interfering.'

'Then why did you bring her here?'

'Because they made me, the ambulance people.'

'And what would you have done, Mr Forrester, if the ambulance people hadn't been at the accident—taken her home?'

'No, of course not. She needs hospital treatment, but not a transfusion. My beliefs won't allow it.'

'Surely your beliefs won't allow a little girl to die?'

'Of course not.' The father looked terribly distressed. 'It's just the blood,' he said.

Julia said gently. 'Look, Mr Forrester, if it was you, refusing for yourself, fair enough. We would try to persuade you otherwise, because that's our job, but at the end of the day we couldn't force you to have a transfusion—but a child's different. There are laws to protect children, and we could undoubtedly get permission to give the transfusion, except that the delay involved could kill Amanda. She's got internal injuries that are haemorrhaging. We must replace the blood or she'll die.'

'No,' came out a strangled cry from the ashen-faced man. 'No, don't let her die.'

'Then please give your consent to her having a

transfusion,' said Julia softly. 'Let us help save your daughter's life.'

Mandy's father seemed to shrink in front of her as a variety of expressions swept across his face. He put his hands up and covered his eyes. 'I can't,' he whispered.

'Please,' said Julia, touching his arm. 'God will understand.'

Mr Forrester raised a stricken face. 'Will He?'

Julia nodded, holding her breath. 'Of course. He understands everything.'

The man said, on a rasping sob, 'All right, give it to her. Don't let her die.'

'Then please sign this,' said Julia, proffering the consent form, still holding her breath.

With shaking fingers, Mr Forrester signed the form and Julia breathed a silent sigh of relief.

She turned to Luke instantly. 'Now, Dr Steel, you may go ahead and give the blood,' she said quietly.

'Will do, Sister, thank you.' He nodded at Julia, and then turned to one of the team. 'Have we cross-matched, Nurse?'

'Yes, Doctor.'

'Right. Let's get on with it, then.'

'Would you like to come with me and have a cup of tea, Mr Forrester?' Julia suggested.

All the fight seemed to have gone out of the man. He gave one last despairing look at his injured daughter, and followed Julia to the duty office.

A nurse brought them tea, and Julia talked quietly, trying to reassure Amanda's father. At last Mrs Forrester arrived, having been fetched from work by the police, and, after explaining to her what was being done at the present time, Julia left the husband and wife together to comfort each other.

By the time Julia went off duty for the afternoon it was nearly three o'clock. She was due back on at five o'clock. She left the unit in Dan's capable hands. Amanda had been transferred to Intensive Care, and the tramps had been admitted by Luke to Men's Medical for rest and treatment. Such was the pressure on beds that it was unlikely that they would be able to stay for more than a couple of days, but even forty-eight hours of rest, warmth and good food would help.

She collected her navy blue trench mac from the cloakroom, slung it round her shoulders, and made to leave by the back exit, when she realised that it was blowing a typical autumn gale. She'd been so busy that she hadn't noticed the rain.

For a moment she wished that she had driven and not walked up to the hospital that morning, though she enjoyed the exercise and the fresh air. She was going to get drenched on the nearly mile-long walk down to the lodge, and she didn't even have an umbrella. Not that it would have stayed up in this wind, she consoled herself.

She stood in the doorway of the staff entrance, looking out at the yellowing leaves being torn from the branches of the oaks that surrounded the staff car park, and decided to make a run for it. With luck she might get a lift.

For once no one seemed to be going down the drive, not even an ambulance leaving the main building.

She had walked about two hundred yards when she heard a car coming from behind, and turned thankfully to wave it down. To her surprise, it was Luke in his red Volvo estate.

He pulled up beside her and leaned across to open the passenger door.

'Jump in, you silly girl,' he said sharply.

Julia stared at him, blinking the rain out of her eyes.

'I'm not,' she said frostily, 'a "silly girl".'

Luke grinned wickedly.

'Really?' he said smoothly. 'Don't you think it just a little foolish that you should have chosen to walk in this weather when you could have asked for a lift? Not the action of our competent manager. Now do, please, get in; you're drenched.'

'I'll spoil the upholstery.'

'Damn the upholstery. What the hell does that matter?' he said explosively. 'Just get in.'

Julia sank thankfully into the soft leather seat, closed the door on the howling wind and rain, and fastened her seatbelt.

'Thank you,' she said. 'I really am most grateful.'

CHAPTER TWO

EVEN moving at the ten-mile-an-hour speed limit imposed on the drive, they reached the lodge within a few minutes.

Julia unbuckled her belt and made to get out, saying her thanks as she did so, when Luke laid a restraining hand on her arm.

'Have you got anything arranged for Saturday night?' he asked.

'No, nothing special; why?'

'I'm going to a house-warming Alistair Gibson is giving. He's recently moved into a rather grand house on the edge of Princes New Town. Come with me; I've been invited to bring a guest.'

Julia was surprised by the invitation. In the three months that she had worked amicably with Luke Steel, he had never shown any personal interest in her. Not that that had bothered her, for she had not thought of him as anything but a good colleague and a super doctor.

Now his invitation, and his hand on her arm, caused her a small thrill of pleasure, which she strove to conceal. No point in letting this rather arrogant, handsome man know that he had succeeded in exciting her.

She said in a calm voice, 'I didn't think that the New Town boasted any grand houses. I thought it was all high-rise and shopping precincts.'

'Well, like many a new town it developed from an

old village, and Alistair's home was the one-time manor house of Princes North.' His deep-set grey-green eyes met hers. 'So, Julia, do you fancy a night out on Saturday?'

Instead of answering direct, Julia asked, 'What about Imelda?'

'What about Imelda?' he said flatly.

'Well. . .' The tonelessness of his voice made her feel flustered. 'Well, what I mean is, have you asked her? Perhaps she would like to go.'

Luke stared at her in surprise. 'No, I haven't asked her; she's working. And why the hell should I?'

'Oh, I just thought. . .' Julia said lamely, wishing that she hadn't taken any notice of the rumours circulating about Luke and the attractive young houseman. From his reaction, there didn't seem to be much in them, and it was none of her business, anyway.

'Well, don't.' His hand was still on her arm, and he gave it a little squeeze, and said with a mocking grin, having obviously sussed out how her mind was working, 'The grapevine isn't always right, you know.'

'Well,' she said sharply, momentarily resenting his manner, which made her feel foolish, 'it's often pretty accurate, and you know the old saying about no smoke without fire. I just thought that I would make sure that I wasn't treading on anyone's toes. And thank you for the invitation; I should love to go to the Gibsons' house-warming.'

'Good.' He nodded and squeezed her arm again before removing his hand and leaning across to open the door.

'Thank you,' said Julia rather breathlessly, as his face came very close to her own, and she caught a whiff of a mix of aftershave and antiseptic. 'And thank you for rescuing me from the elements.'

'A pleasure,' he said, smiling. 'And I'm glad that you're coming with me on Saturday. I'll let you know about picking you up.'

'Fine.' She stepped out into the gusting wind and rain, and returned his smile. 'See you.' She closed the car door and ran up the path to the lodge.

To her pleased surprise, Luke didn't drive off immediately, and she turned to wave goodbye as she reached the front door. He lifted a casual hand in response before zooming away.

Julia let herself into the spacious hallway of the lodge, and hurried up the wide staircase to her flat. Her heart thumped unevenly as she did so, but she knew that it had nothing to do with climbing the stairs, and everything to do with Luke Steel, and those last few minutes in the car.

Once inside her spacious, comfortable rooms, she leaned against the door of her sitting-room, unconsciously clenching her fists. 'Oh, no,' she muttered, half seriously, half crossly. 'Don't be an idiot; don't let it happen again.'

The sexy, masculine smell of him came back to her, as, with unseeing eyes, she stared round the room which usually gave her so much pleasure.

Everything about the Edwardian flat was bright and light. The walls and doors were painted a creamy white, which gave them a warm glow; nothing about it was cold and clinical, just fresh-looking. All the basics were provided by the hospital, but the spacious, high-ceilinged rooms lent themselves to furnishings of almost any period.

The eighteenth-century escritoire, inherited from her godmother, which Julia had brought with her merged happily with the fat, old-fashioned, chintz-covered sofa and two armchairs, donated by her parents when they had moved into a smaller house. They blended with a drop-leaf oak table, and three ladderback chairs. There were various ornaments dotted around, a couple of prints, three full bookcases and an expensive CD player. A bowl of autumn crocuses stood on a small coffee-table.

It was a room that reflected the personality and interests of a modern, successful, career-conscious, professional woman, and Julia loved it.

She pulled herself together, banished the memory of piercing grey-green eyes looking into hers, and brought the room back into focus. A real home from home. Somewhere that she could bring anyone to—someone like Luke Steel, came the unbidden thought. Irritably, she brushed the thought away. Simply because the man had given her a lift, and had invited her out, she didn't have to let it to go her head; it was ridiculous. True, he hadn't needed to bring her home. He wasn't off duty; he seemed to have driven down the drive especially to pick her up, having seen her from his office window.

That signified nothing. He would have done that for any of his staff stranded in the pouring rain, she told herself.

Would he?

He's asked you out to this party on Saturday.

Only because Imelda Robbins is working.

He didn't say that.

He implied it; he said that he knew that she was working.

Like a ping-pong ball, question and answer bounced back and forth in her head. Why such a simple thing as an invitation to a house-warming by a colleague should make such an impact, she had no idea. She only knew that she regretted it if it was going to make complications. She didn't want a repeat of the Howard Snelling episode.

Howard Snelling, her one-time fiancé! She hadn't thought about him for days, weeks even. Princes Park had begun to work its magic, and had made her forget how he had treated her, having affairs with other women when he was engaged to her. She had been so sure of his love. They were both mature people in their late twenties, who knew their own minds, so she had thought, not knowing that her handsome Howard was a perennial playboy, constantly flattered by the attentions of his female colleagues.

She had taken the post at Princes both for advancement and to remove herself from Howard's orbit when she broke off their engagement.

She was angry with the comparisons that she was making between Luke and Howard. The two men were nothing alike, except that they were both handsome and sophisticated, and played the field. But at least, she told herself defensively, Luke did it openly, making no secret of the fact that he enjoyed female company, whereas Howard had always been devious, pretending to be devoted to her only.

Yet in spite of knowing what she did about Luke she was as excited as a schoolgirl at the thought of spending an evening with him. She had accepted few invitations since coming to Princes, but that had been by choice; she wanted a breathing space from events in the past, and time to get settled in at her new hospital and choose her friends carefully. But she had joined the social club, and often had drinks or coffee with the other sisters in the lodge, and had joined parties going picnicking on a couple of occasions, during the last of the summer weather.

In her heart she knew what was bothering her about this particular invitation. She liked and admired Luke the consultant too much to risk spoiling a splendid working relationship by embarking on a social one that might or might not be successful.

Luke had dismissed the question of Imelda without any sign of embarrassment, but Julia was aware that he and the young and attractive houseman had been about together. It was common knowledge in the unit. She had no wish to stir up problems, for, whatever Luke's feelings, and however casually he might view his friendship with Imelda, that lady might have other ideas about him.

That, thought Julia, as she stripped off her wet clothes and ran a hot bath, was the trouble with hospital relationships; they were open for everyone to see, and open to all sorts of interpretations, or, even more likely misinterpretations. She had been down that road before at her old hospital, and had no wish to repeat the experience of forming close ties with a colleague.

Then don't form any close ties, she told herself as she lay in the steaming bath. Just go out with the man on this occasion, and make it clear that you don't want to socialise any more than that. For goodness' sake, woman, you're old enough to do that without offending him and spoiling your working relationship.

She felt better after giving herself a talking-to, and,

after putting on a clean uniform dress, sat down at her desk to write a couple of letters to friends. Then she made herself toast and tea and went back on duty at five o'clock.

She was busy from the moment she arrived back and took over from Dan, who was going off duty.

An elderly lady who had collapsed in a shop in the town had just been admitted. No one was quite sure what had caused the collapse, but it was thought that it might have been a *petit mal*, indicating an epileptic fit, or even a slight diabetic coma, though she wasn't carrying a card to say that she suffered from either condition. Luke was still doing tests when Julia arrived, but was about to arrange the patient's transfer to a medical ward for observation.

Julia explained this to the lady, who they had discovered when she regained consciousness was a Mrs Greenaway.

'But what about my cat, Tigger?' said the old lady. 'He's shut in the house, waiting for his tea. He'll be lost without me.'

'Have you got a neighbour who would look after him for a bit?' asked Julia.

'Oh, yes, Emily—Mrs Knight; she lives next door. But how can she get in to him?'

'Well, I might be able to arrange for one of the social workers to call round to her with the key. Or even the police; they're quite good about doing this sort of thing.'

Julia found that the social worker was just about to go off duty, but he agreed to drop Mrs Greenaway's key in to her neighbour, with instructions about feeding her cat, on his way home.

'Another good deed for the day, Nurse Nightingale,' said Luke with a grin, as a porter came to take a reasonably happy Mrs Greenaway up to the medical ward.

'Good deeds on offer this month,' replied Julia, with a nice smile. 'Now what about this small boy, Kevin, who fell from a swing and has hurt his wrist? It's very swollen, looks as if it might be a Colles' fracture. Do you want him to go to X-Ray before you have a look at it?'

'Yes, he might as well; it'll have to be done anyway. And meanwhile I'll have a look at this busted leg ulcer that Imelda's worried about.' He signed the X-ray request form that Julia had filled out, and she handed it to a nurse, with instructions to see that the boy was taken to X-Ray. She and Luke then went along to the cubicle where a young, pregnant woman lay on the couch, with a bloody leg, looking rather grey and shocked.

A nurse was applying a pressure pad to the wound on the front of her shin, while Dr Robbins was listening with her stethoscope to the foetus, through the woman's taut abdomen.

'Is my baby all right?' the woman was asking as Julia and Luke entered the cubicle.

'The baby's fine, Mrs Jakes. There's no damage there, I assure you,' Imelda said kindly. 'We're just a bit concerned about this varicose ulcer that you damaged when you fell.' She looked up at Luke with relief. 'The consultant here, Dr Steel, will look at it and decide what to do.'

'When's your baby due, Mrs Jakes?' he asked as he bent over to look at the leg. He glanced at the white mound of her abdomen. 'Soon, I guess.' He smiled at the patient, who gave him a tremulous smile in return.

'In ten days' time, Doctor.'

'Ah, then we want to get you back on your feet before then, if possible. Although I must warn you that you're going to have to rest up for a bit. Rest is the only answer, I'm afraid, for leg ulcers. Now let's see what we can do here to start with.'

He examined the injured leg carefully, and had a low-voiced conversation with Dr Robbins, while Julia rearranged the patient's clothing, and reassured her again that the baby was safe.

'Well, now, Mrs Jakes, the vein that was damaged has stopped bleeding and the small varicose ulcer that's been giving you some problems has, being covered, remained relatively clean. I'm going to ask Sister to make sure that it's quite clean and then apply a special dressing, and a long support bandage to your leg from foot to knee. This is necessary because of your condition and the extra weight that you're carrying around at the moment on account of this infant of yours.' He grinned cheerfuly at the now much more relaxed patient. 'Sister will also tell you what you must do over the next few days if that leg's to heal without problems, all right?'

'All right, Doctor, thank you. As long as the baby's OK I don't mind what I have to do.'

'You mums,' said Luke with a laugh. 'Now I'm just going to have a word with Sister, and she'll be back with you in a couple of minutes.'

An auxillary nurse appeared as the three of them left the cubicle and asked Imelda if she would look at a patient who had a foreign body in her eye.

'Will do, Nurse,' said Imelda, sounding and looking very tired as she followed the nurse into another cubicle.

'Poor girl,' said Luke, his eyes compassionate. 'She looks worn out. Not surprising, I suppose, since she's been on duty since the early hours.'

'Well, so have you,' said Julia. 'But at least you had a few hours in bed before that; poor Imelda was called out in the night, too.'

'Yes, there's no doubt about it, being a houseman or a registrar is no picnic. Everyone does more hours than they should, both medical and nursing staff, and I plan to bring this up at the next general meeting, and get something done about it.' His deep voice was firm and decisive; he meant business.

'I'm sure that we'd all be grateful. We survive, but sometimes only just. Now what do you want me to put on this varicose ulcer?'

'An alginate dressing after you've cleaned it up, and a tubigrip foot-to-knee bandage. Tell the lady that she must rest up for a couple of days, and elevate her leg; you know the drill. Suggest that she sees her GP or checks with her antenatal clinic that all is well, though I'm sure it is. Just explain that it is an extra precaution, and don't let her worry about it. But there, you're good at that sort of thing, Julia. There's nobody better. You have a gift for it.'

Julia felt herself flushing at his praise, and bent her head over the treatment card, on which she scribbled furiously. She willed the colour in her cheeks to fade, and raised her eyes to meet Luke's. He was looking down at her, one eyebrow raised quizzically, whether because he'd seen her blush and guessed at the cause, she didn't know.

'Anything else?' she enquired in a cool voice.

'No, nothing. I'm off to my office now, but give me a shout if you need me. I'm going to send Imelda off for a spell when she's finished with this eye job, so I'll be playing at duty officer.'

This return to normal conversation restored Julia to her usual calm. 'Now that,' she said cheerfully, 'is a good idea.'

They smiled at each other and went their separate ways, Luke to his office off the main corridor, and Julia to fetch the trolley containing the various dressings and cleaning agents that she needed for Mrs Jakes.

Imelda looked in the cubicle as Julia was finishing the patient's treatment.

'I'm going off duty, Sister,' she told Julia. 'Dr Steel insists that I have a rest as I'm on call again tonight. He's in his office if you want him.'

Julia was about to say that yes, she knew all that, and then changed her mind. It was quite obvious that Dr Robbins thought that she was ignorant about the arrangement, and wanted to be the one to pass on the news.

'That was kind of Dr Steel,' she said, bending low over the patient's leg. 'But then he's a very thoughtful man, isn't he?'

'He's the best boss in the world,' said Imelda fiercely. 'And a very good friend.'

'Yes,' agreed Julia in a soothing sort of voice. 'We all appreciate what a good boss he is.'

Imelda seemed to hesitate, as if she wanted to say

more, but then shrugged, said goodnight, and left the unit.

Once Mrs Jakes went home in the care of her sensible and loving husband, Julia checked on the other patients in the various cubicles, and then went to her office to start compiling the report for the night staff.

She sighed; hospital work was a twenty-four-hour process. We're like a factory that can't close down its furnaces because they take too long to start up, she thought fancifully, feeling tired now that the end of the day was in sight. If we stopped for even a short while, the system would get overloaded and grind to a halt. There never really was enough time in the day to do all that one wanted to do, work-wise, a reminder that tomorrow she really must finish her stock-taking list.

With that thought, Sonia appeared, and, after handing over, Julia went thankfully out to the car park, only too ready to go home.

It's been a funny sort of day, she mused, as she made her way through the windy darkness to her car, what with Imelda being unusually spiky early on, and Luke driving me home in the rain. Thank goodness it isn't raining now; I would be drenched already. She turned up her coat collar against the wind.

The car park, like the drive and surrounding areas, was well lit, a precaution taken by the management to thwart prowlers. With so many staff, a high proportion of them women, it was a sensible precaution to take.

Julia reached her car and bent to put the key in the lock, and, in the strong lamplight, saw to her dismay that the front, driver's-side tyre was flat.

'Oh, no, I don't believe it,' she said out loud. Well, there was nothing she could do about it tonight. She was quite capable of changing a wheel, but not late in the evening in a gale-force wind.

She stood for a moment, wondering what to do—wait till someone came into the car park and beg a lift, or start walking and stop someone *en route*. The prospect of walking down the drive in the face of a howling wind, even though it was brilliantly lit, didn't appeal. She decided to hang around and wait for another driver to appear. With luck, she shouldn't have to wait too long; quite a few people would be going off duty within the next few minutes.

She got in the car, switched on the courtesy light, and waited, but it seemed an age before she saw the outlines of two men come round the side of the building. Before she could get out of her car and signal for help, she heard the slam of a door, and, in a lull in the wind, heard an engine purr into life, as a sleek Bentley pulled out of the consultants' car parking area.

'Oh, no,' she wailed into the dark night as she struggled out of the low seat of her car. 'Don't say I've missed a lift.'

Someone called from the direction that the Bentley had driven. It was a man's voice, but his words were lost in the wind, which had sprung up again as quickly as it had briefly dropped. Julia ran towards the man, whom she could see in silhouette against one of the lamps. It was only when she was within a few yards of him that she realised that it was Luke Steel, who was standing there beside his Volvo.

'Julia, what on earth are you still doing here? I thought you went off duty some time ago.'

'I did,' confirmed Julia angrily. 'But, would you

believe, I've got a flat tyre, and no way am I going to change it in this weather.'

'What bad luck. I take it you want a lift,' he said, a broad grin belying his words of sympathy.

'If it's not too much trouble,' said Julia, in a throw-away, I'm-not-bothered sort of voice. She was furious that twice in one day she had put herself under some sort of obligation to her boss.

Luke must have guessed at her feelings, for he wiped the smile from his face and said quietly. 'Do get in, Julia. It'll be a pleasure to run you home.'

For the second time that day, Julia lowered herself on to the expensive leather seat of the Volvo.

She managed a smile. After all, it was not Luke's fault that her car had let her down; he had just happened to be conveniently to hand when she needed him.

'Well, at least this time I'm not soaking wet,' she said.

'For your sake I'm glad about that,' said Luke as he started the car, and drove out of the car park.

They didn't speak during the few minutes that it took them to reach the lodge.

Julia debated with herself whether to ask him in for a drink.

'Will you come in for a coffee?' she asked as Luke pulled neatly up at the garden gate.

'I'd love to,' he said, sounding as if he meant it. 'But I have to get home; I'm expecting an overseas phone call.'

Julia felt let down and wondered if she'd sounded too pushy.

'Well, in that case,' she said, not meaning to sound

stiff, but aware that she did so, 'I'll say goodnight, and thank you for rescuing me a second time today.'

'Think nothing of it,' said Luke. 'It was a pleasure, both times.' He smiled at her. 'Now do go and let yourself in. I'm not moving until I see that you are safe inside the house.'

'Nothing's going to happen between here and the front door,' said Julia with a laugh, her spirits raised on account of his concern.

'Indulge me,' said Luke.

'OK, will do. Goodnight.' Julia turned and made her way up the garden path. She turned at the door and waved, and she saw him return her wave from the lighted interior of the car. She let herself into the brightly lit hall of the house, and closed the door behind her. But not until then did she hear him drive off into the darkness of the stormy night.

She took a deep breath. It was a very comforting thought to know that he had waited until she was safely inside the lodge before driving away. He might have something of a reputation where women were concerned, but his manners were impeccable.

CHAPTER THREE

THE next few days were busy ones.

Following the gales that had torn off many of the only half-turned leaves from the great trees that surrounded Princes Park came a spell of calm, sunny weather. The leaves that remained on the trees turned from yellow through orange to red. The beech woods looked especially beautiful, a mass of glowing leaves climbing up the hillside to the north of the hospital.

Sonia was on nights off, and they walked in the woods one afternoon when Julia had a couple of hours off.

'How are things going with you and the boss man?' asked Sonia as they climbed the steep hill, scuffing through a carpet of yellow and red leaves.

'What on earth do you mean?'

'Well, rumour has it that you've got a thing going beween you.'

Julia stared at her friend in amazement.

'Honestly, hospital grapevines are the absolute limit,' she said in disgust. 'Talk about invention.'

'You were seen,' said Sonia with a giggle, 'getting into the gorgeous Dr Steel's car, twice in one day.'

'For heaven's sake, the man only gave me a lift; it was pouring with rain.'

'And in the evening? A little bird told me that he deposited you at the lodge later that same night. And I know that you had your car with you, because you told me so when you handed over to me.'

'Didn't that same little bird tell you that I also had a flat tyre?' asked Julia sarcastically.

'Well, no. I don't think she knew, actually,' replied Sonia, sounding disappointed, and then added cheerfully, 'But I've also heard that you're going with him to the Gibsons' house-warming on Saturday. Is it true?'

Julia looked astonished. 'How on earth did anyone find out about that? I certainly haven't said anything, and I'm sure that Luke wouldn't have broadcast it around.'

'Well, I don't see why he shouldn't. He's probably filled with macho pride at having persuaded you to go with him.'

'Why on earth should he be that?'

'Oh, Julia,' said Sonia, exasperated. 'Because you're stunning to look at—not pretty exactly, but different, striking—and a jolly nice person, and you play hard to get, an irresistible combination for most men.'

Julia stared open-mouthed at her friend.

'What do you mean, I play hard to get?'

'Well, love, let's face it, you do. You haven't exactly made yourself available since you arrived at Princes. You've had hardly any proper dates.'

'I don't believe this,' said Julia, addressing the gloriously tinted beech trees all around them. 'Even my best friend thinks that I've been playing hard to get.'

'Well, it does look rather like that,' said Sonia, eyeing Julia cautiously. 'You used not to be quite so cool and withdrawn.'

'Sonia, a lot of water has passed under many bridges since we were at school together, and quite a few litres since we were training at Kits. We've both grown up since then, surely.'

'But you seem to have been shying away from men since you came here, and that's not like you. Clive says—'

'Your precious Dr Clive Robertson, surgical registrar,' said Julia, trying to inject a little humour into a conversation that she felt was getting too serious, 'should not listen to or pass on the sort of malicious gossip that abounds in the medicos' sitting-room.'

'Ouch,' said Sonia, pulling a face. 'That's telling me to keep my nose out of your business, I take it.'

'Oh, Sonia, of course not. But you know that I had a few problems of the male variety last year, and coming here was partly to put some space between me and them. I'm loving my work; the extended Casualty is extending me, you might say. A real challenge. I really haven't had the time or energy to pursue close friendships. Having you here is a wonderful bonus, and at the moment that's enough, with just a few casual outings thrown in. And a casual outing is what Saturday is all about. Luke was at a loose end, short of a partner; he asked me if I would like to go along, and I said yes. End of story.'

'Oh, well, if you say so. But you're not sort of pining for anybody, are you? There are no untidy ends left over from last year?'

Julia shook her head, refusing to acknowledge the hurt and distrust that Howard Snelling had left her with. 'None whatsoever,' she said firmly. 'I'm just glad to have put it all behind me, and landed up here at Princes, with you to worry the life out of me.'

'That's all right, then,' said Sonia. 'Come on, race you to the bottom of the hill.'

She started to run, but Julia, with her longer legs and slimmer frame, soon overtook her.

Julia laughed to herself as she passed Sonia. I wonder what our juniors would say, she thought, if they could see two staid old sisters racing like five-year-olds.

She waited for Sonia to catch up, and together they walked sedately from the shelter of the trees down the bare slope in view of the many windows of the hospital complex.

'"Nurses must at all times maintain their dignity,"' they quoted in unison, smiling at each other, as they recalled one of the rules of their old training hospital, St Christopher's, a rule of which they were continually being reminded when they were students.

They continued round the main body of the hospital, through the car park, and down the long, twisting, south drive to the lodge and tea in Sonia's flat.

After tea Julia returned to her own flat, and changed into uniform, ready to go back on duty for the evening. As she changed, she considered what Sonia had said about her being withdrawn and cool, and her suggestion that it was a turn-on for the male ego. Was that, she wondered, why Luke Steel had suggested the party on Saturday? Was he just trying to prove that he could persuade her to go out with him when she had refused other invitations? She had no illusions about the medical staff in any hospital, and, good though it was, she didn't suppose that Princes' was immune to the kind of game that was played in other hospitals. Doctors and nurses worked hard and played hard. It was all part of hospital life, who was going out with whom, and for how long, and so on and so on.

She didn't blame Luke Steel if this was what had spurred him on to ask her out, but she experienced a little flicker of disappointment at the idea that he could be drawn into such games.

Never mind, she reminded herself for the umpteenth time, she was only committed to going out with him on Saturday night, and she could cope with that.

She went back on duty at five, feeling bright and refreshed by her walk in the woods.

There had been an accident on the motorway, and there was a crowd in Reception. The room was full with the less severely injured, the police and the beginnings of a number of concerned relatives of the victims.

This was one of the problems of any A and E department, the difficulty of dealing with the relatives of injured persons. Naturally they wanted to know what had happened to their loved ones, and needed to be reassured, but while that was being done members of staff who could have been more usefully employed with the injured had to give up valuable minutes explaining what was happening.

I must talk to Luke about this, thought Julia, as she made her way through the maelstrom of people filling Reception. Perhaps social workers, or extra care assistants good at liaising with people, could be available when there has been a significant accident, personnel who could release nursing and medical staff to treat the victims, similar, on a lesser scale, to the help we have when the hospital is on full alert.

In the cubicles she found injured people from the

road accident, as well as other patients in varying degrees of need, being treated, or waiting for treatment.

Luke was dealing with the worst case, an elderly man, much cut about the face by broken glass, and with several probable broken bones, and in heart failure. Julia looked in, but the crash team was there, and several other supporting staff. There was nothing she could do to help.

She found Imelda in the next cubicle, trying to stem a steady flow of blood from a head wound, while a nurse applied pressure to a bleeding point in a woman's left leg.

'How can I help?' she asked.

'If you can take over up here,' said Imelda, looking immensely relieved by Julia's appearance, 'I can listen to her chest and do reflexes and so on.'

'Right.' Julia placed her hand on the pressure pad that Imelda had been holding to a scalp wound, and began to speak to the virtually comatose patient. 'It's all right, my dear,' she said. 'Doctor is here; she's going to find out what's wrong. It won't be long now.' Deftly, with one hand she picked up a fresh pad of gauze from the trolley, and dropped the blood-soaked pad into the disposal bin. She had a quick look at the wound as she did so. 'It's beginning to clot,' she said to Imelda, who was listening to the patient's chest. 'I think butterfly clips would hold it. Shall I try?'

'Please,' said Imelda, flashing Julia a smile. She nodded as she finished listening to the elderly woman's heart, and said to the patient, who was coming round, 'It's all right. You're doing fine. We'll soon have you feeling better. Now can you tell me your name?'

The patient mumbled something which sounded like Mrs Humphrey.

'Mrs Humphrey?' queried Imelda.

'That's right,' said the patient in a slurred voice. 'My hubby, how is he?'

'Another doctor's with him,' explained Julia, guessing that the husband was the man on whom Luke was working, as all the other people involved in the crash were much younger. 'As soon as I've finished seeing to this cut on your head I'll go and find out how he is.'

She finished drawing the edges of the wound together with tiny butterfly clips, and spoke to the nurse who was dealing with the leg wound, which Imelda was just about to examine. 'You go on helping Dr Robbins, Nurse. I'm going next door to find out what's happening to Mrs Humphrey's husband.'

'Yes, Sister.'

In the next cubicle Julia found Luke with Dan Beatty and a staff nurse working on Mr Humphrey. The patient looked terribly frail and ill, ashen-faced with a tell-tale blue line still round his mouth, but the crash team had gone, and he was out of immediate danger.

'How goes it?' Julia asked Luke softly.

'I think he'll do, for the moment, anyway. But he's generally in one hell of a mess; I want to get him into the ICU as soon as possible. Will you make the necessary arrangements, please?' A smile lit his face and touched his grey-green eyes as he looked round to speak to her.

He turned back to give his full attention to his patient, bending over to remove with tweezers some fine pieces of glass embedded in Mr Humphrey's cheek just below his right eye. Julia felt a little catch in her throat. He looked so caring and gentle, murmuring comfortingly to the patient as he worked. If ever I were involved in an accident, she thought, Luke Steel is the man I'd like to have around.

She went back to Mrs Humphrey in the next cubicle, to let her know that her husband was 'comfortable', though still in shock.

'Both you and your husband are going to need care for a while, Mrs Humphrey,' she explained. 'So you will have to be admitted to hospital. You will both be taken up to the wards presently, but as you are in rather better shape than your husband we'll see if we can arrange for you to see him for a few minutes, when Dr Robbins thinks you're fit enough.'

Imelda said kindly, 'We'll see what can be managed later on, but you've got to stay quiet for a bit, Mrs Humphrey. Now I'm just going to give you something to ease the pain.'

Julia went away to contact Intensive Care and arrange for Mr Humphrey to be admitted there as soon as possible. She also went hunting for a social worker to lay on arrangements for the Humphreys to be visited if relatives didn't turn up.

She was busy up to seven o'clock, helping to treat the other road accident victims and deal with the steady stream of less urgent casualties who arrived. As soon as pressure of work diminished sufficiently, she sent Niri Patel and the little student nurse Celia Ponting to talk to the relatives of the injured. Niri was particulrly good at this, and she had a feeling that Celia, young as she was, would respond well to this sort of nursing chore. It was hard for young nurses to have to deal with bereaved or anxious relatives, but something that they had to learn. Like most of the other branches of nursing, some were 'naturals' at this, and Celia, Julia hoped, might be one of those.

At last she was able to escape to her office and catch up on the mountain of paperwork. The report tonight would take some time, as details of the accident with all the relevant information had to be written up, both on the cards and in the book, and a check made to make sure that all medication had been listed and signed for. As far as possible, this was done as items were used, but occasionally, under pressure, the less important drugs slipped through the net. It was her responsibility to see that this was put right before staff went off duty.

She decided to make a pot of tea to keep her going while she worked, and went through to the little kitchenette to put on the kettle. She had only just got in there when there was a knock on the office door.

'Oh, no,' she groaned out loud. 'Give me a break.' As she filled and switched on the kettle, she called, 'Come in,' praying that her visitor wouldn't keep her long.

To her surprise, it was Luke Steel who entered. Her irritation at being interrupted evaporated, replaced by a warm feeling of pleasure at the sight of him. Suddenly she felt less tired. They exchanged smiles.

'I saw you slip away from the battlefield,' he said, 'and thought that I would beg a cup of tea and a few minutes' civilised conversation before tackling my paperwork. Imelda can manage with the relief junior who's just arrived.'

Julia wrinkled her nose in distaste. 'Paperwork,' she said disgustedly. 'You must have a pile like me.'

'I certainly have, and the infuriating thing is that I had almost caught up with myself this afternoon. I worked in my office virtually undisturbed. Now I'm snowed under again.' He gave her a sideways smile, his eyes gleaming. 'By the way, who won the race? I missed the last bit.'

Julia looked baffled.

'The race?'

'The one that you and Sonia Jansen had in the beech wood.' He twinkled at her, his craggy face full of humour.

'How on earth did you know about that?' asked Julia with a laugh, as she remembered the mad dash down the hill in the afternoon sunlight. Ridiculously, she felt herself blushing.

'I told you that I'd spent hours in my office. It has windows on three sides, remember, and I keep a pair of binoculars there to watch the birds when I've got a minute. Very relaxing. It's usually the winged variety that catch my eye, but this afternoon. . .' His smile grew broader; his eyes danced with fun. 'So who did win?'

'Well, I did, of course.'

Julia put her hands up to her hot cheeks, and laughed again. Somehow she found it exciting, rather than embarrassing, that he should have been watching her and Sonia. It was a good job that he hadn't been able to hear as well as watch them, she thought, wondering what he would have said had he known that he was the subject of much of their conversation. She decided that he would probably have found it amusing. He seemed to have a quirky view of life that was very mature and reassuring. Nothing much would faze him in his personal life, any more than it did in his professional capacity.

She heard the kettle click off, and went to make the tea. Luke followed her into the kitchenette.

Julia put mugs, teapot and milk jug and a plateful of biscuits on a tray, conscious of Luke's eyes upon her.

He rested his hands on her shoulders and turned her to face him.

'I'm looking forward to Saturday,' he said, sounding a little husky. 'Very much. I'll collect you at about seven. All right?'

She liked the feel of his hands on her shoulders; well shaped, strong hands, feeling warm through the thin cotton of her uniform dress. Her mouth felt dry. For a moment she wondered if he was going to kiss her. The kitchen seemed smaller than usual with his large frame filling it. She licked her lips, and looked fully up at him.

'That would be fine,' she said, in an almost normal voice.

He looked for a moment hard into her eyes, and again she thought that he was about to kiss her, but he didn't. 'Good.' He squeezed her shoulders for an instant, and then dropped his hands. 'Here, let me take that.' He moved half in front of her and lifted up the tray. 'After you,' he said, pressing himself against the worktop so that Julia could sidle past him into the office.

He followed her and set the tray down on the desk. Julia wondered if he had felt as strange in the kitchen as she had. Had he been affected by those few moments of closeness? She looked at him from under her lashes as she poured the tea. Perhaps he had. There was a thoughtful stillness about him as he in turn watched her, his eyes on her hands.

She handed him a steaming mug and proffered the biscuits.

'Thank you.' His deep voice had a vibrancy in it that she hadn't heard before. 'May I,' he asked, 'have the only chocolate one on the plate? I have a penchant for chocolate when I'm tired or stressed, very childish of me.' He didn't smile, but the corners of his mouth quirked upwards, and the corners of his eyes crinkled.

Julia nodded, thinking that he looked anything but childish, but it was rather touching, the way he had admitted to this small weakness without losing any of his habitual air of authority. If anything, it enhanced it, proving, if proof were needed, that Luke's masculine strength was rock-solid and could withstand such trivia.

'Are you feeling stressed at the moment?' she asked. 'You don't look it. Or are you tired? You've been on without a break all day.'

'No, I'm not tired, though I felt whacked a while ago, but I was fine when the old adrenalin got going. You know how it boosts one's physical level no end, just as other things lift one's spirit, and add a new level to mundane matters.' He was looking at her intently; his eyes, more green than grey, were serious.

Julia met his gaze unflinchingly. She knew what he meant by 'other things lift one's spirits'. He was obliquely flirting with her. Or was he? Perhaps he was sizing her up, speculating as to what he might expect from her when they went out together on Saturday night.

She continued to look into his eyes. Their tea went cold. He leaned forward. . .

The telephone rang. Julia jumped, and Luke swore very fluently.

Automatically Julia stretched out her hand to lift the receiver. Luke covered her hand with his.

'So much,' he said softly, with a half-smile, 'for spiritual uplift. But thanks for the cold tea.' He swallowed what was left in his mug, and made a face. 'And for the biscuit,' he added. He lifted his hand from hers, and she lifted the receiver to her ear.

'Good evening,' she said, mustering all her self-control to speak calmly. 'This is Accident and Emergency, Sister Manning speaking.' She listened carefully to an enquiry by a relative of one of the motor accident victims.

Luke stood up, leaned across the desk, removed her cap with confident fingers, and dropped a kiss on her shining hair.

'That,' he murmured, his face a few inches from hers, 'is to be going on with. We'll pick up some time from where we left off. But not tonight, or I'll never get any work done. See you tomorrow night at seven.' His eyes were smiling again, his mouth tilted in a half-smile, too.

Julia took a deep breath, and returned his smile with a tremulous one of her own. She said something reassuring to the person on the phone.

'Goodnight, Julia,' Luke said softly. 'Sleep well.'

'Goodnight, and you,' whispered Julia in return.

Luke backed towards the door, put his fingers to his lips when he got there, and then let himself out.

Julia stared at the door, then turned her attention to the caller. 'I think,' she said gently, 'that you should ring Mary Long Ward for the latest information. Your sister has now been transferred there. I'll get you put through.'

When the call had been transferred, she sat looking at her lace cap that lay on the desk where Luke had dropped it only minutes before. She put up a tentative hand to her head, and touched the spot where he had kissed her. If her cap hadn't been lying there as a reminder, she would have doubted that anything as remarkable as a kiss from this strong, rugged man had happened.

It took her a few more minutes to get absolute control of herself, and then, with a shrug of her shoulders and a resolute expression on her face, she started on the report for the night staff.

CHAPTER FOUR

JULIA slept well, and woke feeling marvellous on Saturday morning. She lay in bed, luxuriating in the fact that she didn't have to go on duty. The day was hers to do with as she wished, until the evening, when Luke would pick her up and whisk her off to the Gibsons' house-warming party.

The thought of seeing Luke after what had happened last evening in her office sent a warm glow coursing through her. She hadn't any illusions about the kiss that he'd planted on her head being terribly important, but it had been unexpected, and pleasant. Well, that was fine. Keep everything casual; that was what she wanted. Probably it had arisen because they had both been affected by the trauma of the motorway accident, and the critical condition of some of the victims. That was the trouble with nursing and medicine; one tended to live on highs or lows, according to what was happening to the patients.

Though everyone was told when they were in training that they must not get involved with their patients, the best ones always did, to some extent. It was impossible to care for the sick and injured properly and not do so.

Well, today I'm going to switch off, Julia decided, have a shower, and dash into New Town to pick up something to wear tonight. After all, it is something of an occasion, going out on a proper date for the first time since I arrived at Princes.

She was almost ready to leave when there was a buzz at her front door. For one wild moment she thought that it might be Luke, but then dismissed the thought as ludicrous. He had said that he would see her tonight, and he wasn't the sort of man to change his mind, not, certainly, on account of his mild show of emotion yesterday evening. That he would take in his stride, just as she meant to.

She opened the door to find her twin brother Bill standing there.

'How on earth did you get in downstairs?' she asked, quite taken aback at seeing him. 'You didn't phone to be let in.'

'And it's nice to see you too, sister, dear,' said Bill, contriving a hurt expression. 'Someone was going out, and let me in—as simple as that.'

Julia was immediately contrite. 'Oh, Bill, I didn't mean that I'm not glad you're here; it's lovely to see you. Do come in.'

Bill kissed her soundly on the cheek and followed her into the sitting-room.

Anyone seeing them together would recognise them as being related, perhaps even as twins, for they had the same chestnut hair, and the same smoky blue eyes, though Bill, at six feet tall, was a good five inches taller than Julia. He was also the elder by ten minutes, a fact he often teasingly reminded her of.

Her brother looked appreciatively round the sitting-room. 'I say,' he remarked in surprise, 'they do you proud at Princes, don't they?'

'They certainly do, especially their senior staff. That's why there's always a waiting list to get in here, quite apart from their medical excellence. It's a great place to work.'

'Yes, so I've gathered. I'll have to see what I can do at this interview, then, won't I?'

Julia asked in surprise, 'What do you mean, "interview"? For what? When? Where?'

Bill burst out laughing. 'Now let's see, in order of asking. Senior ophthalmic registrar. When? Monday. Where? Here in the ophthalmic department.'

'Oh, Bill, why didn't you write and say, or at least telephone? I would have liked to know that you were considering the post.'

'You, sister, dear, might have told me that it was on offer!'

Julia looked crest-fallen. 'Oh, Bill, I only heard about it vaguely. And you seemed settled. And it's a bit quick for you to be contemplating a senior reg post at only twenty-nine, surely? Though there's nothing I would like better than for you to be here at Princes.'

'You are sure about that? I wouldn't queer your pitch in any way? You wouldn't mind big brother being around to keep an eye on you? There's no one special you want to keep under wraps from the family, is there?'

'Good heavens, of course not! I've got loads of casual friends, but that's all.'

'Mother's Mr Right hasn't come along yet, then?'

'Oh, Bill, be your age. Mother just has this thing about marriage being the be-all and end-all, and I have no such ideas.'

Fleetingly, as she said this, she thought of Luke Steel, and suppressed it with a mental shrug.

'You're still a career woman, then, regardless.'

Bill had guessed at something; she was sure of that.

That was the trouble about being a twin; your opposite number, as often as not, was privy to your innermost thoughts.

'Absolutely,' she snapped.

'Oh, that's good.' Bill sounded quite innocent; maybe he hadn't noticed anything. 'Like me, you are footloose and fancy-free. A nice state to be in, Julia, don't you agree?

'Definitely,' said Julia. She deliberately turned to mundane matters. 'Do you want breakfast, Bill? You must have left early to get here at this time.'

'Love some. What have you got—bacon and eggs?'

'Sorry, I'm vegetarian, remember. But I can give you eggs, boiled, scrambled, poached, or in an omelette. What would you prefer?'

'Would toast be possible with scrambled?'

'Of course, no problem.'

'You were about to go out,' said Bill, as Julia beat his eggs and turned the bread under the grill in her minute kitchen.

'Oh, I'm not in rush. I can go shopping later.'

'Thank goodness I've caught you off duty.'

'Yes, the first weekend off for weeks.'

'Shopping for anything nice?'

'A dress or something for tonight; I'm going to a house-warming do.'

'Partner you want to impress?'

At first she was going to deny it, but then remembered that this was her twin she was talking to. She couldn't pull the wool over his eyes.

'Yes,' she said flatly. 'The A and E consultant, Luke Steel. He's taking me.'

Bill whistled through his teeth.

'Flying high, sis,' he said with a cheeky grin.

'Very,' confirmed Julia.

'Like him?'

'Yes,' said Julia thoughtfully. 'I do.'

'He's the clever chap who has dual fellowship, isn't he?'

'Yes, physician and surgeon. He is pretty young to have both, only in his late thirties.'

Bill whistled again. 'Yes, that is good going. And he likes to be known as Doctor, not Mr.'

'Yes, especially in Casualty. He says that patients, especially traumatised ones, react more favourably to Doctor.'

'I can see his point. Sounds a nice guy, your Dr Luke Steel.'

'He's not "my" anything, Bill. We're going out for the first time since I started work here, that's all. It's funny; we've been working together for nearly three months and have hardly noticed each other, and then the other day—'

'Cupid got out his little arrow, and wham, got you right here.' Bill put both hands over his heart.

'Don't be such an ass. It wasn't like that at all, nothing so fancy. But we did seem to click, that's all.'

'Well, I hope it works out for you, Julia, however you want it,' he said, suddenly serious. 'I couldn't bear to see you hurt again.'

He was utterly sincere.

'There's no danger of another Snelling episode,' said Julia vehemently. 'It's just the beginning of a friendship, nothing more, and, in any case, he's more interested in Imelda Robbins than me.'

'Imelda Robbins?'

'Junior houseman. At least she seems to be interested in him, though I have heard that she's got a roving eye, so perhaps I'm mistaken about that.'

'Any good to look at, this Imelda?'

Julia laughed. 'You're a shocker, Bill. You're not even working here yet, and you're fishing around.'

'Well, forewarned and all that, you know. There's nothing like being prepared.'

'If,' said Julia solemnly, 'and surely, Bill, it's got to be a big if, you get the senior reg's job, you won't have much time for gallivanting around in the first instance; you're going to be too damned busy working like a Trojan to hold the job down.'

'Oh, Sis, you know that I can work hard, but I can also play hard.' He gave her a pretend leer. 'Now what about this shopping spree? Shall we go in my car? And then I can book myself into the hotel near the foot of the drive, on the main road. That's if it's not too expensive; it looks rather splendid.'

'Oh, Poachers, you mean. It's sort of the hospital local, but I've no idea what their rooms are like. But you don't have to stay anywhere. I can put you up, if you don't mind an inflatable mattress and a sleeping-bag on my sitting-room floor.'

'Do you mean that, Julia?'

'Of course, I wouldn't offer if I didn't, and it means we can see plenty of each other as I have the weekend off, and, except for tonight, have nothing planned.'

'Your Dr Steel won't mind me—' he sketched quotation marks in the air '—"stealing" you on your days off?'

'Oh, do grow up; I've told you he's not my Dr anything.'

'Sorry, point taken.'

'Right, now let's get going, I want to have a really good browse around before I buy anything.'

'Of course you do,' said Bill, sarcastically smooth. 'For this date with this chap who isn't anything special.'

He ducked as Julia aimed a cushion at him.

'A woman likes to look her best whoever she's going out with,' she said scornfully, but her words belied the way she felt about dressing for her date with Luke. Even as she spoke, she realised that she wanted to look special for him, and dressing to please any man hadn't been something that she had done for a long time.

Julia could see in his eyes that buying something to please Luke had been definitely worth while when she opened the door to him at seven o'clock that evening.

'Julia, you look gorgeous,' he said, examining her from top to toe with his cool grey-green eyes. 'Quite a *femme fatale* out of uniform.' He raised one eyebrow appraisingly.

That applies to you, too,' said Julia with a light laugh. 'I've never seen you in evening dress before; you're usually grey-suited or smothered in a bloody plastic pinny.'

They stood in the small hall, and laughed together.

'Give me a twirl,' said Luke, and Julia obligingly did so, showing off to advantage the softly swirling, mid-calf-length skirt of the powder-blue dress.

The dress, in fine wool, with a scooped-out neckline, and off-the-shoulder, elbow-length sleeves, clung to her body smoothly, moulding itself to her high, firm breasts and small waist, until it flared out at the hips in soft folds. She had unleashed her chestnut hair from the usual chignon that she wore on duty, and it rioted like a cloud round her oval face, in tiny curls and tendrils.

Luke took another long, cool look. 'Yes, gorgeous, quite stunning,' he said. He handed her a sheaf of flowers. 'Blue freesias to match your eyes.'

'They're lovely,' said Julia. 'How clever of you to think of a colour match.' She was rather overwhelmed by his thoughtfulness. 'Please come in. I won't be long; I'll just put these in water.'

They went into the sitting-room, and Bill unfolded himself from the armchair. Although Bill was tall, Luke topped him by several inches. If Luke was surprised at finding another man in her flat, he didn't show it.

Julia performed the introductions.

'My twin, Bill; he's staying for a couple of days, Bill, this is Dr Steel, Luke, my boss.'

The two men shooks hands.

'Julia says that I'm her boss, but that's debatable; as manager of the unit, she manages all of us.'

Julia laughed a little self-consciously, and tried to ignore Luke's teasing look.

'I should be so lucky as to manage you,' she said. 'Now I must go and put these in water.' She moved towards the kitchen. 'I'll only be a minute.'

Bill grinned. 'You're quite right about her managing everything and everyone. She's been doing it since we were kids.'

'But I'm sure in the nicest possible way,' Julia heard Luke say as she disappeared into the kitchen to fetch a vase and water.

She didn't hurry. She wanted time to come to terms

with the rush of excitement that had overwhelmed her when Luke had stepped through the doorway. She also wanted to ponder his words about choosing flowers to match her eyes. Had he really taken time and trouble to do that? To her annoyance, her heart gave a little leap at the possibility.

She returned presently to the sitting-room, and placed the nicely arranged vase of freesias on top of her writing-desk. Bill and Luke were in deep discussion about eye injuries, Bill having apparently told Luke why he was at his sister's flat, and what his speciality was.

Luke stood up as Julia entered.

'You know,' he said quietly, looking very hard at her, 'we don't know much about each other, do we, for all that we've worked together for three months? We must remedy that. I didn't know, for instance, that you had a brother in the trade.'

'And a father,' said Bill. 'In the trade, as it were. He's a GP in the West Country, though he's semi-retired now. He and Mother have moved out from the barn of a place in the country, where we grew up, to a small town house near the theatre and shops. So we're almost homeless, aren't we, Julia?' He contrived to look pathetic.

'Take no notice of my silly twin,' said Julia, laughing. 'We still have rooms at home and are always welcome, even at our advanced age. We're a close family, you see.'

'Lucky you,' said Luke seriously, giving them both a wry smile. 'I lost my parents when I was a child, and always envied children with parents who seemed to understand what they wanted to do and be.'

Julia was surprised at this admission from this strong, contained man. She was sure that he wouldn't readily expose his feelings to anyone. He was right about their getting to know each other better; they must. She felt suddenly that she wanted to know much more about him, find out what made him tick, what made him so devastatingly attractive to women. Surely it went deeper than just good looks and an enigmatic sophistication?

'When you say understanding about ambitions, do you mean that you wanted to be a doctor and nobody understood?' she asked.

'Exactly. The relatives who brought me up wanted me to go into the stockbroking business; they couldn't understand how much I wanted to do medicine.'

'How sad,' said Julia sympathetically, picturing Luke as a small, lonely boy growing up with austere relatives.

Luke gave a cheerful laugh. 'Oh, I wasn't badly treated or anything; they were elderly, and kind in their fashion, and my aunt was marvellous when she saw that I was serious about a career in medicine. But I felt a bit hard done by, because I thought that parents would have understood immediately how important it was to me. Of course, I learned later that even loving parents don't always understand their children, but I bet it was different for you two. You must have received plenty of encouragement.'

'We did,' said Julia and Bill in unison. 'Plenty.'

Luke laughed. 'Do you often come out with things together?' he asked.

'Yes, frequently,' they said, as one.

'So I see,' said Luke with a wry smile. 'I'd better be careful what I say to you when you're both together, had I not? I might get the right answer from the wrong person.' He pulled a face in mock-horror, and then spoke to Julia. 'Now if you are ready we'd better get moving.' He gave her an intimate smile that made her heart flip.

'I'm quite ready.'

'Good, let's go, then,' he said.

Julia gathered up a wrap and handbag, and he took her arm and steered her towards the door.

'Have a good time, both of you,' said Bill. 'Look after my little sister, Luke.'

'Oh, I will, never fear,' said Luke, giving Julia's arm a gentle squeeze.

They walked down the stairs and out into the chilly autumn night. The sky was full of stars. An owl hooted not far away.

'I wish I were a poet and not a doctor at this moment,' said Luke, to her surprise.

'Oh, why?'

'Because I could make up some profound lines about you being more brilliant than the stars, and so on.'

'That,' said Julia, catching her breath, reminding herself that he was only teasing, 'would be delightful, but not nearly so special as someone who knows what to do if a patient is in danger of bleeding to death. Give me a doctor rather than a poet any day.'

'Do you mean that?'

'I do, with all my heart. Of course, a poet who was also a doctor. . .now that would be a perfect combination.' She laughed. 'But an unlikely one, I suppose.'

Luke laughed too as he opened the door of the Volvo, and helped Julia in. She sank down into the soft leather of the passenger seat, conscious of the spot where his guiding hand had rested on her arm for a moment. Not until he had settled into the driving seat, and fastened his seatbelt, did he speak again, as he put the car into gear and they pulled away down the drive.

'I'm glad that you prefer doctors to poets,' he said. 'But tell me, how do you rate jazz-playing doctors?'

Julia turned her head to look at him. 'You're a jazz player?'

'I relax with a sax.' His green-grey eyes twinkled at her.

'How marvellous. I adore jazz.' It seemed too good to be true, that Luke was interested in her favourite music.

'I belong to a club affiliated to the cricket club. We play in winter—and in summer when rain stops play. I'm rather hooked. Would you like to come along one evening, as my guest to a play-in? Visitors or new members are always welcome.'

'I'd love that. I belonged to a club when I was at Kit's, though I don't play except the piano, a little, very amateurishly. A jazz session is one of the things that I've missed most since coming to Princes.'

'Good, let's remedy that. I'll let you know when our next meeting is. It'll be great to have an enthusiast like you along.'

Julia felt a wave of pleasure engulf her at his words; he seemed genuinely pleased by her interest. She tried to sound casual as she said, 'I'm interested in drama, too. I've put my name down to join the drama club, but apparently there's a waiting-list. It's awfully well subscribed, but I have been told to expect to be called for an audition within the next few weeks. Apparently they're taking in more members for the Christmas pantomime.'

'One of our traditions, the Christmas panto.'

During this interesting conversation they had travelled through Princes Hollow, and were now on the ring road taking them round the hill on which the hospital stood to Princes North, where the Gibsons lived.

They passed through the outskirts of the town, the light industrial area, made up of single- and double-storey buildings looking quite neat in squares of well kept gardens. Beyond this area began the town proper. There were a few streets of terraced houses, and high-rise flats, most of them looking shabby and run down.

'This is so different from Princes Hollow, with its Georgian squares and elegant crescents,' remarked Julia.

'Yes, and yet in the sixties it was reckoned to be quite a model new town. Everyone was very proud of it, apparently.'

'I wonder how and when it started to deteriorate.'

'That's a leading question. I suppose if the answer to it were known there would be less deprivation and decline in many city centres. I suppose we are even more conscious of it here, because of the comparison with Princes Hollow just over the hill, and even the better parts of the town itself. The differences are striking.'

The dusty, paper-strewn streets in this part of Princes North were almost deserted, except for the occasional person waiting at a bus-stop, or groups of youngsters sitting on walls and looking bored.

'Depressing, isn't it?' said Luke. He took a hand from the steering-wheel and touched her arm gently, reassuringly, as if sensing her momentary sadness. 'We'll soon be through to the old part of town, and that's delightful, and we'll go back by the north drive to Princes, so we won't have to cut through this part of town.'

'I feel ridiculous being so affected by all of this. I suppose it is because much of this part of the world is so affluent that the poverty-stricken areas stand out. If only one could do something for these people.'

Luke was about to reply when they rounded a corner and saw half a dozen skateboarding boys, circling round and round a couple of women, who were obviously trying to walk along the pavement.

Luke took in the situation at a glance. 'I won't be a moment,' he said, grim-faced, as he pulled the car to a halt a short distance from the noisy youths.

In the dark the street-lights, at least those that weren't broken, cast pools of light. Luke strode towards the swirling band of skateboarders as they circled round the two women.

Luke was almost there when the older woman stumbled and fell, and at that same moment one of the youths saw Luke, now running towards them, and shouted to his mates. Within seconds the gang had melted away, as if they had never been there, disappearing into the dark streets opening off the main road.

Julia got out of the car and ran to join Luke, who was kneeling on the dirty pavement beside the fallen figure. The younger woman was just standing absolutely still, looking white and shocked. The face of the woman on the ground was contorted with pain. 'It's me knee,' she was saying as Julia arrived. 'I reckon it's bloody broke.'

Her companion seemed to come out of her shock at the words. She knelt down beside her companion. 'Oh, Mum, you're hurt.'

Luke said quietly, 'This lady's a nurse and I'm a doctor, so we'll do what we can to help. Now may I?' He indicated that he wanted to look at the injured leg, and the woman nodded.

Carefully and gently Luke examined the knee where

the woman indicated that she was in pain. He nodded to Julia. 'Yes, fractured patella.' To the woman he said, 'You're right, Mrs. . .?'

'Candy,' said the daughter.

'Candy,' continued Luke. 'You have broken your kneecap, and I know that you must be in dreadful pain, but I can give you an injection for that while we wait for an ambulance.'

'For Gawd's sake give me something, Doctor; it 'urts like 'ell.'

'Will do,' said Luke. 'Julia, would you be kind enough to fetch my bag, please? And when you've done that, use the car phone to get an ambulance here stat.'

Julia nodded, and ran back to the car, returned with Luke's bag in seconds, and then ran back to the car again and phoned for an ambulance from Princes.

She returned to where Luke was still kneeling by the injured woman. 'I've just given Mrs Candy an injection of pethidine,' he said, 'and sprayed her knee with an anaesthetiser; that should keep her going till they get her into Cas.' She nodded, and silently handed him the car rug that she had found on the back set. 'Oh, well done,' he said. 'That'll help.' Between them they spread the rug over Mrs Candy's recumbent form.

The pain-relieving spray and the injection soon began to have an effect, and by the time that the ambulance arrived the paramedic on board was able to take over and immobilise the knee without causing the patient too much distress.

Everything had happened in less than half an hour, and it seemed no time at all before Julia and Luke, having seen the Candys, mother and daughter, safely into the ambulance were once more on their way to the Gibsons'.

They both looked virtually untouched by what had happened, except that Luke was conscious of having dirt from the pavement on the knees of his trousers.

'It seems,' he said, with a humorous note in his voice and a gleam in his eyes, as they sped towards their destination, 'that we are doomed to be forever on duty, you and I. I must apologise for spoiling the evening. I think that we must make plans to remedy tonight's fiasco by arranging something tomorrow, if you're free.'

'Well, you weren't exactly to blame, were you?' said Julia brightly. 'You went charging in, like the proverbial knight errant to the rescue. But what happened to Mrs Candy would have happened anyway, and would have been much more serious without you to take charge of things.'

Luke's eyebrows shot up. He didn't make any comment on what she had said, but repeated, 'Are you busy tomorrow, Julia? If not, I suggest that you come out with me again to make up for the spoiled beginning to this evening.'

'You don't have to,' said Julia politely. 'And I'm not busy, but I must see something of Bill. He has to go back directly after his interview on Monday.'

'Let's all three go out for a meal in the evening. My treat. I should like to get to know your brother better, hear a few snippets of gossip about how delightful, or otherwise, you were as a child,' said Luke with a grin as they pulled up in front of a tall, elegant Regency-period house. 'Well, we're here,' he said. 'At the Gibsons'.' He helped her out of the car. 'Think about tomorrow night, and let me know later.'

He took her arm and steered her towards the elegant front door of the one-time manor house.

CHAPTER FIVE

JULIA'S first thoughts when she woke up on Sunday morning were not about the party, which had finished at about one a.m., and had been a great success, or about Luke, except indirectly; her first thoughts were about Mrs Candy and her fractured patella. Poor woman; she must have suffered agonies. A broken kneecap was no joke. What a blessing that Luke had been there, and able to deal with it so promptly.

With the fleeting memory of Luke kneeling beside the stricken Mrs Candy, gently reassuring her, flooded back other memories of the evening, and especially of him.

He had been a perfect escort, giving her every care and attention, ensuring that she was introduced to the many Princes staff present whom she had not previously met.

When they had arrived to be greeted by the Gibsons, Olive Gibson had asked where she had trained, and when Julia had admitted to Kit's she had been delighted.

'I trained there donkey's years ago,' she had said. 'We must have a get-together some time.'

'I'd love that,' Julia had replied sincerely, knowing that, even though Olive Gibson was in her fifties, they would no doubt find that they had a few contacts in common at St Christopher's.

That was the beauty of hospital life, she reflected,

lying snug in her bed as the wind howled round the lodge and rain pelted at the windows; hospitals were such tight communities. Sooner or later one would meet up with someone with whom there was a connection.

Hospital friendships were almost like extended families, she thought, and with the thought came a reminder of Luke confessing that he had been orphaned at an early age. Did he feel warmed by the bonds that bound hospital staff together in their own special way? He certainly had a large circle of friends, and was popular with both men and women if last night's party was anything to go by. He had been much in demand.

The evening had been a success in every way, and Luke eloquent, charming and thoughtful.

He had been thoughtful too when they had returned from the house-warming party at something after one o'clock, refusing her invitation to have a drink before making for home.

'No, I won't come in,' he'd said. 'Time's getting on and your brother might want to bed down soon. I understand he's roughing it on your sitting-room floor, poor bloke. But thanks for the offer and thank you for coming with me tonight; it's been a delightful evening.'

His eyes had gleamed in the dim light of the hall, and he had kissed her, first on one cheek, and then on the other, and finally on her moth. Teasing, experienced kisses, undemanding, but full of a sort of suppressed passion. She had been glad that he hadn't been more demanding, not being sure how she would have responded to anything more passionate. A warm, uncomplicated friendship was what she wanted with Luke, she'd told herself, nothing more. But she had been vaguely disappointed when he released her from his loose embrace after a few minutes.

'Goodnight,' he'd said, tilting her head back and kissing her on the tip of her nose. 'See you tomorrow. . . No—' he'd smiled and looked at his watch '—later today.'

He had taken the key from her hand, quietly opened the flat door, and gently pushed her inside. She had watched him take a few long strides to the stairs and then disappear down them two at a time, without a backward glance.

There was a knock at the door, interrupting her thoughts, and Bill entered, bearing two steaming mugs of tea.

'Thought that as you are generously giving me bed and board of sorts I'd bring you tea in bed, with breakfast to follow if you so desire, madam.'

'Idiot,' said Julia, sipping gratefully at the tea. 'This is nice, but I'll get up for breakfast, and then we'll decide what to do for the day.'

A hour later they were out tramping round the grounds, braving the wind and the rain.

'I'd like to get an overall impression of the place,' said Bill, racing her up the beech hill to the little plateau near the top where they could look down on nearly all of the hospital complex that made up Princes Park. Only the lodges at the north and south gates were hidden from them by their own fringe of trees, but the rest of the buildings, even the clusters of bungalows and houses for married staff, were visible in the park-like setting.

Julia pointed out various points of interest.

'That big building over there—' she pointed to a square, modern block, built with softly red bricks to match the original house '—is junior staff quarters, and the smaller building behind it is for senior medical and nursing staff, though there are also rooms and small flats for them in the lodges, and in the Old House, which is there at the dead centre of the complex.'

The Old House was a large Queen Anne mansion of magnificent proportions, built of mellow red bricks, weathered over the centuries to a rosy pink. They even seemed to glow in the driving rain.

'And next to the Old House,' said Julia enthusiastically, 'is the admin block. I believe it was once the stable block, dating from the days when they kept dozens of horses and carriages. You can see that it is pretty big, and almost as elegant as the Old House itself.'

Bill nodded, and peered down at the large mass of buildings radiating in a semicircle from the admin block and the Old House, but separated from them by small courtyards, and connected together by glassed-in corridors.

'So all the buildings connected to each other are wards, and obviously that's the theatre block.' He pointed to the almost windowless building near the tail-end of the east wing.

'Yes, and there's my block, A and E, next door to it, with direct access to the theatres and, via corridors, all the other departments. It's been beautifully designed and thought out.'

'Must have had some good architects in the past.'

'Yes, I dare say, but it is said that Matron Dunn, who has been here forever, has been the guiding hand for over thirty years. Apparently she's been responsible for most of the building programme in all that time.'

Bill whistled. 'She sounds a right old battleship of a matron,' he said.

'She's an absolute darling,' retorted Julia. 'But tough. You know, iron-hand-in-the-velvet-glove sort of thing.'

'Wow, she sounds like some formidable lady.'

'Oh, she is,' said Julia. 'But an absolute cracker just the same.'

They finished their tour of the hospital with a visit to A and E. Bill was quite bowled over by the gorgeous Imelda Robbins, and she seemed to have no inhibitions about flirting with him, in spite of her supposed attachment to Luke. Maybe the stories that Julia had heard about the beautiful houseman were correct, and she was attracted to anything worth looking at in trousers, or to anyone who might advance her career. It was quite a thought.

Julia and Bill lunched in the hospital refectory, a delightful room in the Old House where staff could have their meals in a relaxed atmosphere. It was run like the dining-room of a luxury hotel, and was frequented more by the older and more senior staff, though any Princes resident was welcome to take advantage of the comfortable facilities. The menus were plain, but extremely well cooked and served, and covered most tastes, from meat and fish eaters to vegetarians.

'Stylish,' said Bill, as they ordered their meal.

'Yes, I think that word perhaps sums up Princes Park,' said Julia. 'Stylish.'

* * *

In the afternoon they went back to the flat, where Julia wrote letters, and tried not to think too constantly of Luke and the evening ahead, and Bill caught up with some last-minute revision in preparation for tomorrow's interview.

The weather continued to be stormy for most of the afternoon, although there were occasional flashes of sunshine, and blue skies with high, scudding clouds of snowy-white and gunmetal-grey. During one of the dry periods Julia went out into the garden surrounding the lodge and picked heavy-headed, dripping bronze chrysanthemums, a sturdy display to stand on a windowsill and complement Luke's delicate blue freesias on her desk.

She thought wryly that a psychiatrist would probably say that she was subliminally thinking of Luke as she picked the flowers.

'Hell,' she said out loud to the rain-sodden garden, and smiled to herself. 'There's nothing subliminal about the way I'm thinking. I'm just plain looking forward to seeing Luke tonight, and getting to know him better—just as a friend.' More intimately, you mean, jeered an inner voice, which she tried to ignore. But she couldn't help wondering how last night might have ended if Bill hadn't been around. Would they have remained just friends? Would she have been able or wanted to resist the sophisticated, experienced Luke Steel if he had wanted to seduce her? Would the memory of Howard Snelling have put her off? Had he put her off for good, made her wary of every other man, however attractive and elegant?

For almost the first time in her life, she wished that her twin had been elsewhere, and she could perhaps have discovered the answer to some of her questions. She pushed the thought from her. She was delighted that he might be coming to Princes. They had always been close, and, as the senior registrar's job in ophthalmics also represented a big step up for Bill, then she would be doubly delighted to welcome him to the staff. Anyway, it was probably just as well that she and Luke hadn't been able to experiment, since she was still determined to keep their relationship light.

Luke was picking them up at seven-thirty, though both Bill and Julia had offered to drive to wherever he was planning to take them for dinner. He had been adamant.

'You're my guests,' he'd said. 'And I wouldn't dream of depriving either of you of the delicious wines on offer at the Italian place that I'm taking you to. I'll do the driving.'

It was cold as well as wet, and Julia put on a black velvet trouser suit, for warmth, with a bright-coloured waistcoat and blue wild silk blouse, and splashed on lots of her favourite perfume. Both she and Bill were ready when Luke arrived promptly at seven-thirty.

To Julia's surprise, as she opened the door to him Luke said, without even wishing her good evening, 'You smell nice—flowery; it suits you, that perfume.' He put out a hand and touched her cheek. 'You should wear it always.'

Julia laughed; she was incredibly pleased that he liked it. 'It's my favourite,' she said. 'Thought that I'd try to beat the aromatic scents of an Italian restaurant.' She had a sudden and ridiculous longing to kiss him full on the mouth.

Such a nice mouth, she thought, full and well marked, but very firm. Funny how she was noticing all these things about him now, when, over the months that they'd worked together, she had only seen him as handsome and rather arrogant as a man, and superb and friendly as a doctor.

Once in the sitting-room, Bill brought the conversation down to earth, and gave Julia time to recover herself.

'I've been getting my bearings this morning. We went up the beech hill and looked down on everything, and then had a tour round. It was great,' he told Luke.

'Did Julia show you round A and E?'

'Yes, a neat, very modern unit. Good staff you've got there.'

'Did you meet Imelda Robbins, my houseman, or John Peak, my registrar?'

Bill looked at him a bit warily, as if he expected that this might be a trick question, but Luke was just looking politely interested.

'Your registrar was busy, but I met the gorgeous Dr Robbins. Julia tells me that she's pretty good at her job.'

'Yes. I'll stick my neck out and predict that that young woman's going to go a long way, if she gives herself half a chance and concentrates on work.'

Julia thought that the atmosphere was briefly tense between the two men, and that the reason for it was Imelda. Was Luke warning Bill off? And if so, why? For her sake, as he'd implied, or his?

Fleetingly a wave of sadness tinged with bitterness washed over her, as the possibility occurred to her that Luke was protecting his own personal interest in the young woman doctor. She found herself, against her better judgement, hoping that it wasn't true. So he had taken Imelda out a few times in the past. So what? He was allowed to. His past had nothing to do with her at all.

In the few moments that Julia had been lost in thought, the two men had begun a general conversation about medicine, and the merits of large hospitals like Princes, as opposed to smaller ones. Everything was back to normal, and Julia was left wondering if she had imagined that moment of tension between them.

The restaurant was in Haslemere, some twenty minutes' drive from Princes. It was not very large, all rich velvet hangings and discreet little booths with comfortable padded chairs at the solid tables, and it was aromatic, as Julia had guessed that it might be. The scent of herbs and freshly cooked food met them as they entered.

'Competing with your perfume, Julia,' said Luke softly, as they followed a waiter to the table.

He put a hand on her back at waist-level, to steer her into her chair, and she had difficulty suppressing a shiver of pleasure. The presence of her brother Bill, following behind, however, made her determined not to show her feelings. She was sure that already he was well aware of how she felt about getting to know Luke, and of the tentative, deeper sentiments that were beginning to flourish between them.

They ordered their meals from the elegantly scripted menus that the waiter gave each of them. Julia, who as a vegetarian was frequently used to being offered a rather restricted menu, was delighted with the variety of suitable dishes on offer.

She voiced her pleasure at the long list of fascinating sauces and pasta available.

'There are more dishes here than I've ever come across even in other Italian restaurants,' she said, smiling at Luke.

His eyes were glowing green tonight, dark with pleasure at her pleasure. Their eyes, across the snowy-white tablecloth, locked on to each other. For an instant they were alone at the table. Then Luke murmured, just for her ears, 'I chose this place especially when I learned that you were vegetarian.'

His voice was low and seductive. It was almost as if he were making love to her. Her eyes flickered towards Bill, sitting beside her, but he was absorbed in reading the large menu, and seemed oblivious to his companions.

'Thank you,' Julia said softly to Luke, 'for being so thoughtful.'

'Not at all.' He sat back in his chair and watched her over the top of his menu. 'Take your time,' he said. 'Choose something really exotic.'

She tried out her limited Italian.

'*Va bene*.' She paused. 'Something. . .something. . . *bellissimo*.'

'Yes, Julia, you are *bellissima*.' He, too, flicked a glance in Bill's direction. He leaned across the table. 'Truly beautiful.'

Julia was glad that the lights in the restaurant were dimmed by heavy velvet shades, for she felt herself blushing with enormous pleasure at his remark. She cleared her throat and said in her usual voice, 'I shall have vegetarian *gnocchi* with cream and tomato sauce.'

'And for starters?'

'Oh, garlic bread, please. That is. . .'

'If I have it too?'

'Exactly.'

They laughed together, the implications of the garlic completely understood.

Bill spoke at that moment, and they couldn't be sure if he'd heard the substance of their murmured conversation or not.

'Wonderful place, this, an epicurean delight. May I have the garlic bread as starters, please, mine host,' he said, beaming at Luke. 'And *polpettini* with fried vegetables.'

'*Polpettini*?' asked Julia.

'Meatballs to you, my little ignoramus,' teased Bill. 'But made as only the Italians know how, and in a delicious sauce. Mmm.' He kissed his fingertips suggestively.

'Well,' said Luke, smiling at this easy exchange between brother and sister, 'you've sold me on the *polpettini*. I thought that they seemed. . .mmm. . .' he pursed up his lips as Bill had done, and touched his fingers to his lips, but looked at Julia as he did so, '. . .especially inviting.'

Julia blushed more furiously than before. He's doing it again, she thought, flirting with me like mad, making love to me in a kind of restrained way, the only way possible with a third person present. She gave him a shy smile, wanting to let him know that she understood. He half nodded, and his grey-green eyes widened with pleasure.

'Now, as to wine,' he said, including them both, 'with the food that we're having, I don't think we can better the house wine. It is, in fact, splendid and extremely good quality, and I have that from a friend who is quite a connoisseur. Will that suit?'

The twins nodded in unison.

'Fine by me,' said Bill.

'And me,' echoed Julia, knowing that she would have been intoxicated by mineral water tonight.

The meal was a great success. Bill talked amusingly about his possible chances of landing the senior registrar's post, not exactly monopolising the conversation, but filling in the gaps. Julia and Luke contributed the odd word here and there, but were happy to sit back and study each other silently, and hopefully surreptitiously, letting the conversation flow around them, with either one of them joining in enough to keep the flow going.

Inevitably they ended up talking shop as the meal progressed, though they had agreed at the beginning of the evening not to do so. Bill talked about glaucomas, and the improving methods of dealing with this disease.

'Do you get patients turning up in Casualty,' he asked, 'complaining of stabbing pains in one or both eyes, and believing it to be caused by some outside trauma?'

'Yes, we do from time to time, and we can usually diagnose the problem even before getting an expert down from ophthalmics. We try to explain that a glaucoma is caused by pressure rising within the eye, and destroying the visual nerve fibres. We then reassure them that the condition is largely treatable with drugs or surgery, if caught in time. Fortunately most of the people who come through our department as casualties are experiencing this terrific pain for the first time, but occasionally someone reports in saying that they've had lesser attacks before, and the condition then is usually more advanced,' said Luke.

'Yes, and isn't it a pity that many people soldier on with various aches and pains where the underlying condition could be so much better treated if they gave in earlier?' replied Bill.

'That's human nature,' said Julia. 'You doctors would be surprised at how many people are reluctant to give trouble. You only see them when they've had to give in and seek help, and tell them off for not coming earlier, but you shouldn't, for those who do hang on are often the fighters too, the survivors. Anyway, with the sort of waiting-lists all hospitals have, it's just as well that some people don't rush in every five minutes for treatment.'

'The oracle has spoken,' said Bill, pulling a face.

'And very wisely too,' said Luke, not bothering to conceal his admiration as he looked at her across the table.

Julia got up.

'Excuse me,' she said. 'I must go to the cloakroom.' She picked up her handbag and made for the Ladies.

When she returned some five minutes later, Bill had gone.

'I tried to persuade him to stay for coffee,' said Luke, 'but he flatly refused, saying that he would get a taxi back and that he needed to do a bit more reading before his interview tomorrow.'

'Rubbish,' exclaimed Julia. 'He was working all the afternoon; whatever can he hope to achieve between now and tomorrow? Anyway, it's an interview and not an exam he's going for.'

'All of which I pointed out to him, but he was adamant about going,' said Luke in a dry voice. 'If I didn't know better, I'd say that he had an ulterior motive for making himself scarce, wouldn't you?'

'I don't know what you mean,' she pretended, knowing exactly wht he meant.

'Don't you, Julia?'

She shook her head in pretended ignorance. It was nice to play games once in a while; she was usually so sensible and down-to-earth.

'Oh, come,' said Luke, his voice an octave deeper than usual. 'Isn't it possible that your perceptive brother was giving us time to be alone together?'

She gave in. 'Yes,' she whispered.

'Well, God bless him. Let's make the most of it, then, and have coffee, and talk about us.'

They spent an hour doing just that, talking of incidents that had occurred during their childhoods. Even Luke had a fund of memories up to the time he had been orphaned when he was eight.

Julia's eyes sparkled with tears of compassion as she heard him recount how his parents had taken it in turn to read to him as a small boy.

'How did you learn,' she asked, 'that your parents were dead?'

'My aunt told me, my mother's sister. She was great; she was only twenty herself, but closest to me, since she'd spent quite a bit of time at our house.'

'So she's not much older than you?'

'Jane's dead,' he said in a flat voice. 'She died in an accident two years after my parents. If proper help had been available, she might not have died. Not that I understood that at the time, but it planted the idea of medicine in my mind.'

'Then that's why you're so keen on well equipped ambulances, crash teams and paramedics.'

'That's right. Those first few minutes, and then the next hour or so, are crucial. Not just to survival, but to a fully restored lifeline.'

'Yes,' said Julia quietly. 'That's how I see the role of A and E staff, as immediate sustainers of life, but also as offering the chance of complete recovery.'

She put her coffee-cup down, and Luke took both her hands in his and squeezed them gently. 'I knew you would understand.' He raised her hands to his lips and kissed her knuckles, not once, but several times, and then allowed her to withdraw her hands from his. He took a sip of coffee and looked at her over the rim of his cup, his eyes very dark. 'Will you miss me when I'm away at the conference?' he asked.

She was astonished by the wave of sadness that swept over her at the idea of not seeing him daily, but deliberately avoided a direct answer, surprised by her reaction to his news, and not wanting him to sense it. He was, she reminded herself fiercely, just a friend. 'I thought the conference wasn't until the following week,' she said in a cool voice.

'It lasts a fortnight, but the speaker who was lecturing during the first week can't make it till the following week. I had a phone call asking me to switch, if possible, and do my stint first. It's something of an emergency, or I'd have refused.' He smiled broadly, teasing her, and arched one elegant eyebrow questioningly. 'So will you miss me?' he asked again softly. 'Because to be frank, I have a feeling that I'm going to miss you.' His eyes bored into hers.

His admission surprised her; she hadn't thought that he would be so direct in revealing his feelings.

She opened her mouth to answer, when a waiter appeared, brandishing a coffee-pot.

'More coffee, madam, sir?' he asked.

They both shook their heads, and Luke found a voice, a thick, husky voice.

'No, thank you, no more coffee. The bill, please.'

Julia stood up with an effort, and Luke was immediately round the table and lifting her coat from the back of the chair, and holding it for her to slip her arms into the sleeves. His fingers touched her shoulders, and then her neck, as he straightened her collar. It was like an electric shock. She tingled all over.

'Oh, Julia,' he breathed, and his lips touched the nape of her neck, where her hair, scooped to one side with a comb, left it exposed.

She put up a hand and touched his bent head without turning round.

'Luke,' she said in a trembling, uncertain voice, 'what's happening to us?'

'I believe, dear girl,' he said, speaking into her ear so that his warm breath tickled the lobe, 'that some old chemistry is at work, and we are being drawn together, perhaps against our will.'

They drove home in silence, a silence full of unspoken thoughts and raging emotions.

Arriving at Princes, Luke pulled up in front of the lodge and switched off the softly purring engine. Now it was really silent. Even the wind that had been roaring all the evening dropped suddenly, leaving a dark night sky swept clear of clouds, and filled with flickering stars and an eyebrow of a moon.

Luke released his seatbelt, and turned and did the same for Julia, kissing her on the cheek as he did so.

Julia sat quite still. She felt as if she were in shock. What he had said back in the restaurant had shaken her to the core. Why was it, she wondered, in a detached sort of way, that putting things into words made them seem more real? She must have vaguely known what was happening between them, but until he'd said 'drawn together' she had been able to ignore the steady building up of emotions that she had thought long since buried. Emotions that should never have been stirred churned inside her at the touch of Luke's hand, the sound of his voice.

'It rather hits one for six, does it not?' said Luke, in flat tones. 'I don't know about you, but I'm feeling pole-axed. All I want to do is to take you in my arms and make love to you. I don't feel in the least like I've felt with any other woman for years. If circumstances were different—if we were going to end the evening in your place or mine—perhaps. . .' He shrugged. 'Who knows? Nature would probably take its course. . .'

'And?' murmured Julia.

'Resolve matters for us. The trouble is, having time to stop and think, and neither of us being adolescents, makes one cautious, don't you agree? I feel compelled to try to be sensible, to hold back, to give you a chance, and myself a chance, to come to terms with what seems to be happening to us. I'm not used to long-term relationships.'

'Yes, I feel the same, so unsure of myself. It's

ridiculous; one would think it would be easier to be certain as one gets older.'

'Clearly that's not the case. I suppose the young and innocent have no "past" to make them cautious, whereas we—well, I, at any rate—have.'

'I, too,' said Julia. Luke smiled, a disbelieving, kindly smile, and she added hurriedly, 'Oh, not a lurid past, but a past just the same, and one that I should want to tell you about if. . .'

'If?'

'If we go forward from here.'

'Do you want to?'

'I—I think so. I can't be sure. I wanted us just to be friends.'

'Friends,' he said, and his lips curled into a scornful smile. 'I think that we have passed that point, dear girl. I want to get to know the real you. Not the efficient Sister Manning, but the delicious, desirable Julia.'

'Do you find me desirable?'

'To my surprise, utterly.'

'I think that we'd better say goodnight, Luke,' said Julia in a trembling voice.

He leaned across and kissed her on the mouth, his tongue probing gently, but not urgently, between her lips. Julia let her fingers tangle in his thick black wiry hair as he drew her body as close to himself as the confines of the car would allow. Her taut breasts were hard against the wall of his chest.

After a few minutes they drew apart and, without another word, Luke got out of the car and walked round to the passenger side to open her door.

'I'll see you up,' he said rather abruptly.

'There's no need,' she said conventionally.

'There's every need,' he said firmly, as he gave a small smile.

Outside her flat door they kissed again and clung silently to each other for several minutes.

Luke pushed her resolutely from him. 'Goodnight, my lovely Julia,' he said softly, 'and goodbye for a few days.'

He was frowning as he turned and walked away from her without a backward glance. Julia watched him go and disappear down the stairs.

'Goodnight, my darling,' she said softly as she let herself into her flat.

CHAPTER SIX

THE next few days were going to be hell without Luke, Julia realised as soon as she went on duty. She missed him already. She discovered as the day wore on that she had grown accustomed to hearing his voice, even if she didn't see him, and the very fact that he was there in the building was satisfying, reassuring.

Bill's presence on the Monday helped fill the gap. She encouraged him endlessly over his interview, and when he came back to A and E, certain that he had made irredeemable mistakes during his conversation with his peers, she cheerfully reassured him.

Fortunately for her, although not for the victims, there was an endless stream of injured or ill people to be dealt with all day, and she was frantically busy. Under pressure of work, she was able to blot Luke's absence out of her conscious mind for hours at a time.

The first case to come in after she went on duty was a boy on a bike on his way to school, jostled into the kerb by a passing vehicle which didn't stop. Dealing with this took up some time. The cyclist wasn't too badly injured, as far as they could tell, but the parents had to be located, the police dealt with, and arrangements made for the boy to stay in overnight as he had been concussed.

Next came an elderly lady who had fallen and fractured her femur. The patient was rather deaf, and it took Julia a lot of time and patience to explain that she had broken her hip, and that they were getting hold of her daughter, who would be at the hospital soon.

A baby suffering from convulsions was brought in by a child-minder and was admitted to the paediatric unit while the police tried to locate the parents, who were having a day out in London.

Sandwiched in between these cases was the usual run of patients with foreign bodies in their eyes or ears or throats, which had to be washed, swabbed or plucked out of position.

The pressure began to ease off by late afternoon, and back in her office, doing paperwork, Julia found herself thinking about Luke, wondering what he was doing at that precise moment, and longing for Thursday, when he was due to return. This is only the first day of his absence, she thought wryly, and I'm feeling appallingly bereft. She gave herself a mental shake, and a reminder that she and Luke were only just getting to know each other as people, and that it was ridiculous to feel lonely without him.

She was sitting daydreaming and looking out of the window at the darkening afternoon, and the beginnings of a mist that was rolling across the park, when the telephone rang, making her jump.

She picked up the receiver. 'Casualty,' she said. 'Sister Manning speaking.'

There was a throaty chuckle at the other end of the line, and then Luke's voice said, 'How very proper you sound, Sister Manning.'

'Luke!' She couldn't keep the delight out of her voice. For some reason it hadn't occurred to her that he might telephone. Her heart bumped uncontrollably.

'How are you, Julia? Missing me?'

She gathered the remnants of her pride together.

'We've been busy, you know, usual Monday rush; I haven't had much time to miss you.'

'Liar,' said Luke with great certainty and satisfaction.

'I don't tell lies,' she said stiffly, smiling to herself.

'Not even tiny little white ones that don't matter too much?'

Julia was on the point of saying no, but her innate honesty wouldn't let her.

'Well, not very often,' she admitted. 'Perhaps in a good cause.'

'Am I a good cause, Julia?'

His voice was warm and teasing.

'Let's say that you're a cause, anyway,' she replied, in her turn teasing, but cautious.

'Well, that's something, I suppose. Now tell me, how's Bill doing? Any news yet?'

'No, he's waiting for a decision. Three of those interviewed have been asked to wait, and he's one of them, so he's in with a chance.'

'Oh, that's splendid. I'll ring again tomorrow, before the evening session here.'

'How's it going, the conference?'

'Oh, so-so, a bit early to say yet whether it's going to throw up anything really interesting. Have more news perhaps tomorrow. Wish Bill well for me.'

'Will do.'

There was a small silence; neither of them wanted to ring off.

Luke broke the silence.

'When I get back,' he murmured softly, 'we'll start making up for lost time, and begin getting to know each other properly.'

Properly? What did that mean? There was a knock at her office door.

'Luke, I must go; I'm wanted.'

'Well, that doesn't surprise me. You're always in demand. Goodnight, Julia.'

'Goodnight, Luke.'

They both replaced their receivers at the same moment, just as Bill entered the office. His face told Julia all that she needed to know.

'You've got the job,' she said.

Bill pulled her from the chair and swung her round in his arms.

'Yes, sister, dear, I've got the job,' he said, laughing boyishly. 'Let's celebrate.'

'Oh, Bill, I'm so thrilled for you. It'll be wonderful having you here. Look, if you go away and let me get on with this paperwork I can be off in under an hour. We can phone the parents from my flat, and celebrate at the same time.' She gave him a big kiss on the cheek. 'Oh, Bill, it's wonderful news,' she said.

'I'll give you half an hour, then I'm back with the champers. Where's the nearest off-licence?'

'Down the drive, turn left on the main road; there's an off-licence just past Poachers Inn. Don't come back here; I'll meet you at the flat. And don't get too big a bottle. Remember you've got to drive back tonight.'

'Right, I'm off. Don't be late.'

'See you,' said Julia with a loving and indulgent smile.

She was feeling on top of the world; what with Bill's news, and Luke's phone call, life seemed almost too good to be true. And the knowledge that Luke would be phoning her again tomorrow set the seal on her present happiness.

She settled down to work and made herself put Luke's intriguing call out of her mind, so that she could have a celebratory drink and a meal with Bill. He would have to have something to eat before he left, if only to counteract the champagne, she realised. Should she get him something in the flat, or should they go to the refectory for a meal? One part of her mind mulled this over as she filled in forms and then started on the report.

The sister who was relieving her came on duty a little early, and pressed Julia to go.

'I've heard on the grapevine about your brother getting the ophthalmics job,' she said. 'You must be thrilled to bits.

'Oh, I am. We're going to have a quick celebration before he has to go back to London. That's why I'm only too glad to take you up on your offer, and push off a bit early.'

'On one condition, Manning,' said her colleague, grinning broadly, 'that you introduce me to him the minute he takes up his post. I hear that he's quite a dish.'

'It's a deal,' said Julia with a laugh.

The evening passed in a flash.

Bill had brought in some smoked salmon, lemons and freshly baked brown rolls from the delicatessen in the village when he'd collected the champagne. Julia rustled up a salad, and they sat down to enjoy a delicious supper after they had rung their parents with the news of his success.

Naturally enough, much of the conversation centred on the new job, but just before he left at nine o'clock Bill mentioned the situation between Julia and Luke.

'I didn't realise that you were quite so keen on each other till last night in the restaurant,' he said. 'I thought that you were just getting to know one another.'

'But we are,' said Julia in surprise. 'Sunday was only our second date.'

'So you said, but you gelled so well together, just like a couple; at least, that's the impression that I got. You sort of gravitated towards each other, even when you were sitting on either side of the table.'

'Is that why you pushed off early?'

'Yes, I didn't fancy playing the obtrusive third any longer.' He had been half teasing, but suddenly he was serious. 'It's great to see you happy again, Julia, after last year's fiasco with that skunk Snelling. Don't get hurt this time.'

Julia gave a small laugh. 'It's nice of you to be concerned, Bill, but don't worry; nothing's going to go wrong this time. I'm older and wiser, and intend being cautious, even with Luke, though no one could be more different than he is from Howard.'

'Well, Steel seems a nice bloke, but I imagine that he's quite a guy with the females, a wealthy bachelor consultant with his looks. He must be considered quite a catch.'

'That's true, and he makes no secret of the fact that he plays the field, but I'm sure that he wouldn't cheat if we had a relationship, which,' she added hastily, 'we haven't; we're——'

'Just good friends; yes, I know.' He gave her a hug.

'Anyway, I'll soon be here to keep a brotherly eye on you, and I'll expect a regular report on progress.'

'And that, dear brother, is a reciprocal situation, don't forget. Judging by what I've heard so far about the reaction of the fair sex in this establishment to your imminent arrival, I shall have my work cut out keeping an eye on you.'

Bill pulled a face of pretended horror at the suggestion, and on this happy note he left for London.

Lying in bed waiting for sleep to come, turning over in her mind the events of the last few days, Julia thought of Howard Snelling and of Luke. There were comparisons—they both liked woman and pursued them—but there were also important differences. She had a gut feeling that if Luke committed himself to anyone he wouldn't rat on them as Howard had ratted on her. And surely Luke wouldn't force his sexual attentions on an unwilling partner, as Howard had tried to do when she broke off their engagement.

The memory of that last encounter made her grimace and left a nasty taste in her mouth. Fortunately she had been sensible enough to ignore his sneering remark, 'You've never been very good at it. You're frigid; you never give anything.' She knew that that wasn't true, and common sense told her that it was because she'd been trying to please the wrong man, not because there was anything wrong with her sexuality.

The experience, though it hadn't put her off sex, had soured her feelings about falling in love. She wasn't afraid of love or sex, but she was afraid of choosing the wrong person to share her love with.

What she had to decide before letting a relationship

develop between herself and Luke was whether he was the right man for her. She thought about him as a possible lover, and was suddenly consumed with a longing to feel his hands on her body, caressing her intimately as his own longing took possession of him. Readily she could envisage making whole-hearted physical as well as emotional love to him. He would be gentle and powerful and romantic. She knew, deep inside her, that she would welcome and respond to Luke's lovemaking.

So did that mean, she asked herself—that she was in love with the man? She couldn't be sure, drawn as she was to him. Maybe it was only chemistry that had for some reason manifested itself months after they had first met.

Perhaps only time would tell.

She fell asleep at last, with merging pictures of Luke, Bill and Howard filling her dreams.

Tuesday was quiet, with the usual stream of patients turning up for treatment. There was a minor accident from the motorway, with nobody badly hurt, just cuts and bruises, but brought in by the police because there was an 'incident' that had to be sorted.

Julia had put herself on a split duty to cover the evening, as there was a floodlit football match on in Princes North which often produced a few injured spectators for A and E.

She arrived back on duty early, ready to receive Luke's promised call. All day she had tried to put him out of her mind; now, against her will, the knowledge that she would shortly hear his voice sent her pulse-rate galloping.

Looking her usual calm self, she relieved Dan Beatty, who had been in charge over the afternoon.

'Nothing much to report,' he said when she appeared. 'There's a guy waiting to go to X-Ray, query fractured radius and/or ulna. Some bricks fell on his forearm on the building site where he's working. Then there's a kid in cubicle five who's got minor burns to his legs, from playing about with a bonfire. The burns are being dressed, but he's only marginally shocked, and John says that he can go home soon. And the old lady who is confused, and who came in before you went off this afternoon, is still waiting to be collected. And that's the lot at the moment, apart from a few people waiting to be seen, but nothing dramatic.'

'Right, you whiz off, Dan; I'll take it from here.'

'I'm gone already,' said Dan, leaving the office fast.

Luke phoned a few minutes later.

'I wasn't sure whether I would catch you,' he said immediately. 'I'm a bit earlier than yesterday, but I'm booked for drinks with someone before dinner, and a late session.'

'Like the poor, I'm always around,' she said, bubbling over with happiness at hearing his voice. However hard she tried, she couldn't prevent her pleasure from creeping into her voice. She tried to bring herself down to earth by saying matter-of-factly, 'You sound husky.'

'I'm not surprised; I've been lecturing almost non-stop.'

'Have you got a sore throat?'

'Yes, it's slightly sore.'

'Have you taken anything for it?'

'No, I haven't, Nurse. Stop fluttering like a mother hen, and tell me how Bill got on.'

'He got the job! Isn't it wonderful? He starts in six weeks' time.'

'Well, I'm thrilled for you, Julia, and I bet your parents are thrilled, too.'

'Yes, they're over the moon, already planning a family celebration.'

'How splendid, a family get-together in Bill's honour.'

Julia thought that she detected a wistful note in his voice, and her heart went out to him. It was difficult to imagine somebody without a family to rejoice with, but he had no one close; even the elderly relatives who had cared for him were dead.

She made a bold decision.

'When you get back,' she said, 'if we can get some time off together I'd like to take you home to meet my mother and father.'

There was a moment's silence. Oh, lord, she thought, I've blown it. I'm pushing too hard, too soon. I've put him on a spot. What a daft suggestion.

Then Luke's voice came over, sounding croakier than ever.

'How kind.' He paused. 'Do you really want me to meet them?'

Julia gathered her courage. What the hell? She'd said it now, might as well be honest.

'Oh, yes,' she said. 'I definitely do.'

'Well, thank you. I shall look forward to that immensely and hold you to it.'

'You don't need a show of force. I keep my promises,' she said with a small laugh.

'I'm sure you do.' He paused again, and she heard him muffling a cough. 'Look, I must go now. I'm ringing from the conference hall, and there's someone waiting to use the phone.'

'Well, you've talked long enough with that throat. Look after yourself, Luke.'

'Will do, and you, Julia. I'll try to ring tomorrow. Goodnight.'

'Goodnight.'

As before, they put their receivers down in unison.

She hoped that he would find time to phone her on Wednesday, but took comfort from the fact that he would be back on Thursday night. Perhaps he would ring her from his home.

He didn't ring on Wednesday. She was in the unit all day as they were so busy. A thick autumn fog had suddenly descended at dusk, which should have brought the motorway traffic to a slow crawl, but which instead had resulted in a pile-up of fast-moving vehicles.

The police, arriving just after the ambulances with the third series of injured persons, were scathing about drivers not slowing down in spite of warning signs.

'They just go on regardless,' said a police sergeant, 'ignoring everything.'

He sounded and looked fed up, which wasn't surprising, since this latest accident had produced a mother and baby fatality, and a husband and young girl horrifically injured.

Both father and daughter were admitted to the intensive care unit, while the police set about finding relatives or friends of the family.

When Julia finally went off duty after endlessly giving injections, and dressing cut limbs and broken skulls, it was past eight o'clock. There had been no word from Luke, and she was almost too tired and dispirited to care, though in her heart she knew that a phone call from him would have lifted her spirits. She consoled herself with the thought that she couldn't have spent any time speaking to him, even if he had phoned.

She had a hot bath, fell asleep in front of the television, bestirred herself at half-past ten, took herself off to bed, and slept soundly all night.

When she woke the following morning it was to find that the fog had lifted and had given way to more rain and wind, though the weather forecast was for a mild and sunny afternoon.

She sang as she got ready to go to work, happy that it was Thursday and Luke would be returning, although she had no idea at what time. He wasn't due on duty till Friday, but she was sure that he would at least phone her when he arrived home.

Luke rang her in the early afternoon. 'I'll see you at about seven,' he said in a hoarse whisper. 'May I call at the lodge?'

Thrilled to hear his voice, and even more thrilled at the prospect of seeing him that evening, Julia nevertheless felt that she ought to put him off. Obviously the sore throat that he'd had on Tuesday had worsened, and the best thing that he could do was to go home and go to bed.

She said, 'You sound as though you should be in bed, Luke, not visiting after a tiring journey.'

'Do you want to see me?'

'Oh, Luke, you must know that I do, very much.'

'Then that's all there is to it. I won't stay long, just time enough to say hello. All right?'

'All right, but once here you must stay for supper; you'll need it after travelling.'

* * *

Julia got herself off duty just before six, rushed down to the lodge, showered and changed into a red cashmere sweater and corduroy trousers, and was ready to prepare supper by six-thirty.

Thinking of Luke's sore throat, she decided to give him soup as a starter. It would have to be tinned, but, laced with sherry, should be quite drinkable. For the main course she made a quick recipe macaroni cheese, which smelt delicious as it began to brown under the grill, and for pudding decided on fresh tangerines with ice-cream. Nothing there that he wouldn't be able to swallow.

The coffee was just percolating perfectly when the intercom sounded, and moments later Luke was ringing at the door of her flat.

Julia, her heart thumping madly and a wide smile on her face, opened the door.

Luke stood there, looking gaunt and ill. He was shivering, and he was not alone. Beside him stood a tall, elegant-looking female with a slight, peevish smile on her coldly classical face.

For the briefest possible moment Julia was stunned into silence, and then she opened the door wider, and said, 'Good evening,' in a perfectly normal voice, smiling at the Nordic beauty by Luke's side. 'Please, do come in. Luke, go and sit down; you look dreadful.'

'He shouldn't have come up,' said his companion in a cross voice. 'But he insisted.'

Luke walked slowly to the nearest chair, and sank down upon it.

'Julia, sorry about this,' he croaked. 'I'm afraid that my condition has rather worsened since I spoke to you earlier. Grace kindly drove me down—she didn't think that I was up to driving myself—and I must say that I was grateful for the offer.' He gave them both the semblance of a smile. 'Grace is an old friend and colleague, who was by great good fortune at the conference, and took pity on me.' He looked from her to Julia. 'Let me introduce you to each other. Ms Grace Townsend, Julia Manning, manager of our accident and emergency unit.'

The two women shook hands rather warily.

'It was kind of you to drive Luke all the way back,' said Julia.

'Not at all,' replied Grace coolly. 'It was the least I could do, since we are such old and close friends.' Her large pale blue eyes seemed to Julia to harden. 'We go back a long way, and anyway, I planned visiting Princes. It was meant to be a surprise for Luke after he'd spoken at the conference next week. I didn't know that he was switching with the first lecturer.'

Luke said huskily, 'The coffee smells good, Julia. Is it ready?'

'Percolated to perfection,' she said quietly, grateful for the interruption. 'I'll fetch it.'

She went through to the kitchen. What was this Grace woman implying? she asked herself. She spoke almost as if there was something special between her and Luke, or had been. So what if there had been? His past is nothing to do with me. But his past turning up now might be, nagged a small voice. She had so looked forward to Luke's return, to pursuing the intimacy that they had developed over their few phone calls, and she knew that Luke had felt the same. Had he really needed someone to drive him back, or had the Nordic beauty forced herself on him? That, she had to admit, was unlikely; she couldn't see Luke agreeing to the arrangement if he didn't want to. Well, only time would tell how matters stood, or had stood, between them; she would have to be patient. At least he had insisted on visiting her on his way home; that was some small comfort.

She returned from the kitchen with the tray. 'Now, hot coffee first, and then something to eat when you feel up to it, Luke.'

'Oh, we won't stay to eat,' said Grace firmly. 'I've got to get Luke home and in bed as soon as possible. He needs rest, warmth and probably antibiotics. I shall phone his GP when we get to his cottage.'

Luke said just as firmly, though hoarsely, 'I'll phone my GP, Grace. You just get me home after I've finished my coffee.' He smiled at Julia and took a sip of the fragrant liquid. 'This is delicious. I'm so sorry that I can't do justice to a meal, but I'm afraid Grace is right: the only sensible thing for me to do is to go home to bed and start on a course of antibiotics. My chap will probably give me umbrella cover to start with, and then perhaps decide on something specific after doing tests. I've certainly got a chest bug of some sort, or more likely a spot of viral pneumonia.'

'Well, at least it's more treatable than flu,' said Julia, pleased that he had made the point about talking to his doctor himself, and not through Grace, who so obviously wanted to keep matters in her own hands. He clearly felt indebted to her for making the long drive down from the north, and there was certainly a rapport between them, but were they, or had they been, really important to each other, or just close colleagues?

She was even more pleased when he said, 'Let's be grateful for small mercies,' and touched her hand in a gentle and familiar gesture, as if emphasising his closeness to her. 'Come and see me tomorrow; I'm going to be off for a bit, I'm afraid. Will you explain the situation to John Peak first thing?'

'Of course. But you will be in touch with him later, won't you? He's a super registrar, but inclined to be touchy about protocol. He'll expect to hear from you direct.'

'Naturally. Give him my apologies, ask him if he can continue to cover for me, and tell him I'll ring as soon as I've got some treatment sorted out and might have an idea when I'll be back in business. I'm sure he'll understand. I just don't think that I can tackle any other problems pro tem.' Suddenly Luke looked infinitely weary, and his drawn face was glistening with perspiration. 'Look, Julia, I'll leave it to you; say and do what you think. I have every confidence in your judgement. All I want to do is get to my bed, and fight off this beastly bug.'

Grace, who throughout this exchange had sipped at her coffee, put down her cup briskly.

'Well, thank goodness you've come to your senses, Luke,' she said sharply. 'That's what you have staff for, so you can delegate. Now let's get going, and leave Sister Manning in peace.'

'Julia,' reminded Luke. 'Not Sister Manning; we're off duty.' He was still touching Julia's arm, and now, as he stood up, transferred his hand to her wrist and pulled her towards him. 'Come and see me tomorrow.'

'Will do.' On an impulse she stretched up and kissed him on the cheek. 'Take care,' she said softly.

'I will.'

'I'll see that he does,' said Grace coldly. 'Let's get going, Luke. The sooner you're home and in bed, the better.'

Luke said as fiercely as his throat would allow, 'Don't fuss, Grace; I'm coming.' He gave Julia a lop-sided smile. 'Take care of the shop, and don't forget to report in tomorrow.'

'I won't.' She was sure that, had they been alone, he would have kissed her then, if he'd had the strength.

But he didn't; he simply squeezed her wrist a little tighter and, with a gleam in his eyes, said, 'Promise?'

'Promise!'

Grace moved restlessly from one foot to the other, and Luke turned and gave her a sharp look.

'Sorry to keep you, Grace,' he said drily, 'after you have been so kind, but Julia went to a lot trouble preparing a meal. I hate to rush away without making proper apologies.'

Julia shook her head. 'It was nothing,' she said. 'I'm sorry you feel so poorly. Let's hope that once you start on some medication you'll feel better.'

'I'm bound to,' he said. 'I'll soon be back to normal.'

Grace gave an exasperated sigh. 'Not unless you hurry up and get home to bed,' she said in a flat voice.

'Grace is right,' said Julia. 'Do go and rest. I'll see you tomorrow, and don't worry about the unit. Everything will be fine.'

'Right. Goodnight, Julia.'

'Goodnight, Luke, Grace.' Julia smiled at them both as she opened the flat door. 'Go carefully,' she added as she watched them descend the stairs. 'It's quite foggy.'

Luke, following behind Grace, turned for a moment halfway down the stairs, and raised his hand in a farewell gesture, and then touched his fingers to his lips.

'Goodnight,' he mouthed silently.

Julia stayed on the small landing until the sound of the car engine in the quiet night faded away, but not until it had did she go back into the flat and close the door.

She cleared away the food she had prepared, generally tidied up, and then watched, without really taking it in, her favourite programme on television. Eventually she switched off the set and went to bed, expecting to lie awake for hours mulling over the evening's events, and especially the significance of the presence of Grace Townsend. But she didn't. Amazingly, she fell into a deep and dreamless sleep the moment that her head touched the pillow. Her last thoughts were of Luke looking lean, handsome and rather predatory, with his beaky, prominent nose much in evidence in his drawn face, as he had turned on the stairs and wished her a last goodnight. How foolish and wonderful of him to visit her when he was feeling so ill; no wonder Grace had been so cross with him for insisting on doing so.

She was awoken the next morning by the telephone ringing, and when she picked up the receiver she heard Luke speaking in a whisper.

'Julia, as I expected, I won't be able to get in today. Conciliate John Peak and ask him to continue to cover for me, please, as we discussed, and tell him that I'll phone later. My GP visited last night and confirmed pneumonia, though it doesn't seem severe, thank God, and is easily treatable, or he'd get my good friend Gregory Hurst in for a second opinion. Our esteemed medical director is, after all, the local guru where chests are concerned. But fortunately that won't be necessary. The worst should be over in a few days, though it'll be a while longer before I'm back at work.'

'I'm glad your doctor's got it in hand,' she said, somehow controlling the tremor in her voice as she thrilled to the sound of his. 'Take care, Luke; I'll be thinking about you. Don't speak any more; save your strength.'

She didn't want to stop talking to him, but knew that she must for his sake. She was about to ring off when Luke coughed and said huskily, 'You are coming to see me today, as promised, aren't you?'

'Of course,' she said immediately, and then remembered. 'But I don't know where you live, Luke.'

'Thatches, Friday Street; go east from the end of Princes drive. And Julia, do come before five if you can. Mrs Crowe, my daily housekeeper, will be here. She's a treasure. She'll let you in.'

'Right. Take care.'

She rang off to stop Luke trying to talk further. He really must take care of that raw throat, she thought, trying to be down to earth and serious. But she couldn't stop her heart bounding with delight at the thought of seeing him, even sick and bed-bound, in the knowledge that he wanted to see her. She was thrilled to bits, and this feeling remained with her as she prepared for work.

The thought dawned on her as she was getting showered and dressed that Grace Townsend might have stayed at the cottage overnight. She had seemed determined to take control of his care last night. But if she had, it didn't seem, from what Luke had said about his housekeeper being in the house during the afternoon, that she would be around then. She hoped not, though even this possibility failed to squash her elation at the prospect of seeing Luke.

This warm, glowing feeling at the mere thought of seeing someone must be what being in love is all about, she thought. In love? She pulled herself up with a jolt. She wasn't in love with Luke; she couldn't be. They were only just getting to know each other, in spite of having worked together for months. They were just good friends, as she'd explained to Bill.

And Luke had said nothing about love. He'd made it plain that he liked her, admired her, wanted to get to know her better, but he hadn't said, 'I love you,' and neither had she. They had come a long way in a comparatively short time, and there was definitely something special in their relationship, but love? She mustn't anticipate that, not until she was a hundred per cent sure of him and he of her. She wouldn't repeat the Howard Snelling fiasco and fall in love with the wrong man, or with a man with a roving eye, or a man with too fond a memory for old girlfriends, showing up out of the blue. This time everything must be right for loving, or temptation must be avoided altogether.

On this rather sobering resolution she accelerated up the hill between the line of Spanish chestnut trees turning red and gold in the October sunshine, making up her mind, as she turned into the staff car park, to concentrate on work, and only work, for the next few hours.

CHAPTER SEVEN

THE moment she arrived in the department, Julia became involved with an aggressive alcoholic. At first he was reeling round the waiting area, bending over worried patients and being obnoxious, but keeping his aggression verbal. Suddenly, however, just as Julia and Dan approached, speaking quietly and trying to persuade him to enter one of the cubicles, he became violent, lashing out at both of them.

John Peak was in the nearest cubicle, and rushed out to help, as did one of the staff nurses. Between the four of them they got the man under some sort of control, but not before he had caught Julia a glancing blow on the side of her face. By the time the man had vomited, been given an injection, and was reasonably quiet, Julia's face was red and slightly swollen.

'Here, let me have a look at that,' said John. 'Make sure that the skin isn't broken. That bloke's hands were none too clean.'

They went into one of the cubicles, and John examined her cheek carefully.

'There's the tiniest of cuts on your cheekbone just below your left eye, but it only needs a spot of antiseptic cream on it, I think. But you're going to have a nasty bruise, Julia, and it might even extend to a black eye of sorts. Let's just have a look at your pupils and make sure that the jarring didn't cause any damage.' He examined her eyes with the ophthalmoscope, paying special attention to the one on the damaged side of her face. 'They're fine,' he said, as she had expected, and added in his rather pedantic fashion, 'But as you well know, you can't be too careful about a blow to the head.'

'No, of course you can't, John; thanks for looking at me. I'll have to fill in the staff accident book. Will you sign it, please, later?'

'Of course.' John looked at his watch. 'I wonder where Luke is. It's not like him to turn up late without letting me know.'

'John, I'm sorry. I haven't had a minute to tell you, but Luke won't be in today. He's off sick. A mild case of pneumonia, according to his doctor. He phoned me just as I was leaving this morning, and asked if I'd give you the message. He wants you to hold the fort, please, said he'd speak to you later.'

John Peak looked hurt or offended, or both, as she had feared.

'Of course it's not your fault, Julia, you had to know as manager, but I think the boss might have spoken to me personally.'

Time for one of those little white lies that Luke had teased her about, thought Julia. Well, this was definitely in a good cause, keeping her boss and his registrar on good terms.

'Your phone was busy, John, and his throat was so bad that I think he was afraid of losing his voice altogether if he didn't leave the message with me.' She crossed her fingers behind her back and hoped that John would be convinced.

Apparently he was, for his face cleared at once, and he looked his normal, rather sedate and pleasant self.

'Oh, of course, I didn't think of that; the phone was busy. Now I must get back to work. Are you sure you feel OK, Julia?'

'I'm fine,' she replied, heaving a sigh of relief. 'I'll write up the accident book, and then I'll be with you.'

The morning sped past, and then much of the afternoon, and it was after three before Julia was free. She rushed off duty, and changed into a tan skirt and blue sweater in the space of twenty minutes, then set off to look for Thatches. In spite of her determination to be cool and careful about allowing herself to fall in love, she had difficulty in suppressing a rising tide of excitement at the thought of seeing Luke.

His directions had been clear, and within a short while she had found the thatched cottage, tucked away in a lane leading off the main road.

She parked in the driveway beside the house and walked round the hedged garden to where a wooden gate gave on to a brick path leading to the front door.

She was only halfway up the path when the door was flung open by a teenage girl in tight jeans and a red cotton T-shirt that strained across her pert breasts.

'Yes?' she asked sharply. 'What do you want? The doctor's ill, can't see anybody.'

She stood there filling the doorway, hands on slim hips, an aggressive, fierce young woman, looking little more than a schoolgirl.

Surely this couldn't be Mrs Crowe, Luke's treasure of a housekeeper? This girl looked more like a bright-eyed, full-breasted robin.

'Are you Mrs Crowe?' she asked. 'The doctor is expecting me.'

'You Sister Manning from the hospital?' asked the girl, ignoring Julia's question.

'Yes,' replied Julia, trying a friendly smile, which clearly didn't work, as the girl, though she moved slightly to one side, only grudgingly opened the door wider to let her in. 'How is Dr Steel this afternoon, Mrs Crowe?'

'You've got to be joking,' said the young woman. 'D'ya think that I look like a Mrs anybody? My mum's Mrs Crowe; I'm Mandy.'

Julia was relieved. Thank goodness this girl-cum-woman wasn't Luke's housekeeper. The idea of Mandy looking after him daily, making his bed, washing his clothes, was unthinkable.

'Oh, you're holding the fort for your mother.'

'That's right. She's gone shopping for the doctor. He's pretty sick, you know. I don't think that he ought to have visitors. If it was up to me, I'd say no visitors.' She looked unflinchingly at Julia, as if daring her to disagree.

Julia didn't know whether to laugh, or to be angry. It was quite obvious that the girl had a crush on Luke, and was being over-protective, especially, she guessed, where female visitors were concerned.

She said placatingly, 'But I'm a nurse, you see. Not like an ordinary visitor. The doctor needs to see me about his work at the hospital.'

It was amazing the change that came over Mandy. The disappearing frown left her face clear and almost childish, and very pretty

'Oh, that's different; it's what you might call business, I suppose. You're not like the other woman who was here this morning, supposed to be a doctor. Didn't look like a doctor.'

'Well, I am a nurse, I assure you.' In fairness she added, 'And if the lady's name was Townsend, then she is a doctor; I can vouch for it.'

'Oh, well, I suppose she is, said she was a friend of the doctor's.' The girl gave an exaggerated sniff. 'Would you like a cup of tea? I was just gong to make one for the doctor. He's got to have lots of fluids, to help his temperature come down, so his doctor told him. Isn't it funny, a doctor having a doctor?'

While she was talking, Mandy was leading the way through a long, low, comfortable sitting-room, with casement windows at both ends, beams across the ceiling and a number of prints and original paintings on the walls. It was an orange and brown room. An autumn room, Julia decided. A fitted mushroom-coloured carpet stretched the length of the room, and old-fashioned looking easy-chairs covered in autumnal-tinted cretonne were dotted around. In front of the wide brick fireplace filled with huge logs of wood stood a rich brown leather button settee, with orange cushions ranged along its length.

There were several doors leading from the sitting-room, and one of these Mandy opened to reveal a short, narrow staircase leading to the floor above.

'The doctor's up there, second door along the right-hand passage. I'll bring the tea up in a jiffy. He's having his with lemon. Do you want yours like that, or ordinary with milk?'

'I'd love lemon, please.'

Julia started up the stairs, unaccountably feeling

nervous about seeing Luke now that the chattering little Mandy was no longer there.

Don't be such a fool, she told herself. You're just visiting a friend and colleague who is sick.

But that, she knew, was not quite true. They had got beyond the just good friends stage, in spite of last night, and Grace's presence at the flat.

Where, she found herself wondering, was Grace? Had she stayed the night, or had she left once his GP had called? Mandy had said that Dr Townsend was here this morning, but perhaps she had just been visiting. She had no idea; only Luke could give her the answer.

She tapped at the door, and heard a muffled, 'Come in.'

Luke was lying half propped up against a mound of untidy-looking pillows. 'Thank goodness it's you,' he said throatily. 'I thought for a moment it was Mandy, my ministering angel, come to torment me with more suggestions for improving my condition.'

Julia looked towards the door and put a finger to her lips.

'She'll be coming with tea any minute now. The poor girl, she's got a crush on you, and she's only trying to help, you know. She has your best interests at heart.'

Luke gave a theatrical groan.

'I know,' he croaked. 'She has ten times more brain than her mother, but half the practical efficiency.'

Julia looked down on Luke and then, without thinking and very naturally, bent swiftly and kissed him on his hot forehead.

'You've got a hell of a temperature,' she said, 'but it won't hurt you to move. At the risk of making you furious, I'm going to suggest that you visit the bathroom while I'm here, and have a wash and brush-up, while I tidy your bed and turn your pillows and so on. OK?'

Luke looked at her in pretended horror. 'My God,' he said, 'you are infinitely worse than Grace, who is a splendid doctor but a rotten nurse. At least she had the sense to retire to Poachers after my doctor visited last night, and didn't start chivvying me around.'

Julia felt a surge of relief at hearing that Grace had not spent the night at the cottage.

'Well, each to our own trade,' she said lightly, holding up Luke's dressing-gown as he got out of bed. 'Making patients comfortable is a nurse's work. Now go and make yourself presentable; you'll feel tons better afterwards.'

'Just as you say, Sister,' he said with pretended reluctance, pulling a face.

He had just disappeared when Mandy arrived with a tray of tea and biscuits.

'Dr Steel is in the bathroom,' explained Julia. 'Just leave the tray if you will, and I'll make sure that he drinks his tea.'

'I'd better make his bed while I'm here,' said Mandy, bustling across the room.

'No, it's all right,' said Julia. 'I'll see to it. I'm sure you have other things to do.'

'Well, if you're sure,' said Mandy dubiously, 'that you can manage.'

'Leave it with me,' said Julia kindly, giving the girl a friendly smile.

Mandy nodded. 'OK,' she said, and left the room.

Julia whipped over to the bed, stripped off the duvet

and sheets, turned the mattress, and was tucking in the bottom sheet when Luke reappeared.

'Sit there,' she said, 'by the window for a minute, while I finish the bed.'

'Yes, Sister, no Sister, three bags full Sister,' he said raspily through his painful throat. 'Perhaps I'd be better off left to Mandy's ministrations.'

'Shall I call her?' enquired Julia sweetly.

Luke sat down gingerly in the chair by the window. 'You dare, woman,' he said, with a sardonic grin.

Julia relented. 'I won't be a minute,' she said. 'Bear with me; I'm going to make an armchair with your pillows, prop you up well, to help your chest.'

'I'm sure it will be worth waiting for.'

'Of course it will.' She busied herself with the sheets and pillows. 'There, all ready; you can hop in now.'

'I'll stay here a bit longer,' he said decisively, settling himself back in the chair.

'No,' she replied, equally decisive. 'You're on bed rest, remember, your own doctor's orders.'

'My dear girl, I am a doctor too. Do allow me a little leeway in interpreting orders.'

Julia said firmly, 'I shall go, Luke, unless you get back to bed now. I didn't split my guts getting here to give you tea and sympathy, but professional support, friendly help and—' she bent down over the chair, her smoky blue eyes smouldering as she looked into his '—advice,' she added emphatically.

Without warning, he snaked a hand up and pulled her head down on a level with his, and pressed her cool cheek momentarily against his hot one, and then cupped her face with both hands. 'Julia,' he whispered huskily, 'you're wonderful. Such passion. You're a real little virago when you get going, aren't you?'

'You'd better believe it. Either you go back to bed or. . .'

'Or what?' He smiled, and brushed his thumbs gently over her cheekbones, and she winced as he touched the bruised area. 'What's wrong?' he asked sharply as she straightened up and took a step backwards. The light from a wall lamp already on against the afternoon gloom fell across her face.

'You're hurt,' Luke exclaimed angrily. 'How the hell did that happen?' He rose to his feet and stepped towards her.

'It's nothing,' she said, touched by his anger. 'Someone—a drunk—socked me this morning, that's all.'

'That's all? And what the hell was everyone else doing while you were getting beaten up? Where the devil were Peak and Beatty?' He grasped her arms and pulled her nearer the lamplight. Being ill had not apparently affected his strength, as he held her in a grip of iron.

'John Peak's seen it. It's perfectly all right, I assure you. There's no real damage. It's just a bit sore.'

Luke took no notice of this remark, but looked hard and long at the bruise and softly tested the slight swelling and cut beneath her eye with long, gentle fingers.

'Hmph,' he said at last. 'Should never have happened, but there doesn't seem to be too much damage, thank God.' He put his hands on Julia's shoulders and pulled her close, dropping a kiss on the top of her head. 'Such lovely hair,' he murmured. 'Burnished chestnut. Why don't you let it down the way you did when we went out to supper? You're not on duty now.' His fingers plucked the comb and clips that held her neat chignon in place, and her hair cascaded in a bright curtain down her neck and framed her face.

'Beautiful,' he murmured, running his fingers through the heavy, shining mass of hair. She shivered with a deep and wondering pleasure at his touch. He tilted her face to meet his and showered small, hot-lipped kisses on her cheeks, and chin, and nose and brow. 'When I've got rid of this beastly bug I shall make a much better job of this with proper kisses,' he said softly.

She leaned against him, her heart thumping, her legs useless, almost giving way. His body felt hot beneath the thin silk dressing-gown. He'd got a fever; he must go back to bed. She tried to say as much, but he trailed a finger across her lips, and shook his head. His grey-green fathomless eyes caught and held hers for an immeasurable period of time, the quiet ticking of the small clock on the bedside cabinet receded, and a thick, meaningful silence possessed them and the room as they drowned in each other's gaze.

It was Julia who broke the spell first, carefully and reluctantly easing herself away from Luke's febrile body.

'I haven't long,' she whispered. 'I'm on duty this evening.'

Luke looked down at her, his eyes still glowing. 'Just as well,' he said gruffly. 'You're sending my temperature sky-high.' He brushed another kiss across her forehead.

'You must go back to bed,' she said unsteadily, resisting the temptation to snuggle up against him again, and hear the wild drumming of his heartbeats, and run her fingers through the curly, silky hair on his chest, just visible in the V of his pyjama jacket. She could imagine the feel and look of it as it tapered down towards his navel. Strong black masculine hair. . .

'Your wish is my command, dear, lovely Sister Manning. To hear is to obey.' He strolled towards the bed, slipped out of his dressing-gown, and sank back against the neat armchair of pillows that Julia had arranged. 'Bliss,' he said softly. 'Absolute bliss.' He closed his eyes, and added, 'Would be heaven if you were beside me.' He patted the bed and opened his eyes glinting with humour. 'Can I tempt you, Florence Nightingale?'

She didn't need tempting, she thought; she was ready to fling herself down beside him, and let him make wild, passionate love to her. Not that there was any question of that with Luke's high temperature, and his occasional rasping breaths, but the thought filled her with delight. Her self-cautioning thoughts about falling in love deserted her. With a surge of excitement she realised that she was on the verge of wanting sex, of longing for this tall, handsome man to teach her all the nuances of sexual fulfilment.

She said shakily, but trying to sound in command, 'Regretfully, can't be done, Luke. I have to go soon, and you need your rest. You look all in; you've done enough.'

It was true. His hot skin, with a sheen of sweat glistening on it, was pulled taut across his face, throwing up planes and shadows in the lamplight. His eyes looked more piercing but more sunken than usual. He was still a sick man needing rest.

She moved over to the bed and bent swiftly to kiss his burning forehead. 'I'll come again tomorrow, and stay longer,' she whispered. 'Don't forget to drink plenty. Have some more orange juice now.' She poured juice into the glass and held it to his lips, and he gulped it down greedily.

'Thanks,' he said as he emptied the glass. 'You're a great nurse, Florrie.' He chuckled, but his chuckle turned into a cough. When it subsided he said, 'That is a promise, about coming tomorrow?'

'Of course. I'll take the afternoon and evening off.'

'We can have supper together.'

'If you're well enough.'

'I've only got a mild pneumonia. It's being treated; I'll be on the mend tomorrow.'

He was obviously determined to treat his condition lightly.

'Right.' She smiled rather tremulously, not wanting to leave him. It had been magic being with him even for a short while.

'Goodnight, love, see you tomorrow.' His eyes were drooping with fatigue, but he found her hands and kissed both palms before letting them go.

'Goodnight, Luke, sleep well.' Quietly she let herself out of the room and made her way downstairs.

Mrs Crowe was back from her shopping trip and busy unpacking a pile of groceries.

Mandy, who in spite of the abrasive welcome she had first given Julia had good manners, introduced her mother.

'This is my mum,' she said, and to Mrs Crowe, 'This is the nice nurse who came to see the doc, Sister Manning.'

The two women shook hands. Mrs Crowe, thought Julia, was much more what she had expected of a treasure of a housekeeper. She was a motherly-looking woman in her fifties, neatly dressed and quietly made up with a little powder and lipstick, a proper house-keeper who could be relied upon to look after Luke in any circumstances.

'It is nice to meet you, Mrs Crowe, and I feel happier now that I know that Dr Steel is in such good hands, yours and Mandy's.' Mandy looked pleased. 'May I ask you to do me a favour?'

Mrs Crowe nodded, and said, 'Anything if it will help the doctor. He's such a nice man, lovely to work for.'

'Well, if I leave my telephone number, both the casualty department one and my personal number, will you phone me at any time if you think that he's poorly, but not ill enough to get the doctor?'

'Yes, of course, Sister, any time. In fact it would be a relief to know that there was someone else I could call on.'

'Thank you. I wish I could stay now, but I'm due back on duty. Will you be off soon, Mrs Crowe?'

'Oh, no, I'm going to stay on a bit tonight, Sister, to make sure that the doctor has some hot soup. They can manage at home for once, and Mandy's going to help me here.'

'That's awfully good of you, Mrs Crowe, and you, Mandy. I'm sure that the doctor wil be very grateful. Tomorrow I hope to be here for the evening and prepare supper if I can arrange time off, so you'll certainly be able to get away on time then.'

Mandy said, 'You don't have to worry; Mum and I

can take care of the doc. I expect you've got other things to do with your time, Sister, haven't you?'

Clearly Mandy wasn't gong to relinquish her hold on Luke too readily. Julia decided to use the same ploy that she had used earlier, putting the emphasis on work; perhaps she could swing it again.

'The thing is, Dr Steel is worrying about a backlog of paperwork, and I'm going to help him sort it out.' Another little white lie in the name of diplomacy, she thought.

It seemed to work a second time, for again Mandy visibly relaxed, and said with a smile, 'I suppose he's what you might call a workaholic, the doctor.'

'Yes, he is that right enough,' replied Julia, grateful to be able to confirm something that was undeniably true. 'Now I really must go, or I shall be late on duty.' She said her goodbyes and left.

She drove back to Princes through the gathering dusk of the October evening, mulling over, long and lovingly, the delights of the afternoon. She could hardly believe that she had enjoyed Luke holding and caressing her with such suppressed passion. She had liked the feeling of his hot body pressing against hers, and if he had not been ill. . . Surely they were right for each other? Surely Grace Townsend meant nothing to him? Luke was no Howard Snelling; he wouldn't be so crass as be involved with two women at the same time, would he? It had been purely an accident that he and Grace had met up at the conference, at least on his part. She of course had known that he would be lecturing there. Was that what had taken her there—the chance to hear Luke, an acknowledged expert in his field, lecture on trauma in injury? Was that perhaps Grace's field too? Was she a casualty officer?

The traffic on the road began to build up, and it had started to rain. She forced herself to stop daydreaming and concentrate on driving.

Once back at Princes, she had no time to dream; it was a rush to change and get to the unit by five, but she just made it. She did the rounds to check on the current situation. There was a young man, Trevor Blake, in cubicle five, having a rectal bleed, probably from internal haemmorhoids, and suffering from shock. He was waiting to be seen by the registrar from Men's Surgical, where he might be admitted prior to surgery later that evening if intervention was considered necessary or desirable fairly soon.

Dan Beatty was with him, making all the right reassuring remarks.

Julia confirmed what the charge nurse was saying and then asked Dan if he could come to the office for a few minutes. 'We'll send another nurse in to stay with you till the consultant comes,' she told the patient, and on the way back to her office instructed an experienced auxiliary nurse to special Mr Blake.

Dan and Julia went over the afternoon's list, and then Julia asked him if he would swap his half-day, and cover for her the next afternoon.

'Why, sure, Julia, I haven't got anything planned particularly, and my wife's working; I don't mind swapping. Something special you want to do?'

Julia hesitated for a moment, and then decided to take the plunge. After all, it wouldn't be long before the grapevine was even more busy about herself and Luke—it had already begun to hum.

'Luke's pretty poorly with this pneumonia thing,' she explained. 'I visited him this afternoon. His housekeeper is good, but I've promised to relieve her tomorrow afternoon if possible.'

'Poor old Luke. It's times like this when it's not so good to be a bachelor type living a free and easy life, and playing the field. A good and loving wife comes into her own, doing those little extras.' Dan gave her a sly grin.

'Failing a wife, I suppose a girlfriend might do,' said Julia with a laugh.

'Admirably, I should think,' said Dan. 'But——' he tapped the side of his nose '—keep a look-out for the opposition.'

'What on earth do you mean by that?'

'Oh, come on, Julia, you must know that Imelda's got a thing about Luke. And there have been others in the past, as you might expect with a great guy like him.'

'Well, of course I know about Imelda—who doesn't?—but I thought she was already looking elsewhere, and her feelings for Luke had faded, as it were.'

'With Imelda, things don't fade; they have to be prised away from her, though it might be different in this instance.'

'Well, I'm not going to do anything as undignified as fight over a man with another woman. It's ludicrous.

'But worth it, perhaps?'

'It won't be necessary,' said Julia stiffly, wondering if she should say anything about Dr Townsend's appearance on the scene. She decided against it. There was, after all, nothing concrete to discuss. 'Luke and I are just good friends,' she finished rather lamely.

'Want to bet?' asked Dan.

* * *

Lying in bed much later that night, Julia reviewed her day. The afternoon with Luke had been fantastic and unexpected, his anger over her bruised cheek gratifying, and his gentle, teasing way with her afterwards an absolute delight. Even the slight irritation that Mandy presented had been easily dealt with.

The young woman had a crush on Luke, but that would pass. What might not pass so easily, if Dan Beatty was to be believed, was Imelda's more mature crush on him, and, of course, Grace's presence, of which Dan was ignorant. Did either of them present a threat? Imelda was young, but not so young. She might have real designs where Luke was concerned, and the equipment to deal with it: a bright, intelligent mind in a mature and beautiful woman's body. As for Grace, she was an unknown quantity. Julia acknowledged that the only edge that she herself seemed to have over the other two women at this moment was a purely chemical one, the chemistry of sex, which caused one person to be attracted to another for no sound or practical reason. That, she and Luke seemed to have in abundance at present, but would it last? She had no way of telling.

She had thought Imelda cooling towards Luke, and he seemed only mildly interested in her, and yet now, in the darkness of the night, she was not so sure. Imelda's striking beauty seemed an almost insuperable boundary. After all, Imelda had been around and had known Luke before she, Julia, had arrived at Princes.

And what about Grace, and the other women that Dan had hinted at in Luke's past? Not that she would expect a man of his age to be entirely without a past. She had a past herself, so why shouldn't he? For her, past and present didn't mix, but what about Luke?

Since her arrival at Princes, the grapevine had reported him as having fleeting and mild affairs with several attractive women.

So what? That was nothing to do with her. All she should be concerned about was how he felt about her now. That he liked, admired and desired her was only too plain, but was that enough?

On these muddled thoughts, she eventually fell asleep.

CHAPTER EIGHT

THE following morning was quiet in A and E. The weather, of course, always played a large part in road accidents. On this particular October morning it was mild and sunny in a smoky, autumnal sort of way, and the nearby motorway was for once free of early morning collisions.

There were only three patients in the waiting area when Julia went on duty, and three cubicles occupied. She took the night report from Sonia and left her office to check on what was happening in the cubicles.

Imelda was in cubicle one, removing a long splinter from under a fingernail. The finger had already been frozen, and Imelda was carefully and confidently drawing out the sliver of wood when Julia entered. As always, Julia admired Imelda's skill when performing any surgical procedure, however small. She had neat, narrow, but strong hands that she seemed to know unerringly how to use for the patient's benefit. It would be a pity if she didn't take up surgery as a speciality; she certainly had the ability and the brains, and was perhaps better suited temperamentally to being a surgeon, rather than a physician. Her skills were more in the mechanical than the emotional side of medicine, Julia thought, as she watched the splinter being finally withdrawn.

'I think we ought to have this finger X-rayed, Sister, don't you?' said Dr Robbins to Julia when she realised that she was present. 'To make sure that there's no damage further down, though it seems to have come out quite cleanly.' She seemed to be in a good mood this morning, for she smiled at the patient, and held up the splinter for him to see.

He made a face, and said, 'Blimey, I didn't realise it was that long. You made a good job of getting that out doctor, I reckon.'

'Dr Robbins is an expert at this sort of thing,' said Julia, smiling at both patient and doctor, hoping to keep Imelda in a good mood for the rest of the morning. To Imelda she said, 'I'll arrange about the X-ray, and I'll just put a loose dressing round the finger for now.'

She filled in the necessary forms, and sent the patient along to the X-ray department, and then followed Imelda into the next cubicle, where a little girl was waiting to be assessed for possible admission.

The child was lying quietly, comforted by her mother, who, at first sight, looked more in need of attention than the child. She was obviously in shock after witnessing her little girl falling from a swing and hitting her head on the swing support post. There was also a nurse in the cubicle.

Julia wished everyone good morning in her calmest fashion, and then spoke to the nurse who had been left with the patient.

'Take Mrs. . .' she checked the accident-action card '. . .Mrs Connel to the office for a few minutes, and fetch her a cup of coffee, while Dr Robbins examines Lucy. I'll stay here and help.'

Mrs Connel protested that she wanted to stay.

'It would be better if you didn't,' said Julia quietly but firmly. 'Doctor wants to do a few more tests now that Lucy has rested for a bit, and you need a hot, sweet drink. I promise that I'll let you know as soon as you can return. We won't be too long.'

The nurse led a somewhat reassured Mrs Connel away.

Imelda decided after her second examination of Lucy Connel that she should be admitted to the children's ward for twenty-four hours' observation. Julia went to tell Mrs Connel and arrange for Lucy's transfer to the ward.

In the third cubicle, swaddled in blankets, and being fed a hot drink by a student nurse, lay an elderly lady suffering from hypothermia. She had been found sleeping rough, and had been brought in by police, and was in such a poor state of health that even the mild weather hadn't saved her. Imelda decided that she should be admitted to the geriatric ward, if and when a bed became vacant.

'Perhaps you would arrange that, Julia,' she asked in the nice way that she had when she was in a good mood.

'Of course,' said Julia, and went off to phone the ward in question.

The sister there told Julia that they couldn't admit Mrs Adams until the afternoon, when a patient was being discharged into a rest-home.

'Oh, that's all right; as it happens, we're pretty quiet here. We'll keep the poor old duck in a cubicle, unless it gets hectic, and send her up this afternoon.'

She put the phone down, and went to explain to Mrs Adams what was going to happen, and then asked one of the nurses to keep looking in on that particular patient until she was moved after lunch. 'I'll let Catering know that we need a patient lunch for here,' she said. 'And you go and fetch it, please, at twelve o'clock, and in the meanwhile take regular hot drinks in to Mrs Adams.'

'Yes, Sister,' said the young student nurse meekly.

Julia went back to her office. She could always find jobs to do that had to be shelved during their many busy spells, but was sorry that it was quiet this morning from a purely selfish and personal point of view. She wanted the hours that must elapse before she visited Luke to fly by, and from experience she knew that they only did that if one was up to one's eyes in work, hard, demanding work.

There was to be no such reprieve today. There were always casualties coming in, but this morning they did so in a trickle, and were all minor injuries that could be dealt with by other staff.

She immersed herself in the perennial paperwork; order forms, patient statistics, duty rosters, all time-consuming, but dull, dull, dull. Nothing to stop her mind wandering and her thoughts drifting towards Luke and what he might be doing at that very moment.

He would still be resting for the next few days in bed, but as soon as the antibiotics got to work he should show signs of improvement. He might be fit to start work in a couple of weeks. Meanwhile, she guessed that he would be working at home as soon as possible. She knew that he had been asked to contribute a series of articles for a medical magazine on advanced A and E practices, and she was sure that he would be wanting to try out some ideas.

She looked at her watch. Twelve-thirty. Dan Beatty was relieving her at two, and, had they been busy, she would have skipped lunch. But they weren't busy. There was no reason why she shouldn't go to lunch now and leave one of the staff nurses in charge.

She made her arrangements with Staff Nurse Patel, and went to the refectory in the Old House, meaning to find a secluded table and commune with herself as she ate. It was not to be. Imelda Robbins caught up with her as she entered the house.

'Shall we share a table?' she asked.

Without being downright rude, Julia had to agree.

'That'll be nice,' she said falsely.

It wasn't that she didn't want Imelda's company particularly; she just didn't want to lunch with anyone. She wanted just to think and dream about Luke and the visit she was making to him that afternoon, and fantasise a little as to what might happen. The knowledge that hopefully, unless the Townsend woman put in an appearance, they would be alone in his house, just the two of them, added a piquancy to her thoughts that was stimulating and exciting. Be your age, woman, she reminded herself silently. Stop acting like a schoolgirl in love; you're nearly as bad as Mandy. She smiled inwardly at the thought of the nubile Mandy and her crush on Luke.

'What are you having?' asked Imelda, as a waitress came to serve them.

'Oh, the vegetarian casserole,' said Julia, hardly glancing at the menu, and making an effort to squash her wild imaginings.

'I'll have the fish, the turbot,' said Imelda to the waitress. 'I'm surprised that you didn't choose that,' she said, turning to Julia. 'You're like me, aren't you, a fish-eating but otherwise vegetarian person?'

'I don't feel like fish today,' she explained.

Neither do I feel like chatting, she thought, but naturally kept the thought to herself. In a way, although she wanted to eat and think about Luke, she was both surprised and half pleased that Imelda wanted to share a table with her. It meant that the doctor was still in a good mood, and that boded well for the department over the afternoon. It was always a relief to be able to go off duty knowing that all was as well as it possibly could be. Not an easy proposition for A and E, where the situation and the patients could change from minute to minute, but at least to know that the staff were in good form was something.

Fortunately Imelda kept up a flow of conversation that mostly required just a 'yes', 'no' or 'really?' reply, so that half Julia's mind could dream blissfully about her afternoon and evening with Luke. She would cook him supper. She knew from having seen Mrs Crowe unpack the groceries that both the fridge and the larder were well stocked. What about a cheese surprise, one of her mother's specialities; layers of thinly sliced potatoes and cheese with tinned tomatoes and onions spread between each layer, nicely spiced, and some broccoli or broad beans to garnish? And for starters, melon with white wine, well chilled, and for a pudding. . .

Imelda was leaning across the table and saying something which obviously required a more intelligent answer than yes or no.

'Sorry,' Julia apologised. 'I didn't hear what you said.'

Imelda positively hissed. 'Don't look now, but two tables away to your left is Grace Townsend.'

Imelda was very excited, and was looking at Julia in a rather strange fashion, as if she expected some reaction from her.

'Ah,' said Julia, interested, but not surprised. 'Grace Townsend.'

Imelda looked at her curiously. 'Do you know her?' she asked in surprise.

'We've met,' said Julia, hiding her pleasure at having surprised Imelda.

'But she left Princes about four or five months ago, before you came here. She was the registrar on A and E, and left just before John Peak took over. I started as houseman just a few weeks before that. She got her fellowship, and was doing some statistical research that interested a hospital group in Florida, and she was invited there on a lecture-cum-work tour. I didn't think anyone knew she was back. How on earth did you meet her?'

'She called in with Luke to my flat on their way back from the conference.'

Imelda looked astounded. 'She and Luke called in to see you?'

'Yes,' said Julia calmly.

'But how strange that they should want to see you,' Imelda said, unaware that she sounded rude. Julia forgave her, knowing how surprised she was. Imelda recovered herself a little and tried to explain. 'What I mean is, I heard that they had quite a thing going between them, but it was fizzling out when I started working in the unit. They were always having rows. It was something to do with Grace wanting to go to the States, I think, but I'm not sure about that.'

Julia felt a trickle of apprehension down her spine.

Was that what Dan Beatty had meant when he talked about Luke and other women? Had Grace figured so largely in his life, as Imelda was suggesting, or was she being malicious or just speaking out of ignorance? Why hadn't Luke mentioned Grace if she had been important to him? She answered herself—because he's not had the chance to do so, because we're only just getting to know each other. I haven't told him about being engaged to Howard, so why should he tell me about his past? It's dead and finished, isn't it? He must feel the same about his affair with this woman as I feel about my engagement to Howard: that it's in the past, a regrettable but dead incident. Yes, of course, that's what it is. If there was the slightest possibility of him getting back together with this Grace, he wouldn't have behaved as he did with me yesterday, surely? He must consider his affair, however serious it might have been, was a thing of the past. As long, of course, as Grace felt the same way.

One thought after another chased around in her head, blotting out sounds, even the sound of Imelda's voice. Julia could see Imelda's lips moving soundlessly, but had to concentrate hard to make out what she was saying.

She was in fact telling Julia that Grace was going.

She leant still further across the table, and whispered fiercely, 'You can look now; she's off.'

Julia cautiously turned her head and saw the back of the tall, statuesque blonde woman who had invaded her flat on Thursday night leaving the room together with three other doctors. She had an impression of a dark-tailored suit on a superb figure before the little party disappeared.

'Surrounded by men as always,' said Imelda, leaning back in her chair with a sigh. 'That's what I remember most about Ms Townsend. One of the first things I ever heard about her was that she had half the men at Princes after her, those who were free, and those who were not so free.'

'But Luke was the lucky winner?' Somehow Julia made the words come out sounding coolly interested, with no hint of the tumult that was going on within her. The very last person she wanted to start guessing at how she felt was Imelda.

In fact Dr Robbins's reaction to the return of Grace Townsend was a surprise. She was excited, but only in a gossipy sort of way, not as if she was afraid of competition. It was strange, since until very recently she had been throwing herself at Luke, and, though she had cooled off over the last week, Dan had thought that she still had hopes where Luke was concerned. Yet nothing in her manner now indicated this. Presumably this meant that she had set her sights elsewhere.

Almost as if she had read Julia's thoughts Imelda said, with a pleased smile, and a 'cat's got the cream' look, 'I'm so pleased that I decided to finish with Luke. He's really too old for me; he needs an older woman, or women.' She looked slyly at Julia. 'And of course, now that Grace is back—"the Nordic beauty", she used to be called—well, no one else will get a look-in anyway.' She shrugged her shoulders, as if to imply that it was a foregone conclusion that the gorgeous blonde would have him if that was what she wanted.

Julia felt numb, and could only mumble some nonsensical answer to Imelda's suggestion, and try to look indifferent.

Imelda looked at her curiously.

'Don't you mind,' she asked, 'about Luke and Grace?'

'Mind? Why should I mind?' Her voice was rock-steady, though her heart was thumping madly at the thought of what the question implied. The grapevine had obviously been busy, or had Dan Beatty let it be known that she and Luke might have something going between them?

'Well—' Imelda sounded uncertain '—I thought that you and Luke. . .' Her voice trailed off.

So she didn't know anything.

'Luke and I had a meal together the other night, with my brother. You remember; you met him—Bill.'

Imelda actually blushed.

'Yes, I remember,' she said softly. 'You brought him round A and E. He's smashing; I'm glad that he's got the reg job in Ophthalmics.'

Julia frowned and looked at her quickly, wondering how interested Imelda already was in Bill, then she looked at her watch and feigned surprise.

'Gosh, is that the time? I must fly. I've got to hand over to Dan at two, and there's oodles to do.'

'Are you off?'

'Half-day.'

'Doing anything nice?'

Was there a knowing look on Imelda's face? Does she know that I'm going to visit Luke? wondered Julia.

'I'm going to drop in on Luke,' she said, 'see how he's progressing.'

Imelda frowned briefly, and then smiled.

'Give him my love,' she said, 'and tell him to get well soon. We need him.' To Julia's relief, she sounded no more than mildly interested, and certainly not jealous. She seemed to be out of the running where Luke was concerned.

Julia hurried from the refectory, her mind in turmoil. Was the returned Ms Townsend, the 'Nordic beauty', a threat? From the little she had seen of her, she looked stunning, but looks weren't everything. She had got the impression when she and Luke were in her flat that Grace Townsend was somehow brisk, abrasive. Surely Luke would not be interested in such a woman? He would want someone with a core of softness—feminine, gentle, loving. Or was that just wishful thinking? she asked herself. Were the woman's other attributes enough to outweigh these virtues?

Somehow she got through the rest of her duty period until two o'clock, when Dan relieved her. It took but a few minutes to hand over the report, and then she was away, down to her flat to change into something special for her visit to Thatches.

She showered to wash off the unpleasant memory of Grace Townsend having lunch with a band of adoring males, and consoled herself with the fact that at least she wasn't with Luke. Some inner, almost guilty compulsion made her feel it necessary to compete with the beautiful consultant in matters of dress, less for Luke's pleasure, though she hoped that he would notice how she looked, than a silly desire to prove that she was capable of competing. The fact that the chances of seeing Grace again before she herself saw Luke were remote, most unlikely, mattered not one jot.

When she reached Luke's thatched cottage, the unlikely happened, and, to Julia's utter amazement, the door of his cottage was opened by Grace Townsend.

She must have come straight to the cottage from the refectory.

Julia hoped that her mouth was not hanging open in surprise, and was glad that she'd spent some time choosing what to wear—a soft wool, long-skirted suit in orange tan over a turtle-necked sweater of heather-purple, with soft leather tan boots to complete the outfit. It made her feel good: comfortable but well dressed. Just right, she judged, for the muted sunshine of an autumn afternoon. She had hoped that Luke would appreciate her efforts, and now, faced with the sophisticated Townsend woman, she was doubly glad that she had dressed with care.

Grace was dressed as she had been at lunch, in the elegantly tailored black suit and white silk shirt blouse. The black and white complemented the ash blonde hair, drawn back into a complicated chignon, and the remote classical features, and the china-blue eyes.

Cold-looking blue eyes, Julia decided, as they swept over her as she stood in the porch, unreached by the conventional smile that hovered round her lips.

They bade each other good afternoon, both in rather cool voices, and then Grace opened the door a little wider, and stood to one side. It was almost like a repeat of the greeting that Mandy had given her the day before, Julia thought.

'Do come in,' said Grace. 'We are expecting you.'

The 'we' was proprietorial.

'I know that Luke is,' said Julia with a glimmering of a smile. 'He asked me to come.'

'Yes, so I believe. You're going to cook or something, aren't you, and bring him up to date with what's happening at the unit?'

'Oh, it's more a friendly visit than anything to do with work,' Julia said smoothly, resenting Grace's attitude. 'As I'm sure you know, Luke asked me to come and spend the afternoon and evening with him for company. And I offered to relieve Mrs Crowe and Mandy and prepare supper.'

'The housekeeper and that awful daughter of hers. I sent them away. Luke has had his lunch; I shall see to his dinner.'

Julia said coldly, all at once certain of herself, and hoping that Grace hadn't offended the Crowes, 'No, I shall see to Luke's dinner; it has already been arranged. You are of course welcome to stay, or to return later to share the meal with Luke and me.'

For the briefest of moments Grace looked angry and undecided, then she said with a trill of laughter, 'Well, I'm sure that you're a much better cook than I, so we'll not quarrel over who's going to cook the meal. Actually, I have some other people to see at Princes, so I'll be returning there presently, and leaving Luke to your tender mercies, Sister Manning. I dare say he could do with bit of nursing care now. Everything's been done for him medically that can be done.'

With difficulty Julia kept down the flush of anger that she was feeling, determined to remain polite and not let the gorgeous-looking Grace see that she was affected by her jibe. The Townsend woman was obviously implying that what she considered the minor role of nursing was what Luke now needed. She gritted her nice white teeth in suppressed fury.

'Yes, well, I'll go up and see Luke,' she said firmly, 'and have a chat with him before I think about preparing a meal. Why don't you,' she suggested sweetly, 'go and see those important people at Princes, and come back for dinner at sevenish?'

Grace gave a barely perceptible nod, as if she accepted the inevitable, and was letting Julia win that round. 'I'll take you up and tell Luke that I'm going out for a bit,' she said, as if Julia couldn't be trusted with the message, 'and say goodbye to him for now.'

Julia all but snorted derisively. Grace's words and actions were plainly meant to show that she was in charge where Luke was concerned, and somehow implied that he found this acceptable. She couldn't believe it, not after the way he had behaved yesterday afternoon. He'd been so tender and concerned about the small injury to her face, and had been so adamant about her coming again today so that, ill as he was, they could spend more time together. He'd said nothing about Grace returning to the cottage, or suggested that there was anything more than friendship between them now, whatever there might have been in the past. Neither had he mentioned that Grace had been his registrar, a close working relationship. But then perhaps he didn't consider that any more important than the fact that they had been more than friends. It was all in the past. He wouldn't deliberately conceal any of these facts, knowing that once Grace was back, albeit briefly, Julia would be bound to learn all that there was to know, and perhaps more, through the overactive grapevine.

How true that was. Imelda had already started the ball rolling at lunch today, and there was no doubt that other rumours would follow, thick and fast.

How was Luke taking Grace's return? Julia wondered as she followed the coolly beautiful woman in her elegant black suit up the stairs.

Was he bothered or not? He didn't readily give away his feelings; it would be difficult to tell, unless they spoke of it openly.

He was lying looking much as he had done on the previous day, flushed and uncomfortable, but this time exasperated and rather angry too in an aloof, dignified sort of way. Had she walked in on a row of some sort between him and Ms Townsend, or was he just suffering general frustration and for once not bothering to conceal it? The atmosphere in the room crackled.

Luke's flushed face lit up when he saw her. 'Hello, Julia, love,' he said throatily. 'I hoped it was you. Can you do something about these damned pillows? They are bloody uncomfortable.'

It was a lovely greeting, Julia thought, as she crossed to the bed. His words made her feel confident, no longer overshadowed by the beautiful Grace. She dropped a light kiss on his still hot forehead, and smoothed his hair back from his brow.

'Yes, they are in a dreadful mess, aren't they, my darling?' she said, slipping in the endearment as though she used it regularly. The words, like the kiss, seemed to come naturally. 'Here, let me help you. Lean forward so that I can tidy them.'

'Thank you,' he said. 'That'll be great.' If he was surprised by the warmth of her greeting, he didn't show it. Julia slipped her arm beneath his and eased him forward, away from the pillows, which she took out one by one, shook, plumped, and turned, leaving the cool side uppermost, as she arranged them in armchair fashion. Then she rolled him gently from one side to the other and straightened the bottom sheet.

When she had finished, Luke lay back for a moment with his eyes closed, and them mumbled softly, 'Heaven. The Nightingale touch.'

Grace, who had seemed rooted to the spot during Julia's rush of activity, now walked over to the bed and smiled down at Luke, and then across at Julia.

'You've made a wonderful job of making Luke comfortable,' she said, sounding rather patronising, but quite genuinely complimentary. 'I wish I had your touch. I suppose nursing teaches you that; medicine doesn't.' For a moment she looked almost wistful and certainly less frosty as she studied Luke's relaxed form, as if she wished that she could have performed this small, intimate act for him.

Julia shrugged, surprised by the other woman's unexpected mildness. Perhaps she wasn't as hard as she looked. Her kind heart made her reply gently, 'Making patients comfortable is an art,' she said. 'Some people have it, some don't.' She met Grace's blue eyes, which now didn't seem quite so cold and expressionless. Perhaps she had misjudged her. She returned her smile with a tentative one of her own.

Luke opened his eyes; they were actually twinkling with amusement. He looked from one to the other of them. 'That's better,' he said raspily. 'You're talking to each other.' He raised one eyebrow; the look of exasperation and anger that had been on his face when Julia arrived seemed now to have completely vanished. 'There's no reason why we shouldn't be civilised about this. I dare say, Julia, you have heard on Princes' busy grapevine, if not more directly, that Grace and I had a thing going once?' He took her hand and squeezed it gently.

'Yes,' she said in a somewhat trembly voice, surprised at how quickly he was getting to the point, 'I had heard.'

'But it's in the past. Grace is just visiting me as a friend.' He turned with a smile to look at the beautiful blonde woman. 'That's so, isn't it, Grace?'

Grace's face was almost expressionless, but she nodded, compressed her lips, and said in a low, flat voice, 'Yes, Luke, it's all over; we're just friends now.'

Julia felt sorry for her, and wondered what had been said before she arrived that had obviously turned Grace's world upside-down. Had she come to see Luke expecting to be received with open arms, and had he immediately rejected her because of what she had done in the past, or because he had simply changed his mind? Was she herself one of the reasons that Luke had finished with Grace, or had this been determined before they had ever met?

It looked as if Luke was the only person who could answer these questions. Well, there would be time enough for answers in the future. For the moment, don't press it, some inner instinct warned her. Luke was putting a cool and dignified front on it, and so was Grace, but cutting oneself off from the past couldn't be easy, however it came about. Julia's tender heart felt for both of them, but surprisingly especially for Grace. Luke kindly but firmly had made her admit that their intimate relationship was over, but everything about her attitude earlier had indicated that she had hoped for a reunion.

Grace said quietly, 'I'd better be going, Luke. I've several people to see at Princes.'

'Right,' said Luke in his croaky voice. 'Sorry I can't see you out. Julia will do the honours.'

'No, it's all right, I can see myself out. And Julia, I'll skip dinner after all,' she said rather sadly. 'Goodbye, Luke; get well soon.' She bent and kissed him on the forehead. 'Mustn't get your viral pneumonia bugs,' she said, with a hint of laughter in her cracked voice. She turned to Julia and extended a hand.

Surprised, Julia took it.

'Goodbye; look after him.' She turned away from her and left the room, closing the door softly behind her.

Luke and Julia stared at the closed door.

Silence settled on the room, an uneasy, crowded silence, full of things unsaid, vibrant with frayed emotions and raw surfaces.

Julia felt like running away and leaving the room and the smooth, sophisticated scene behind her, but Luke still held her wrist in a light but firm grip. It would almost have been better, she thought for a moment, if everyone had given way to their feelings, and ranted and raved. It was almost too civilised. It was a broken relationship, however neatly handled, and two people—no, three, if she counted herself—left mauled by the experience. She dragged her eyes from the door through which Grace had just disappeared, and looked down at Luke, automatically assessing whether what had happened had affected his condition, and just for a moment she saw him as a patient and nothing else.

He was looking drawn, the planes of his face pronounced, with a fierce frown drawing his eyebrows together to meet over his high-bridged nose, but otherwise he looked no worse for the experience.

He uncreased his forehead and smiled faintly at her. 'We had a great thing going for a while and a lot in common,' he said quietly. 'I thought that we were going to make a go of it.'

Julia eased her wrist from his grasp.

'Well, as long as you're sure about breaking off your relationship, I don't think that you could have done anything to make things easier. You both did your best to be, as you wanted, civilised.' Her voice was cool, distant. She couldn't for the life of her infuse any warmth into it, give Luke any grain of comfort, though one part of her wanted to do just that—comfort him, this man with whom she was falling daily, in spite of her determination to be cautious, deeper in love.

She felt momentarily detached from what had happened, and for a brief moment regretted everything; working at Princes, meeting Luke, and discovering her growing love for him. Why couldn't they have remained just good colleagues, working harmoniously together as they had until a short while ago? Why indeed? She felt guilty, as if she were the other woman who had tempted Luke away from Grace, but common sense told her that this was not true, and Luke's next words confirmed this.

'We had sorted it, Julia, before you arrived on the scene. It's an old story, and Grace accepted the consequences before she went off to America.' He seemed to sense her uncertainty, and took her hand. 'Believe me, our relationship was over months ago. We didn't agree on ccrtain fundamentals, like having a family and a domestic life. Grace didn't want any of that; she wanted us both to pursue our careers to the exclusion of all else.'

'Didn't she want children?

'No.'

'Because she was afraid of having to give up her work?'

'No, there was no question of that, and she knew it. I didn't ask her to give up the work that she loves for good—I'm not a monster—but I hoped that she would be prepared to take some time out to have a family.'

Julia looked at his long, gaunt face and compassionate grey-green eyes, and thought about him being an orphan. It would be harder for him than most men not to father a family. He had made it clear, that Sunday night in the restaurant, that it was something he had always longed for. Grace's ruthlessness in denying him this must have been shattering.

'Perhaps,' she said softly, 'Grace would have come round to the idea in time.'

'No. She didn't want children, not ever. Even today, trying as she was to put the clock back, trying to recreate the past, I could see that nothing had changed. She just wanted to pick up where we left off.'

Julia's heart plummeted. Had he and Grace actually talked intimately this afternoon about marriage and raising a family, and would he have welcomed her back if she had changed her mind?

Of course not, she reasoned; he wouldn't be so cruel, or so unthinking.

She knew from having worked with him for months that he was an intensely compassionate man, in spite of his cool, sometimes arrogant veneer. Repeatedly she had seen him in the unit go much further than he personally needed to assist and reassure a patient or relatives. Luke the man was just as compassionate as Luke the doctor. He must have a reason for telling her about himself and Grace.

He squeezed her hand, and, as if he knew what she had been thinking, said, 'I've only told you all this to give you a clear picture of the situation as it was, and as it is, between Grace and myself. You had nothing to do with my breaking up with her in the past, but, even had she changed her mind about having a family, you would have everything to do with my refusing her now—everything.' He shook her arm gently. His deep-set grey-green eyes were luminous with some tender, deep emotion which he was willing her to understand. He said in his quiet, deep voice, 'Do you understand what I am saying, Julia?'

Julia stared at him silently for a moment, as if puzzled, her face serious, thoughtful, then as the true import of his words flooded over her she began to smile. It was a smile of pure happiness, a tremulous, tentative, quivering smile, as she realised that he was telling her that he loved her. She felt tears of joy pricking the backs of her eyes, and blinked to dispel them. 'Oh, Luke,' she murmured huskily, and it was all that she could say.

The room was very still. Golden, hazy autumn sunshine beamed through the small lattice window, illuminating Luke, pale-faced and stern, propped up against his pillows. With a strength that belied his illness, he pulled her down on the bed beside him. His face softened; his finger traced the outline of her lips. 'You have a lovely mouth, Julia, but I won't kiss it, not now, even though my wretched chest thing is well under control. I'll make do with this.' His hot lips trailed across her brow, and her cheeks and her eyelids. He leaned back against his untidy pile of pillows, looking exhausted. 'There, my love,' he muttered, 'you'll have to make do with that for the time being. I'm less capable than I thought myself, but I'll make up for it in the not too distant future.'

'I'll keep you to that,' said Julia breathlessly, lightly, suddenly overwhelmed, wanting to make a token resistance, for some reason feeling that she should show some reticence. She planted a matter-of-fact kiss on his cheek, and struggled up from the bed. 'At this moment,' she said firmly, nurse-like, 'I'm going to tidy you up again and then make us both a nice cup of tea, and discuss what we are going to have for supper.'

His eyes gleamed knowlingly, and she wondered if he had read all or part of her mind. He gave her one of his nicest smiles, and her heart lurched painfully.

'Tea,' he said with a grin. 'The British panacea to all ills. I could murder a cup.'

CHAPTER NINE

THE next morning, getting ready to go on duty, Julia pondered over the events of the previous day and evening. Her evening spent with Luke had been wonderful, full of warmth and understanding and a building up of the rapport that existed between them.

She had made him comfortable with her usual skill, and he had dozed while she prepared supper, and after supper he had rallied enough to discuss the articles that he had been commissioned to write for a medical magazine.

She had got over the shock of learning how close he and Grace had once been, and the even greater, if exhilarating shock when he had explained his present feelings for her. She simply hadn't expected him to be so frank about his feelings, so soon. For, although he had heavily hinted at how he felt when he had phoned from the conference, she had expected a slow, cautious approach. But his words and actions at the cottage, presumably triggered off by Grace's appearance on the scene, had made a nonsense of this. He had all but said, I love you, and before she left he had made his feelings even plainer.

'Don't let's waste any more time,' he'd said. 'As soon as I am up and about again in a couple of weeks' time, let's seriously discuss our future.'

Julia sighed with happiness, and went to work in a state of euphoria that remained with her for many days.

* * *

Luke improved rapidly over the next week or so, and Julia noticed a difference in him each time she visited.

'Behold,' he said happily in a teasing manner, surprising Julia by meeting her at the front door ten days after the advent of his pneumonia. 'You see before you an almost fit man. According to my doctor, I've made a remarkable recovery, all due to good, clean living, and the fact that I am a superb physical specimen, and with just a little help from antibiotics. I'll be back on duty next week; it'll be great to be hard at it again, and working once more beside my favourite lady.'

He was in an exalted, ebullient mood, obviously delighted at feeling so well, and free of the lassitude that his illness had produced. To her utter surprise and delight, he gave her a long, lingering kiss, and let his hands rove lightly over her body as he held her close to him. He touched her breasts and buttocks until she was weak with longing and he was hard with desire.

After a while she eased herself out of his arms, and said breathlessly and with a little laugh, 'I hate to dent your ego, darling, but you can't be *that* fit yet, and isn't Mrs Crowe in the kitchen?'

'For one wonderful moment,' he said, 'I thought we were alone. As to being fit enough. . .' He shrugged and raised his eyebrows in a pretended leer. 'I wish I had the opportunity to prove it. I feel fit enough for anything, though, I admit, Mrs Crowe presents rather a problem.'

They smiled at each other in complete accord, understanding that if it had been possible they would have made love there and then; emotionally and physically they were ready. Luke was wearing a rather splendid quilted Paisley dressing-gown. He had just shaved and smelt of cologne, and his black, wiry, grey-speckled hair was neatly brushed.

'I thought,' he said, leaning against the wall, looking thin and elegant, if still rather haggard, 'that we might take tea down here today, make a change from the everlasting bedroom scene.'

Julia, having recovered somewhat from his passionate embrace, giggled. 'I thought it was the bedroom scene that you were interested in,' she teased, inwardly still glowing from his masterful greeting.

'Aren't I just?' he said, with a lop-sided grin. 'But I'm afraid conditions for that aren't perfect for the moment.' He waved a hand towards the kitchen, and then leaned forward and trailed a kiss across Julia's mouth. 'Another time,' he whispered. He put a hand beneath her elbow and steered her towards the big leather settee in front of the blazing fire. 'Let's make ourselves comfortable while we wait for Mrs Crowe's superb tea,' he suggested as he sat down beside her. He patted her knee. 'Now before I lose control and ravish you again, bring me up to date on all the gossip at Princes and particularly in A and E,' he said.

Mrs Crowe came in at that moment, and placed a delicious tea of hot buttered scones and newly baked cake in front of them.

They thanked her, and when she had returned to the kitchen Julia said, 'Well, Imelda's showing an interest in the new junior registrar on Orthopaedics, but he hasn't deflected her from her work; she is pulling her weight in the department.' She smiled shyly at him, and added, 'Everyone's working hard; we miss you dreadfully, you know.'

'And you most of all, I hope,' he said gently, laying a hand for a moment on her knee.

'Yes, I do.' His pent-up passionate embrace had made her bold, and she didn't mind revealing her feelings. She said softly, looking at him lovingly, 'I like knowing that you're around. John Peak's great, very reliable, but he's not you, and I don't feel the same about him.'

'I should think not indeed,' replied Luke in a teasing voice, and leaned across the small gap between them and nuzzled her ear. 'And long may it remain so.'

She gave a little gasp of pleasure as his tongue tickled her earlobe, and then said, pretending to be severe, 'Do you want to hear all the news or don't you?'

Luke nodded. 'Yes, please,' he said deceptively meek, and gave her an unabashed smile.

'Well, Dan Beatty's gone off sick. He looked rotten. High temp. and so on. One of his kids has got mumps; it seems to be going around. Poor Dan, it looks as if he's got it too; apparently he didn't have it as a child, and hasn't had an injection against it. He's terribly worried about side effects—sterility and so on—although he knows only too well that it only occurs in very severe cases, and even then rarely. He said all this himself. I tried to reassure him how unlikely it was, and he agreed, but he went home still bothered. I must ring his wife later to find out how he is, and hope that she can make him see sense.'

'Poor devil, I can guess how vulnerable he feels. I would feel the same. Oddly, it doesn't matter how informed one is; most men are anxious when they have mumps. I'm damned glad that I had it as a child.'

Julia smiled. 'So am I,' she said, and, blushing a little

added, 'I should hate to see you with mumps, and it's nice to know that your virility is quite intact.'

Luke made a face. 'It had better be,' he growled.

Julia looked sad for a moment. 'Poor Dan, I wish he weren't so worried, but, if the worst should happen, at least he's got a family already; it would be worse if he hadn't.'

Luke put out a hand and stroked her cheek. 'Yes, infinitely.' He paused. 'What a lovely, kind, sympathetic woman you are, Julia,' he said in a low, thoughtful voice, and a kind of magic understanding flowed between them as he spoke and touched her. A different sort of magic from the earlier passion, this was calm and quiet.

The grandfather clock in the corner of the room chimed five o'clock.

Luke dropped his hand, and Julia stood up. 'I must be off,' she said in a small, breathless voice. 'With both you and Dan away. . .well, you know what it's like at this time of year.' Suddenly she knew that if she didn't go soon she wouldn't be able to tear herself away from him.

'Yes,' replied Luke, his voice a little deeper than usual. 'A plethora of accidents in this season of mists.' He stood up beside her, lean and handsome, looming over her, his grey-green eyes brilliant. 'I look forward to seeing you tomorrow, Julia.'

'And I you.'

He took her in his arms and kissed her gently. His mood had softened; he was less forceful than earlier. 'I do love you, my darling,' he said quietly. 'So very much.' His thumb traced a pattern across her palm and along the inside of her wrist, making her tremble with longing and some deep-buried primitive desire to melt into him, to be absorbed by him. 'Do you love me?'

'Yes,' she whispered. 'Oh, yes, I do.'

'Good.' He cupped her chin in his hands and tilted her head so that their eyes met. 'Don't stop loving me, dear girl, now or ever, whatever happens.'

'I won't, I promise.'

Luke dropped his hands and gave her a lop-sided grin. 'I'm behaving like a maudlin idiot,' he said. 'Blame it on the remnants of this blasted bug. Now away with you, love, and take care.' He knew that if they didn't part now they would give way to their passion, Mrs Crowe or no Mrs Crowe.

A few minutes later he waved her off and she drove away into the soft golden radiance of the October sunset which perfectly matched her mood of glorious undiluted happiness.

He loves me, he loves me, her heart sang; Luke loves me.

Casualty was so busy over the next few days that Julia didn't have time to visit Luke. She telephoned to explain, and he was flatteringly disappointed, and pressed her to try to get away the following day. They exchanged loving remarks before she had to ring off. But the second time she phoned to say that she still couldn't visit, Luke's response was totally unexpected and shattering. He sounded cool and almost indifferent, not at all the man who had so passionately kissed her a few days before, and a cold trickle of foreboding ran through her as she listened to him. Instead of voicing regret that she would be unable to visit, he seemed almost relieved when she explained that she couldn't come.

He was brisk and matter-of-fact.

'Don't worry about it,' he said tonelessly. 'I of all people understand, you should know that. And I'll be back at work soon; I'll see you then.'

'Luke,' she said, shocked and surprised by his manner more than his words, 'is everything all right, are you all right?' She felt hollow inside.

'Of course, I'm fine. Don't fuss, Julia.' He sounded impatient.

She swallowed threatening tears, shaken by his attitude, and said in an even voice, 'I'm not fussing, Luke. I just want to know why you sound. . .' Her voice trailed off.

'Sound what?' He tried to speak levelly, but she could sense his tenseness, his anger. He sounded strange, hard, bitter, not the Luke she knew and loved.

'Different,' she said lamely, unable to be more explicit. Almost in a whisper she added, 'Different from what you were the other day. It's as if you don't care any more about us.'

Luke gave a bark of a laugh. 'Well, I warned you that I was maudlin, didn't I, on account of feeling so much better? I was a bit high.'

'And now what's happened to make you different, Luke?' With difficulty she stoppd her voice from shaking.

His voice softened a little. 'Call it post-pneumonia blues, Julia. Give me a bit of space.'

Space. He wanted space. The word sounded like doom. If he loved her, why did he want space? The word whirled round and round stupidly in her head, leaving no room for anything else.

She went to work the next morning feeling like nothing on earth. She had spent most of the night mulling over their telephone conversation and Luke's strangeness, falling asleep eventually after deciding that he was probably suffering from slight depression, as he had suggested. It was, after all, quite common following an illness, and she shouldn't be surprised that he had succumbed to it, although he seemed, on the face of it, an unlikely candidate. But if he wanted 'space' she would give it to him.

She put on her professional smile, and went through to her office for the hand-over report, where she found Sonia looking, for once, ruffled.

'We've had a hell of a morning. Started at seven,' she told Julia as she handed over. 'A bloke on a motorbike skidded on wet leaves, and ran into a queue of people waiting for a bus. The rider was injured, query arm and leg fractures, at present down in X-Ray, and five other people hurt. Two just superficial cuts and bruises, one child fractured collarbone—he's with his mum, she's very pregnant, and the accident might have started things off; the registrar from Maternity is with her to assess—and there's one other elderly chap with angina. With luck and treatment, he should be OK in an hour or so.'

'Is that all?' asked Julia sarcastically.

'By no means; do you want a list of those waiting to be seen?'

Julia held up a hand. 'No, thanks,' she said. 'I'll wait till I get to them.'

'Wise girl,' said Sonia. 'By the way, you'll be glad to get your boss back today, with a start like this.'

'Luke?' asked Julia in surprise, her heart skipping with pleasure at the sound of his name and the thought of seeing him, in spite of yesterday's devastating telephone conversation.

'He phoned just now, said that he was much better and would be in later this morning. I thought that he might have already been in touch with you,' she added slyly, 'since rumour has it——'

'Rumour,' said Julia enigmatically, 'has a lot to answer for.'

Sonia looked hopeful, but Julia was not to be drawn even by her best friend, and Sonia went off duty no wiser about the situation that existed between Luke and Julia.

With a tremendous effort of will, Julia put aside her personal feelings and the fact that she would be seeing Luke soon, and concentrated on work. She just prayed that his decision to return meant that even since last night he had got over his depression. After all, it had descended on him fast enough; why shouldn't it disappear just as fast? She gave a sigh, rolled up her sleeves, put on a plastic apron, and went to the aid of one of her nurses struggling with a patient who was vomiting copiously.

'Right, Nurse,' she said briskly, 'let's get this lady cleaned up and into a fresh gown, and ask Dr Peak to come and look at her as soon as he's free.'

From then on, work and her patients claimed her full attention, and she was glad of it.

The patient who was being sick had taken an overdose of paracetamol tablets, not enough to kill her at the time, but probably enough to cause damage to various internal organs. It was doubtful if she would survive long-term; she might very well bleed to death by internal haemorrhage. Julia, feeling desperately sorry for someone obviously crying out for help, arranged for her admission to the intensive care unit.

The next patient she saw, a large, tough-looking man in one of the cubicles, had a dislocated elbow. Imelda had apparently examined it, and had quite rightly decided that she wasn't strong enough to manipulate such a powerful arm without perhaps doing further damage to the patient.

'I'm waiting for John to manipulate it,' she told Julia, 'when he's finished with his present patient.'

'Very sensible,' said Julia, and tried to explain to Mr Brack why he had to wait a little longer for treatment.

'You mean,' said the man sneeringly, 'that you women ain't strong enough ter do it.'

'Quite right,' said Julia, giving him a nice smile. 'You're a big man and have strong arms. It makes much more sense to let another man loose on it. It needs some brute force as well as skill to reduce a dislocation—and men are usually better at applying brute force than women,' she couldn't resist adding sweetly.

''Ere, it ain't gonna 'urt more, is it? It's bloody murder at the moment,' said Mr Brack, looking anxious.

'No, of course not,' she said reassuringly, already regretting her snide remark. It wasn't like her to let her professional façade slip. 'We're going to give you a pain-killer. You've probably got a nerve pinched. That should do the trick, Mr Brack; you'll be much more comfortable.'

Mr Brack looked suspicious, but quietly allowed Julia to give him an injection to ease the pain while he waited for Dr Peak to do the reduction.

It wasn't in the end John Peak who did the job, but Luke. He had arrived while Julia was in the cubicle, and now suddenly appeared beside her as she was disposing of the used syringe and needle in the special container.

'Morning,' he said to both Julia and the patient. 'I understand that we have an elbow to reduce.'

Julia quelled her thumping heartbeats and the flush that had risen to her cheeks when Luke appeared.

'That's right,' she said calmly. 'Mr Brack has a dislocation caused by carrying a very heavy load in the wrong position. I've just given him an intramuscular injection of Pethilorfen written up by Dr Robbins. It should begin to work quite soon, and make the joint less painful.'

They looked at each other across the examination couch. Luke, thought Julia, looked drawn and hollow-eyed, but otherwise normal.

Julia, thought Luke, looked drawn and sad, and shadowed beneath her eyes. He wished he could do something to restore her to her usual serene and happy self, and felt guilty knowing that he was the cause of her sadness. But there was nothing he could do, not yet anyway. Perhaps in a few days if. . . He became aware that both the patient and Julia were looking at him, waiting for him to speak.

'I'll just have a word with Sister, Mr Brack, while the pain-killer is taking effect,' he said with a smile for the patient.

He pulled aside the curtain, and indicated that Julia should precede him from the cubicle.

Once they were outside, his eyes met hers again, and he gave her a faint smile. 'Are you all right?' he asked abruptly, knowing that it was a silly question.

'I'm fine.'

'You look sad,' he said in a softer tone.

Julia put a hand up to her face, as if to wipe away any expression. She didn't want him to know how badly what he had said on the phone and his changed attitude was affecting her. She smiled brightly. 'It must be your imagination. I'm fine, absolutely fine.'

'Really? You could have fooled me,' he said flatly.

She would have liked to have said, Well, whose fault is that? but of course she didn't.

A nurse came out of a neighbouring cubicle, and apologised as she almost collided with them.

For a brief moment they stared silently at each other. In spite of his words and concern, Luke's eyes were blank, giving nothing away. He motioned towards the cubicle, and they re-entered to see how their patient was doing.

'That injection's worked a treat, Doc,' said Mr Brack. 'Nothing like so much pain now.'

'Good, that's what I wanted to hear.' Luke sat himself down on a chair. 'Now I want you to sit in that chair opposite me, and we'll see what we can do about getting this elbow back in position.'

Mr Brack looked at him as if he were mad.

'You want me ter get down and sit there,' he said, nodding at the empty chair.

'That's right, Mr Brack. Sister will help you down.'

Julia moved forward and offered an arm.

'If you'll sit here, Mr Brack, Doctor will be able to manipulate your elbow back into position. He'll place your injured arm over his knee like this—' gently she placed the man's forearm on Luke's knee '—and very gradually he'll extend it until, at a certain point, it will click back into place.'

Luke began to manipulate the injured arm, pulling it gently against the firm support of his own thigh.

In spite of the pain-killing injection, Mr Brack began to sweat, but before the pain had become unbearable there was a click, and the joint slipped into place.

'Bloody 'ell,' said the patient. 'It's back.'

'Yes, it's back all right,' said Luke, 'and it should stay that way. You shouldn't have any more trouble with it.' He examined the arm carefully. 'Just a bit of bruising beginning to show round the joint, but that's all. Just go easy with it for a couple of weeks. Sister will put a little protective pad over the elbow and fix you up with a sling. Move your fingers from time to time so that they don't get stiff. You can dispense with the sling in a fortnight or so.'

'And that's all?'

'That's all; you're free to go as soon as the effects of the pain-killer have worn off. You may feel a bit muzzy. Give it a quarter of an hour or so and it should be fine, but of course do come back if it gives you any trouble.'

Julia fixed the pad and sling in position and gave the patient a reassuring smile. 'Goodbye, Mr Brack; go and sit in the waiting area for a little while before going home.'

'Well, goodbye, Sister, thanks, and you too, Doc.' A relieved Mr Brack went on his way.

Luke flexed his hands. 'My God, that bloke had

strong muscles. Thank goodness Imelda didn't try to manipulate; she would probably have done some damage to herself in the process.'

'Yes, especially as I don't think the patient would have been so co-operative with a woman doctor. I think he has a poor opinion of females in the medical and nursing professions.'

'More fool him,' said Luke flatly, almost indifferently.

Julia's heart felt like a lump of lead. She longed for him to respond to her as he had at the cottage. What had happened to change him? He had been warm, and loving, and tender. He'd said that he loved her, and yet here he was, being cool and indifferent. She couldn't believe the change in him. She wanted to reach out and touch him, make him come back to her instead of keeping his distance.

She didn't know what to make of his sudden change of attitude. It was hard to believe that post-pneumonia depression was at the bottom of it, but what other reason could there be? Men, it seemed, and particularly this one special man, were unpredictable. She was in such an unhappy muddle.

Luke was saying something to her, and she dragged her thoughts back to the immediate present.

'I'm so sorry,' she said. 'What did you say?'

'That I thought you might be pleased to see me, since the department is so busy.'

'Well, of course I am.' She went on tidying up the cubicle, glad to have her hands busy and avoid his eyes.

He gave a tight-lipped smile that didn't reach his eyes. 'In spite of my post-pneumonia blues?'

'In spite of that.' She managed a smile of sorts. He

seemed to be trying to be friendly in a professional fashion at least; she would have to try too. 'It is good to have you back.'

Luke ran a hand through his hair, leaving it looking shaggy and untidy.

'You need a haircut.' The words came out without her thinking. Why had she said that, when what she wanted to do was ask him why he'd been cold and distant with her on the phone, and yet seemed now to be less distant and trying to make contact. She looked at his strained, stern face. He was obviously wrestling with an insoluble problem that he couldn't confide to her. But why couldn't he, if he loved her?

Luke gave a harsh laugh. 'I haven't thought much about haircuts,' he said shortly. 'They're pretty low on my agenda at present.' He turned and walked out of the cubicle.

The unit remained busy all the morning, and, apart from bumping into each other occasionally as they worked, they didn't have the opportunity for further conversation. Just before lunchtime, however, when Julia had made up her mind to have a sandwich and catch up on paperwork, Luke appeared in her office.

'Julia,' he said abruptly, 'dine with me tonight; I've something to tell you.'

She looked up and straight into his steely grey-green eyes, which gave nothing of his feelings away.

'Yes,' she said at once, not pretending to prevaricate. 'I'll dine with you.'

'I'll pick you up at eight and we'll go out to eat.'

'Fine, I'll be ready.'

He went away after this stilted conversation, and she

heard his footsteps receding down the corridor. What, she wondered, had he to tell her that was causing him so much soul-searching? The only possible problem that she could think he might want to discuss was his relationship with Grace. But surely that was all finished and done with; he'd made it perfectly clear when he was first ill that there was nothing left between him and Grace.

A cold hand clutched at her heart. Was he going to tell her that everything was now over between him and herself? After all, he had talked about being maudlin and had once said that he didn't go in for long relationships. Was he now regretting the fact that he'd told her he loved her? Had that been simply a result of his illness and his slight dependency on her nursing ability when she visited him? What rubbish; of course it wasn't that. He had been interested in her before he went to the conference; it had nothing whatsoever to do with his being sick. She knew, though, that until she met him tonight and he explained himself it was pointless to speculate.

Firmly squashing her fears, she put the problem from her, and got on with her paperwork.

She had been hard at it for about half an hour when there was a knock at her door, and Sonia appeared.

'Can I beg a cup of caffeine, either tea or coffee?' she said as soon as she saw Julia. 'I'm luxuriating in the fact that I'm on nights off, starting from tonight.'

'I thought that you weren't due to be off till tomorrow?'

'Polly Peters asked me to swap with her and bring my nights off forward, so I have. Only too happy to oblige. Her husband's due home from Ireland at the end of the week, after several months away.'

'Is it right that he's been recently promoted?'

'Yes, he's a major now. Quite a step up for him, I understand, but it's got its drawbacks: apparently he'll get another overseas posting, and Polly might have to decide between her career here, or going with him.'

'Is there a contest?'

'Well, you know, she is in the running for night supervisor, something that she's been aiming at for a long time. She's worked as hard for that promotion as presumably her husband has for his. I can understand that she wouldn't want to give that up lightly.'

'Yes, but she must have known when she got married that her husband might be sent abroad and would want her to go with him.'

Sonia sighed. 'The trouble is, who thinks that far ahead when they're in love.'

'Yes, who indeed?' replied Julia, and continued to ponder on the nature of love and the extraordinary effect it had on a person when she was back with the patients and involved in bouts of feverish activity.

Luke went off at five o'clock, reminding her that he would pick her up at eight. His manner still gave nothing away. He looked rather more tired and drawn, not surprising after putting in hours of hard work for the first time since his illness.

'Are you sure that you feel up to going out to dinner?' asked Julia anxiously. 'We can put it off if you like, or I could cook something at the cottage.'

'No,' he said shortly, 'that won't be necessary. I'm quite fit enough to go out for a meal, and I'd prefer it to be somewhere neutral.'

Julia's heart sank. There seemed no getting through to him; he remained stiff and withdrawn.

There was really no need for her to stay on duty as things had quietened down after the earlier bustle, but she was reluctant to go back to her flat until the time had come to get ready for her date with Luke. She would only spin useless thoughts round in her head. It was much better, she decided, to keep busy, and keep her unhappy thoughts at bay.

Most of the cubicles were empty, and she helped the nurses tidy these up. Two cubicles were occupied, one by a woman having stitches put into a cut in her hand, caused by a carving knife. In the other cubicle a middle-aged man was waiting for the freezing process to work before having a boil on his neck lanced. Julia asked him why he had come to A and E for what was a routine procedure, something that his doctor could have carried out.

'I'm a rep,' he explained, 'and I've only stopped off overnight. This thing was giving me gyp. I think that my collar's been rubbing against it all day and made it worse. I knew that I wouldn't sleep if I didn't get something done about it; that's why I came here.'

Julia looked at the badly inflamed boil.

'Well, I'm glad that you decided to get something done about it,' she said. 'Another day or two and it would have been a real mess.'

'Yeah,' said the man ruefully. 'I've already had a rocket from the doctor.'

At that moment Dr Peak appeared. He seemed surprised to see Julia.

'I thought that you'd gone ages ago,' he said.

'I should have,' Julia said briskly, with false cheerfulness. 'You know what it's like when you're having fun, but I'm off now. Goodnight.' She nodded to both the doctor and the patient, and left. She really had no excuse for staying longer, anyway; she just had time to shower and change to be ready for Luke to pick her up. Her heart fluttered at the thought of seeing him, even though she wasn't expecting much from the evening, except, perhaps, stilted explanations.

A few minutes later she drove down the drive to the lodge. Lights were blazing and music blaring from the ground-floor rooms, and as she let herself into the hall she was met by a crowd of people all milling around with glasses in their hands. Both doors to the two front flats were open, and there were more people obviously partying inside both flats.

'What in the world is this all about?' she asked Sonia, who had appeared and was thrusting a glass of wine into her hands.

'It's Jake and Ann; they've got engaged at last, and they're getting married next month.'

'I don't believe it! How long have they been going around together?'

'Oh, years.'

'What's brought this on, then, and why so sudden?'

'Ann's just discovered that she's pregnant—you know, the best-laid plans—and they're both delighted, and, hey presto, they decided to make honest parents of each other.'

'Well, that's wonderful. Where are they? I must go and wish them well.'

Ann and Jake were in Ann's sitting-room, sitting side by side on a sofa, apparently indifferent to their friends seething all around them.

Sonia, who had followed Julia, said, 'Look at them, like two young love-birds. You'd never think that they were both in their thirties and had been going out together for years, would you?'

Julia shook her head. No, she thought, you wouldn't; they look so radiantly happy. And it was at that moment that she knew that she wanted to marry Luke, no matter what. She had no doubts. She was prepared to take any risks. She just wanted the chance to see Luke looking as happy as Jake was looking at this moment. Nothing else was important. She didn't know what he was going to say to her that evening, and she didn't care. All she knew was that she must convince him that they were meant for each other. She had never felt so certain about anything in her life.

Presently she went up to her flat, showered, and changed into a floaty silk dress, all pastel greens and smoky blues, and was reminded of Luke buying blue freesias to match her eyes. She put on high heels, a little mascara and dark red lipstick, swamped herself in her favourite perfume—the one that he liked—slipped a blue velvet jacket round her shoulders, and waited for Luke to arrive. The party was going strong, with couples dancing in the hall to music coming from systems from both downstairs flats, when her intercom doorbell rang. It had to be Luke. She pressed the buzzer to let him in, and went down to meet him.

She saw him at once, head and shoulders above everyone else. He was standing in the hall, surrounded by a crowd of people, when she walked down the stairs, and someone was pressing a drink into his hand. As if knowing that she was there, he looked up as she started down the last few steps, and pushed his way through to her.

He put his glass down on a table at the foot of the stairs and held out both his hands.

'Julia, you look marvellous, but tonight is hardly a celebration.' He sounded sad. His eyes swept over her and he said softly, though she could hear his voice through the din, 'You look lovely, delightful, very feminine. The colours are perfect—your colours. And you're wearing that delicious perfume again.' He frowned. 'But it's all wrong for what I have to say to you.'

She was glad that he didn't sound stiff and distant. She said boldly, surprising even herself by her words, 'It's never wrong to dress up for the man you love.'

'Really?' said Luke drily, looking grim. He stared silently at her for a moment, and then shrugged and gave a half-smile. 'Oh, well, so be it.' He looked around him, and changed the subject. 'What's this madhouse all about?' he asked with raised eyebrows.

Julia gathered herself together, determined not to be put off by his strange manner. 'Oh, it's a party for Ann Sibley and Jake North,' she explained. 'They've just got engaged; they're going to get married next month.'

'Good lord, are they really, after all this time?'

'That's right; their long, ongoing relationship has blossomed. They're expecting a baby, and have decided that the time has come to get married. Isn't it wonderful?' And that, she thought, was a silly, unsophisticated remark to make to a man like Luke.

There was a moment's silence, then he said quietly in a surprisingly gentle tone, 'To be in love and expecting a baby has got to be the best of all possible scenarios. Lucky them.'

'That's what I thought,' Julia murmured, startled by the unexpectedness of his comment and the tone of his voice. Then quite suddenly she remembered what he had said about wanting a family when he'd explained one of the reasons why he and Grace had split up. 'She didn't want children, not ever,' he'd said sadly.

He took her arm and steered her to the door. His face was again stern, rigid. 'Come,' he said. 'It's time we were on our way; we've a lot of talking to do.'

CHAPTER TEN

IN SILENCE Julia and Luke drove through the calm October night, mild as summer. There was a huge moon rising in the eastern sky, a harvest moon.

Luke drove to the end of the drive and turned left on to the main road. Julia was pleased that he didn't stop at Poachers, that favourite haunt of Princes' staff, but continued on into the centre of the town. Her mind was busy wondering about the conversation that they were going to have as she tried to guess at what Luke might be going to say to her. She suppressed her fears that it was going to be something that she would dread hearing, and reminded herself of her determination to marry Luke at all costs. They loved each other; that was all that mattered.

She watched his competent, sinewy hands on the steering-wheel, hands that she had seen performing minor miracles on injured people, and felt comforted. She recalled his remark when he had heard Ann's and Jake's news, and was further reassured. It revealed the gentle, very human man beneath the polished façade. A man who could feel that way about love and marriage would not brush off what had passed between them as nothing, whatever was bothering him at this precise moment.

He spoke at last as they drew up in a small square outside an Indian restaurant.

'I thought,' he said, sounding like a polite stranger,

'you would enjoy one of their light vegetable curries at this time of night, a house speciality. Well worth trying if you haven't had it before, though they have a good menu if you want something different.'

'The curry sounds perfect.'

The interior of the restaurant was dim and discreet. Their table was tucked away in a corner in a little pew-like box, with bead curtains giving it privacy. Luke was obviously known and respected by the Indian owner, who came over to greet him as they sat down at the table. Luke introduced him to Julia, and discussed the wine that they should have with the meal. A very light, dry white wine that would complement the curry was decided upon. They chose starters of chilled melon and guavas, marinated in a tart lemony sauce.

Wine and starters were served to them by smiling, soft-footed waiters, who then withdrew behind the bead curtains.

'Perfect for preparing the palate for the curry,' said Luke, forking up a mouthful of melon. 'Do eat, Julia.' The light from the small glass lamp on the centre of the table glimmered in the grey-green depths of his eyes, and threw his prominent, handsome nose into relief. He gave her a tight smile that barely quirked the corners of his mouth, the only indication that he was not fully relaxed, as his eyes met hers above the narrow table. He put out his left hand and lightly touched her wrist as she obediently raised her fork to her mouth. 'Now,' he said in a very deep, serious voice, 'let's talk. I want to explain, now that I am quite fit, how I feel about us.'

Julia gulped down her mouthful of delicious fruit. Fear of what he might be going to say made swallowing difficult. She nodded. 'Yes, you said that we would discuss our future once you were well, but that was before. . .' She hesitated and frowned as she tried to think of the right words to use.

A shadow passed across Luke's face. 'Before. . .?' he prompted, wondering if she had any idea what he was going to say to her.

Julia was still silent, still groping for words, looking at him intently, her smoky blue eyes tender with love. 'Before, Julia? Before what?' he repeated.

She found her voice and said, gathering her courage, 'Before you asked for space, before your manner towards me changed and over the phone you became cool and distant, as if you had stopped loving me, after all that you said at the cottage that last afternoon. It doesn't make any sort of sense, Luke. You said that you loved me then, and I believed you; I still believe that you love me. Please, Luke, tell me that I'm right.'

Her lovely eyes pleaded with him.

Before he could say anything, the beads on the curtain rattled and a waiter appeared to collect their plates and bring the next course. They carried on some sort of meaningless conversation as he whisked in and out.

Luke nodded at their plates as the waiter left. 'We'd better eat,' he said, 'and go back to Thatches later and talk some more. It's impossible here.'

Julia looked at him and tried to guess what was going on behind his bland expression. What would happen when he took her back to his home? Would they just talk, or would they—a trickle of excitement ran down her spine—would they make love? Would he forget whatever it was that was bothering him, and realise that all she wanted was him and his love, that she cared not a jot about anything else?

Luke was watching her. He thought he had some idea of what was going through her mind. 'Eat,' he said softly. 'And then we'll go home.' At least there, he thought, we won't be interrupted. It had been a mistake to come to the restaurant, even though he had hoped to avoid an intimate confrontation. Saving Julia distress was his prime concern.

Home! Luke's home. It had become a haven when he was ill, a haven of love and intimacy. Julia looked down at the steaming plate of curry. She didn't feel hungry, but perhaps to please Luke and fill in the time until he was ready to leave she could manage something. Tentatively she picked up her fork, and her hand hovered over the succulent-looking vegetables. Luke stretched a hand across the table, took the fork from her uncertain fingers, and speared a bright green bean and a slice of tomato and a few grains of rice.

'Open wide,' he said with a smile, as if speaking to small, much loved child, and, as she did so, popped the offering into her mouth. He handed the fork back to her. 'Now try again, love. You've hardly eaten all day, and you've been working flat out.'

She laughed softly. She felt a new woman. How gentle and caring he was. Whatever he had to say, he couldn't hide that.

'I'll try,' she said.

Surprisingly, once she had started to eat she began to enjoy the delicately spiced food, and her appetite slowly returned. Nothing had been resolved between them, but the heavens hadn't fallen in. She still hadn't a clue as to why he was prevaricating, but deep within her she knew that it wasn't because he didn't love her. Love. Such a small word, meaning so much. She turned it over and over in her mind, wondering at it, and the fact that he'd said it.

Her thoughts had been so busy, and Luke had kept up such a flow of conversation, in his usual composed fashion, to which she had answered in monosyllables, that she hadn't noticed the waiter coming and going, and changing dishes.

She looked up from her empty plate in astonishment, and found Luke smiling at her in a quizzical fashion just as she finished her sorbet.

'You see, you were hungry,' he said in his deep voice. 'You needed to eat.'

For a moment Julia was struck dumb. How could a whole meal have come and gone without her noticing it? She had been so wrapped up in her thoughts, and so calmed and relaxed by Luke's gentle conversation, that time had not registered.

All of a sudden she wanted to be back in the car with him, alone with him, and speeding towards Thatches. Some instinct told her that only there would she learn the truth about Luke's seeming withdrawal from her. She longed to feel his strong, sinewy hands touching and exciting her as they had before. She felt herself blushing, and with an involuntary gesture put her hands up to her cheeks.

Luke's eyes met hers, and, as so often before, he seemed to read her mind. His wide, tender mouth curved into a smile.

He said softly and quite naturally, 'How delightful—a woman who can still blush.' He stood up and came round the table, and offered her a hand. She put hers into it as she rose from her set. 'Let's —'

There was a crash of glass and crockery from beyond the bead curtains, and a murmur and then a crescendo of voices.

Luke moved swiftly, dropping Julia's hand and parting the curtains in one easy movement. 'Somebody's collapsed,' he said over his shoulder. 'We'd better see what we can do.' He moved out into the main restaurant, and Julia followed him.

'Good lord,' he said as he knelt down beside the body lying on the floor. 'It's Cliff, Cliff Roberts; he's a friend.'

A woman in the circle of people standing round them cried out. 'Luke, oh, thank God you're here. What's wrong? Please help him, please.' She crouched down on the floor beside Luke.

'Miriam, my dear, I don't know what's wrong yet, but I'll do what I can.' He turned to Julia. 'Cliff's wife,' he said briskly. 'See that someone looks after her; I need your help. And ask someone to ring for an ambulance.' Julia put an arm round Mrs Roberts. 'Come on,' she said gently. 'Sit down and let Luke and me get on. I'm a nurse. We'll do all that we can.'

Willing hands guided Miriam to a chair, and Julia knelt down by the stricken body opposite Luke.

Luke took charge. The stunned people who had been sitting at the table with the sick man stood back. Cliff Roberts had fallen sideways when he collapsed. He was overweight and of early middle age, judging from his fair, almost grey hair. He was lying on the floor, looking glisteningly pale, with a bluish line round his mouth.

Luke felt for a pulse. 'Stroke, I think,' he muttered

to Julia. 'But heart's gone too; there's no pulse. He's stopped breathing. Let's resuscitate.'

Julia lost count of time as she and Luke worked on the stricken man together, he compressing the chest, and she, after clearing the airways, giving mouth-to-mouth resuscitation. They worked rhythmically on opposite sides of the body in an effort to restore the man's own ability to breathe. The ambulance arrived just as he took his first shuddering breath, and they were able to hand over to the paramedic and his team with all their up-to-date equipment.

'I'll have to follow the ambulance up to A and E,' said Luke, 'as he's a friend. And as you can see, Miriam's pretty shaken. She'll go with him in the ambulance, but I'll have to see what she wants to do afterwards, and do a bit of reassuring; it's the least I can do.'

'Of course.'

Luke squeezed her hand and smiled into her eyes as they got into his car a few minutes later. 'The best-laid plans. . .' he said.

'Don't worry about it; it can't be helped. I'm glad you were there to do what you did as a doctor and a friend.' She felt a mixture of frustration and relief that their evening had to come to an end without resolution. She was as much in the dark as she had been at the beginning of the day.

'I'll drop you off at the lodge, and tomorrow we'll pick up from where we left off.'

She nodded.

'And Julia?'

'Yes?'

'I'll do what I can to explain matters, my word on it.'

'All right.'

They smiled at each other, and Luke touched her cheek briefly with a gentle finger. He was no longer cold and distant. She felt immensely comforted by his words and the small gesture.

The journey back to Princes, following the ambulance, didn't take long, and they spoke only of their patient and what his chances were, deliberately avoiding any more personal conversation. The incident had clearly marked the end of their evening, and Luke's recent attitude. She was none the wiser about what Luke had been going to divulge, but his last words had helped to reassure her. The future began to look less bleak. There were still hurdles to be surmounted, but at least it looked now as if they might overcome them together.

He pulled up in front of the lodge, and she released her seatbelt immediately, and made to open the door to get out, knowing that Luke wouldn't want to delay getting up to the hospital.

He put a detaining hand on her arm. 'Thanks for all your help,' he said softly. 'I couldn't have managed without you. You're beautiful, Julia, a super nurse, and a lovely womanly woman. Remember that.'

He leaned across the small space between them and kissed her very gently on the mouth, and then unlatched and pushed open the door. She got out and closed the door, and he released the handbrake, put the car into gear, and sped away up the drive.

'Goodnight, you dear man,' she whispered into the still, moonlit night. 'Good luck with your patient.'

* * *

In spite of the party still going on downstairs, and the muddled, inconclusive thoughts left by her evening with Luke, Julia slept well and dreamlessly. Perhaps it was on account of the physical effort she had put in helping to resuscitate the collapsed man, or perhaps it was because Luke's parting words had made it clear that he loved her, whatever hang-up was keeping him from her at this moment. Whatever it was, it had lulled her into a sense of security.

When she woke, faint signs of dawn were creeping round the curtains. Her tummy immediately knotted with excitement and anticipation. One way or another, today was going to be special. Luke and she would meet at work as usual, but there the similarity with any other day would vanish. Because they were professionals, they wouldn't let their personal affairs spill over into work, but they would each be conscious of the other, and of the events of the previous night. And this evening, when work had at last finished, what then? Thatches, and Luke's explanation of his reasons for demanding space, which only the coronary collapse had prevented him from revealing last night? And after that, what?

She pulled back the curtains. A grey, foggy world met her eyes. The trees, with the last few leaves clinging to them, were beaded with moisture. The drive was almost hidden by a blanket of mist. Well, at least she would be too busy to dwell on personal matters, as almost certainly the fog meant accidents of one sort of another.

The phone by her bedside rang, and she knew that it was Luke.

'Julia, how are you this morning?' His voice was matter-of-fact, but immediately her spirits rose.

'Fine, and you?' Her heart did its usual mad thumping at the sound of his voice.

'Oh, I'm fine too.' She fancied that she could see him shrugging his shoulders, as if his answer didn't matter.

'How's your friend?' she asked.

'Holding his own in Intensive Care. Gregory Hurst's looking after him. He couldn't be in better hands.'

'No.'

'His wife, Miriam, asked me to tell you how much she appreciated what you did.'

'Thank you.'

The phone was silent for a moment, and then he said, 'I don't know if you've noticed, but there's one hell of a fog. I think that we're going to be busy today, if past experience is anything to go by. I'll be leaving within the next few minutes. See you at work; take care.'

'I'm only going up the drive.'

'Nevertheless, take care.'

'And you,' she replied. 'Bye.'

'Bye.' He rang off.

A very brief, businesslike conversation, she thought, but his concern for her safety on her short journey was almost lover-like, and his concern over the day's work ahead good reason for not prolonging his call. He might have said more had he been less practical, less concerned. But early morning was not the time to resolve personal problems; they would have to wait.

* * *

She heard a couple of ambulances wail up the drive while she was getting showered and dressed. The holocaust, she thought grimly, has begun.

A and E was frantically busy from the moment that she arrived on duty. At some point Luke arrived, but they had barely time to exchange more than rather guarded glances before they were caught up in work. It was impossible to know what had happened to the morning and half of the afternoon, for it was three o'clock before the seemingly endless stream of accident victims stopped arriving.

The motorway injuries were generally the worst, because speed as well as impact played a large part in battering bodies, but there were, too, quite a few other victims that morning. Two elderly people had slipped on the greasy pavements and fractured bones in legs and arms. A child who had run out in the road in front of a car, unseen by the driver in the thick fog, had multiple injuries, and was still being assessed, and the driver was being treated for shock.

The list, thought Julia wearily as she disposed of the umpteenth pair of plastic gloves, was never-ending. But it wasn't. Suddenly, or so it seemed, the ambulances stopped heralding their arrival at the door, the waiting areas began to thin out, and the fog, so she heard, had eventually cleared. With luck, from now until dusk, when there was likely to be more fog, A and E would be relatively quiet.

Julia had requested, and received, during the morning, more medical help in the shape of a junior houseman and the registrar from the rehabilitation unit, Guy Lloyd. They had both worked hard, and Julia, with

Luke's agreement, sent them for a short break. When they returned, they could hold the fort, while she and the regular doctors took a rest and caught up on notes for their records. Both young doctors were happy with this arrangement, and, together with several nurses, made for the duty room for sandwiches and coffee.

Imelda, who in spite of her willowy and slender figure was always hungry and could tuck away mountains of food, said to Julia, 'I do hope they leave some for us; I'm famished.'

'Don't worry,' said Julia, laughing at Imelda's forlorn-looking face, 'there's a huge plateful of sandwiches being kept nice and fresh for us in my office.'

'Thank God for that,' said the pretty young doctor piously.

John Peak came out of the cubicle where he and Imelda had been working on the small girl who had been struck by the car and who was now being taken up to the ICU. He looked tired in the way that they all did at times, not so much through the volume of work, but by the nature and cause of the injuries with which they had been dealing, most of which could have been avoided with a little more care and thoughtfulness.

He stared at Julia for a moment, and then said bitterly, 'Bloody waste, what a bloody waste.'

'Isn't she going to make it?' asked Julia.

John shook his head. 'If she does,' he said, sounding unutterably sad, 'God knows what sort of a mess she'll be in for the rest of her life.' He peeled off his plastic apron and gloves and tossed them into a bin. 'I'm going out for a breath of fresh air,' he muttered, striding towards the outer door.

'Sandwiches and drinks in my office when you come back, John,' Julia called after him.

He held up a hand in acknowledgement, and passed out through the doorway.

Luke came out of another cubicle, looking rather drawn, but quite cheerful.

'Nice old lady in the last car in the pile-up,' he said. 'Not too badly injured—cuts, bruises and shock mostly—and her husband's in a similar state. They'll both do.' He smiled at Julia and Imelda, but his eyes lingered on Julia. 'Well, Sister,' he said, the warmth in his eyes as they rested on her at odds with his professional tone, 'have you managed to supply us with some goodies in your usual brilliant fashion, or do we have to go foraging?'

'There's food in my office, Dr Steel,' she replied, holding back a smile, determined to be as formal as he in front of Imelda. The grapevine was quite busy enough as it was without giving it more ammunition. 'Dr Lloyd and the houseman will be back shortly. Why don't you and Dr Robbins make a start? I'll just sort my nurses out and then I'll be with you.'

Before she finished speaking, Imelda was already on her way to the office. 'Food, glorious food,' she called over her shoulder. 'I'll probably scoff the lot.'

Luke took hold of Julia's arm and looked down at her, his eyes bright, commanding. Just for a moment they were alone together in the short corridor beyond the cubicles. 'You'll be coming along soon, won't you? I want a word about tonight,' he said in a firm voice. 'We have to meet at your place or mine to get some privacy.'

Julia nodded. His touch had unnerved her. Her heart

was in her mouth, her pulses bounding. Speech was, for the moment, beyond her.

Her place or his? Hers, she decided. She would feel firmer, safer on home ground, whatever he had to tell her.

At eight o'clock Julia, Imelda and Luke were due to be relieved by the night staff, but just before then a Mr and Mrs Kent and their two grandchildren were admitted. They had been involved in a fire caused by a faulty gas fire. Fumes and smoke had taken their toll of the old couple, though the children were only suffering from mild shock.

It was nearly nine o'clock before Julia and Luke finished dealing with the Kent family. They handed over to the night staff to complete the arrangements for the warding of the two elderly patients, already beginning to respond to initial treatment. The Kents' son and daughter had been tracked down by the police, and would soon arrive to take their children home.

Wearily, but with a feeling of triumph that things had not been worse for their patients, Julia and Luke disposed of their aprons and gloves, and discovered that, in spite of the protection, they were still grimy. Somehow old Mrs Kent had managed to get her sooty fingers everywhere when she had been thrashing about, and they were both covered with black marks.

They grinned at each other as they made for Julia's office.

'To say the least, we need a wash and brush up,' said Luke. 'You have soot on your nose.'

'And in my hair,' said Julia. 'Ugh, I had forgotten how the smell of smoke clings. I need a shower and a hair wash, and a bath, and then another shower to get rid of the stench.'

'And I,' said Luke, 'feel contaminated from top to toe.'

'You are,' said Julia, feeling rather light-headed. 'Your white coat isn't white any longer, Dr Steel, sir.'

Luke pushed her gently ahead of him into her office, where the night sister, Polly Peters, was sitting at the desk, going through the report and the card file, looking incredibly neat, and starchy-clean.

'Evening,' she said cheerfully as Julia and Luke reeled into the room. 'You poor things, you must be exhausted, and you look pretty gross.' She sniffed. 'And smell it,' she said with a laugh.

'Just stop the chit-chat and pour the coffee, Peters,' said Julia, sinking on to a chair. She grinned and nodded towards Luke, who was lowering himself into another chair. 'Our esteemed boss needs his shot of caffeine.'

'Coming up, O, master,' said Polly Peters with a giggle. She handed them both a mug of coffee. 'Now I'm going to love you and leave you, and do my rounds. Leave any other info in the book, Julia. I'll pop in later to check up.'

She went away, and silence descended on the office as they both relaxed, cupping their mugs of coffee and sipping at the steaming contents. After a while Julia began scribbling away in the report book.

The room was blissfully quiet after the outside bustle. They sat in a companionable silence, compounded of weariness and hard work, and the pleasure of being alone together.

After a while they smiled at each other, their eyes full of longing.

Luke said in a quiet voice. 'Have you nearly finished?'

'Yes.'

'Good. I'll do my paperwork tomorrow.'

'Right.'

Luke asked in a low voice, 'Do you still want to talk, Julia?'

'Yes, I do,' she said firmly. 'I don't think that I can bear the uncertainty any longer. I know we both need to shower, but I'd rather forgo that and make do with a quick wash, and go to my flat and talk, Luke.'

'Your flat? I'd rather we went to Thatches,' Luke said quietly. 'It's more private than the lodge.' He'd either forgotten or ignored the fact that he'd given her the choice of her place or his earlier. He gave her a broad, teasing smile that made his eyes twinkle with fun, and Julia found herself smiling back. 'And if you change your mind about a shower, I've a very nice roomy one that you're welcome to use.'

It wasn't worth arguing about, and he was quite correct: his place was more private. 'We'll go to Thatches,' she said, giving in gracefully.

'Good. I'll just go and collect my things from my office and sluice off the worst of the grime. See you in ten minutes.'

Half an hour later they drew up outside Luke's cottage, where a soft orange-coloured light glowed above the porch.

The fog had lifted, and a few stars and a full moon

half hidden by wispy clouds floated overhead. Thatches in the moonlight looked incredibly romantic.

Luke put his key in the lock, pushed open the door, and stood back to let Julia through.

'Do make yourself comfortable,' he said, like the perfect host that he was, adding, 'I'm going to have a stiff whisky, and I suggest that you have a very weak one, or coffee or tea since you'll be driving later. What would you prefer?'

'Tea, please. I seem to have drunk gallons of coffee today.'

'Right, I won't be a moment.'

'I can make it; please let me. I know where everything is.' She needed to be doing something with her hands. She followed him through to the kitchen.

Luke shrugged. 'If you insist,' he said. 'I'll pour my drink.' He stared hard at her for a moment, and then went back into the sitting-room. It was almost, she thought, as if he suddenly couldn't bear to be close to her.

A few minutes later the kettle boiled, and her hands shook as she poured the water into the teapot. Now that they were about to talk, she rather wished that she hadn't insisted on knowing the truth about his withdrawn state. It might have resolved itself. What if, after all, it was just post-infection depression? She might be stirring up a hornets' nest of uncertainty for nothing.

She poured her tea and returned to the sitting-room. Luke was sitting on the leather settee.

'Come,' he said, to her surprise, patting the space beside him.

'I'd rather sit here,' she said, sitting in one of the armchairs beside the fireplace.

'I'm not going to rape you, for God's sake,' said Luke wearily. 'I just thought that it would be easier to talk sitting next to each other.'

'Sorry, I feel more comfortable here,' replied Julia, knowing that she would find his nearness too disturbing if she sat beside him.

Luke gave her a wry smile. 'Scared of me?'

'Not at all.' She clenched her hands round her mug of tea. 'Are you going to explain, Luke, why you suddenly changed from a loving person to a cold, indifferent one in the space of a couple of days?'

'I wasn't, and am not, indifferent, my dear. Never that, not where you're concerned, believe me. But I was, and am, frightened for you.'

'Frightened?'

'Yes, because you're loving and loyal and will want to stick by me whatever happens. I didn't want to put you into that position. I thought that if I prevaricated, seemed less loving, you might back off at least for a little while.' He gave a thin smile. 'I might have known better. You don't fall in and out of love at the drop of a hat.'

'No, I'm a pretty faithful sort of person, and I'm a one-man woman. Besides, you asked me to love you whatever happened.'

'So I did. But you see, Julia, your sort of unselfish, untarnished love makes you very vulnerable. You're too generous, and how will I know that it's love that you're offering, and not just compassion, when you learn what I have to tell you?' He looked at her questioningly across the small space between the settee and the armchair.

Julia went cold. What on earth was he trying to tell

her—that he had inherited or was suffering from some dreadful condition that he was afraid of passing on to any children he might have? No, common sense told her, it had to be something that he had only recently learned about, or he would never have allowed himself to speak of love in the first place. But what could it be that was so frightening?

She got up and went and sat beside him. 'I don't really know the answer to that,' she said softly. 'I only know that I love you, and want you to love me, whatever happens. And if compassion enters into it, who cares? We all need a little of both in our lives some time.'

He reached out and took her hand and caressed it gently. 'Julia,' he said evenly, 'could you love me if I were sterile, infertile, unable to give you children?'

'Of course; why not?' she said without hesitation. She was astonished by his question. 'Why on earth do you ask?'

'Because I think I may be sterile.'

'You? But why? You had mumps when you were a boy; surely you would have known if that attack had produced side-effects?'

'No. It was a severe attack, but my aunt probably didn't even discuss that possibility with my doctor, and I was too young to think of such things. I've never given it a thought before, knowing how rare it is, or I'd have had tests done. Hearing about poor Dan, and talking to you about marriage and families, simply brought it into focus. I have got tests under way now, by the way, and I'll have full results in a day or two.'

Julia stood up and prowled restlessly round the room and came to a halt facing Luke. She was angry and relieved, and she wanted to cry. She blinked back the tears.

'And you put me through days of misery wondering if you had fallen out of love with me, because of a little thing like that?' she uttered at last. 'Oh, Luke, how could you, how could you? Why on earth didn't you tell me what was the matter? Even if you *are* sterile—and that's a pretty remote possibility—what does it matter if we love each other?'

Luke stood up. He seemed taller and thinner since his illness, his face more lined, and yet more handsome. Such a strong face, Julia thought, taking a deep breath. He put his hands on her shoulders, and looked down into her anguished face. 'It matters,' he said softly, 'because you want children.'

'I want *you* more. Don't you understand, Luke? For me that's enough.'

'Now, perhaps, but in the future. . .'

'I shall always want you more, and we can always adopt children.' She looked up at him, her eyes wide, still glistening with unshed tears, and produced a tremulous smile. 'Anyone would think,' she said shakily, 'the way we're talking, that you had asked me to marry you.'

'I can do that any time, but wouldn't you rather wait till the tests come through, just to be sure, love?' Luke's voice was even deeper than usual, and throbbing with emotion. His hands tightened on her shoulders.

'No,' she said firmly. 'Please ask me to marry you.'

Luke drew her closer. 'I don't ask,' he said. 'I demand that you marry me. Say that you will, Julia.'

'I will.'

Luke gathered her into his arms and bent to kiss her.

'You smell horribly smoky,' he mumbled as his mouth found hers.

'And so do you,' she muttered when he released her lips for a few moments. Pent-up emotion made her giggle. 'It isn't very romantic, is it?'

'There is a remedy.' His eyes gleamed down at her.

'What?'

'We can take a shower. I told you that I had a spacious shower.'

'"Roomy", you said.'

'Roomy enough for two,' said Luke with a wicked gleam in his eyes. 'I suggest that we wash off all this grime, and then, my dearest, darling, lovely girl, when we are all scented and shiny clean, I'll propose to you all over again. How does that sound?'

'It sounds wonderful, very poetic, almost too good to be true,' said Julia in a husky voice, revelling in his loving words.

'Oh, my darling, it's true enough; make no mistake about that. I'm breaking the habit of a lifetime asking you to marry me, so why shouldn't I be, just for once, the tiniest bit poetic, a man of romance rather than a man of science?'

'No reason,' whispered Julia breathlessly. 'No reason at all.'

A few minutes later, to Julia's utter surprise, they stood together, naked and taut with love, under the hot needles of water of the shower.

Luke soaped her gently all over, his hands lingering lovingly on her breasts and thighs, until she was aching with love for him and she longed to make passionate love to him. She wanted him as much as he wanted her. It was a wonderful, healing revelation after her days of unhappiness and doubt. Her instincts told her it would be a perfect coming together.

'Will you marry me, Julia?' he asked softly. 'I love you so very much.'

'Oh, yes, please,' she murmured, her hands stealing up over his shining wet shoulders and neck until her fingers tangled in the thick mass of his hair. 'Oh, yes, please, just as soon as possible.'

And there, under Luke's shower for two, they made at first gentle, and then passionate love to each other.

A few days later the result of Luke's tests came through and he learned what Julia had been certain of all the time—that he was healthily fertile.

They were married at the end of November in the hospital chapel, with Julia's family and the many friends that they both had among the staff of Princes present.

Matron Clare Dunn was there, and Gregory and Erica Hurst, who had themselves been married in the chapel in May. And representing the paediatric department was a radiantly and imminently expectant Poppy Fordyce with her husband Nicholas. They had married in February. Also present, from the rehabilitation unit, were Babs Becker-Brown and her fiancé Guy Lloyd, who would be married in the spring.

Sonia was Julia's bridesmaid, and Bill, Julia's twin brother, Luke's best man.

Julia reflected happily, as she walked down the aisle on Luke's arm, that this year had been a good one for Princes and romance.

As they came out of the chapel the mist which had been shrouding everything all the morning suddenly lifted, and a shaft of sunlight illuminated them both as they stood in the porch.

Luke took Julia in his arms and kissed her. 'Isn't there an old song,' he said, 'which says something about the sun shining on a happy bride?'

'I don't need sunshine to make me happy,' said Julia firmly. 'I just need you.'

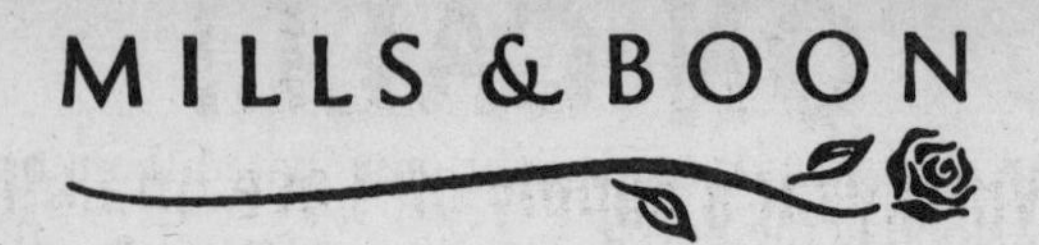
MILLS & BOON

ON CALL!

Win a year's supply of 'Love on Call' romances ABSOLUTELY FREE?

Yes, you can win one whole year's supply of 'Love on Call' romances! It's easy! All you have to do is convert the four sets of numbers below into television soaps by using the letters in the telephone dial. Fill in your answers plus your name and address details overleaf, cut out and send to us by 30th Sept. 1994.

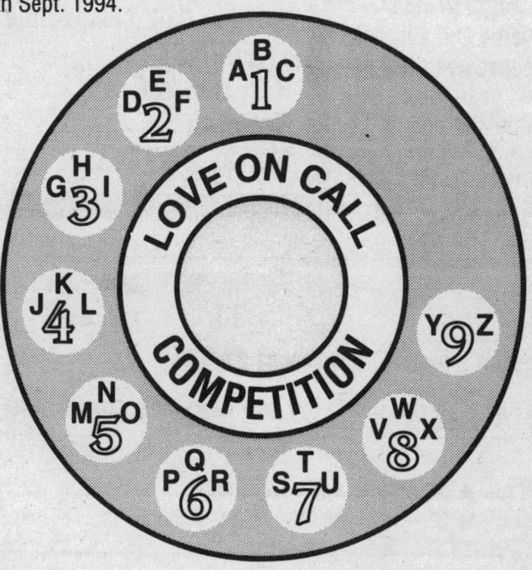

1 5233315767 ______________________

2 3552 152 1819 ______________________

3 165547322 ______________________

4 2177252267 ______________________

Please turn over for entry details

MILLS & BOON READER SERVICE COMPETITION!

ON CALL!

SEND YOUR ENTRY NOW!

The first five correct entries picked out of the bag after the closing date will each win one year's supply of 'Love on Call' romances (four books every month - worth over £85). What could be easier?

Don't forget to enter your name and address in the space below then put this page in an envelope and post it today (you don't need a stamp). Competition closes 30th Sept. '94.

'Love on Call' Competition
FREEPOST
P.O. Box 236
Croydon
Surrey CR9 9EL

EPLQ

Are you a Reader Service subscriber? Yes ☐ No ☐

Ms/Mrs/Miss/Mr ______________________

Address ______________________

____

____

Postcode ______________________

Signature ______________________

One application per household. You may be mailed with offers from other reputable companies as a result of this application. Please tick box if you would prefer not to receive such offers. ☐
Offer valid only in U.K. and Eire.